T0197308

THE DEVIL
MAY LIE

THE DEVIL MAY LIE

MIMA

THE DEVIL MAY LIE

iUniverse books may be ordered through booksellers or by contacting:

iUniverse
1663 Liberty Drive
Bloomington, IN 47403
www.iuniverse.com
1-800-Authors (1-800-288-4677)

ISBN: 978-1-5320-7184-3 (sc)
ISBN: 978-1-5320-7183-6 (e)

Library of Congress Control Number: 2019903371

Print information available on the last page.

iUniverse rev. date: 03/27/2019

ACKNOWLEDGMENTS

Special thanks go to Jean Arsenault for helping with the grueling editing process. I would also like to thanks Mitchell Whitlock and Jim Brown for helping with the back cover description.

Thank you as well to the West Prince Arts Council for help with this project. Your support is greatly appreciated.

CHAPTER 1

We love power. It's addictive. It starts when we're children on the playground and ends with our death. It's human nature to crave power. We lust after it as if it were the flesh of a lover and it haunts our dreams at night. It sends a roaring fire through our veins that ignites our heart. It makes us bold. It excites us with an intense passion that overflows into all areas of our lives. Without power, where would we be?

We're all animals and as such, it's natural for us to want to devour our enemy. A lion has no conscience about killing an antelope because it's his true nature. The only difference is that humans are expected to be more civilized than wild animals, but it's not true. Watch the news and see what is taking place around the world. Civility isn't in our nature.

Jorge Hernandez knew this all too well. Having been a major player in the Mexican drug cartel for over 20 years, he had seen and participated in many uncivilized acts, but to him, this was part of the game. In fact, this was how he took over the Canadian marijuana industry. His company, Our House of Pot, was as familiar throughout the country as popular grocery and hardware chains. It wasn't to say that he was the only player, but he was the definite leader in the industry. Those who had tried to cross him were quickly reminded how he had become such a powerful man in the first place.

"So you tell me that my daughter, she has this other girl try to strangle her but you suspend my Maria for defending herself but not the other girl?" Jorge spoke abrasively as he leaned forward in the chair, his dark eyes blazing in fury as he glared at the middle-aged white woman on the other side of the desk. "So this here, this is how you run your school? I must worry about the safety of my 11-year-old daughter?"

"Mr. Hernandez, we have a three strikes policy in this school," Mrs. Rabin spoke slowly, calmly, as if it was going to change the sense of urgency in the room. "This means that we try to give the children a fair chance to learn from their mistakes before we take more severe actions."

"So what," Jorge shot back. He lurched ahead in his chair as Mrs. Rabins posture tightened up. "You wait until this fucking kid kills my daughter, is that it? Or sends her to the hospital? Or is that still only *one* strike?"

"Obviously, we wouldn't allow it to get to that point," Mrs. Rabin replied curtly as her face turned pink, her fingers gripped a pen. "We have cameras…"

"Yes and your fucking cameras have a way of catching everything my daughter does," Jorge replied, his dark eyes narrowing. "Yet, you seem to miss it when another child tries to strangle Maria. Why is that exactly?"

"We just didn't catch it as fast as…"

"What? Is this other kid," Jorge cut her off and pointed toward the door. "She the kid of someone in government? Someone with a little power, maybe?"

"We don't reveal the name of the parents due to privacy…"

"Privacy," Jorge snapped, his voice getting louder. "You got to be fucking kidding me, lady! You better believe I am going to the parents because someone has to do *your* job."

"You don't understand, Mr. Hernandez," The principal made another attempt to explain even though it was clear that her carefully composed mask was cracking. "We like to handle everything within the school."

"You mean, do nothing?" Jorge asked as his voice continued to get louder as his heart raced in fury. "So this other kid, she comes to school tomorrow like a little *princesa* and my daughter, she is suspended. What is the…how do you, say, punishment? Is there no punishment for this other child?"

"Of course, we will have a stern conversation with her," Mrs. Rabin insisted as her eyes narrowed. "Mr. Hernandez, you'll have to calm down..."

"You, lady, got no right to tell me to calm down," Jorge snapped back and felt his English growing poorer as he grew angrier. "My daughter was on *your* property when she had another kid attack her and you tell me that I need to calm down? There has to be something wrong with you."

"Mr..."

"Let me ask you something," Jorge cut her off. "If this was your kid that someone tried to strangle, would this fucking 'three strikes' policy, would it be ok with you? I'm curious, do you *even* have kids?"

"I...I have a son, he's in university but..." She stammered nervously.

"Yes, so, your son goes to class and let us say someone tries to strangle him," Jorge spoke calmly while his eyes stared through the woman on the other side of the desk. "Would you agree to these same rules? Would it be a 'three strikes' policy in that case as well? I'm wondering, Mrs. Rabin, how would it *feel* if it were *your* son that someone attacked?"

She fell silent.

"I want you to think about that for a minute," Jorge continued to speak with forced restraint, his eyes not looking away from hers for a second. She eventually glanced down at her desk and back up again, clearly flustered. "Let us be reasonable here. I do not know about you but where I come from lady, there are *no* three strikes."

"How...." Mrs. Rabin's voice shook as she spoke. "How do you feel that this situation should be dealt with, Mr. Hernandez?"

Before he could answer, the door opened and his wife walked in. Paige Noël-Hernandez automatically sent a wave of serenity through him, her presence was a combination of strength and tranquility. Her blue eyes met with his and a peacefulness flowed through him followed by a sense of power that was much more comforting than his original, erratic fury.

"Excuse me," She spoke in an even tone as she closed the door behind her and walked toward the desk. "I was just speaking to my step-daughter and I would like to know why she has marks around her throat?"

"This is what I have tried to understand," Jorge said as he loosened his tie, the original fury in his voice returned. "And why my Maria will be punished and this other child is not. Do I not pay enough for this school that you can make sure my daughter isn't harmed?"

"Mr. Hernandez, Mrs.." The principal started to cough and reached for a glass of water as Paige sat down, her presence creating a certain unease in the room. "Excuse me, sorry. Please, as I was saying earlier, there's a three strikes policy and since Maria has had…. issues before, this is her third strike and because the other child has never had any other issues.."

"Any issues you saw," Paige quickly corrected her with a softness in her voice that was almost too calm for the situation as she pushed a strand of blonde hair aside. "But from what Maria was telling me, this child taunted her for most of the school year. She used racist terms, suggested Maria was….sexually active and told her to 'go back to her country' on several occasions. Is none of that considered a 'strike'? I'm just curious."

"Yes, however, Maria did not bring this to our attention," The principal replied. "If she had, certainly, something would've been done."

"She said it often happened in front of one of your teachers, who did nothing," Paige countered.

"I'm sure the teacher didn't hear otherwise, we clearly would've taken care of the matter," Mrs. Rabin replied, her eyes avoiding Jorge as she focused on Paige.

Paige took a breath and shook her head. "That's not acceptable."

The principal opened her mouth but nothing came out.

"We'll have to come up with a better solution," Paige continued.

"Look," Mrs. Rabin said. "It is clear to me that you are not happy with this school's policies. I can understand that but my hands are tied."

"*Untie them*," Paige spoke bluntly, her assertiveness grew as her eyes narrowed.

"The best I can do is to talk to the child and her parents," Mrs. Rabin said, only briefly glancing at Jorge, before returning her attention to Paige. "And hope they punish the child at home or get her the counseling she needs."

"Oh, do not you worry about the parents," Jorge insisted. "*I* will take care of the parents."

The principal hesitated before replying as her eyes widened.

"As I said, due to privacy issues, we don't.."

"I don't need your help getting the parent's names," Jorge interrupted her. "I got my own resources."

"Maria told me the child's name," Paige continued, her voice smooth as honey. "I'm certain we can find the parents on our own."

"We don't encourage you to…"

"Lady, I don't got to take orders from you," Jorge abruptly cut her off. "We will talk to the parents since your *hands are tied* and meanwhile, I suggest you be reasonable with my daughter."

"The school year is almost over," Paige offered. "I think that we can compromise here."

"Exactly and next year," Jorge glanced at his wife. "We find a more *suitable* school for Maria, maybe one with zero tolerance for bullying."

"We do have zero tolerance here," Mrs. Rabin boldly reported. "We have to take the situation into consideration. Punishment isn't always the answer. Maybe the child has a mental health issue."

Jorge didn't reply at first, he abruptly reached in his pocket and pulled out a pack of gum. Looking up at Mrs. Rabin, he noted her face went pale until she saw the green package. Perhaps his reputation preceded him.

"Mental health issues?" Jorge asked. "Let me guess, it was a white girl?" Glancing at Paige, he watched her nod.

"That is what I thought," Jorge commented as he shoved a piece of gum in his mouth and glared at the principal. "So, again, I will use your child as an example, Mrs. Rabin. Your son, you say he's in university? What if someone jumps out of nowhere and attacks him? Maybe tries to strangle him, do you let the attacker go because maybe he had mental health issues? I am *just* curious."

"I don't think that's the same…"

"You tell the students here that they aren't children but 'little adults'," Jorge cut her off and noted the nervousness in her face. "So, I would think, you would treat this situation the same, am I right?"

The principal considered his words briefly and looked away from the couple. With terror in her face, she cleared her throat.

"I think we can come to an understanding, Mr. Hernandez," She finally spoke in a hoarse voice.

A grin crossed Jorge's face as he turned to his wife. Reaching for her hand, he looked into her eyes. "These Canadians, always so accommodating."

Twenty minutes later, the family silently climbed into the SUV. This was after Jorge inspected his daughter's neck and gave her a comforting hug and kiss. Maria insisted she was fine but Jorge was still enraged that someone had tried to hurt his child.

"Maria," Jorge spoke up as they drove home. "What happened to you, it was not acceptable. This child, she cannot hurt you."

Her big brown eyes briefly met with his in the mirror and she nodded.

"*Papa*, she has tormented me for *months*," Maria spoke earnestly, dramatically swinging her hand in the air. "Today, I had enough, so I shoved her."

"You shoved her?" Jorge asked in surprise. "What? This here, this was not reported to me by Mrs. Rabin."

"She doesn't know," Maria replied as she crossed her legs in a ladylike fashion.

"Did their fancy cameras, did they not pick up on this?" Jorge asked as he glanced at Paige. "I do not understand."

"I made sure we were away from the cameras," Maria replied and although Jorge didn't show it, he was proud of his daughter. She was definitely a Hernandez. Glancing again at his wife, he noted the smirk on her face. "Paige always says that you must look for the cameras."

"Now Maria, you know I didn't mean it that way," His wife spoke evenly but one glance at her and Jorge had to bite back his laughter. Ah!! The women in his life made him proud!

"Well, at any rate," Maria continued as she sat up a bit straighter. "I got sick of her attacking me, so I shoved her and told her next time would be worse."

"And Maria, she did not tell this to the principal?" Jorge asked as he stared ahead at the traffic.

"I said it wasn't true and pointed out that there were no witnesses."

This time Jorge couldn't suppress his grin but said nothing. Parenting magazines and so-called experts could say whatever they wanted about the proper way to bring up a child but in Jorge Hernandez's world, there was only one way; you taught them to be smart, you taught them to be strong and most of all, you taught them to be powerful.

CHAPTER 2

Jorge dropped Maria off at home. It was as they drove away that the couple shared a look.

"Clara can only stay for a short time," Paige reminded him as they headed back toward the highway and Jorge merely nodded. Of course, Clara wasn't just their occasional babysitter but what their inner circle referred to as the 'cleaning lady', or the person in charge of checking for listening devices in their homes and offices. "She and her husband have plans later tonight."

"This here, will not take long," Jorge gestured toward the street ahead. "Just a friendly conversation between parents."

Paige grinned and reached over to run her hand through his black hair just long enough to make him smile.

"What about Alec? Aren't we supposed to meet later?" Paige inquired, referring to the federal politician they helped get elected the previous fall. "I can't even keep track of the simplest things anymore."

Jorge's expression softened as he reached out and touched her arm, sharing a look while stopped at the light.

"I tell him to come to the house later," Jorge replied as traffic started to move again, his focus returning to the road. "He does not mind. This is fine with him."

"And Diego, he's doing well?" She quietly inquired about their associate and friend. "Were you in contact today?"

"All is well," Jorge insisted. "Him and Michael, they will take care of everything."

"I asked him earlier this week about his *vacation,*" Paige spoke calmly as they eased forward. "He said the weather was beautiful in Colombia and they're having fun."

"This means the business transaction, it is going well," Jorge replied as he turned their SUV on one of Toronto's richer neighborhoods. "It is the first time he has returned to his home country in years. I was unsure how he would feel about going."

"I think he needed this," Paige insisted with confidence. "It was something he had to do. Also, I think he wanted Michael to see where he came from."

Paige was referring to Diego's boyfriend. The two had been together for close to a year and although some guessed it wouldn't last, things had progressed ahead. Not to suggest there weren't bumps in the road.

"Perhaps that will help their…problems," Jorge spoke thoughtfully, his eyes scanning the lineup of expensive homes as they passed. "This here, this is the kind of neighborhood we must move to. The house we have, it is a dump compared to these places."

"They're kind of elaborate, aren't they?" Paige asked and they shared a quick look. "Do we need something so big?"

"We can afford it so we should have it," Jorge replied. "Now that the company has grown so rapidly, your nosey Canadian government won't be so concerned with us having a rich home. Our income on paper represents this kind of neighborhood."

"If that's what you want…"

"Yes, *mi amor,* with everything you've given me, you deserve a beautiful home like this one," Jorge drove up the driveway to an enormous house surrounded by a perfectly manicured lawn. He winked at her before parking the SUV and reaching for the door.

"Jorge, are you sure you want to do this," Paige seemed hesitant. "And at his home?"

"*Mi amor,* I am told he works from home," Jorge replied and nodded. "And yes, we must take care of this now or it may get out of hand. We managed to save Maria from suspension but this here," He glanced toward the house. "This is where the real problem is."

The couple got out of the SUV and headed up the walkway. Paige was reluctant but Jorge boldly stepped ahead and rang the doorbell. After a brief pause, the door opened and a young, beautiful woman stood on the other side. The voluptuous white woman wore a girlish dress with her hair up in a large bun on the top of her head. She looked Jorge up and down with interest, only briefly glancing at Paige before saying anything.

"Can I help you?"

"I'm here to see Monty Harrison," Jorge instructed.

"About?" The young woman seemed unsure as she tilted her head to one side.

"About his fucking kid that tried to strangle my daughter in school today," Jorge sharply replied, causing a look of shock to cross the young woman's face. "And lady, I don't got all day."

"Ah...I....I'm the nanny...just a second," She stumbled and rushed away, leaving the door open ajar, which that was all Jorge needed to push his way in. Glancing around, he noted that the house was immaculate, if not boring.

"For the record," Paige said as she followed him inside and closed the door. "If we ever hire a nanny, she's not gonna look like that."

Jorge glanced at his wife, giving her a quick wink and grin just as the young woman returned.

"He will be here in a moment."

Jorge didn't thank her but merely nodded as she slipped away.

Monty Harrison was an older man, probably well into his 60s, something that surprised Jorge but he still remained expressionless when he appeared in the room. His eyes glanced from the Mexican man wearing a shirt and tie to the blonde lady standing next to him and shook his head.

"Yes? Can I help you?" He appeared perplexed as he focused on Jorge. "I was told you were here about Genevieve."

"Is that your daughter? The girl who tried to strangle my Maria today at school?" Jorge spoke aggressively. "Is this how you bring your children up? To harm others?"

"I understand that there was an....incident at school today but I generally allow the girl's mother to take care of these things," Monty Harrison spoke without emotion, something that Jorge found rather strange. "If you wish to speak to her when she returns later…"

"No, you don't get it," Jorge lowered his voice, his eyes narrowing on Monty. "I'm here *now* and I'm going to talk to *you*. Now, this bullying my kid, it is going to stop."

"I will pass this message on to my wife and…"

"No, you pass this message on to your daughter," Jorge shot back, his voice rose in frustration. "What? You don't talk to your own kid?"

"In this family, the woman is in charge of the children," Monty Harrison spoke as if it was the most logical explanation. "We don't believe that men get involved in child rearing."

"Well, you might want to start *rearing* your own kid because your wife," Jorge spoke dramatically with his hand swinging around. "She ain't doing a very good job. You do not believe me, I got a picture of marks around my daughter's neck that proves it."

Without giving Harrison a chance to speak, Jorge immediately grabbed his phone and found the picture in question, flashing it to the dumbstruck man standing before him.

"Oh, that certainly is disturbing," Monty Harrison replied as his posture became tense.

"Disturbing isn't the word I would use," Jorge countered, his anger grew when faced with this man's stoic expression that lingered in the world of dissociation. "Do you not get that your kid could've killed my daughter? Do you not fucking get this?"

"I think," Paige cut in, her hand reaching out to touch Jorge's arm as if trying to calm him. "What my husband is trying to say is that we have a concern that you're failing to see the seriousness of this situation. This isn't simple name-calling on the schoolyard, your daughter has a violent streak that should be addressed. We didn't go to the police this time but if anything further happens, this is an option we might consider."

"One of *many* options we might consider," Jorge spoke viciously and for the first time in the entire conversation, Monty Harrison showed some emotion. With fear in his eyes, he nodded rapidly, almost nervously as he backed away from the angry Mexican. "Now, do we have an understanding? There won't be any more of this bullshit from your daughter?"

"Of course, I will take it up with her mother," Monty continued to speak as if they were talking about a stranger and not his child. Jorge was at the end of his rope and merely shook his head before turning toward the door.

It wasn't until they were outside and in the SUV that Jorge blew up.

"What the fuck is wrong with that man?" He ranted as they pulled back on the road. "Why did he keep talking about his daughter as if she were some stranger's kid? As if the mother was the only one involved in his fucking kid's life?"

"It sounds like that *is* the case," Paige remarked as she tapped on her phone. "I wonder how common this is in Maria's school."

"Maria's *former* school," Jorge corrected her. "This year is almost finished and we will find her another school. That fucking place has pissed me off all year. At first, I thought it was Maria because we know how headstrong she is but then, after that weird religious video thing..."

"Oh, you mean the pro-life seminar from the right-wing group?" Paige asked and shook her head. "That was odd. Then Maria disagreed with the presenter and was given a poor grade as a result."

"I thought this was an... an inappropriate topic for an 11-year-old," Jorge complained. "Who decides on such a thing for a school?"

"The board? Maybe you should look into joining," Paige joked and reached out to touch his arm.

"I somehow doubt that I fit the profile they are looking for," Jorge replied with a grin, his body relaxing as his wife teased him. "Former cartel kingpin with a tendency toward violence....."

"A *tendency*?" She continued to tease. "That's putting it mildly."

"Hey, things, they get a little...messy," Jorge replied and winked at his wife. "How about you? Former assassin of the world? Maybe you can find a creative way of dealing with this problem with the school."

"I think it's best that I don't get involved," Paige replied. "I have enough on my plate these days."

"You sure do, *mi amor,* that is certainly true," Jorge's voice now full of love. "Speaking of which, we must get home before Clara has to leave. Alec should be along soon."

"I sent him a text about Monty Harrison," Paige said in a smooth voice. "I'm interested to see if he knows this man."

As it turns out, he knew a lot.

CHAPTER 3

"*Mi amor,* I am getting too old for this," Jorge commented after they arrived home and Clara left. The couple was in their kitchen, while upstairs, Maria could be heard dancing and singing to music. "This is why people, they have children in their 20s so that they are grown up by their 40s. I do see this now."

Paige didn't reply at first, merely raising an eyebrow while Jorge climbed on a nearby stool. The constant roller coaster never ended; work challenges, people attempting to disrupt his business and of course, his personal life wasn't always easy. Although he spent most days feeling on top of every aspect, there were times when he craved the simple life.

"Not to suggest that I regret being a father," Jorge was quick to get back on track as he watched Paige make a pot of coffee. She showed no judgment as she listened, one of the many beautiful qualities of his wife of almost two years. Paige was calm and brought much-needed peacefulness to his life. "It is just that this here, it is the one area of my life where I do not always know what to do."

Paige didn't reply as she flicked on the coffee pot and turned in his direction. Pushing a strand of hair behind her ear, she gave him a gentle smile and nodded in understanding.

"*Ser padre es difícil.*"

"It is difficult," Paige agreed as she crossed the room just as the coffee maker started to make noises. "But you're doing fine."

"But did I handle things well today? Maybe I should've been more forceful with the father? Should I have taken Maria to the hospital even though she said she was fine?" Jorge glanced toward the ceiling to indicate his daughter and shrugged. "I do not know."

"Well, you did say that if we went to the hospital then they might call the police," Paige reminded him. "If that's the route you wish to take..."

"*Mi amor,*" Jorge spoke gently as he reached across the counter for her hand. "You know that this is not the route I ever wish to take. The *polica*, they will do nothing. *I* will take care of this."

Paige merely grinned as he squeezed her hand.

"The school nurse checked her out and said she's fine," Paige gently reminded him. "Plus, I think you took care of the principal and Harrison,"

"*Si,*" Jorge reluctantly agreed.

"I know something that might cheer you up."

"Oh, *mi amor,* you know exactly how to cheer me up," he spoke in a low, seductive tone. "This is not something new."

Paige laughed as he let go of her hand and she headed toward the stairs. Glancing at his phone, Jorge noted that Alec was on the way to the house. Although having the Greek man in place within government was helpful, he often wondered if it was worth the efforts it took to get him elected. Although compliant and easy to control, there was one fact that was hard to swallow about Alec Athas and that was his past with Paige. The two once had a relationship and although it was over 20 years ago, it still irked him.

"Look who's awake?" Paige sang out as she walked downstairs with an infant in her arms. Barely a month old, their son had made an early arrival at the beginning of May. Just the sight of him caused Jorge's heart to soften; his *familia* was the only thing that kept him human in light of his many dark deeds. "He must've heard his father's voice."

"Are you saying I'm loud?" Jorge teased as Paige approached him with their baby. Standing up, he reached out and carefully took his son from her arms. There was a sense of fragility that surrounded the infant that went beyond his early arrival and small birth weight but also his name. Miguel.

There was never any doubt that their son would be named after Jorge's younger brother, who had died as a child. A terrible accident had taken the 10-year-and for that reason, Jorge would always blame himself. If anything positive had resulted from that terrible day in his childhood, it was that he was now more protective of his own family. No one and nothing would ever hurt anyone he loved. Even a threat would have consequences as the past had proven.

"Ah, *mi amor,*" Jorge looked into his son's brown eyes as he walked into the living room toward the couch, where he sat. Paige silently followed. "I do not care what you say, he looks like you too. I can see it in his eyes. He calms me just as you do every day."

"Do you think?" Paige quietly asked as she stood nearby and watched the father and son together. "I look at him, I only see you."

"Ah, but he will grow, change in his looks," Jorge reminded her as he briefly glanced up to see the pride in her face. He then carefully touched his son's cheek; the baby's skin was so soft, so smooth, everything about him was absolute perfection. Jorge paused and fought a wave of emotion that overtook him unexpectedly. "I see Miguel too. My brother. It is not just the name they share. He's here. I feel his presence each time I look at my son."

Paige's eyes watered as she listened. This wasn't the first time Jorge had confessed feeling that way. The morning of Miguel's birth, his emotions ran high from the first moment he held their son. The same nurse who appeared mildly afraid of Jorge when he arrived in the delivery room, aggressively instructing them to do their job properly, was later shocked to see the same man sobbing as he held his new baby. It was the most powerful moment of his life.

"You have given me the greatest gift, Paige," Jorge spoke emotionally as the child's eyelids began to droop and he yawned. "Each time I pick up my son, I feel that I am healing from what I did to my brother."

"It was an accident," Paige reminded him. "You were 12. You made a mistake. You didn't mean to hurt your brother."

"But I did, *mi amor,* I did," Jorge reminded her. "It was my stupidity. I told my brother to get on that dirt bike. I did not know how to drive it but you know me, even then, I was full of piss and vinegar, as they say…"

Paige laughed and wiped a stray tear away. "Some things never change."

"But my son," Jorge looked down at the baby just as Maria walked down the stairs, glancing at them with interest. "He will be better than me. Just as my daughter will be too."

"*Papa,*" Maria spoke up as she approached them. "Did you go to see Genevieve's father?"

"Yes, *niñita,*" Jorge assured her while continuing to stare at his son. "I felt that we needed to have a…discussion."

"She's telling everyone that my 'crazy' father went to her house and threatened him."

"I did not threaten him, Maria," Jorge insisted and looked up at her daughter. "I simply suggested that he start to discipline his child. However, it did not seem like he had any part in doing so."

"Her mother does it all," Maria commented and made a face. "Her family is old-fashioned. Her father barely talks to her."

"Well, Maria, maybe we have just discovered why this child is so troubled," Jorge commented and his daughter shrugged.

"*Papa,* can I hold the baby now?" Maria asked as she moved closer and glanced at the infant. "I've barely seen him all day."

"Yes," Jorge said as he slowly eased the child into his sister's arms. "But be very careful."

"I know, I know," She replied and giggled. "*Papa,* you tell me every time."

"She'll be fine," Paige quietly insisted.

The love in Maria's eyes when she picked up the infant was undeniable. Originally, Jorge feared she wouldn't react well to Paige's pregnancy but it was the opposite. He could see that the siblings would be close and that filled his heart with joy.

The doorbell rang as Maria headed upstairs with the baby and Paige rushed to answer it. Jorge took a deep breath. Exhausted from the day, he was now rejuvenated by his son. Perhaps his earlier estimate that children wore him out was a bit presumptuous. Maybe it was the opposite.

Hearing Alec's voice from the hallway did little to inspire him as he stood up and headed toward his office, where the three would conduct their meeting. It was important that he showed his strength when dealing with the politician. Business associates who weren't in his inner circle couldn't see his weak side, his vulnerabilities and for this reason, Jorge rarely had his children around when Alec dropped in. Although he was slightly closer to the family than most politicians he had in his pocket, it was better to show caution.

Paige and Alec were chatting when they entered his office and Jorge merely nodded when the Greek man said hello, quickly finding his usual spot on the opposite side of the desk from Jorge. Paige sat beside him.

"Thank you for meeting us here," Jorge automatically jumped in, his voice full strength. "Things have been hectic lately so this is better."

"I would prefer to meet in private," Alec spoke earnestly as he opened his jacket to display a shirt and tie. "I don't want anyone suggesting that we are colluding."

"As it turns out," Paige cut in and gestured toward Alec. "He knows Harrison from his political circles. I was telling him about our day."

"Ah, yes!" Jorge grinned. "Interesting man."

"Perhaps if you want to relive the 50s," Alec commented evenly as he relaxed. "Harrison is one of these extremists that believe that we need to return to 'simpler times'."

"What does this mean?" Jorge asked with interest.

"There's this idea that the world is spiraling out of control and for that reason," Alec hesitated and glanced between the couple. "That we need to step back and return to the way things used to be when men and women had more defined roles. He thinks that this is the only way to get this country back on track."

"So, what?" Paige said with laughter in her voice. "Women stay home and cook and clean while men go out and work?"

"Basically."

Jorge threw his head back in laughter.

"Hey, you might laugh but many Canadians feel the same way," Alec insisted and beside him, Paige appeared stunned. "We've been doing surveys and a lot of people believe that we need more conservative values, that our culture doesn't have enough structure."

"Are you fucking serious?" Jorge countered. "Look around you, turn on the television, people, they do not want conservative values."

"Unfortunately, there *is* a wave taking over and it's gaining popularity," Alec spoke seriously. "That's my biggest challenge now. How do we listen to the voters but keep in line with our party values?"

"I wasn't aware that you ever listened to voters," Jorge said as his eyes lit up. "But conservative values, this is a fad. Who cares?"

"But, here's the problem," Alec countered. "If these people start to restructure the political landscape, it might mean problems for you. Do you think these ultra conservatives want Our House of Pot in their neighborhood? Rumor has it that our opposition is working to bring back *traditional* values and if that's the case, one of the things they're playing around with is making pot illegal again."

"Over my dead body, they will," Jorge fumed. "So, these fucking conservatives think they're going to make my company illegal? Not a fucking chance! I will take each and every one of them down."

"Looks like you might've unknowingly started that today at Harrison's house," Paige spoke gently and Jorge took a deep breath and listened. "He clearly fits in with this group."

"He's working the angle too," Alec commented as he tapped on his phone. "Did you know Harrison is on your daughter's school board? That means he's influencing the curriculum."

Paige and Jorge shared a look.

"They're insidious," Alec bitterly continued. "They have people on school boards in both private and public schools. Why do you think sex education was removed? It doesn't go along with this conservative wave. Parents complain to me but it's a provincial issue and I'm federal."

"Really?" Paige appeared concerned. "So they can influence what our children learn?"

"They can influence a lot of things," Alec corrected her. "This is a powerful group."

"So we talking like *Handmaid's Tale* kind of crazy?" Jorge still appeared angry, if not slightly humored, at the same time.

"Maybe not that extreme but if you get these people on boards for various companies, that could mean they decide to hire fewer women… fewer minorities….judge people on their sexuality. I mean, anything is possible," Alec paused for a moment. "Remember, they want to go back to when things were *supposedly* better. Of course, what they mean by *better* is when everyone knew their place. They just have to find someone to represent their values to eventually lead the country."

"So how does someone counter such a movement?" Jorge was curious.

Alec hesitated for a moment before answering.

"We get ahead of them."

CHAPTER 4

"Paige, I do not like this," Jorge spoke bluntly as his wife rushed around their bedroom while he fixed his tie. Their eyes met briefly and she shrugged. "This here, it is too much. With a new baby and Maria. Do not worry. I will take care of it."

"Jorge," She suddenly hesitated as if searching for the right words. "When we talked about Harrison last night and these conservative values, this affects all of us. If women aren't ready to fight it, where does that put us in the future?"

"I know, *mi amor,* I know," Jorge insisted as she approached him, her head tilted slightly as if trying to read his expression. "However, you must take care of yourself and our family. Let me handle this. I do not want you to overdo it."

"I'm fine," Paige reminded him as she touched his arm. "Just because I had a baby doesn't mean I've lost my edge."

"I did not say such things, Paige," Jorge insisted in a softer voice. "What I mean is that you are exhausted since the baby arrived. It took a lot out of you and that is normal but now, you must allow yourself to get back to where you were before. We will find you some help with the baby and of course, whatever else you need."

"I need to fight these right-wing assholes," Paige assured him with a small grin, her eyes lit up in response. "I don't want my children growing up in these people's twisted version of the world and that means I need to help you fight."

"Ok, *mi amor,* but today, I will talk to Chase," Jorge referred to another one of his associates, a young indigenous man who took care of the company's high-end club *Princesa Maria.* "He can do the research needed on these people and later this week, we will come up with a plan. But please, Paige, for today, can you stay home and look after yourself. Maybe see if Clara is available to babysit and spend a day at the spa? Meditate? Whatever you need, *mi amor.*"

"I don't want to fight you on this...."

"Then don't," Jorge gently insisted as he pulled her close and kissed her on the forehead. "Sometimes, your husband, he knows what he is talking about. Perhaps humor me? Just for today, *si?*"

She didn't reply but her eyes said it all.

With some relief, Jorge kissed his two children before heading out. Jumping into his SUV he tore out of the driveway and made his way toward downtown Toronto, where he would meet with Chase at the *Princesa Maria.* On the way, he decided to call the IT expert for Hernandez-Silva Inc.

"Good morning sir," Marco Rodel Cruz's voice was suddenly booming through the SUV as Jorge sat in traffic. The Filipino immigrant had been with the company for well over a year and was as valuable as a hacker as he was in running the company's IT section. "How are you today, Mr. Hernandez?"

"It is a beautiful day," Jorge insisted and forced a smile on his face. "But Marco, my son, he robs me of my sleep."

Smooth laughter filled the SUV and Jorge couldn't help but grin.

"Sir, I did tell you that a new baby, he would cry a lot and usually at the most inappropriate hours," Marco reminded him with humor in his voice. "It is hard to get accustomed to, yes?"

"Yes, Marco but we must take the bad with the good," Jorge replied and glanced toward the next vehicle. "It is the sweetness that takes away all that is bitter in life, would you not agree?"

"I certainly would sir," Marco spoke graciously. "It will be fine, Mr. Hernandez. He is healthy, this is most important."

"Indeed, Marco," Jorge decided to switch gears as he inched his way toward the club. "I must have you help me with a project. Would you be able to pop by the *Princesa Maria* this morning? I am on my way there now to meet with Chase and I might have something for you."

Of course, he would never discuss anything in detail on the phone. Only a moron took such a chance.

"Yes sir, that is no problem."

"See you soon then?"

"I will be there."

Jorge ended the call, satisfied that he was getting his ducks in line, however, his brain continued to race. He made another call.

"*Buenos dias,* sir," Jesús Garcia López spoke slowly into the phone as if he had just woke up. The two men had a long history working together and in fact, he was one of Jorge's most reliable foot soldiers. "How are you this morning?"

"*Perfecto,*" Jorge replied as his eyes scanned the traffic ahead. "Jesús, I must schedule a meeting for later this week. Something of great importance was brought to my attention. Plus, I do believe it is time for us all to touch base on our many projects."

"Boss, the summer pot festival, it is organized with exception to a few minor details," Jesús referred to the event that gained international interest. The festival would include popular music, food and of course, lots of marijuana. It was an opportunity for enthusiasts to gather together in Toronto to connect with their tribe. Although it wasn't Jesús who organized the event, he had overseen it since conception.

"Ah! Wonderful! It will be beautiful," Jorge insisted with pride in his voice. "You have done well, *amigo.* Have you spoken to Diego recently?

"Sir, I believe his much-deserved vacation, it is going well," Jesús replied. "He and Michael, they are seeing all the sights."

Jorge grinned. This meant Diego was meeting with some of the country's most dangerous people to assure they continued to meet customer demands at Our House of Pot. Not to mention, the Colombian product was cheaper.

"Perfecto," He replied as he reached the club and parked in the VIP section. "We will talk again soon. I will organize a meeting."

"Very good, sir," Jesús replied before ending their call and Jorge turned off the SUV. Grabbing his phone, he jumped out and locked the vehicle before heading for the club. Finding his key, Jorge made his way inside and glanced around the empty bar. As usual, a pile of bottles sat in the corner but other than that, the place was flawless in appearance.

Heading toward the office located behind the main bar, he saw Chase already seated at his desk. The young indigenous man, who was in his late twenties, glanced up from his laptop with a smile on his face.

"Good morning, Jorge," Chase said as he sat up straight and pushed his laptop aside. He stretched, yawned and this, in turn, caused Jorge to do the same before collapsing in the chair across from his associate. "Miguel is still waking up a lot at night?"

"That is putting it lightly," Jorge replied as he ran a hand over his face. "It is hard to adjust. With Maria, I was away a lot but I do not remember it being so hard to be a new parent."

Chase gave a compassionate smile as he fixed his tie and nodded.

"But, it is fine," Jorge continued, pushing those thoughts away. "My son, he is a blessing, so I will not complain."

Chase studied his face and nodded. Jorge felt he had no right to complain considering Chase's two boys were in another province and barely kept in contact.

"So, it was brought to my attention that we might have a new problem," He pushed ahead. "This was after my daughter, she had some issues at school again yesterday."

"Yes, she texted me about it," Chase spoke evenly but there was humor in his eyes. Slightly uncomfortable, Jorge looked away. Maria had a crush on Chase that was somewhat troublesome at times even though the young, indigenous man was harmless, yet protective of Jorge's daughter. "She said you took care of things and she's back in school today?"

"Yes, well, you know me," Jorge said with a smirk on his face. "I have a way with words."

Chase laughed.

"However, that is not the problem," Jorge spoke just as Chase's phone beeped.

"Marco is outside," Chase said as he rose from his chair, his large frame leaned over the desk as he tapped something in his phone. "Be right back."

After he left the room, Jorge glanced at his own phone to see a photo of Diego and Michael on a beach. Grinning, he slid it back in his pocket just as Chase returned with Marco in tow.

"Ah, Marco!" Jorge immediately turned in his direction as the upbeat Filipino walked in the room. Rarely in a bad mood, he was an obedient and reliable employee. "You got here fast."

"I bike, sir."

"Bike?"

"Yes, sir, it is often faster especially with traffic."

"Smart," Chase commented as he returned to his chair.

"So, this issue, we must discuss," Jorge jumped right in, glancing between the two men as Marco sat down. "It was brought to my attention that there is apparently a conservative wave taking over the country? This is what they tell me."

"Yeah, I saw that on the news a few time," Chase replied. "Like polls that say people think things are moving too fast especially with technology?"

"Oh sir," Marco cut in. "Those polls, they can be fixed. Is that what you wish for me to do?"

"Well, that is a possibility in the future," Jorge considered. "However, for now, we must start investigating before these *conservative values* take over. It is said that they want to make pot illegal again and I do not have to tell you that I am not pleased."

"Can they do that?" Chase asked skeptically. "Just turn over a law?"

"It's government, they do whatever the fuck they want," Jorge complained. "I had a long conversation with Alec Athas last night and he made me understand that this group, it is slowly moving into various areas from schools to private enterprise and of course, they eventually want to get into government and pull us back in time. I know what I must do but it will take a lot of work."

"But why change?" Marco asked. "I do not understand. Canada, it is very progressive. This is what I love about this country."

"This is what these people *don't* love about this country," Jorge replied and noted the concerned look in Marco's eyes. "They believe that things were better long ago and people are too confused now."

"Confused?" Chase asked and shrugged. "I don't get it."

"About many things, my friend," Jorge said and recalled the previous night's conversation. "They say that young people are confused about their sexuality, about their roles in the world. Women, they are confused about whether to marry, have children, work…..men, they believe we are confused about whether to wash the dishes or fix their car."

"I have done both," Marco spoke honestly.

"Me," Jorge glibly replied. "I don't wanna do either but that is not the point, these people, they think that we no longer know our roles and that society, it wishes to have someone come in to tell them what they're supposed to do."

"If Diego were here," Chase began to laugh. "He'd say they want us to all be sheep."

"Ah yes!" Jorge laughed. "And the wolf himself just sent me a text from a Colombian beach, so I suspect that is good news for us. This was how he was to communicate with me that they were successful in their mission."

"He already had the contacts so it was much easier for him," Chase reminded them. "Diego was determined to get this done."

"So, sir, I do not mean to interrupt," Marco asked and turned toward Jorge. "But what is it you would like me to do?"

"Marco, I am so happy you asked," Jorge replied and leaned back in his chair. "I need you to hack a website. This conservative values group that I was speaking of, I need you to get into their emails. See what you can learn. Of course, this is a big task so Chase, I will need you to help. I would like you to read some of the information Marco is able to find, sift through messages boards, various Facebook posts, comments on news sites. I need to get a feel for what is going on. What do people *really* want?"

"Sure," Chase agreed while Marco nodded.

"Also, you mentioned that polls can be hacked?" Jorge asked and Marco quickly nodded. "Can you do that to work more in my favor?"

"I will try, sir," Marco nodded enthusiastically. "Let me look."

"This here, it could be a problem so it is up to us to make sure it doesn't become one," Jorge moved to the edge of the chair. "We have to send a strong message to these right-wing assholes that we are not fucking around."

Everyone knew what that meant.

CHAPTER 5

"It's interesting that one of the things we're fighting against is women being oppressed and yet," Paige paused briefly as they got in the elevator. "You wanted me to stay home today with the baby and do wifey things like cook dinner."

She spoke with no judgment in her voice which caused Jorge to grin and give her a look.

"*Mi amor,* my English is not always so good but I do not believe that's the definition of oppression," Jorge teased and reached out to touch her arm. His wife was wearing a soft grey fitted skirt and a white blouse. "And by the way, you look sexy as hell in that outfit."

"I could barely squeeze my ass into this skirt," Paige spoke hopelessly, causing Jorge to glance at her hips with interest. "I was reading in a magazine that if you have a child at my age that losing the weight is more of a struggle with hormones and being older."

"Paige, let me guess," Jorge commented as the elevator door opened and they walked out. "You read this article and then on the next page, there was an ad for some weight loss product? These stupid magazines, they only make women hate themselves."

She didn't reply but looked sad as they walked toward the office of Hernandez-Silva.

"Paige," He stopped her in the quiet hallway. "Please, do not worry so much. You look beautiful. I do not know why you do not believe me when I say this."

"But, my body, it looks like a train wreck," Paige said and her face turned a light shade of pink.

"Paige, your body, it is beautiful," Jorge insisted, surprised by how self-conscious his wife grew since the pregnancy. She had never been this way before. "Remember, it has only been a month since Miguel was born. Be fair with yourself."

She didn't respond.

"Also, I am not trying to *oppress* you," He continued. "I do think you are exhausted and you know me, I worry."

"You were like this for the whole pregnancy," She quietly replied.

"Yes, but *mi amor,* you were shot at the beginning," He gently reminded her as his eyes glanced at her arm. "It was…how do you say, not serious but still, it scared me. I will always be protective of you."

Her eyes softened and he reached for her hand as they walked toward the door.

Once swiping his passcard, they entered the office. Met by a hurried vibe, the energy level was high at Hernandez-Silva Inc. which pleased Jorge. Walking into the boardroom, they immediately found Diego Silva excitedly talking to Jesús about his vacation. In turn, the overweight Mexican man was squinting and nodding, as if he wasn't able to keep up with the excitable ramblings.

However, as soon as Diego spotted Jorge and Paige at the door, he immediately stopped speaking and flew across the room. Rushing past Jorge, leaving a wave of cologne behind him, the Colombian embraced Paige with a powerful hug.

"Me, I am here too," Jorge reminded him. "You run past me as if I'm the dirt on the ground."

"Paige!" Diego spoke excitedly to his best friend while ignoring Jorge's comments. "How is the baby? How are *you*? You look tired. Is Miguel sleeping through the night yet? Oh, I have *so* much to tell you!"

He talked so rapidly that Jorge felt like his head was spinning, noting that Diego's final comment appeared to be directed at him. His black eyes were wide while a deep tan gave him an unexpected healthy appearance.

"Diego, you must relax," Jorge abruptly commented. "I tell you to go to Colombia to *get weed*, not to snort all the cocaine in the country."

Diego merely laughed and pulled him into a strong hug before suddenly letting go and rushing away.

"I have the coffee ready!" He commented while Paige and Jorge sat in their usual places, across the table from Jesús, who nodded before reaching for his phone. Although he was the same age as Jorge, his extra weight and limited hair made him appear slightly older.

Diego poured them each a coffee and continued to excitedly ramble on.

"Everything went perfectly," He rattled on. "The weather, the food…"

"Diego, do you not remember why I sent you there?" Jorge cut him off. "Did you do the business we spoke about?"

"Yes, of course," Diego insisted. "It was *perfecto.*"

"It is hard to believe it would go so smoothly," Jesús spoke in his usual tone, his words drawn out. "These here, are not always the easiest people to work with."

"I got contacts," Diego reminded him. "Plus Jorge, his name is known in Colombia."

"This isn't my first rodeo," Jorge commented just as Chase Jacobs walked in. The young man's presence was quiet, yet powerful at the same time. Behind him was Marco, holding an opened laptop. The two took their usual seats at the table.

"Good morning, everyone," Marco commented then nodded toward Jorge then Paige. "Good morning Mrs. Hernandez."

"Morning Marco." She replied before nodding at Chase, while Diego rushed ahead to fill the coffee cups of the newest arrivals.

"What are we waiting for? Jolene?" Jorge asked as he glanced around the table. "That is all we are missing? Michael, he is at work?"

"Yup, he's at the station today," Diego said as he rushed to return the coffee pot to its place. Everyone at the table was reaching for cream, milk, and sugar while Jesús sat down his phone and took a drink.

Jorge merely grinned. Diego's boyfriend, Michael Perkins was a dirty cop. He came in handy on more than one occasion and proved his loyalty. However, it was when he helped save Jorge's wife that he was able to win his place at the table.

"Sorry, I am late, I know," Jolene Silva rushed into the room, her heels clicking loudly on the floor. The Colombian femme fatale closed the door behind her and quickly grabbed a seat beside Paige. It was interesting how the women had grown from hating each other to become friends but Jolene had more than proven her loyalty in past months.

"Paige, you look tired," She spoke in a lower voice as she pulled her chair ahead and brushed a strand of her long, dark hair aside. "You must get a nanny."

Noting that his wife looked slightly defeated with this comment, he quickly cut in.

"Ok, we aren't here to have tea and discuss our lives," Jorge was abrupt, grabbing everyone's attention. "We are here to talk business. There's lots to do, so let us get right to it."

"Let me start," Diego immediately cut in, fidgeting at the head of the table. "Colombia, it was a success. We will have no problem meeting our targets, especially for the festival this summer. They're fully on board."

"I have taken care of getting it into the country with no hassle," Jorge confirmed as he sat back in his chair. "The government, it won't be a problem."

"At least, not yet, sir," Jesús spoke up and glanced at his own laptop. "This here information that Chase has sent us, it looks like this conservative group, it is going to push to make pot illegal again."

"Yeah, I've noticed one of their commercials on television again last night," Chase spoke for the first time since his arrival. "They're a non-profit group that wants more conservative *family* values because this supposedly will make us sleep a little better at night."

"This here, it does not comfort me," Jolene replied as she slipped on her glasses and glanced at her phone. "I do not like."

"None of us like it, Jolene," Jorge insisted and reached for his coffee. "Their family value bullshit is going to try to take us down. As Alec said, they want to criminalize pot again and you know what? That's not fucking happening."

"What's the fuckers name?" Diego's voice grew more agitated as his eyes bulged out. "Who's behind this?"

"The leader, it is a woman," Jolene spoke with surprise in her voice as she looked up from her phone. "I do not expect."

"Well, *Jolene,*" Diego spoke with aggravation in his voice as he glared at his sister. "Why is that such a surprise."

"I do not know," She snapped at him. "I guess I just think it is always men who want to control everything."

"Ok," Jorge put his hand in the air, knowing an argument was about to break out. "I do not care if it is a movement by a man, woman or a fucking dinosaur, I do not wish to deal with it."

"Are we gonna take her out?" Diego spoke abruptly. "That would be my first choice."

"No, Diego, not yet," Jorge replied and turned his attention to Chase. "What is her name again?"

"Elizabeth Alan," Chase replied, shaking his head. "She leads this group called Canadians for Conservative Values. Her goal is to make Canada boring again."

Everyone laughed.

"Well, yes, that is what these groups usually want," Jorge replied with a grin and raised his eyebrows. "They are not exactly about sex, drugs and rock n' roll."

"So, this group, are they associated with a political party?" Jesús asked.

"No, not officially," Chase replied. "However, they do have a lot of political influence. It seems like no one really paid attention to them in the beginning but now, they're making waves."

"This woman," Marco spoke up. "She has experienced issues with her son. He was addicted to cocaine and this is why she started this group."

Everyone looked at Jorge.

"What? I didn't shove it up his nose," Jorge said with a shrug. "And me, you know I'm not so much about cocaine anymore."

"But sir, in fairness, we are still associated with the cartel," Jesús replied.

"I really hope that Clara was in today," Jorge suddenly thought of the company's 'cleaning lady'. "We got this room checked out, right?"

"Sir, she was in before you arrive and no listening devices," Jesús confirmed and continued. "So, this lady, her son snorts cocaine and she starts this group?"

"Her son *died* of a cocaine overdose," Chase replied as Marco nodded. "So, she started this movement and that's also why she wants to criminalize pot. She believes her son started with pot."

"Ah yes, the supposed 'gateway drug'," Jorge rolled his eyes.

"But the *cocaína*," Jolene spoke up. "He chose to take, right?"

"It is still our fault," Jorge reminded Jolene. "It is us 'pushers' right? It is not like these kids come looking for it."

Jolene let out a sharp laugh.

"So what do we do?" Diego loudly countered, startling Jorge while beside him, Paige let out a snicker. "We can't let this get out of hand."

"Oh, we will not be letting anything get out of hand, *amigo*," Jorge replied and turned to his longtime friend. "I got a plan."

CHAPTER 6

Losing my son was the most painful experience of my life. The fact that he would even consider taking an illicit drug like cocaine shocked me. My husband and I did everything to make sure we brought him up with good, Christian values.

Jorge automatically turned to Paige and rolled his eyes. Having been in the drug game for a long time, he knew that most users didn't exactly advertise their habits, let alone to their families. It was a dirty, secret, underground world for a reason. She gave him a vague smile, as he raised an eyebrow before returning his attention to the middle-aged white lady on the laptop.

After his death, it was a long time before I could go into his room. I don't know if it was as a source of comfort to just feel near him again, even if it was in the smallest way but God told me to go in his room. That I had to do this and what I found, shocked me. It was on his computer. I found violent video games, pornography, violent movies, music that focused on drugs, sex and money. I was shocked! This wasn't the son I brought up.

"Well, lady, if I've learned anything as a father," Jorge spoke to the screen and over Elizabeth Alan's voice. "It's that these kids, they have minds of their own."

"They sure do," Paige spoke softly and touched his arm as she leaned in closer. "Especially Maria."

"You're right, *mi amor,*" Jorge winked at her. "As usual, you are right."

...is contaminated. We've allowed our society to get this way and we're all responsible. It's time that we brought back good, Christian values. We live in a country where pot is legal, temptation is all around them and where our children have easy access to demoralizing materials on their electronic devices. It's time we fight to bring up our children in a more civilized, moral world. If I can help just one person...

Jorge abruptly slammed the laptop closed and pushed it across their kitchen table.

"Enough of this bullshit," He grumbled and shook his head. "As soon as I hear anyone say, 'If I can only help *one* person, I want to vomit.'"

"Well, maybe she's sincere," Paige replied showing no judgment. "But it seems kind of dramatic."

"*Mi amor,* there is money behind this," Jorge assured her and leaned in to give her a quick kiss. "Who stands to make money here? What is she trying to sell?"

"Supposedly, values and morals," Paige quipped with a grin on her lips, her blue eyes studying her husband's face.

"What's going on," Jorge insisted. "This here is a woman who either started off small and had someone swoop in and sponsor these videos, or she has the cash because it is a little overproduced. You know this, Paige, because when you did your videos for your life coach site, did they look like this?"

He pointed toward the silver computer on the table and she shook her head.

"I was thinking the same thing."

"Paige, your videos, they were good but it was easy to see you record them with no bells and whistles, this lady, she's got bells and whistles."

"I wonder who is backing her?"

"We gotta search for the money tree," Jorge insisted. "Marco and Chase are still looking into it but maybe we might have to get someone on the inside to find out, unless of course, Marco can hack further to learn more but so far, it looks on the up and up."

"I think you're right," Paige softly replied. "There's definitely someone pulling the strings or at the very least, helping her get more attention."

"Me, I think it's political," Jorge replied and turned toward his wife. "I believe, this lady will either come out to endorse a party in the future or will run. I got a feeling."

"Alec might have some thoughts when he comes here later," Paige suggested. "He knows the political landscape better than us."

"Me, I know everything," Jorge insisted. "This lady is working to create a name for herself and when the time is right, she'll join a party. She will play a role. I guarantee it."

"So what do we do?"

"We must counter," Jorge replied and paused for a moment. "We must make sure her group sinks. There is no way that this woman or anyone else is going to fuck with my business. When she picked a fight on our Canadian morals, she started a war with me."

"So, her, we need to…" Paige allowed her words to drift off.

"Paige, I think we need to wait, see who is behind her before we act," Jorge spoke softly, his hand reaching out to caress her arm as his breath grew heavy. "We must first find out who is on top….and then we must work our way down."

"I find that often to be the best plan of action," She spoke with a seductive tone.

Jorge leaned in to kiss her, his desires growing quickly while a soft moan rose from the back of her throat. Lost in his own lust, he was taken aback when Paige suddenly moved away with a pleading look in her eyes.

The baby was crying. Paige began to rise from her chair.

"Oh, *mi amor*, I do love my son but he does not have, what you say, the best time?" He shook his head and cleared his throat. "He does not want us to ever be intimate again."

"I think that's a bit of an exaggeration," Paige grinned as she started toward the hallway.

"It does seem to happen a lot, does it not?"

"He's probably afraid you will get me pregnant again," Paige joked as she headed toward the stairs.

"Oh *mi amor*, you would be pregnant like that," He bragged and snapped his fingers and winked at her just before she was out of sight.

Grabbing his phone, he sent a message to Chase.

Reviewing some videos. Who stands to make money here? That is what I wonder.

Seconds later he received a reply.

Good question. Someone is benefiting.

Overly produced videos.

I know.

Setting his phone down, he thought for a moment and grabbed it again. He would send a message to Tom Makerson, the editor or *Toronto AM*. This man had been a huge influence in the media when Jorge was pushing to have Alec Athas voted in the previous year. Makerson always had his ear to the ground and perhaps was aware of something they were not.

Hey, we got to talk. I got something for you.

Seconds later.

No problem.

Hearing his wife walking downstairs, Jorge pushed his phone aside. The sight of his son continued to have a calming effect on him; even when he cried, even when he wouldn't eat, even when he shit right through his diaper, Miguel was perfection. He was an angel to Jorge.

"Ah! My beautiful baby is awake," Jorge automatically reached out for the infant and noted his big eyes staring back. "This here, is the center of my world and you know what? I would not want him growing up in the boring place that Elizabeth Alan wishes for all of us. Let him discover, explore and see everything the world has to offer. And you know why? Because we do not bring up our children to be so easily influenced. That, to me, is the real problem."

"Sheep," Paige spoke quietly.

"As Diego always says, so many sheep, so few wolves," Jorge looked in his son's eyes. "But my son, he will be a wolf. He will rule the world someday."

Paige let out a laugh.

"Maybe we should wait until he's at least out of diapers before we start encouraging him to take over the world," She suggested as she headed towards the kitchen. "Do you want to feed him?"

"Of course, my love, nothing would make me happier."

"Nothing would make *me* happier," Paige insisted as the baby continued to stare at Jorge and Jorge, in return, smiled. "He doesn't want to eat for me. Or sleep for me. Or stop crying for me."

Hearing the defeat in his wife's voice, Jorge looked up as she prepared Miguel's bottle.

"Paige, do not be so hard on yourself," he reminded her. "It is not you. Babies, they are finicky."

"I feel like we aren't bonding," She admitted with sadness in her voice. "Jorge, I don't think I'm a good mother. I think he hates me."

Her words upset him.

"Paige," Jorge was in stunned disbelief. "This is not true! Do not be silly."

"He fusses as soon as I pick him up," Paige complained. "He won't eat for me and half the time, he's barfing on me."

"Paige, of course, he loves you but you," He stopped and considered his words carefully. "*Estas nervioso*. The baby, he must sense this from you."

Paige didn't reply but when she returned, her face was full of sadness. It broke his heart. She handed him the bottle.

"I do not say that to hurt you, *mi amor*," He reminded her since they had this conversation regularly. "It is because you are scared and have been since the first day of your pregnancy."

"I never thought I would be a mother so this...I don't think I'm good at it."

"It is not that my love," Jorge said as he started to feed the baby. "You must relax. Maybe spend more time on your meditation pillow, *si?* I think you must calm and he will too."

"But you're never calm," She pointed out as she sat down. "And he's great with you."

"Yes, but Paige, you must remember that he calms me," Jorge replied as he looked down at the baby sucking on the bottle. "So, this here calms him too. That is why. It is not because I'm the best father or you're the worst mother, it is just you are too worried."

"I know," She sadly admitted.

"*Mi amor*, it is how I always tell you," Jorge reminded her. "You must first take care of yourself. How about you relax today? Go shopping with Diego or whatever girly things he wants to do."

Paige laughed.

"Laugh! Yes, do some of that. Diego, he is dying to tell you about his crazy trip," Jorge said as he continued to look down at the baby, occasionally glancing at his wife. "Go, spend a day with him. I am here. The baby, he will be fine."

The doorbell rang and Jorge looked at his wife.

"It's probably Alec."

She rose from her chair as Jorge noticed the baby had stopped sucking the bottle and moved it away. He wasn't sure what to do next. Did he burp him? Feed him more? Considering this was his second child, this was something he should know but he was clueless. Unfortunately, Paige was even less experienced with children.

Alec and Paige could be heard talking and Jorge decided the baby looked like he wanted more milk, so returned the bottle to Miguel just as Alec walked in the room. Paige followed seconds later.

"I'm glad I caught you," Alec glanced down at the baby and continued. "Or is this a good time?"

"*Amigo,* I've run one of the largest cartels in the world," Jorge boldly reminded him. "I think I can feed a baby and carry on a conversation at the same time."

"Ok, fair enough," Alec laughed. "You're right about Elizabeth Alan she's definitely connected to a right-wing group and they're trying to find a party to hitch their wagon to and bring us down in the next election."

"Already?" Paige asked. "We just had an election."

"Yeah, well, there's some stuff going on but it doesn't matter because we're always looking ahead," Alec insisted and glanced at the baby who was resisting the bottle. "Jorge, I think he might need to be burped or something.

"I read online that babies have to sit up first so they don't vomit," Paige spoke nervously. "I think…"

"I don't know…" Alec spoke uncertainly.

"This baby, he is fine," Jorge insisted as he sat the baby up. "And you were saying."

"Their goal is to find a party and someone who people support, who people feel safe voting for that pushes their values," Alec spoke passionately.

"They want the ultra-conservative version of Jorge Hernandez. Someone who is strong, charming, persuasive…"

"Handsome?" Jorge teased. "This is me except I'm not about to help those motherfuckers out."

"Jorge, the baby…" Paige pointed out as he lifted the child up to his chest and rubbed his back.

"My love, Miguel is a Hernandez," Jorge teased and winked at her. "Him learning bad language should be the least of your worries."

It was then that he felt hot liquid on his chest. Looking down, he realized Miguel had spit up on him.

"Wonderful, this is another shirt in the garbage," Jorge said in a defeated voice as he moved the baby away and Paige grabbed some paper towels.

"Take it off," She instructed. "I'll try to get the stain out before it sets in."

"No no, wait!" Alec insisted and they both looked up at him in disbelief. "I have an idea."

CHAPTER 7

They shared a silent look in the elevator. It was a strong moment of eye contact that said more than any words could but yet, no one else would've been able to read it. The beauty of their relationship was that communication went beyond words and affection but into a deeper level that Jorge never would've thought existed had he not experienced it with Paige.

Neither said a thing when the elevator stopped. Jorge reached out to gently take her hand and they walked in silence toward the office. It was outside the doors that Paige hesitated as if she wanted to say something but didn't. Jorge took this as his cue to finally speak.

"You know, Paige, this is not something we need to talk to the others about yet," He quietly suggested as he squeezed her hand. "Perhaps it is too soon."

"I would rather we didn't talk about it at all," She quietly countered. "I don't think you've fully thought this through. I wish Alec hadn't brought it up."

"Alec, he knows," Jorge insisted and leaned in to kiss her. "It is not a huge deal. We will see but in the end, if he is right then perhaps, this is something that must be done."

"It *is* a huge deal," Paige insisted, her eyes begging. "The fact that you don't think it is, suggests you need to give it more thought. *Much* more thought."

"I cannot believe that you question Alec, of all people," Jorge attempted to tease her but it was clear she wasn't seeing the humor so he stared into her eyes. "*Mi amor,* this can be done and if anyone can do it, it is me. You know this is true."

"It doesn't mean it's a good idea," Paige insisted just as a figure showed up on the other side of the glass door. Diego Silva gave them both a funny look before roughly pulling the door open and inspecting their faces.

"What's going on? Are you two fighting? Is something wrong? Is my god*son* ok? Paige is…"

Jorge immediately cut off Diego's ramblings by putting his hand in the air and abruptly speaking over him.

"Diego, please, this is nothing, here," He gestured toward his wife. "We were discussing what to do for dinner tonight. Everything, it is not a drama, you know?"

Paige smiled beautifully and Jorge winked at her as they entered the office. Diego appeared unconvinced.

"You'd tell me, right?" Diego spoke gruffly, his face twisting into an odd expression as he fixed his tie. "You guys, you aren't holding back are you?"

"Diego, do we not tell you everything?" Jorge countered as they made their way toward the boardroom where he glanced in to see the others waiting. "The baby? Who was the first to know? Us eloping, who was the first to know? Diego, I assure you, when there's something to tell, we will let you know."

With that, the three of them entered the boardroom and headed for their usual seats except for Diego, who rushed to pour them each a coffee. Jorge noted that Jesús was squinting over his phone while Marco spoke to him in a low voice. On the other side of Jesús sat Chase, who was talking to Jolene about his kids in Alberta, which was interesting considering there had once been a great deal of tension between the two. Diego's boyfriend, Michael was at the table today and sitting on the other side of Jorge. The young black man leaned in while the Colombian scurried around the table to serve the coffee before sitting at the head of the table.

"Heard you had some problems at Maria's school?" Michael asked and raised an eyebrow. "Want me to go over and scare the shit out of the kid? Sometimes even having a cop car in front of someone's house is enough to shake their tree."

Jorge grinned at the idea and gave it some thought.

"You know, although I do appreciate the idea," He spoke evenly. "Maria has not had problems since that day so it is possible, I got my message across to the father."

"I don't know. From what Diego was saying, this Harrison guy is one strange fuck."

"Religion," Jorge said bluntly. "Is it not the root of all evil?"

Michael answered by raising an eyebrow and grinning.

"Ok, let us get this show on the road," Jorge spoke up with his usual abruptness, causing everyone to stop their independent conversations and focus on him. "What's everyone got for me today?"

"Sir, may I speak first?" Marco raised his hand slightly with uncertainty.

"Marco, you are new to our meetings," Jorge spoke respectively. "But have you not noticed that we are pretty uncivilized so there is no need to be formal."

Marco's face automatically relaxed as he began to laugh and nod while the others showed some form of amusement.

"Yes, sir, I do understand," He paused for a moment before continuing. "I wanted to say that Chase and I continue to do research and it seems that we may have found a connection between this Canadians for Conservative Values group that Elizabeth Alan is part of and some right-wing politicians. Remember, sir, that man who made the racist remarks during the Christmas holidays?"

"The *gringo* that was caught on someone's phone saying that Canada is a Christian *only* country?" Jorge glanced at his wife.

"Oh, that guy," Paige spoke evenly. "He felt that only Christians should be allowed in the country and then later said it was taken out of context?"

"That is the one, Mrs. Hernandez," Marco said and vigorously nodded. Across the table, Jorge noted that Chase was rolling his eyes. "Anyway, he seems to be in regular contact with this woman."

"I'm not surprised," Chase jumped in. "That whole party's a bunch of racist knuckle draggers."

"To me, every party has racist members," Jorge spoke with assertiveness while reaching for his coffee. "None of these parties, I do not think, care about multiculturalism. They care about getting the votes and will say whatever their polls tell them to say. If they think it will get followers by saying the moon is made of dog shit, they will say it. That is politics."

"There's no more integrity," Diego sharply commented and nodded while scrunching up his lips. "That's probably why voters are apathetic."

"Diego, do you think there ever was integrity in politics?" Jorge countered. "I do not care where any of us are from originally, we can all say that about our home countries. Paige, Chase, you have lived in Canada your whole lives, what do you think?"

"I think we're getting off track," Paige smoothly replied and gave him a look, causing Jorge to laugh.

"*Mi amor,* as usual, you are right," Jorge said and took a moment to regroup. "So what you are saying, Chase, is that this woman, her intentions are less than sincere?"

"Basically," Chase nodded and glanced around the table. "I'm only reading between the lines but her emails leaves me with the impression that she was approached to start this group."

"Either that or she started a blog to discuss her grief," Paige jumped in and glanced at Jorge. "And maybe someone saw it and encouraged her to take it a step further."

"She was clearly a willing participant, no?" Jolene spoke uncertainly. "But also, if she had grief in her heart, maybe she not see that these people were bad?"

Everyone fell silent for a moment. Knowing that Jolene had suffered a loss herself, it made sense to Jorge that she would best understand and took her words into consideration. Beside her, Chase gave a knowing glance and Jorge looked away. He couldn't imagine losing one of his children as he had. The world would never be a safe place if he lost anyone he loved.

"Well, this is a good point, Jolene," Jorge said and fell silent.

"Not necessarily," Michael cut in with skepticism in his voice. "You gotta see what I see at the station. You wouldn't believe how convincing people can be when it suits their agenda. For all we know, the kid could've taken some of her stash. Don't be bought in by the window dressing. People, they *lie* and some are fucking good at it."

Jorge noted the bitterness in his voice.

"Regardless, we gotta move on here," He was curt in his reply. "The bottom line is I am not having this conservatism shoved down my fucking throat and I am sure as hell not going to see marijuana criminalized again. Do not get me wrong, I'm gonna sell it either way and actually, it might be easier to not deal with government regulations if it was illegal. But I have invested too much time and money to backtrack now."

"Our sales keep going up every month," Diego jumped in. "Especially now that we resolved the supply issues we dealt with over the winter."

"It is hard to keep up with such crazy numbers but that is why we contacted our friends in Mexico and now," Jorge glanced at Diego who was nodding. "Colombia. This here is perfect, we can be assured of meeting demand this summer with the tourists and of course, our festival."

"We are the only pot business out there that is able to keep up with demand," Jesús reminded them. "That is why we have such a strong lead in the industry."

"And it's going to stay that way too," Jorge insisted. "This Christian fucking lady and her conservative values won't stop me."

"But sir, how can she anyway," Jesús asked as he scratched the bald spot on his head. "I do not understand. We are now one of the leading industries in the country. You were featured in that national magazine recently as one of our strongest businessmen in Canada and the government, they are making so much in taxes so it does not make sense to criminalize it again."

"Unless," Michael cut in just as Paige was about to say something. "Unless people feel it is doing more harm than good. If they can make it sound like it's a gateway drug and causing more crime, people will be for criminalizing it again. That's how the government works and that's how the law works."

"But if that were the case, we wouldn't have alcohol either," Chase countered and Jorge noted that his wife was pursing her lips as if in thought. "There are more problems stemming from alcohol than pot."

"But it is more socially acceptable," Jolene seemed to stumble over her words as her Colombian accented grew thicker. "With my addiction group, they say that it is more difficult with alcohol because it is ok with the people. It is accepting by the people."

"Accepted," Diego corrected her, automatically causing Jolene's eyes to narrow in anger. Jorge jumped in before the two could start an argument over her broken English.

"Ok, so, yes, this is a good point," Jorge agreed. "We are not quite there yet with pot."

"You have to also consider that if they find out our weed is coming from Mexico and now, Colombia," Paige reminded him. "This could be held against us since they are countries recognized for a lot of murder and mayhem surrounding the drug trade."

She gave him a warning look that he knew extended beyond this conversation.

"This, my love, I do see but they have always had a blind eye to the drugs coming into this country," He calmly answered. "The people at the top, they are making too much money to care."

"We need to find a way to be reassured," Diego said as he sat up straighter. "We can't have the government pulling a fast one."

"Let me worry about the government," Jorge replied as his eyes evaluated everyone around the table. "And in turn, they should worry about *me.*"

CHAPTER 8

Tom Makerson had been the editor of *Toronto AM* since the sudden death of Robert Sturk Junior the previous year. He had proven very helpful to Hernandez especially when Alec Athas was running in the last federal election and needed a boost in the polls. Although Jorge saw the media as a necessary evil, he did approve of how Makerson ran his paper.

After dropping Paige off at home, Jorge met with the young editor at a small coffee shop, not far from his office in the downtown area. Although the two men hadn't seen each other much since the fall election, it was good knowing he was only a phone call away.

"So tell me," Jorge jumped in as soon as they sat down, both with a coffee in hand. "What's the deal on this group, Canadians for Conservative Values and that lady, Elizabeth Alan? What do you know?"

"I would say," Tom spoke stiffly, glancing around as if to make sure no one was nearby. "They're definitely gathering some steam."

"See, to me, a country that's ok with marijuana being legal isn't exactly conservative in nature," Jorge said before taking a drink of his coffee. "It does not make sense. Perhaps, you can enlighten me."

"Well with all the murders in the city in the last year, I guess people are worried," Makerson spoke thoughtfully as he ran a hand through his strawberry blond hair. "Especially after those men died in cottage country, remember the fire? Rumor has it that they were all shot too but the police didn't bother to investigate and basically labeled it as an unfortunate forest fire."

Jorge nodded in silence. Tom looked into his eyes and quickly looked away.

"And ah…yeah, so there's that but there have been some other random murders like that old woman from the pharmaceutical company…"

Makerson once again looked into Jorge's eyes and quickly looked away.

"And you know…others…." He drifted off.

"Well, death, it is always unfortunate, is it not?" Jorge replied while challenging Makerson's eyes. "But it is a part of life."

"The point is that this, along with drugs on the streets and the rise in violent crimes has made people nervous," Makerson began to speak slowly as if choosing his words with care. "I think this conservative group is playing on people's fears and I think that Elizabeth Alan is the perfect spokesperson since she lost her son to drugs. She seems like a sympathetic character."

"Seems?" Jorge caught the last word and jumped on it. "You know something that I don't?"

"I heard stuff…"

"*Amigo,* come on, don't hold out on me," Jorge spoke in a gentle tone. "If you know something, you must share it with me."

"Well rumor has it that she was a party girl at one time," Makerson said and then quickly added. "Of course, I'm not sure if this is true and regardless, it has nothing to do with her son's death."

"Was he an addict or some kid playing around not knowing what he was doing?" Jorge countered. "Rich, white boy, chances are this wasn't his first time doing a few lines."

"No, I'm hearing he liked to party," Makerson leaned in. "And that he was into some pretty interesting stuff."

"Drug wise?"

"No no, I'm talking otherwise," Makerson said as he shook his head. "Her son was no saint. He liked to party a lot…with girls and boys."

"So bi?"

"Yup and at the same time," Makerson said in barely a whisper. "I couldn't get anyone to back me up on the story but rumor had it that when emergency responders arrived, there were a lot of fucked up kids, semi-dressed, if dressed at all, together in the same room. I'm guessing that's not the part of the story that Elizabeth Alan wishes to talk about."

Jorge grinned and shook his head. "Oh *amigo,* as usual, you do not disappoint."

"As for this group she's linked to," Makerson said as he relaxed in his seat. "They seemed to come out of nowhere. I never heard of them until a few months ago. Suddenly, she's being linked to them."

"As I recently said to my wife," Jorge spoke thoughtfully as a young couple walked by and he waited until they sat in the corner to continue. "This is not because it interests these people. Someone is going to make money otherwise, why would they bother?"

"It depends, what are they pushing for specifically?"

"I heard they might want to criminalize marijuana again."

Tom Makerson laughed.

"As if that would ever happen," He shook his head. "The government is making a shitload of money in taxes."

"That is what I said too but there must be an angle," Jorge replied.

"Well, what does conservatism mean?" Makerson spoke thoughtfully, glancing at the couple in the corner. "What do they want?"

"Well, my daughter, she recently got into some trouble at school with this other kid," Jorge said and thought for a moment. "This other kid tried to strangle her and when I went to see the parents, it seems that only the mother takes care of the child and the father acted as if it wasn't his 'job' to get involved. That seems pretty conservative if not going back in time. Do you think it is the same?"

"That's interesting although very extreme," Makerson thought for a moment. "I wonder if he's connected to this group. I would guess having greater control over the people would be a benefit to someone but who?"

"Well, the pot side of it, I would say Big Pharma," Jorge replied. "They are losing money since legalization other than the synthetic shit versions of cannabis."

"Well, never underestimate Big Pharma but it sounds like something more at work here," Makerson spoke thoughtfully. "Let me do some digging and see what I can come up with."

"No one digs better than you."

Makerson merely grinned.

Jorge returned home to find Jolene feeding Miguel while beside her, Maria was rattling on about her plans for the summer. Glancing around, he immediately noticed his wife wasn't in the room.

"Where is Paige?" He abruptly asked, cutting into his daughter's story. "She is not home?"

"She's upstairs," Jolene pointed toward the ceiling and lowered her voice. "I drop in to see the baby and I told her to go sleep. Jorge, she does not look well, you know? Maybe she is low in a vitamin or something?"

He didn't reply. Noting the look of concern on Jolene's face, Jorge immediately headed for the stairs.

In their bedroom, he found Paige lying down. She opened her eyes as he approached the bed.

"*Mi amor,* is everything ok?"

"Yeah," She quietly replied. "I'm just tired."

"The baby, he is wearing you out," Jorge said as he sat down beside her. "We must get a nanny to help. This is too much for you."

"It shouldn't be," Paige started to rise from the bed. "Other mothers do it and most have no help and more children."

"You are not other mothers," He quickly pointed out. "Do not compare yourself. Maybe you need to visit the doctor?"

"I'm fine," Paige insisted as he reached for her hand and leaned in to give her a quick kiss.

"You don't look fine to me," Jorge replied. "Jolene is right, you look tired."

"It's normal," Paige insisted. "The baby is only a few weeks old. The labor was hard, Miguel doesn't like to sleep much at night and he's so fussy with me."

"He's fussy with us all."

"But me," Paige shook her head with sadness in her eyes. "He's so detached from me. Even Jolene is down there cuddling and feeding him with no problem. Maria doesn't have a problem. You, Chase, Diego....even Jesús has no problem. But me..."

"Paige, it is as I said, you are nervous with him," Jorge insisted. "Do not take it to heart. You're his mother. Of course, he isn't detached from you."

"I don't know, this doesn't feel right." She spoke sadly.

"Paige, you read these terrible magazines and watch these silly movies with Maria," He countered. "And they tell you that you have a baby and everything is beautiful and wonderful and there's an instant attachment but you know, that isn't always the case. You will see. It will get better."

She appeared unconvinced.

"I used to feel the same when Maria was born," Jorge pointed out. "I felt attached to her but when I would hold her, she would cry. I assumed it was because I was away so much but look at us now, we are very close."

"She is talking about auditioning for parts this summer," Paige quietly changed the subject and Jorge immediately grew tense, shaking his head.

"This fucking acting thing," He complained. "I do not want my daughter involved in such a shitty business and yet, what does she choose?"

Paige shrugged. "I hate to say it but maybe she has to experience it to see it's not always glamorous."

"But *mi amor,* I also do not want to hurt my daughter," Jorge considered her idea. "These auditions, they can be brutal."

"I know but I think she has to see it for herself because she won't listen to us," Paige reminded him. "She's pretty headstrong."

"I wonder where she got that," Jorge teased Paige. "Obviously, not me."

"Obviously," Paige rolled her eyes and laughed.

"Yes, well, if she insists, I guess that is what we must do," Jorge replied and looked toward the closed door. "Jolene, she is good with the baby."

"I know, who ever thought we would let her near our child?" Paige said thoughtfully. "This time last year…"

"This time last year, there would be no way in hell we would allow her into the house let alone near our son," Jorge replied while squeezing his wife's hand. "but she is the godmother and Diego is the godfather, both would do anything for Miguel. Jolene was there when you went into labor and took good care of you till I arrived."

"She did."

"I would think that Jolene would have issues, since…you know," Jorge said. "It has not been that long since her miscarriage."

"She told me that it heals her to be with Miguel," Paige spoke with emotion in her eyes. "I can't even imagine losing a child after having my own. How does a mother get over that?"

"She grew stronger," Jorge said and squeezed his wife's hand again. "And you, my love, you will get stronger too. You're a Hernandez. Nothing and nobody holds us down for long."

Her blue eyes shone and a smile crept on her lips.

CHAPTER 9

"Papa, as you know the summer is quickly approaching and I've given my plans some thought," Maria spoke up at breakfast the next morning while Paige poured herself a cup of coffee and Jorge looked up from his phone. The sound of the television in the next room briefly caught his attention but he quickly glanced back at his daughter.

"That is good, Maria," Jorge encouraged her while out of the corner of his eye he could see Paige giving him a sideways glance. "But you know, you are also allowed to enjoy your summer. Last year, you worked very hard in acting classes with no break to have fun."

"Oh, but *Papa*, acting classes *are* fun," Maria insisted, her brown eyes widened in excitement. "It's my passion in life."

Jorge opened his mouth to comment but hearing his 11-year-old daughter talk about 'passion' somehow left him unable to speak.

"This summer, however, is my time to shine," Her eyes lit up as she spoke. "This summer, *Papa,* I would like to audition for some television roles."

"Maria, I don't know…"

"*Papa,* I'm ready and we cannot waste time," Maria was insistent. "It's important that I get out there and gain some experience when I'm young."

"Maria, you are 11-years-old," Jorge reminded her. "This is too young to get in the acting world."

"But *Papa!* This is my *passion!*" She spoke dramatically, waving her arms in the air. Paige gave him a warning glance before rushing toward the stairs with a cup of coffee in hand. "I'm almost twelve and a teenager! You can't hold me back from growing up."

"Maria, we have this discussion again and again," Jorge complained, no longer holding back his frustration as he spoke sternly. "Twelve is not a teenager, twelve, it is still a child. You are too young to get mixed up in this acting world. It is not what you think Maria. I have met actors and it can be a cruel business."

"I can handle it," Maria spoke stubbornly, sitting up taller. "You will see."

"Maria, Paige and I are busy," Jorge continued to grasp at straws. "We do not have time to take you to auditions and we certainly will not be leaving the city to do so either."

"There are lots here in Toronto," Maria countered. "And I can find the auditions myself and if you and Paige are busy, I'll ask Chase or Jolene or Diego or Jesús…"

"Maria, I don't know…" Jorge felt himself cave in and shook his head. His daughter had no idea what she was asking. "Why do you want to do this? I do not understand."

"Because I love to act!" She insisted. "Please, *Papa!*"

"Ok, I will think about it," Jorge promised as he glanced toward the living room to see a familiar face on television. It was Elizabeth Alan. "Maria, just a second, I must see this."

Getting up from his chair, he rushed into the next room and grabbed the remote. Turning up the volume, he listened carefully.

"…..values were strong when I was a child. My parents had strict rules and we knew that it was necessary to abide by them. Parenting now is much more difficult and we're suffering as a society. Our kids are growing up with no morals, no values, no social skills and, no respect."

"How would you suggest that we change this? What do you think we need to do?" The young reporter countered.

Elizabeth Alan paused for a moment.

"We need more structure. More defined roles in the family. We need more discipline and go back to the old ways that worked for our parents,"

Elizabeth shook her head. "We need higher expectations for our kids. Right now, we're letting them down and it's affecting everyone."

"You say that this was brought on by your son's death," The reporter continued. "Do you think this structure would've helped him?"

"I do," Elizabeth spoke with conviction. "I allowed him to explore the world and I was quite liberal when it came to parenting and look where it got me. I no longer have my son."

"Your movement has some controversial ideas," The reporter continued. "For example, you suggest that the male and female roles in a household should be clearly defined in order to not confuse the child. Why is this necessary?"

"Kids need to see structure within their home at an early age," Elizabeth spoke stiffly. "If they grow up knowing 'Mommy does this' and 'Daddy does that' then there's no confusion. Right now, our children are lost with no clear gender roles."

"Your ideas, however, go beyond the family unit," The reporter pushed. "You have also suggested that school and government need to make some changes."

"Canadians for Conservative Values believe we're getting much too liberal in this country," Elizabeth shook her head. "For example, legalizing pot? How could legalizing a proven gateway drug be a good idea? Our government has gone way too far this time. If it wasn't for marijuana, my son might be alive today."

She teared up.

"He started with pot and it led to more harmful drugs. They can say it isn't a gateway drug but I know better..."

"*Papa,* who is this crazy lady?" Maria approached him holding a cup of coffee in her hand.

"Maria, why are you holding a cup of coffee?" Jorge changed the topic while suppressing his frustration with the woman on television.

"I drink coffee now," She replied then carefully brought the cup to her mouth and took a sip. "It helps me stay alert."

Jorge decided that this wasn't a battle he wanted to fight and instead turned his attention to his ringing iPhone on the table. Rushing back, he noted it was Diego calling him.

"Yeah," He answered abruptly.

"Hey, did you see the conservative *puta* on the news," Diego spoke with his usual vigor. "Michael said that's the lady you were talking about the other day. Why did they let her on the news?"

Another call interrupted Jorge's thoughts and he glanced at his phone. It was from Tom Makerson.

"I gotta go, Diego."

Without saying good-bye, he took Makerson's call.

"Did you see the news?"

"Yup," Jorge answered abruptly while he watched his daughter saunter across the floor, drinking her coffee.

"She's getting national attention now so that could be a problem," Makerson suggested. "We need to do an article that counters everything she said but *you,* as the CEO of Canada's largest pot retailers, you need to get on television and shut her down. I'm going to make some calls then do a feature in *Toronto AM* this weekend."

"Ok," Jorge replied without a second thought. "But will people listen to this lunatic?"

"They might," Makerson said with a heavy sigh. "Look, I've been doing some digging and she's really got her claws in and I suspect that someone pretty powerful is pushing their agenda. We know Big Pharma wants to own the market but I don't think it's them this time. It could be completely political but I'm still looking into it. The point is that we have to act right away before this woman starts a fire we can't control."

Jorge agreed and ended the call. His daughter was staring at him.

"Do you not need to get ready for school?" He glanced at her and suddenly realized she was still in her robe.

"I thought I would take a personal day to think about my future goals," She replied.

"Maria! Get upstairs now and get ready for school!" Jorge hollered causing his daughter to jump and spill some coffee on the floor. "And clean that up! Enough of this ridiculous crap. You are not missing school."

Upstairs, the baby started to cry and downstairs, his daughter did the same as she rushed to grab some paper towel and clean up the coffee.

"But *Papa,* with the new baby and everything, I need a day to.."

"Upstairs, Maria!" Jorge ordered as he watched her finish cleaning up the mess. "You have 5 minutes."

Glancing at his phone, he saw text messages, voice mails and wanted to throw his phone across the room. It was only early and already his day was frustrating. Maria ran upstairs and slammed her bedroom door. The coffee pot was making a sizzling noise and he realized it was empty and quickly rushed across the room to unplug it.

Jorge then rushed upstairs, noting that Maria's door was still closed, he headed to the end of the hallway. There, he found Paige in the baby's room, attempting to calm Miguel as he screamed while she cried in frustration. Rushing across the room, he gently removed the baby from her arms and tried to console him.

"Oh Miguel," He stared into his son's eyes and noted that the baby began to calm while Paige only cried harder. Glancing at his wife, then his son, his attention suddenly hijacked when Maria showed up at the door with her backpack in hand, her uniform on.

"I'm ready!' She snapped and glanced at Paige. "You made her cry too?"

"Maria!" Jorge snapped back, causing the baby to cry again.

"See! You make us all cry!" Maria complained.

"That's not the case," Paige sobbed and Maria rushed to her. Jorge took the baby out of the room. "Things are just really stressful right now…"

It was while he comforted his child in the hallway that it suddenly hit him; Elizabeth Alan may have had an angle but so did he. That *puta* was going down with one fierce swoop.

CHAPTER 10

Jorge shuffled in his seat. The overpowering lights were hot, causing beads of sweat to form along his hairline. He reached for a bottle of water on the nearby table, relieved he had worn a strong deodorant under his suit because the studio felt like a sauna. Jorge barely had taken a drink when, a tall, heavy woman rushed in and swept a brush of powder on his face before quickly disappearing. He sat the bottle down and glanced at Paige waiting on the sidelines. She wasn't happy when he was in the spotlight but always supported him.

Jorge was asked to move a bit to the right, then a little to the left until a man came over and showed him exactly how to sit. The host, Meghan Willa strutted in wearing heels that resembled something he'd expect to see wrapped around a pole and not on a serious news reporter. They shook hands and she shot a fake smile before sitting across from him. In person she appeared apathetic and tired, wearing layers of makeup that didn't hide much because little is hidden on television. At least, not to the discriminating eyes.

Up until the time of the interview, he remained quiet, stoic even, as he observed the woman about to interview him. According to Tom Makerson, she wasn't respected among journalists, merely a pretty face who picked up a job with the network and *somehow* moved up the ranks. Makerson didn't hide the fact that he was looking forward to the fierce Mexican taking on the flakey reporter.

As soon as the camera started to record, a smooth smile took over his face as Meghan introduced him as the CEO of Our House of Pot, the largest pot retailer in Canada. Out of the corner of his eye, he noted her fingers were fidgeting with a pen and he felt his own inner strength increase. He fed on other people's anxiety.

"Good morning and thank you for joining us, Mr. Hernandez," Meghan said with a bright smile on her face.

"It is my pleasure," Jorge replied courteously.

"You've been very busy since marijuana was legalized," Meghan pointed out as her green eyes widened as did a disingenuous smile on her lips. "Our House of Pot has grown quickly and the company's sales are far beyond what many people predicted. Was this a surprise to you?"

"Not at all," Jorge replied with a slight shrug. "In fact, I believe this is something Canadians have wanted for a long time. Unfortunately, the government wasn't always listening."

"That's interesting," Meghan remarked, her fingers continued to fidget with the pen. "So you feel that legalization should've been introduced before it was?"

"Absolutely," Jorge calmly replied and with a sudden burst of fire, he continued. "I believe the lineups on the first day is proof that Canadians were *more* than ready for legalization. The government, unfortunately, it often does not listen to its people. We live in a democracy but yet, do we really?"

"So, you feel that *our* Canadian government doesn't listen to its people?" She asked defensively, and that was when Jorge knew he had Meghan Willa exactly where he wanted her.

"No, Ms. Willa, I feel that *no* government listens to its people," Jorge corrected her. "In Mexico, it was the same and when I worked in the United States as a salesperson for my father's company years ago, I noticed it was the same as well. No matter what country I've visited, the people often have similar complaints."

"Fortunately," He continued. "The Canadian government finally did as the people asked. That is why this is such a beautiful country."

He could see Meghan Willa pale beneath the bright lights. Jorge knew little about journalism however, he was quite sure that it was up to the reporter to control the interview and at that moment, it was him that was in control. But he continued to smile. He continued to show his fake charm as he sat up a bit straighter, his eyes challenging the nervous woman who sat across from him.

"It was a bold move, politically," Meghan seemed to regain her confidence. "There are many who opposed the decision including Elizabeth Alan, who's with Canadians for Conservative Values."

Jorge merely nodded.

"She feels," Meghan continued as her eyes grew in size. "that Canadians are heading in the *wrong* direction and that marijuana is a gateway drug. What are your thoughts on this, Mr. Hernandez?"

"With the utmost respect to Elizabeth Alan," Jorge replied. "I disagree. I believe that Canada is one of the most progressive and forward-thinking countries in the world. We cannot allow unjustified fears to hold us back. I do not believe that marijuana is a gateway drug. We must remember that it is now legal but people have used cannabis for many years and not necessarily to get high but also as a medicine. This is not a new, experimental drug but something that is natural and has been a part of our culture for decades."

"But just because it has been part of our culture," Meghan spoke confidently while her fingers continued to fidget. "That doesn't mean it hasn't been a gateway drug. Elizabeth Alan and many others have spoken out to say that their children started out smoking pot and eventually moved on to use much heavier drugs."

"Let me be direct with you, Ms. Willa," Jorge spoke slowly, his eyes staring into hers, while a fake smile sat on her face. "It would be naïve of us to believe that without marijuana, that these same people would not try hard drugs. Rather than laying the blame, should we not instead be looking at the bigger picture? Why are these people feeling the need to take drugs when they know the risks involved? What is wrong with our society to cause such things? Do we need more resources in mental health? Do we need to look at the legal pharmaceuticals that are causing devastating addictions? Perhaps, this is where our focus should be."

"Are you suggesting that no one who smokes pot won't move on to heavier drugs?"

"Not at all," Jorge was quick to reply, his comment sharp as he swung his hand in the air. "What I am saying is that it is easier to lay blame than to find real solutions. If you removed marijuana from the conversation, if tomorrow it no longer existed, completely unavailable, do you *really* believe there would be no addiction problems?"

Meghan Willa appeared stunned by his reply.

"That is a great point," She answered with another fake smile and suddenly cut him off. "Thank you. We were speaking with Jorge Hernandez, CEO of Our House of Pot."

As soon as the camera stopped rolling, the reporter's expression fell flat and she glared at him.

"Mr. Hernandez, you're clearly not aware how interviews work but you do *not* ask me the questions, it's the other way around," The reporter snapped as she jumped off her chair while across from her, Jorge gingerly rose from his seat with a sanctimonious smile on his face.

"Well, Ms. Willa," Jorge countered as he removed his microphone. "I do believe, it is the reporter's job to keep the interview in line, am I not correct? Perhaps, you would be better suited for a different career and asking people questions merely be, how do you say, a hobby?"

With that, Jorge placed the mic on his chair and began to walk away. Before he was able to join his grinning wife, the director rushed up to him.

"Mr. Hernandez," He hurriedly approached him. "Please accept my apologies for Ms. Willa, her reaction was completely inappropriate and does not reflect this network."

"I see," Jorge replied without giving the man any room to wiggle

"There are no excuses for her behavior and I will be speaking to her shortly," The small man commented, rubbing a hand over his bald head as he took him aside, his voice lowered. "You had some very strong views on the topic and perhaps she wasn't expecting such a reaction."

"I understand," Jorge nodded dismissively and started to once again walk toward his wife. "Now, if you will excuse me, I must go to another appointment."

"Of course," The man replied. "Thank you again."

"Wow," Paige muttered when he finally reached her and they started toward the elevator.

"You know me, Paige, I do not hold back," Jorge replied in a low voice, as he glanced around at curious eyes one last time. "If they want to put my business up for target practice, then they better have their best soldiers. That woman, back there, she was nothing. She would be better suited to do shows about gardening not playing reporter."

"You're right about that," Paige commented as they got in the empty elevator and for a moment, while the door closed, neither said a thing. Her voice soft, gentle, she continued. "I thought it was sexy."

"You thought it was sexy?" Jorge asked, surprised by her reaction as the energy changed between them. "What do you mean?"

"You were bold, strong, you had that fire in your eyes," Paige replied as her hand slowly slid up his arm and she moved closer to him. "I thought it was sexy how you put the reporter in her place. You're so confident. No one fucks with Jorge Hernandez."

She whispered the last words in his ear, sending a shot of desire through his body. Jorge slid his hand around her waist, taking a detour to cup and squeeze her hip as his breath grew labored just as the door opened.

Walking into the parking garage, he glanced around, his mind racing. If they went home, a crying baby would await them allowing them no privacy.

"I especially loved it when you made her look like a fool in the interview," Paige continued as he reached for her hand. His eyes widened as he listened, his libido stirring with desire and his heart raced. He cleared his throat as she continued to speak softly. "You took over and she didn't have a hope in hell."

Jorge stared at his wife as she raised an eyebrow.

"Anyone watching the interview will see that she was ill-equipped as a reporter," Paige said with a smirk on her face.

"But the interview," Jorge finally found his voice as his eyes glanced around looking for his SUV. "They will cut out what they want. There will be nothing left. They will never make their reporter look bad."

"Wanna bet?" Paige asked as Jorge looked in her eyes. "That was a strong interview. They aren't going to cut a thing."

"Oh, *mi amor,* I do not know," His breath continued to grow labored as he thought about everything he wanted to do to her; their sex life had been fast and furious, if not rare since the birth of Miguel but at that moment, he knew it was time to revive it. "We have to go somewhere."

Looking into his eyes, Paige replied. "You know I would go *anywhere* with you."

"A hotel?" Jorge asked, his voice grew vulnerable, his body weak. "Across the street, there is a hotel. I want to go there with you. We need some time alone away from everything. Just us. That is what I want, *mi amor,* more than anything else in the world."

"Then that's what we should do," Paige replied. "Unless you have..."

"Diego, the others, they can wait," Jorge commented grabbing his phone. "I will say I got tied up at the studio with something. We will meet them later...."

"Sounds good to me," Paige replied as she pulled him close and their lips met. Their kiss started soft and gentle and quickly grew in passion, as his hands ran up and down her body, he suddenly stopped and moved away from her.

"We must go, now, *mi amor,*" He spoke breathlessly as he read the lust in her eyes. "I will message them all, you, can you take care of Clara. Do you think she can stay?"

"She'll stay," Paige assured him as she reached in her purse. "We got this covered."

"And Paige?" He spoke gently as her blue eyes looked up. "I will devour you."

CHAPTER 11

They were barely in the room when their lips met with unexpected aggression that hadn't existed since the birth of their son. In fact, Jorge had shown reluctance to express the same fierce passion that normally dominated their sex life in the past. Even during the pregnancy, he was hesitant until Paige assured him that she wasn't fragile and sought the same intensity that had been a consistent theme throughout their relationship.

"Mi amor," He suddenly stopped as she threw his tie aside and began to work on the buttons of his shirt. "Perhaps, we should be cautious. I know that this isn't the first time but maybe we need to be…"

Her blue eyes focused on his face, quickly scanning down to his lips as she swooped in to kiss him. This time he didn't fight back, his tongue quickly darting into her mouth as his hands worked to unzip her dress that quickly fell to the floor. He noted she stepped away from the material while he removed his shirt and she unzipped his pants. Jorge immediately felt his desires multiple, as he stepped away to finish removing his clothes.

Suddenly shy, Paige pointed toward an opened blind. "Can you close that?" She now stood self-consciously and he made a point of not looking toward her stomach. That had proven a bad idea in the past even though Paige had a way of bringing attention to it. He merely nodded and followed her instructions.

Deciding it was best to approach her as if there was no awkwardness in the room, Jorge lurched forward, his lips quickly taking over where they had left off moments earlier. He showed no shyness when touching her body, no reluctance to remove her bra, sliding his lips down to her breasts. His tongue barely touched her nipple, he was surprised when she let out a small gasp. It was a different sound. One she had never made before so rather than moving on he continued, his tongue increasing the intensity as her nipple grew hard as his hand reached for her other breast, his fingers working gently at first, he instinctively began to pinch the nipple and Paige gasped loudly, her body twitching as her breathing rapidly increased. His tongue working harder, his fingers moving quickly, Jorge witnessed Paige experience waves of pleasure that was clearly an unexpected surprise.

He finally moved away, seeing her flushed face, his lips roughly returned to hers, his tongue slithering in her mouth, he pulled her body close as they both moved toward the bed. He stopped kissing her long enough for them to get on top of the covers before his powerful return, noting that Paige was meeting his passion with the same intensity she always had, with no hesitation. His hands ran down her smooth skin and over her hips. Noting that she was still wearing panties, he began to pull them down and she repositioned herself, helping to remove the only barrier between them.

Falling on his back, he pulled her on top of him. Since Miguel's birth, he had been cautious, allowing her to lead the way, nervous of hurting her, pushing things a little too far, as he often had a tendency to do in the bedroom. He was hardly a gentle, romantic lover but a man who saw the act as a carnal experience that required the buildup of lust with a powerful release, that sent him and his partner to a secret world of pleasure that could be felt in every inch of their bodies.

Positioning herself on top, Paige leaned down to kiss his lips as she started to grind against him, causing his desires to mount until Jorge thought he was going to lose his mind. How many times had he laid next to her, unsure on whether or not to express his needs, fearful of being selfish, knowing she was exhausted and overwhelmed. It built up slowly, almost painfully in the weeks since Miguel's birth until the point that a less loyal man would've probably cheated.

Now, he was getting his reward. Feeling her tongue trailing down his body until the instant perfection when it touched the end of his penis. Her mouth was a pleasurable warmth that worked a magical bliss that caused his breath to grow heavier.

Merely a short introduction to the main show, she moved away and crawled back up his body, while he stared into her eyes, silently communicating how much he wanted her. As she lowered her body, he closed his eyes briefly as she slowly, tortuously moved him inside her, causing him to gasp when she finally sat on him and began to rock. His hands reached out to grasp both sides of her hips, he expected their usual, slow encounters since both were nervous since she gave birth but this time she quickly picked up the speed and he felt her squeeze her hips together causing him to let out a loud moan that filled the room.

Her movements quickened, as she roughly rocked her hips and began to lift them slightly, causing him to squeeze her ass and thrust his own hips forward. Paige began to moan loudly, a whimper of pleasure that turned to loud cries as she leaned back slightly, her face flushed, she finally stopped with one last moan and he pulled her body down hard while lifting his hips one last time, letting out a loud gasp as she collapsed on him.

"Oh *mi amor*! That was beautiful," Jorge replied as waves of pleasure filled his body. It was the most satisfying experience he had in weeks, as his heart pounded, his legs felt weak. He pulled her close and closed his eyes. "Let us stay here all day. Fuck everyone else. Fuck the meeting. Fuck everything."

"What about the kids?" Paige whispered.

"They'll be fine," Jorge assured her as euphoria flowed through him. "Clara, she will stay. Maria is home today, so there is no need to pick her up, all will be fine."

Paige giggled.

"You know, this here was a great idea," Jorge continued. "Maybe we must do this more often. Have a room."

"We have a room at home," Paige teased.

"Yes, with a crying baby in the next room," Jorge reminded her. "As soon as I get an erection, I swear, that baby wakes up and cries. I had one in the shower the other day and he started to cry. He's probably at home crying right now."

Paige laughed and moved away to look in his eyes.

"I think that might be a bit of a stretch," She smiled, her eyes lit up for the first time in weeks. "So what did you do about the shower situation?"

"I jerked off but I didn't enjoy it," Jorge replied and boldly moved forward to kiss her. "I love my son but he does not want me to have sex ever again."

"I think it's a stage," Paige replied and her face grew somber. "Just like his clear dislike for me."

"Paige, he does not dislike you," Jorge said and pulled her close again, kissing her forehead. "You need to relax and you know what? More days like this, where we schedule time alone, away from the kids, this might be exactly what you need. What we both need."

"Maybe you won't rip apart a reporter as often," She teased and he laughed then winked.

"Oh no, that has nothing to do with sexual frustration," He countered. "That is just Jorge Hernandez being Jorge Hernandez. That woman was ill-prepared for a serious interview. People want the truth. They want the blunt answers and no nonsense. That is who I am. That is what she got."

His interview was on the news that evening. As Paige predicted, the network kept it in its entirety with some light editing so that the audience didn't see Meghan Willa's nervousness. However, Jorge's dominance was clear. Paige gave him an approving look while Maria wrinkled her nose.

"*Papa,* you disagree with me being on television and then you do this interview," She immediately grew obnoxious, causing Jorge to flinch. "Why is this ok for you and not me?"

"Maria, this was an interview," Jorge reminded her. "I was not acting in a program. I was asked to defend my business and this is the only reason why I am on television. *Bonita,* this is different and you know it."

"But can you not see why I love being on television?" She countered as her brown eyes watched him. For a moment, he saw her mother Verónic crossing her face and it made him angry. The woman was dead and continued to haunt him from hell through their daughter.

"No, Maria, in fact, I do not," Jorge sternly insisted. "It was not fun. I do not enjoy being on television and I guarantee if you go online now, you will see criticisms of me all over social media. This is why I want you to think twice about getting into this silly industry."

As if accepting the challenge, Maria grabbed her iPad from the coffee table and began to gently tap on the screen.

"Hernandez was right. The government never listens to us and the legalization of pot was long overdue. Bravo!"

"Maria, that is one," Jorge insisted. "You continue to look and you'll see many criticisms of me, my industry and probably the suit I chose to wear."

"Meghan Willa showed bias in this piece and was no match for Hernandez. This is an experienced business person who quickly reminded her that he rules in this industry for a reason."

Jorge pause for a moment. Surprised by the positivity, he continued to insist that it was only luck that she had found nothing negative so far; after all, it was social media. However, as his daughter continued to read, the positive comments flowed through the room. Paige even moved closer, reading over her step-daughter's shoulder.

"Jorge, there are a couple here that are complaining but," She appeared as surprised as he felt. "Maria is right, most of these are positive. People like you."

"You seem surprised, *mi amor,*" Jorge teased and winked at her. "It is difficult to believe, I know, but some like a powerful man."

"This one woman says you were sexy," Maria giggled. "Paige must've wrote that!"

Jorge laughed along with his daughter.

"The women in my life, always underestimate me," He teased as his phone beeped. Glancing at it, he noticed that he had a few missed messages from Diego, Jesús and Alec Athas. A call was coming in from Makerson. Jorge reluctantly answered.

"Hola."

"Wow! You put Meghan Willa in her place!" Makerson said with humor in his voice. "That made my day!"

"And this, it surprises you?" Jorge snickered as he watched Maria and Paige continue to read the comments.

"No," Makerson quickly replied. "But you did it with the right amount of finesse so you didn't come across as an asshole but yet you were forceful, powerful, this will work in your favor."

"This is a role I've been playing for some time," Jorge replied and stood up to walk into the next room. "It is just for an audience this time."

"People liked it," Makerson spoke excitedly. "I was on social media and the YouTube video is picking up steam quickly. People are commenting, liking, sharing."

"See this here, it means nothing to me," Jorge insisted. "Silly social media."

"Silly social media that is raising your profile."

Jorge laughed and heard a beep. Checking his phone, he saw Alec Athas was on the other line. Ending his call with Makerson, he answered.

"We gotta talk," Alec said immediately. "It's important."

CHAPTER 12

"Tell you the truth, I just want to defend my business," Jorge shrugged casually as he focused on his breakfast while across from him, Alec Athas ignored his own food. They met in a well-known restaurant that was popular for early morning business meetings with Toronto's elite. "Me, I do not care about social media likes and this nonsense. It is irrelevant."

"It *isn't* irrelevant," Alec leaned in and lowered his voice. "Trust me, that's the strongest indicator of what people think. It's how we get a sense of which way people are leaning and what they're thinking. And now, they're thinking that you're on to something."

Jorge laughed before digging into his eggs and glancing out the window at a small crowd waiting at a nearby bus stop.

"Just hear me out," Alec continued as he picked at his breakfast. "Look, I know you only did that interview to defend the pot industry, to essentially say Elizabeth Alan is an alarmist and hey, we both know that her whole group is only propaganda for the far-right."

"She," Jorge cut in, pointing his finger at Alec. "She's got money backing her and I'm going to find out where it's coming from. Look at her website, her videos, you gotta have money to put it together."

"You have to remember, she has supporters," Alec calmly replied and picked up his toast. "There's a lot of regular people who think the same way as her. The more she picks up steam, the more money they give her."

"Yes, see me, I don't believe that," Jorge shook his head as he glanced at the waitress when she stopped to see if everything was fine. After she left, he continued. "Sure, she's got some *dinero* coming but there's more. She didn't start this site and suddenly have thousands of followers. She's not that interesting and people, how would they find out about her? She's got help. I promise you that. There's someone out there that has something to gain."

"She tackles a lot of topics so the only group that benefits is the party that aligns with her values," Alec said and raised an eyebrow. "She's like their test market."

"Test market?"

"Yes," Alec thought for a moment while Jorge continued to eat. "Rather than going out on a limb and potentially pissing off people, they send out this woman to see public reaction. If she crashes and burns, they've lost nothing but if she's a success, they can suddenly hitch their wagon to her and say they believe the same."

"Now that," Jorge said with a grin as he dug a fork in the last of his eggs. "That does make sense. But let us take it a step further, who benefits if that specific party gets voted in?"

Alec thought for a moment while he chewed his food.

"This is what I am wondering," Jorge continued. "Who benefits from all of this?"

"I keep coming back to the rumor that someone wants to introduce a bill to criminalize marijuana again."

"But this here, it is too easy," Jorge suggested with a shrug. "We say it's Big Pharma losing money but that sounds a little too simple, you know? Plus, I get the feeling that this is more general."

Alec nodded but didn't reply.

"I believe there is more," Jorge stared into space and bit his bottom lip. "This Elizabeth lady, she talks about men and women having more defined roles. Isn't that very old days? You know, back in a different time? Why do people find it appealing to do such? This does not make sense to me."

"She claims it simplifies life," Alec took a drink of his coffee. "At least that's her selling point."

"Her selling point, yes," Jorge nodded. "However, what does this mean? If women only cook and clean and men go out and work, let's say, for example, who does this appeal to and why?"

Alec shook his head.

"Who stands to make money?" Jorge changed the question.

"I'm not sure that's the right question," Alec finally answered. "I feel that this is about power. It's about regaining control."

"But why?" Jorge replied as he finished his breakfast. "Why does it matter? You do not think that someone will be making money from all of this?"

"Maybe," Alec seemed unsure. "But who?"

"This is what we must figure out, my friend," Jorge said as he pushed his plate aside and focused on his coffee. "This here is about restructuring society but again, there has to be a reason and in my experience, the reason is usually money. So, again, I ask you, who will be making money if these changes take place."

"It depends how far it goes."

"Let's say," Jorge said and leaned back. "Marijuana is criminalized again. Who gains?"

"Big Pharma for sure," Alec automatically answered. "You're taking some of their business away."

"Who else?"

"Well, liquor sales are going down so I would say they would see an increase."

"True, anything else?"

"Fewer people go to jail because it's not a crime to smoke and grow a small amount now."

"Hmm....you may be getting warmer, *amigo*," Jorge considered. "But the police, they will find another route. They will arrest people driving high. They will grab someone smoking it in a park....meanwhile, another person is probably getting mugged on the other side of that same park, but whatever, right?"

Alec merely grinned in response.

"So this, we must continue to think about," Jorge said and shook his head. "Me, I do not know the answer. I see business increase. Edibles will be the future for those who don't want to smoke pot. I was talking to that French bakery, remember the one that Diego once introduced me to? With the delicious pastries? I thought maybe they would be interested in potentially working with my company to create a line of product. That is one example of how companies can make more money. Me, I see the benefits and how to increase business so I cannot understand why someone would want to criminalize it again unless someone is losing money. This is what we must figure out."

The waitress returned to refill their coffee and once she left, Alec finished his food and slid his plate away.

"That aside, about your interview," Alec said and shifted gears. "People like you. They like that you're direct and are willing to call the government on what they lack."

"It was only a short interview," Jorge replied with a shrug.

"It was powerful though," Alec replied and leaned forward. "You have no idea how much attention you've captured by saying that the government doesn't listen to the people. You came across as strong, progressive, honest and that's something that Canadians want."

Jorge didn't reply.

"Look, I know that you aren't interested in what I've been suggesting but hear me out," Alec continued and displayed a certain vulnerability as he spoke. "The world is changing. There are some powerful forces that are attempting to interfere with democracies, like ours in Canada. We need someone who not only can lead but can stand up to the bullies and tyrants. It's not just about leading a great nation but protecting it."

Jorge continued to listen.

"Instinctively, Canadians know that," Alec pointed toward the window. "They see what's taking place globally, what's on the news every night and they're well aware how important it is we are ready for anything."

"To me, the news is scaring tactics," Jorge interrupted, shaking his head. "The world always had many of these problems but people weren't aware or interested in seeing it."

"True," Alec reluctantly agreed. "But obviously, the problems are deepening now."

Jorge shrugged as he thought about Alec's recent proposition.

"Ok, but first, it does not matter because we just had an election so there is no need to even consider such things. And also, it does not mean that I should become involved. Paige, she hates the idea. It is too public and I have a lot of reason, *amigo,* to stay under the radar."

"Whether you like it or not, you're the CEO of one of the largest companies in Canada so you already are a public figure," Alec countered. "Plus you supported me in our last election. Some people were more intrigued with you than me."

"Perhaps," Jorge agreed. "But I do recall you were once reluctant yourself."

"I was wrong," Alec insisted. "But this time, I am right."

"Again, it does not matter," Jorge decided to repeat his former point. "There is no election coming."

Alec looked away.

"Unless you know something that I do not?" Jorge continued, sensing Alec was holding back. "Tell me, why are we even speaking of this?"

"There might be some circumstances….I can't talk about them now," Alec confirmed as he leaned in and spoke in a low voice. "But there might be some sudden changes in the future. And if that's the case, it will happen very quickly."

"Ok, so say, this sudden change does happen," Jorge said with a smooth grin on his face. "I am controversial and there are some skeletons in my closet."

"As I told you before, you're already being considered," Alec replied. "Your name has come up several times."

Jorge hid his surprise. Although he often pompously commented that he could've been the president while living in Mexico, it never occurred to him that a Canadian political party would seek him out. It felt surreal.

"Me…with my past?"

"We only know rumors and speculation," Alec reminded him while shaking his head. "You have no arrests in either here or Mexico. You've come to Canada and in a short time, managed to take over the pot industry and employ thousands across the country plus you've had other business successes. You're a family man, married to a Canadian woman. You're an immigrant."

Jorge didn't reply, his mind racing.

"Think about it," Alec leaned in again. "You could have the immigrant vote, definitely the Latino vote. If you talk about women's issues, especially as a new father who's involved with his family, you could have the female vote. You're pro-pot so you may inspire some votes there too. You have a lot to offer because of what you stand for and who you are."

"This is a good point," Jorge slowly began to agree. "I am also a self-made man. My family was quite poor, so I know what it means to work hard to get ahead."

"You're courageous," Alec continued to encourage. "You take on challenges. Your presence is strong but yet, you're charming. Many people think the party leaders we have are too soft. People would rather someone direct and blunt, even if that means sometimes being rude."

Jorge continued to think and didn't reply.

"I'm telling you now," Alec continued. "If you got in the political game, you would win."

CHAPTER 13

"We need some help," Jorge told Paige when he arrived home to find her rushing around the house while the baby cried upstairs. "This here, it is too much for you."

"But other women.." Paige attempted to say but Jorge was already shaking his head.

"I do not care about other women," Jorge sternly replied and shook his head. "It is *you* that I care about and soon, Maria will be home for the summer too."

"And she can help me," Paige offered as she headed toward the stairs.

"*Mi amor*, you know she will cause you more headaches when she's home all day," Jorge reminded her as she rushed upstairs with a desperate expression on her face. "You know how strong-willed and relentless she can be."

Reaching in his pocket, he grabbed his phone and called Diego.

"*Hola!*" He picked it up on the first ring.

"Diego, I have a job for you," Jorge instructed. "I need you to help find a nanny for Paige. This is too much for her."

"Oh, I agree!" Diego spoke gently when the topic of his close friend arose. "I was there the other day and…"

"Yes, I know, Diego, I know," Jorge glanced toward the stairs as Miguel continued to cry. "She doesn't agree with me but she needs help. We must find someone who we can trust."

"Of course," Diego agreed. "Should we look for someone from Mexico?"

Jorge thought a moment.

"Maybe....I would prefer Spanish-speaking."

"I will get back to you."

By the time the baby stopped crying and Paige came back downstairs, Jorge had Diego on the job and he was cleaning the kitchen.

"I thought you were going to the office today," Paige asked as she entered the room while Jorge put some cups into the dishwasher. She headed toward the coffee pot.

"You know me, Paige, I cannot stand sitting in an office," Jorge replied. "Fortunately, with today's world, much of what I need to do can be done offsite. Diego is at the office now."

Paige merely nodded as she poured a coffee.

"How's Miguel?"

"Fine, just a diaper change," Paige replied as she turned and headed to the fridge.

"*Mi amor,*" Jorge started with some reluctance. "I have asked Diego to find you some help."

"Jorge," Paige swung around and was shaking her head.

"My love, please listen to me," Jorge cut her off. "Trust me on this one, you need help and I think it will be good for you to get back to your old routine."

She seemed to soften with that comment and nodded before reaching in the fridge for a carton of cream.

"So, this morning," He slowly began to speak again. "I had a meeting with Alec."

Paige exchanged looks with him before putting cream in her coffee.

"Paige, please hear me out..."

"Jorge, I know what he wants," She insisted and shook her head. "You have enough. Look at everything you've done in your life."

"It is not about getting more," He gently corrected her as she sat on a nearby stool, looking sadly into her cup.

"It's about power," She quietly replied.

"I understand why you see it this way," Jorge said as he moved closer. "But Paige, Alec has a good point. We need strong people with a clear vision to run this country. People who can take on their enemies and win."

"Jorge, this isn't like the cartel," She reminded him, her eyes widening as she spoke. "You have to be humble. You can't kill the leader of another country because he's giving you problems."

"I was thinking more about torture," Jorge teased her and shook his head. "I am joking, Paige. Of course! I know the rules are different but yet, some things, *mi amor,* some things are the same."

"You know I never discourage you from anything you want to do," Paige reminded him as her eyes searched his face. "But this isn't a good idea. If you have a more public image, this could mean some people will dig into your past. You have a lot of skeletons."

"None proven," He reminded her as he moved closer and looked into her eyes.

"It's risky," She whispered as she reached out and touched his arm. "You're flying a little too close to the sun. Don't let Alec play with your ego and you know that's what's going on here. He's trying to get you to do what is good for his party, not what's good for you."

"Alec?" Jorge asked, taken aback by her comment and began to tease her. "Paige, I never thought I would hear you say such things about the Greek God?"

"He's different since getting into politics," She observed and reached for her coffee. "They're right, politics changes people."

"Well, *mi amor,* see you do not have to worry about me," Jorge reminded her. "I am who I am. Politics, they would not change me."

"If anything," Paige said with a small grin. "You'd change politics. It would never be the same again."

The upcoming days didn't allow him much time to consider the idea again. Jorge was busy going over final details for the upcoming marijuana festival as well as working with the Colombian company that would help meet Canadian's demands for pot. And of course, he also assisted Diego in finding some help for Paige with the baby.

In the end, it was a familiar face that was hired for the nanny position. Juliana was a Mexican woman who had worked with Jorge in the past and was happy to return as a caretaker for both Maria and Miguel. Surprised that she was willing to leave Mexico again, Jorge was willing to do whatever he could to make this decision permanent.

"If you can help me become a Canadian citizen," Juliana asked Jorge in a phone conversation. "I will stay."

"Of course," Jorge insisted. "We can arrange this."

Paige continued to insist that she didn't need help but her reluctance was half-hearted at best. Juliana would live in their basement apartment, which had been empty since Jorge's mom stayed in it the previous year, before her sudden death.

With many challenges sorted out, Jorge suggested that he and his wife escape for a weekend.

"*Mi amor,* life is good," Jorge reminded her one evening as they got ready for bed. "It has been a busy and now that Juliana is back to help us, we can go out of town and enjoy some time together. It will be beautiful."

"I feel uncomfortable being away from the baby," Paige admitted and glanced toward the door. "He's just starting to bond with me so maybe I shouldn't leave now."

"Miguel will be fine," Jorge insisted as he glanced at his phone before throwing it on the nightstand and removing his tie. "How about we go to a hotel here in the city? That way, we are close but yet, away from the house?"

She appeared content with the idea and he immediately made the arrangements. He found a beautiful suite, just like the one they met in two years earlier. Of course, bringing up the topic always made Paige cringe. The fact that she could've accidentally assassinated the man who would one day become her husband simply wasn't funny to her. Jorge thought it was hilarious. He joked that destiny brought her right to his door.

The week finished off on a positive note as the couple threw a few items in their suitcases, looking forward to some time alone. Jorge felt confident that the children would be fine under Juliana's care. If anything went wrong, the Mexican woman could handle it. Not that this was likely since their home had a superior security system.

Everyone was warned to not contact them unless there was an emergency. That's why a ding on his phone late Saturday night grabbed Jorge's attention. Sliding his body toward the nightstand, he glanced at

Paige sleeping beside him before grabbing his phone, assuming it was Maria. He instead found an unsettling text from Makerson.

Naked, he rose from the bed and headed out of the room, gently closing the door behind him. Before he could call Makerson, a second text came through, this one with a link to an article entitled, *"Our House of Pot CEO and His Cartel Connections."*

Anger shot through his veins as he read how he was now importing marijuana from cartels in both Mexico and Colombia. He had investors from Canada who would not be impressed with this article.

His heart racing in fury, he quickly made a phone call.

"You saw?" Makerson answered.

"I saw," Jorge muttered. "This here, it is not true."

"I can counter it in Monday's paper," Makerson remarked and cleared his throat. "The editor is a guy named Jeremy McNair and he's an extreme right-wing conservative asshole."

"Jeremy McNair," Jorge repeated his name. "This is good to know."

"I would suggest you do another television interview," Makerson reluctantly commented. "I know you aren't crazy about the idea but if there ever was a time, this would be it."

"I may not have a choice," Jorge angrily replied. "I must do what is right for my company and investors."

"Last time you did an interview, it was with a soft network," Makerson reminded him. "In the meanwhile, I have an idea. Check with me tomorrow."

Ending the call, Jorge quickly contacted his sources to look into the reporter. Jeremy McNair.

CHAPTER 14

"This here, it is all new to me," Jorge commented as he prepared for an interview with Makerson, which would stream live on social media. The *Toronto AM* editor was typing something on his laptop while Jorge fixed his tie and glanced at Paige, who sat on the other side of the office with an iPad in hand. "Paige, she knows all about this kind of thing, after years as an online life coach."

Paige silently grinned. The life coaching business had merely been a coverup for her many years as an assassin; it provided a way to launder her money and to look legit to the Canadian government.

"There's nothing to it," Makerson replied as he finished typing, his eyes scanning the screen briefly, he turned to Jorge. "It's no different from a live television interview although it's somewhat more relaxed. It's a way for us to get your side out immediately before Monday morning's paper hits the shelves. We want to act fast to counter McNair's article."

"Sounds good," Jorge replied as he sat up straight.

"And Paige, can you check the comments?" Makerson glanced across the room. "If you see anything that we should address, let me know but I don't want to pay much attention to comments during the interview. It's a distraction."

"Isn't that the idea?" Jorge countered. "If we see their reactions, we can act accordingly."

"To a point but we also don't want to get too off course either," Makerson insisted. "Remember that our goal is to discuss comments made by McNair and to knock him back on his ass."

"Do not worry about McNair," Jorge insisted. "I will look after him."

Makerson merely raised an eyebrow but didn't comment.

"Ready?" He asked Jorge with a grin on his face.

"Me?" Jorge replied. "I'm always ready for anything."

"Then let's get started."

Makerson tapped a button and began to talk. He thanked people for following, gave a brief introduction to Jorge Hernandez and went on to welcome him.

"Thank you for taking time on a Sunday afternoon to do this interview," Makerson spoke with a smile glued to his face, his eyes full of excitement. "I know you were away for the weekend with your wife when this story broke but you felt it was necessary to discuss the accusations right away."

"Yes, of course," Jorge replied with his charming smile that quickly turned serious. "However, our weekend away was still within the city. It was more of a weekend away from the kids."

Makerson laughed on cue and replied, "So, a short break to regroup?"

"I like to think of it as an extended date with my wife," Jorge answered with a mischievous grin on his face. "A new baby and a teenage daughter, sometimes it is nice to spend some quiet, alone time."

"That *does* sound nice," Makerson said and nodded. "Well, thank you again for dropping by the office for this interview. I know it was originally meant for tomorrow's edition of *Toronto AM* but sometimes, we like to shake things up around here."

"Life is about the shakeup," Jorge replied and continued to smile as he glanced at the screen and back at Makerson.

"I wanted to discuss some rumors that Our House of Pot has cartel connections in both Mexico and Colombia," Makerson continued, his face growing serious while Jorge did the same, he slowly nodded his head. "It was recently suggested that you're connected to organized crime, that you have been for some time and that you're in Canada to take advantage of our legalized marijuana industry."

"This, of course, is not true," Jorge spoke firmly and could see Paige nodding out of the corner of his eye. "It is unfortunate that people assume that I have connections to the drug cartel that plagues my home country. Having grown up in Mexico, I am well aware of the death and destruction the cartel has caused and I certainly do not support such things. I am very disappointed that the Canadian media would make such unfounded reports."

"I believe the specific article in question suggested there were rumors of these connections especially now that you are buying some product from both Mexico and Colombia."

"Unfortunately, Canadian suppliers were unable to meet our great demand, as we saw on the first day of legalization," Jorge calmly replied and paused for a moment. "We had to think outside the box. Having grown up in Mexico and having spent time in Colombia, being familiar with conditions, I naturally thought that this would be a great place to grow the marijuana. It would help meet with demands but at the same time, be able to keep the price down."

"Just so my audience knows," Makerson glanced toward the laptop as he spoke. "What kind of work did you do while living in Mexico and how did you eventually come here to Canada?"

"My father, he founded a coffee company that grew over the years and I worked closely with him as an international sales rep," Jorge replied and tilted his head slightly to the left and took a breath before his face filled with sadness. "He, unfortunately, decided to sell the company before his death a couple of years ago."

"Did you consider taking over his business?" Makerson asked.

"No, the idea of carrying on the company without my father did not appeal to me," He replied and bounced back from his moment of vulnerability on camera. "It would never be the same once he left, so I told him he should sell. By this time, I had invested in some Canadian businesses and was looking forward to a new chapter in my life."

"So what made you decide to move to Canada and invest in our marijuana industry?" Makerson asked as he leaned back slightly in his chair. "Why not stay in Mexico."

"Love, my friend, *amor!*" Jorge spoke enthusiastically and Makerson laughed on cue. "I met my wife and she, of course, was a Canadian woman and as I said, I already had investments here so it only made sense that I come here too. Also, my daughter, she wanted to study at a Canadian school and who am I say no to the most important women in my life?"

"But why take over the *pot* industry?" Makerson pushed. "What was it about this industry that appealed to you so much?"

"Ah, well, as we said earlier, I do come from a country where the cartels have destroyed many lives," Jorge replied, his expression once again grew serious. "Canada, in its decision, is essentially trying to shut down this black market. I thought that it was forward-thinking and progressive, being one of the few countries in the world to take such a strong stand. I wanted to be a part of it."

"But why take over across the country?" Makerson reminded him of the original question. "Why not, for example, just take over in Ontario?"

"I feel that to do something right, you must make things consistent," Jorge insisted. "In the beginning, of course, there was a lot of confusion about laws, inconsistencies between provinces and I wanted to put everyone on the same page. I worked with the government to make this so and I feel that now, it allows the industry to run much smoother than how the government originally set things up."

"Do you think it wasn't planned out properly?"

"I think when it comes to government, sometimes," Jorge thought for a moment and wrinkled his forehead. "Sometimes, they have a way of getting too many people involved, too many opinions, too much politics." Jorge hesitated and laughed. "You know, the government, it has a way of taking something so simple and making it too complicated and this was one of these cases. I merely stepped in with a more logical solution. I believe that at the time, they did the best they could however, it was new territory so it was not so easy."

"So, what is the future of pot?" Makerson asked. "You have a festival coming up this summer?"

"We have a festival coming up this summer," Jorge agreed and sat up a bit straighter. "All the information is on our website. Lots of experts in the industry will be there, musicians, there will be food, a great time."

"And you continue to work on new ideas?"

"I continue to envision our future and I do believe it will be beautiful," Jorge replied with a nod.

"Thank you again for taking time on your Sunday to drop by," Makerson spoke in a relaxed tone.

"It is my pleasure," Jorge spoke earnestly.

"For more on Jorge Hernandez, check out our Monday edition of *Toronto Am,"* Makerson spoke to the screen while Jorge smiled in the background. "We'll have the full story. We'll also include the details on where you can find Our House of Pot online, social media and all that good stuff. Thanks for watching."

The green light turned off and Makerson closed the laptop.

"Just like we rehearsed it," Jorge commented with a nod. "That should work."

"I thought it was best to not speak too much to what McNair said but merely refer to it as a 'rumor'," Makerson commented as he scratched his head. "We don't want to give him much attention because we would've seemed too defensive. This way, it was downplayed."

"The comments were both good and bad," Paige said as she looked up from her iPad. "Some people ranted about the government or how pot should only be grown here in Canada but for the most part, people were unusually reasonable."

"Well, that in part was thanks to Marco," Jorge said with a grin. "Our hacking genius, he has many accounts on social media, as it turns out. This is helpful to us."

"Regardless, the sense I'm getting is mainly positive," Paige replied and as her finger ran up the screen. "People for and against it. People complaining about the government being ill-prepared." She glanced up at Jorge. "A lot agreeing with what you said too, about price and restructuring the system, across the country."

"It had to be done," Jorge replied. "There were inconsistencies but my government friends, they were listening."

"Or you made them listen," Makerson quietly replied and Jorge merely raised an eyebrow. "What you did was good but we'll continue to monitor the comments and see where it takes us. We need to gauge what people think and see what our next move will be."

"Ah! The online world is so complicated," Jorge replied as he stood up and reached for his phone. Glancing at it, he grinned. "Maria seems more taken with the fact that I referred to her as a teenager in the interview than anything else her *Papa* has done."

Paige laughed.

"And Diego wants us to meet him at the bar."

Paige nodded. "Let's go."

CHAPTER 15

"We *never* get together anymore except for business," Diego complained from behind the bar when Paige and Jorge walked into the *Princesa Maria*. Still early in the day, the club was closed to the public. "Paige had the baby, then Michael and I went on vacation, Jesús is busy with the festival…."

Jorge didn't respond but grinned as the couple sat at the bar while Diego automatically poured them each a coffee.

"It's nice being back in a routine," Paige agreed as she ran a hand through her hair. "I love Miguel but I felt like my old life was a distant memory and I missed it."

"Paige, you do not adjust well to change," Jorge reminded her. "Remember when we first met and things, they happen so fast. There were times, I could see in your eyes, that you were overwhelmed and I saw that again since the baby. It is difficult for you."

"I don't know why," Paige replied as she reached for the coffee Diego passed her. "I've certainly had a lot of changes in my life."

"There is just some people who do not adapt as well," Jorge commented. "You know, we are all different."

"Me," Diego jumped in as he poured his own coffee. "I think age makes a difference. I could fly by the seat of my pants when I was 20, now…not so much. I like a nice *routine*."

With his exaggerated emphasize of the last word, Jorge grinned and glanced at his wife, who smiled.

"I think we can all relate to that one," She replied.

"A new baby, it is a lot," Jorge commented as he took a drink of his coffee. "Miguel is an angel but when he starts crying, I sometimes think he's the devil."

"Well, he would get that naturally enough," Diego teased. "He got his father's lungs, that's for sure."

Paige laughed and seeing her relax, Jorge did the same without commenting.

"But he's better now?" Jorge glanced at Paige. "I see a big difference when you are with him."

"Big difference," Paige agreed as her eyes widened. "Having Juliana back is amazing. I didn't think I needed it but I guess I did."

"I think you put too much pressure on yourself," Jorge reminded her. "It is a lot and Maria will not be easy this summer, I'm afraid. She has been relentless.."

The door opened and they turned to see Chase walk in wearing gym clothes. Realizing he had interrupted their conversation, he appeared hesitant.

"Chase, hello," Jorge turned slightly in his seat. "We were talking about Maria and how she wants to audition for television. But I suppose, she has told you that. You are, after all, her best friend."

Chase laughed as he moved stiffly across the room.

"She mentioned something about it," Chase replied as he went behind the bar and reached for the coffee pot while Diego looked on. "She made it sound like it was agreed she would be going on auditions."

"No, I wouldn't say that exactly," Jorge countered and glanced at Paige. "I do not know what I can do with this child. She is strong-willed."

"That's not always a bad thing," Diego reminded him.

"It can be a problem as well," Jorge said and shook his head. "We have to keep a close eye on her because she is very impulsive."

"Wow! Where would she get that?" Diego spoke with sarcasm in his voice and glanced at Paige, who began to laugh.

"Yes, yes, Diego, we know where she gets that from," Jorge replied with his hand in the air. "But you know...Chase, what is that on the back of your neck?"

"What?" He asked as he stirred his coffee. "What do you mean?"

"It looks like claw marks except much more painful," Jorge commented and leaned forward. "Do not tell me you are back with that sadist from Maria's school?"

"Was that a teacher?" Paige spoke up with interest. "I don't think she actually taught Maria, did she?"

"No, thank God," Jorge replied and returned his gaze to Chase. "I knew you were walking funny this morning."

"I'm not back with the....sadist..." Chase hesitantly replied with an awkward shrug while beside him, Diego appeared somewhat aggravated. "It's this other girl I met."

"You seem to have a type," Jorge reminded him. "This one, where did you meet her, at an S&M convention? A torture chamber?"

"I met her online," Chase shrugged as he turned around with his coffee in hand. "She's actually.....umm...deaf."

"Deaf?" Jorge nodded. "So this, it works out perfectly because she cannot hear you screaming as she tortures you."

Paige almost choked on her coffee and attempted to hide her laughter while Diego gave Chase a strange look.

"It's not that bad," Chase insisted.

"*Amigo*, I would suggest that perhaps you think about why this is the kind you like so much," Jorge reminded him. "Like you, Chase, I also had issues when I was a young man but I worked through them."

"You did?" Paige appeared surprised.

"Yes, I went to a counselor in Mexico."

Everyone looked stunned.

"*You,* you went to a counselor?" Diego spoke up and his eyes bugged out. "You?"

"Yes, Diego, me, me, me, I went to a counselor," Jorge insisted. "It was after my daughter was born and I realize that I had a terrible relationship with women. It was important to learn how to resolve this before it maybe affected my daughter."

"I didn't know that," Paige appeared surprised. "You've never mentioned it."

"I haven't thought about it much in years," Jorge replied. "But it was important. I see that my abandonment issues made me detached. Of course, I had to fix that so I did not have this problem with my daughter."

"I can't picture you going, voluntarily, to counseling," Diego appeared shocked. "That doesn't seem like you. Are you teasing us?"

"Diego, no, does this seem like a joke?" Jorge asked and saw the look of disbelief on their faces. "It is important to me. When I see how much I loved this baby girl, I did not understand why my mother turned against me after my brother died or how she could let my father beat me. I decided that it was time to fix it."

"You obviously didn't fix things with your mother," Diego muttered.

"No, this is true," Jorge spoke regretfully. "Unfortunately, she was impossible when it came to this subject but I was able to express myself once my father had passed. They were miserable people and you know, there is nothing I can do about that but for me, it was about not being the same kind of parent to my children."

Diego opened his mouth to say something just as the door swung opened and Jolene walked in, followed by Michael.

"Look who I found in the parking lot," Jolene piped up as she headed toward the bar. "He act like he did not see me."

"I didn't see you, Jolene," Michael said as he followed her. "I was about to text Diego to let me in."

"You are a police officer?" Jolene asked. "Are you not to be more vigilant? You know, aware?"

"Ok, let us get to business, shall we?" Jorge cut them off and pointed toward the office where they would hold their meeting. Jolene rushed behind the bar to grab a coffee, while Michael merely followed Diego into the office. Chase held back to talk to Jorge.

"I was thinking," He started. "I might suggest to Maria that she start recording herself practising lines, so she can then play it back and perfect her acting before going out on auditions."

"Chase! This is wonderful," Jorge said as he patted his arm. "If she can do this, then she may her forget the auditions this summer."

"At least a good part," Paige commented as she approached the two men. "Yes, please suggest it, Chase. She won't listen to us but she *will* listen to you."

"Sure," He agreed. "I just wanted to check first."

The three of them headed into the office, closing the door behind them.

"Now, let us make this fast," Jorge spoke abruptly as he sat beside Paige and Chase went behind his desk. The others were seated. "We got a problem with this Jeremy McNair, who decide to write an article in his paper suggesting I am with the cartel."

"Yeah, well you don't gotta worry about McNair," Michael commented. "We had a little conversation earlier and ah.....I think he's now more focused on his health."

"I see, so you did find him," Jorge asked with interest.

"I found him," Michael replied with a smirk on his face. "He took a tumble down the stairs."

"A slip fall?" Jolene piped up. "Sometimes, this causes them to hit their head and they think differently."

"He hit more than his head," Michael assured her. "Buddy is in the hospital recovering. I warned him that the good news was that he would have time to think about what he had done. If it happens again, he ain't gonna have time to think about nothing."

"And the cameras?"

"No one will see a thing."

"And did he see you?"

"I sprayed his eyes first," Michael replied. "He didn't see nothing."

"*Perfecto!*" Jorge replied and noted that Diego was nodding, his lips twisted and a look of satisfaction on his face.

"This is good, thank you," Jorge replied. "Now, this Elizabeth Alan. I must learn who is the money that is backing her ideas. Jesús is out of town, working on something for me but he was attempting to find some skeletons in her closet too. I must touch base with him soon."

"Where is he?" Diego asked. "I saw him yesterday."

"Mexico," Jorge replied. "We may have learned who it was that kidnapped my mother last year and extorted over a million dollars from me. When we do, this man, he may find that I have my own justice."

"You already have a reputation in Mexico," Diego reminded him. "You would think that this man would already know this."

"I think, Diego, that sometimes they forget since I am no longer in my home country," Jorge stated. "This here, it will be a reminder that no one fucks with me. It will send a strong message."

"I thought he was down there checking out the marijuana," Jolene commented. "Is that not what he said to me yesterday?"

"Officially," Jorge replied. "Remember, Jolene, we must always cover our tracks."

"We are each many people," Paige commented and they shared a look while the others sat in silence.

CHAPTER 16

"I still can't believe you went to counseling," Paige commented as she climbed into bed that night. Across the room, Jorge was checking his phone. He stopped and looked up at his wife. "It just doesn't sound like you."

"Paige, as I said earlier, this here, I forgot," Jorge replied as he glanced at his phone again before sitting it down to undress. "I am glad that I did think of it though. I hope that Chase takes my advice. These relationship he has, are often with demented women. When the sanest person he has been with is Jolene, you know there is a problem."

Paige giggled. "In fairness, she's much better now."

"I once thought that would never be the case," Jorge replied as he removed his shirt and laid it on the chair and unbuttoned his pants.

"It makes me think," Paige continued. "There are so many things that we don't talk about, things in our past. Like, my life as an assassin and your days in the cartel. Maybe we should."

"*Mi amor,* perhaps it is better that we do not speak of such," Jorge commented as he removed his socks and headed toward the bed, only wearing his boxers. "But if you wish, of course, we can."

"I was just thinking about Jesús being in Mexico," Paige continued as Jorge climbed into bed. "You know, whoever kidnapped your mom, what if it's an old enemy? This is the kind of thing that I would like to know if these people crop up again."

"Oh, Paige, the person who did this wasn't an enemy but someone trying to extort money," Jorge replied and looked away. "As for enemies, some are in prison but most are dead. The life of someone in a cartel, it is often a short one. I am one of the exceptions. Well, me and the one I have worked for but that is because most see him as a powerful man with no connections to the cartel."

Paige looked troubled but before she could speak, Miguel started to cry in the next room.

Jorge started to stand but Paige was already out of the bed.

"We'll continue this later," She commented before heading out the door.

Glancing across the room, Jorge realized his phone was next to his clothes on the chair. Groaning, he slowly rose from the bed and went to get it. He was awaiting some news from Jesús in Mexico but so far, there was nothing. His only message was from Makerson, who sent a link to an article from his earlier interview. Scanning it quickly he skipped ahead to the comments.

Reviews were mixed. Some thought he was a great man who revolutionized the Canadian pot industry while others saw him part of the problem, insisting he was only out to make money. People continued to associate him with the cartel but most pointed out that if this were true, Jorge Hernandez never would've been allowed in Canada. It went on and on. Some comments were simply ridiculous but none upset him. To Jorge, social media was silly and meaningless, regardless of what anyone thought.

Going back to read the article, he noted that Makerson, as promised, used a lot of words that created the impression that he was merely an immigrant who seized an opportunity in Canada. He built him up as a hero, which worked perfectly.

Feeling his eyelids grow heavy, he quickly forwarded the article to Diego and sat his phone aside. Sinking into bed, he could hear Paige's gentle voice speaking to the baby in the next room. Although he fought off sleep until her return, he quickly drifted off.

The following morning, he awoke to discover Paige wasn't beside him in bed and for a moment, it sent a stab of fear through his heart. It wasn't until he glanced at the nearby clock that Jorge realized that he had overslept. Paige was downstairs, talking to Maria.

Grabbing his phone, he quickly touched base. A late night message from Jesús sent relief through his body.

Sir, everything is going well at the new location here in Mexico. I am spending time with old friends tonight and give you more details when I return.

Knowing that this was code, Jorge quickly went into his browser to find a well-known Mexican news site to glance over the headlines. It took a few minutes but he found it.

Four Men Found Hanging From Bridge in Los Cabos

Glancing through the article, Jorge saw everything he needed to know.

….signs of torture….

….tongue cut out while another had missing toes, police say…

….with no teeth, police say it will be difficult to identify the bodies…

…no leads but police assume this is a cartel-related crime.

Perfecto.

Of course, the police automatically blamed it on the cartel. The public hanging was the result of four, pathetic men kidnapping his mother the previous year and thinking they would get away with it. Of course, Jesús and some of their old associates in Mexico took care of them. However, this fight had nothing to do with the cartel.

In fact, since he was no longer a narco, most of his former competition wouldn't inflict harm on either him or his family, especially now that many made money through his grow-ops in Mexico and Colombia. Although everything looked legit on paper, the truth was that you simply did not grow marijuana in a Latin American country and think you weren't dealing with the cartel. The Canadian government had a blind eye to such things and as long as they continued to do so, everyone would be happy.

"*Papa,*" Maria came bouncing into the room. "You are still in bed and it is late. Are you sick?"

"No, *bonita,* I guess I was just tired," Jorge admitted as she plopped down on the bed and he sat his phone aside. "Today, is it not your last day of school?"

"Yes, thank God!" Maria spoke dramatically. "This will allow me to focus all my energy and time on my acting career."

Jorge merely nodded, unsure on how to approach the topic.

"And *Papa*, Chase has made an excellent suggestion to me," Maria continued, her brown eyes expanding in size. "He thinks I should record myself practicing my acting then watch them back to see my strengths and what I need to work on."

"This is a great idea," Jorge spoke enthusiastically as Maria jumped up from the bed. "Maria, do you receive your report card today?"

"I think they will be emailing it to you," Maria replied as she headed toward the door. "I must run *Papa*, I will be late."

"What, no *besos?*" Jorge asked as he leaned forward.

Giggling, Maria rushed back and gave him a wet kiss on both cheeks before skipping out the door. Jorge laughed as he rose from the bed. Hearing his phone beeping again, he reached for it. This time it was Makerson.

Lots of comments on the article this morning. I'm afraid not all are good. I'm guessing it's the conservative right and Elizabeth Alan's crew.

Jorge shook his head and sighed. He jumped on the article just as another message came in from Alec Athas echoing Makerson's comments. The remarks he discovered this time suggested that many opposed Jorge and didn't view him as a self-made businessman but the devil himself. This was a suspicious change from the previous night.

Not that he cared. Placing his phone on the table, he headed for the shower, where he would give the entire scenario some more thought. If Elizabeth Alan was behind this situation then he had to deal with her head on. Although thoughts of possible torture and intimidation crossed his mind, Jorge wondered if perhaps the best results would come from direct and public confrontation. He suspected that if placed face to face with him, she wouldn't stand a chance.

As soon as he got out of the shower and got dressed, he headed back into the bedroom and grabbed his phone.

What if I debate this issue with Elizabeth Alan in person? What do you think?

He sent this message to Makerson followed by Athas. He considered sending it to Diego but instead forwarded him the article and suggested that he read the comments.

Interesting idea.

This was from Makerson.

Let me think about that. It would make a great live online event but we must make sure that we have enough people on our side jumping on to comment.

Jorge thought for a moment.

We could advertise it on Our House of Pot's website and perhaps social media, so our supporters are ready to contribute in comments?

Before he heard back from Makerson, Athas replied to his earlier text.

Could be tricky. You would take her down in one swoop and that might work against you.

Jorge didn't reply. Meanwhile, Makerson sent another message.

I think you might be on to something. There's no way potheads are going to want to turn back the clock on legislation.

Jorge agreed and replied.

Athas fears that I will eat her alive and in turn, make myself look bad.

He waited for Makerson's reply. When he received it, it only made him laugh.

You won't have to. Leave that to your followers. If we have people who make compelling arguments, others will jump on the bandwagon. Trust me, I know how social media works. It's easy to manipulate.

CHAPTER 17

"I am glad you are here early," Jorge ushered Jesús into the house and pointed toward his office. "Paige will let the others in when they arrive but first, we must talk."

"Boss, it went smoothly," Jesús commented as they walked into his office and Jorge closed the door. "But sir, the man who led it, it was your cousin, as we suspected. He would not have seen your mother, so she wouldn't have known but he was the man who came up with the idea. The others, they received a share of the money and were living quite well."

"When they were living," Jorge laughed as he walked behind his desk and sat down while Jesús joined him, sitting on the other side. "I will admit, they did get away with it at first because, at the time, I had too much on my plate, however, I knew that whoever did it would eventually slip up. When they thought it was safe, they would talk and unfortunately, my cousin, he talked to the wrong person."

"And sir, I checked everything out," Jesús confirmed. "The snitch, he was telling the truth. All the facts check out. I have, in turn, rewarded him for his honesty."

"I believe that is fair," Jorge replied as he leaned back in his chair. "For me, it was never about the money but disrespect. It is important for people to know not to disrespect me. They thought they would kidnap my mother and get away."

"Sir, they made many excuses for what they did," Jesús confirmed and nodded. "It was as if they felt it was their right to kidnap her. To your cousin, it was a normal business transaction to do so and extort money."

"Easy money, Jesús," Jorge replied and nodded. "It's about doing as little as possible and making a lot of money. This generation, they want it all without doing the work."

"This is true," Jesús replied with a nod.

"But I must talk to you about something else before the others arrive," Jorge remarked as he sat forward in his seat. "It has been bothering me for some time."

"What would that be, sir?"

"Paige," Jorge started and glanced toward the door. "When she was shot last year. I need to know who did it."

Jesús showed no expression and nodded. He, of course, was referring to a shootout that took place when they ambushed white supremacists in cottage country. At the time, Jorge assumed it came from the enemy but of course, he wasn't certain.

"But sir, do you think it was someone on purpose targeting Paige?" Jesús asked with concern. "Or do you think it was one of the men from the cabin? Did one of them not have a gun?"

"See, that's the thing, Jesús," Jorge replied as he leaned back in his chair. When the doorbell rang, he quickly sat forward and lower his voice. "I have never been convinced. At the time, I was more worried about Paige and didn't want to alarm her, especially since she was pregnant with Miguel. I thought it was better to let her believe that I thought it was from the cabin but it has crossed my mind, what if it was not?"

Jesús didn't reply as voices could be heard approaching the office door.

"Jesús, if you could…"

He didn't reply but nodded while his face grew serious.

The door opened and Diego continued to chat with Paige as he entered the office with Michael following behind.

"The best limes I've had in my life!" Diego bragged. "And from my tree!"

"We have three goddamn lime trees in our condo," Michael shook his head. "You can barely move without running into one."

"You are lucky Diego does not have a jungle in your condo," Jorge commented as the two men approached the desk and sat in their usual seats.

"Don't give him ideas," Michael complained. "Those so-called miniature trees are enough."

"You gotta admit though," Diego cut in. "They produce some beautiful limes."

Michael shook his head and didn't reply.

"Is Jolene and Chase coming too?" Paige asked as she leaned against the doorway.

"Yes, I believe so, *mi amor,*" Jorge replied and glanced at his phone. "Jolene, she is almost always late and Chase may be tied up at the club."

"Should we start without them?" Diego loudly asked as he began to twitch nervously. "If they can't be here on time maybe we should. As a lesson."

"Relax, Diego, we can wait one extra minute," Jorge grinned. "Or do you have something very pressing today?"

"I have things to do at the office," Diego insisted and lurched forward. "I'm running your company, remember?"

"And, you do it well," Jorge replied and stretched.

"You need to drop by more," Diego insisted. "Now, you pop in occasionally. You don't even have an office. It's weird."

"When I go in, I just go to the boardroom," Jorge reminded him. "You know me, I do not like to be tied down to one place for long."

From the doorway, Paige could be heard laughing.

"He wants to find a new house already," She commented. "Because looking for a place the first time was such a blast."

"That is the thing, my love since we do not need one right away," Jorge said with a grin on his face. "We can casually look. That is my goal for this summer, to find somewhere new. This place, it's just ok."

"It's huge," Diego reminded him.

"Yes, but it is just ok," Jorge repeated. "Maybe I will have to design and build my next place."

Diego rolled his eyes while Michael laughed. Jesús nodded but appeared troubled since Jorge mentioned his quest to find Paige's shooter.

Jorge was about to comment when the doorbell rang again and Paige immediately rushed toward the main entrance. Jolene's loud voice could be heard along with her loud, clicking heels.

"Is the baby, is he awake?" She was asking and Paige could be heard responding as they arrived at the office.

"Miguel is sleeping," Jorge insisted with one hand in the air. "Please, it is not often, so we must leave him. Poor Juliana is napping as well. That baby makes sure we never forget he is in the house."

"Sounds like you," Diego said with bugged out eyes and smirk on his face.

"As if you could ever forget such a beautiful *bebé*!" Jolene commented as she hugged her breasts as if to demonstrate snuggling a baby. "I could not."

"If you lived here, you wouldn't have much of a chance to," Paige commented as she stood in the doorway again.

"Paige, come sit down," Jorge instructed. "When Chase arrives, I will get it."

"He's running late," Diego sharply commented as Paige sat beside him. "Probably forgot."

Jorge glanced at his phone. "Oh, he said to start without him, he got tied up at the bar."

"Well, at any rate," Jorge continued. "I will visit him later today and we will talk. It is a busy time at the bar."

"So, what happened in Mexico?" Diego asked immediately. "Did you find out who did the kidnapping."

"It was," Jesús began and turned slightly in his chair. "Jorge's cousin and some of his friends. They wanted to make some money and thought this would be a good way."

"And hey, they enjoyed my money for a while," Jorge spoke with wide eyes and glanced at his wife, who merely smirked. "However, like all good things, it had to come to an end. Of course, I will never see that money again but I do feel better knowing who my enemies are….ah, were.."

Diego's eyes grew in size as Jorge spoke.

"Can't trust family," Diego's boyfriend was the first to comment. "I don't care what anyone says, blood is *not* thicker than water."

"Yes, Michael, I must agree," Jorge nodded and leaned back in his chair. "Family are only those you choose"

Noting the solidarity in the room, he continued.

"Anyway, this situation here, it has been taken care of," Jorge continued and moved on to the next thing. "Now, I also wish to speak about my recent interviews with Makerson and that dingbat at the network. There are mixed reactions to what I have said, of course, my understanding from Makerson is social media is often manipulated. It is sometimes hard to say what the average people are thinking."

"Sir, would it be a good idea to maybe have a survey on our website?" Jesús asked. "Perhaps this would be better?"

"But still, that only tells about our customers, not the general perception," Jorge reminded him. "It may not help us find what we are dealing with."

"When did you start caring about social media or what people think?" Diego countered as he shook his head. "You do what you want anyway."

"Ah, yes, Diego, I agree," Jorge said and nodded. "However, my concern is that this far-right movement will try to close down my business by manipulating people on social media. Of course, it is all perception, each will see what they want anyway."

"Nah, the sheep will follow mindlessly as they always do," Diego insisted and shook his head. "That's why these far-right people target the super religious because a lot of those same people, mindlessly follow religion."

"Diego, it is not that they follow religion mindlessly," Jolene interrupted. "They follow faith and that is why not because they are dumb."

"I never said they were dumb, Jolene, I said that they follow along with whatever their preacher or…whatever says," Diego replied while swinging his hand in the air. "Look at these wacko fundamental Christians. In the US, they actually tell them how to vote at their church."

"Anyway," Jorge cut into the argument between the siblings. "The point is that Diego is right, many people do not think, they listen to the loudest of voices and believe it to be true."

"I don't know if they follow the loudest voice necessarily," Paige spoke up. "I think it's that they follow whoever makes sense to them."

"That is a good point, Paige," Jorge nodded. "This is true, people believe what makes sense, what is logical."

"Why are we talking about this again?" Michael shook his head. "Is this a philosophy class?"

"Our lives are a philosophy class," Diego insisted and made a face.

"The point is that we must make sure that pot isn't criminalized again and social media is very influential," Jorge spoke with frustration in his voice, causing everyone to grow serious again. "We are not fucking around with the Elizabeth Alan's of the world. I want to take them head-on now. I'm not leaving this."

"So what are you gonna do?" Diego asked.

"I have spoken to Makerson and overall, the interview went well and we are getting mixed, although primarily positive comments on social media," Jorge said and paused for a moment. "So, my wish is to have a live debate with Elizabeth Alan since she is the face of the conservative extreme."

"That's an interesting idea," Michael commented while the others showed various reactions. "I suspect that you will clip her wings pretty fast."

"I will fucking destroy her," Jorge said and his face darkened. "That woman and her supporters, I will take them on, one by one and until there is no one left standing."

He didn't have to ask if the others were on board. They were.

CHAPTER 18

"I thought you say, you like that I am bold," Jorge spoke into the phone the following morning. Sitting in his office, a cup of coffee on the desk, he could hear Paige and Maria moving around the house. Their voices were a vague muffle from behind the walls. "This here, is me being bold."

"I'm concerned you'll go a little too far," Alec Athas confessed on the other end of the line. There was a slight pause before he continued. "You have a tendency to be...aggressive. Like that interview with Meghan Willa, some people thought you were too abrupt with her."

"I thought people liked that I was direct," Jorge reminded him as he glanced toward the window. The sun was pouring through indicating another hot day ahead. "You tell me that Canadians like that I say what they think themselves and yet, now you're saying what?"

"Yes, people like your bold statements but they aren't crazy about your abruptness," Alec replied and paused for a moment. "Especially since she is a woman."

"What? Are you kidding me?" Jorge said and began to laugh. "Now, these women want equal rights but yet, be sensitive to their feelings? If this Willa lady wants to do soft interviews, she should be interviewing fucking celebrities and that kind of nonsense. This, this is not my problem."

"I agree," Alec was quick to point out. "But our recent poll says that people feel you're too abrupt."

"Well, that *amigo,* is me," Jorge countered with no apology. "Take it or leave it. I do not care what your polls say. I do not shape who I am to make sensitive people happy."

"I'm not saying that," Alec insisted. "What I'm saying is be cautious. It's not that you have to make everyone happy but when you're in public relations, even if it's for your company, you have to play the game to a point and you know that."

Jorge hated to agree but he was right.

"So," Alec continued. "If you want to do this debate with Elizabeth Alan, please keep that in mind. That's all I ask. You don't want to seem like a vulture because people take pity on the underdog. They always do. People will see her as this poor woman who lost her son and you as this powerful CEO who is ripping her apart on television."

"Well then, I will meet her in private and rip her apart," Jorge suggested. "Me, I do not care. I am not dying to be on television again."

"I think this should be public," Alec surprised him with his suggestion. "I think when there's a fire under her, she'll melt. Just be careful how high you turn up the flame."

Jorge considered his suggestion as the day moved forward however, it was a call from Makerson that afternoon that put a halt to it.

"She doesn't want to do it," He said as soon as Jorge answered the phone just as he was about to enter *Princesa Maria*. "Elizabeth Alan doesn't feel that she has to justify her position."

"Is that so?"

"She feels that there is nothing constructive or positive about the two of you debating it in a public forum of any sort," Makerson continued and took a deep breath. "That's why I need your statement that I can tweet and see how things fall into place."

"My statement?" Jorge asked and took a few steps back. "My statement is this. If she feels that marijuana should be illegal again then she better be ready to face the man who's CEO of the largest retailer in Canada and if not, then she should shut the fuck up."

"Ok, well, we might paraphrase that slightly," Makerson laughed in the phone. "How about 'The CEO of Canada's largest pot retail store is ready to have a public debate with Elizabeth Alan of Canadians for

Conservative Values over the issue of legalized pot. Jorge Hernandez says it's time that Alan either takes on this challenge or drops the subject.'"

"I like that," Jorge agreed and thought for a moment. "You writers, always so smooth."

"That's our job," Makerson replied. "That'll put a fire under her and challenge this whole movement she's preaching. If she can't debate it in public, she doesn't have a leg to stand on."

"And she clearly knows she cannot fight me," Jorge suggested. "Otherwise, she would not be backing down."

"That's where you want her," Makerson insisted. "We want her to back away because if she does, it sends a message to whoever is behind this shit."

"Let us hope so," Jorge said and took a deep breath. "Keep me posted."

He finally went into the club, where the staff was preparing for the opening later that afternoon. No one looked surprised to see him there but merely carried on with their work. Jorge locked the door behind him before heading toward Chase's office behind the bar. After a quick knock at the door, he went inside.

Sitting at his desk, Chase looked exhausted. He closed his laptop as Jorge walked in and shut the door.

"What? Your sadist keep you up last night?" Jorge immediately asked as he sat down. "You look like hell."

"I had to come in last night," Chase replied and shook his head. "There was a fight and the police showed up, so I had to come to check the situation."

"A fight?" Jorge asked. "What the hell happened?"

"I don't know, a couple of guys got into it at the bar," Chase shook his head. "My night manager was here but things got out of hand fast and the police were called."

"By us?"

"No, I think by another customer," Chase replied as he sat back. "You know we don't tend to call the police."

"It was resolved?"

"Yes, the police carted the guys off," Chase replied with a yawn.

"So, you didn't sleep after that?"

"Not much, I had to come back this morning when the orders arrived," Chase said and took a deep breath. "I gotta talk to you about something."

"Oh yeah, what's that?" Jorge asked as he relaxed in the chair.

"Remember the other day when I suggested to Maria that she practice her acting skills and not go to auditions yet?"

"Yes."

"She did and she sent me a few," Chase replied as he opened up his laptop. "So, that was fine. Then today, she sent me this."

After tapping on the keys for a moment, he turned the laptop around to show Jorge a YouTube channel. It took him a minute to realize it belonged to Maria.

"You got to be fucking kidding me," Jorge growled as he sat forward in his seat and pulled the laptop closer. "What the fuck is she doing on YouTube? Isn't this illegal? She's a child."

"A lot of kids get discovered on YouTube," Chase reminded him. "So I think that's what she thinks will happen to her too."

"This here," Jorge spoke loudly as he glanced over the site and shook his head. "This is coming down *today*."

"That's what I thought," Chase said and appeared hesitant to continue. "I wanted you to know this wasn't part of my suggestion."

"Oh, *amigo,* this I know," Jorge assured him as he shook his head. "This here, it is my daughter's idea."

"She's dying to be famous."

"I wish she would change her goals," Jorge admitted while feeling defeated. "I cannot seem to fight her on this idea of acting."

"I'm sorry."

"This here, it is not your fault," Jorge reassured him while sliding the laptop back toward him. "I must go talk to her now. This channel is coming down immediately."

"Was there anything else you needed to see me about?" Chase asked as Jorge jumped to his feet.

"Oh, *amigo,* nothing urgent," Jorge replied as he headed toward the door. "We will talk later. Right now, I must go home and speak with my daughter."

Heading out to his SUV, he grabbed his phone and sent a quick text to Paige.

Maria has a YouTube channel! I am on my way home. Please tell me she is there.

He was in the SUV and on the way home before receiving a response. *She's in her room. When did this happen?*

Jorge didn't reply. He was too angry when he thought of how vulnerable it made her to the sickos on the Internet. He loved and hated his daughter's determination. If only she wanted to do something other than acting.

Arriving home, he wasted no time. Barely in the door, he glanced at Paige holding Miguel on the couch with an alarmed look on her face.

"*Maria!* Get downstairs now and bring your laptop with you!"

"I couldn't even find it," Paige whispered as Jorge headed in her direction. "How did you find it?"

"Chase, she sent it to him, of course," He muttered in response as footsteps could be heard and Maria walked downstairs with a look of despair on her face, laptop in hand.

"Yes, *Papa?*"

"This YouTube channel, it goes, now!"

"But *Papa!* I need it for my work!"

"You, you do not have work," Jorge reminded her. "You are a child."

"I need to be on there so some agents can see me or maybe a famous person."

"Maria, *no!*" Jorge shot back at her. "Open the laptop and remove the account *now!*"

"I can't, I need it," She argued with tears in her eyes.

"Maria do you not know what kind of sick perverts go online looking for children such as you?" Jorge countered and watched as Maria's face turned pale. "It is very dangerous. You are not to be on there."

"Maria," Paige attempted to ease into the conversation as she rocked the baby, who watched in interest. "Maybe it would be better to wait. Perfect your acting and someday, after you are doing it professionally, then you'll have agents and people who can do this for you. I think that's how it usually goes."

"But that's how kids are discovered now," Maria countered. "On the Internet."

"Your father is right," Paige immediately backed him up. "There are some sick people on the Internet and he wants you to be safe."

"Yes, Maria," Jorge replied and attempted to calm himself. "We cannot take a chance. You are a very pretty, interesting young woman but unfortunately, that is what these old sickos look for and I will not have them preying on my daughter."

Maria looked physically ill as she silently opened the laptop and deleted the channel.

"Now, no more channels," Jorge insisted. "This here, it is not to happen again or I will take your laptop away."

"*Papa…*"

"Maria, this is not a game," Jorge cut her off. "I am serious about this."

"I didn't think Chase would tell you," She complained. "I even had a stage name."

"Maria, it is not about your name," Jorge spoke evenly. "It is about you. Chase did not tell me to tell on you, he mentioned it because he was concerned about your safety, as he knew I would be too."

"He said that?" Maria brightened up slightly.

"Yes, he did," Jorge confirmed and glanced at Paige who smirked as she looked down at Miguel. "Now, please, you can audition and practice but not on the Internet, do you understand?

"Yes, *Papa,*" Maria nodded and closed her laptop just as Jorge's phone rang. He answered it.

"She's going to do it," Makerson blurted out in excitement. "Elizabeth Alan is on board for a live debate."

Jorge grinned and turned away from his family, walking toward his office.

"*Perfecto!*" He replied. "Get in the ring, bitch."

CHAPTER 19

Before the open discussion on legalized marijuana session began, Jorge was already sizing up his opponent. Elizabeth Alan didn't appear weak and vulnerable as she did in her many online videos. If anything, there was an almost obnoxious arrogance coming from her side of the room. Another white woman whispered something to her, causing Elizabeth to glance in his direction then abruptly look away as if he were offensive to her eyes.

"She's a piece of work," Paige muttered as she leaned in, a cup of coffee in hand. Her eyes shot back toward his opponent. "I see her looking this way as if she's wondering who I am."

Without giving it a second thought, Jorge turned around and gave his wife a quick kiss on the lips. Looking into her eyes, they shared a smile.

"We're going to get started in a minute," Makerson could be heard from behind him while Paige started to move away.

"Have fun," She muttered before walking across the room to sit in an empty chair on the other side of Makerson's desk. Things were moved to set up everything for their live streaming event on social media. Jorge had no idea how it worked but didn't care. He knew what to do.

Elizabeth Alan walked toward him with a friendly smile on her face. She politely introduced herself to Jorge and they shook hands before returning her attention to Makerson.

"I have an appointment at 3 so can we keep this brief?"

"Sure," Makerson replied in his usual, good-natured way as Jorge sat down. "That shouldn't be a problem."

He watched Elizabeth sit down, smoothing out her light blue dress, she cleared her throat. Jorge glanced toward his wife who gave him a quick eyebrow flash, causing him to smile. Two seats from Paige sat the woman who was with Elizabeth Alan. Glancing at her phone, she appeared uninterested.

"Are we ready to go?" Makerson asked another man, who kneeled in front of the desk, typing something on the keyboard. The young intern with a long beard turned around and nodded.

"Yup, all set when you are."

"Let's do this," Makerson replied and sat down between the two as red numbers flashed on the screen showing a countdown to start.

"Good afternoon," Makerson spoke toward the laptop. "I'm Tom Makerson, editor for *Toronto AM* and I'm here with Jorge Hernandez, CEO of Our House of Pot and Elizabeth Alan with Canadians for Conservative Values. Today we're having an open discussion on legalized marijuana in Canada. As you can imagine, my two guests have opposing views on the matter. Elizabeth, let's start with you."

A smile lit up her face as she turned toward Makerson.

"You have been very vocal on this topic," Makerson spoke in a friendly tone. "You feel that marijuana is a gateway drug that causes more harm than good. Could you explain your position for those who aren't familiar with you?"

"Yes and thank you, Tom, for allowing me the chance to discuss this matter," Elizabeth spoke softly. "I became involved with a group called Canadians for Conservative Values around the time marijuana was legalized in this country because I felt the government had a casual attitude about this known gateway drug. I quickly realized that many others felt the same and my goal now is to create awareness over the matter and hopefully make people realize that this was a dangerous decision for our country."

"Why do you feel it is dangerous?" Makerson spoke with no judgment in his voice. "Many people compare it to alcohol and feel that if used responsibly, it causes no real risk."

"I *know* it's dangerous because I lost my son from drugs," Elizabeth said and took a deep breath as if to compose herself. "And it started with marijuana."

"And you feel that if it wasn't for pot, that he wouldn't have tried more dangerous drugs later?"

"Absolutely not," Elizabeth spoke confidently. "I never had a problem with my son before he started smoking marijuana. He tried it once and it was *downhill* from there."

Jorge bit his lip but remained silent.

"You believe this was where his addiction started?" Makerson continued to show his professionalism.

"Yes and he would be with us today if it hadn't been for marijuana," Elizabeth appeared assured. "I know it."

"Jorge," Makerson turned in the other direction. "Of course, as the CEO of Our House of Pot, you obviously have an opposing view on pot legislation. What do you think when you hear a story like the one Elizabeth just shared with us?"

"I think it is quite unfortunate that she has lost a son," Jorge replied immediately showing compassion in his voice. "And I am sorry *however*, I do not feel that it reflects the experiences of most people."

His reply was blunt causing Elizabeth to lean back, her eyes full of shock while Makerson appeared unfazed by the comment.

"You don't feel that most people think it's a gateway drug or you don't feel that it has a negative effect on most people's lives?" Makerson asked with a touch of humor in his eyes.

"Both," Jorge replied with no apology. "It is unfortunate and again, I am sorry for your loss," He directed his comment at Elizabeth Alan. "However, you cannot blame marijuana for the decisions that your son made and considering most people, they do not turn to heavy drugs after smoking pot, it is not reasonable to place the blame on the entire industry."

"Are you implying that it's my *son's* fault that he died?" Elizabeth quickly lost her original composure, leaning forward, she faced her opponent.

"No, of course not," Jorge countered. "But what I am saying is that marijuana, for most, is *not* a gateway drug and regarding your son, there is no sufficient proof of that either. In fact, this is really just your opinion."

Makerson leaned back slightly as if to make way for the argument to continue.

"So you think my son, who never did drugs in his life," Elizabeth fumed while Makerson glanced down and raised an eyebrow. "Would have even considered doing anything stronger if he hadn't tried pot first? Are you serious?"

"Yes, I am *very* serious," Jorge spoke in a condescending tone, frustrated with her ignorance. "I assure you, if pot didn't exist, people would still do other drugs and that, of course, includes some of the most dangerous drugs, which are pharmaceuticals. Many addictions and deaths every year are the result of Big Pharma not marijuana, so if you really have an issue with the people who cause a lot of death and destruction, why not start with them because as you know, they are *also* legal."

Makerson quickly jumped in. "So you think Big Pharma contributes to the problem of addiction?"

"And *death*," Jorge replied with a nod. "Take a look at the news, how many people has Fentanyl killed? Why is this on our streets? Why is it so easily accessible? These are the questions we need to ask instead of making pot the villain. That is, how you say, like bringing a gun to a knife fight."

"You feel that it's not receiving adequate attention?" Makerson asked.

"Not even close," Jorge noted that Elizabeth Alan had tears ready so he upped the ante. "Look, I will be honest with you in this matter. My oldest child has lost her mother because of the devastation of Fentanyl. Do you know what it is like to have to explain to a little girl, a child, why her mother has abandoned her?" He stopped for a dramatic pause. "Then try to explain why she is dead because of an addiction?"

No one said a word so Jorge turned his full attention back to a stunned Elizabeth Alan. "And I assure you, Ms. Alan, she did not start with pot."

Makerson finally spoke with compassion in his voice. "I'm very sorry, I had no idea that this was an issue in your family as well."

"It is," Jorge insisted. "It is an issue in many families."

Makerson glanced at Elizabeth Alan's infuriated expression and quickly ended the interview.

"I know you have somewhere to be, Ms. Alan, so would you like to make any final comments before we wrap this up?"

"I still maintain my position," Elizabeth answered rigidly as her face turned red. "I know Mr. Hernandez will attempt to justify his company but a mother knows her child and I know my son would still be here today if he hadn't started smoking pot."

Of course, her comment fell flat after Jorge's speech, something Makerson couldn't acknowledge until after the live event ended and Elizabeth Alan and her friend were gone.

"You fucking nailed this one," Makerson said as he closed the laptop and moved the desk back to its original position. "I had no idea you were going there. Was that even true about your daughter's mother?"

"It was," Jorge admitted while glancing at Paige who was smirking. "It was not a lie. This conservative bitch may have her sob story but I beat her at her own game. I don't fuck around with her kind."

"That interview ended when you told your story," Makerson seemed gleeful as he pulled his chair up to the desk. "That was what you call a 'mic drop moment' if I ever saw one. Holy fuck, her face! Did you see her face?"

"She was pissed," Paige offered as she stood up. "You got her on that one. I didn't know you were going there."

"I had to fight fire with fire," Jorge replied. "I would prefer not to bring up my daughter in the media however, in this case, it was necessary."

"You didn't say her name," Paige pointed out. "I can see why you did it."

"It will be fine," Jorge insisted. "This will be fine. It worked out exactly as it had to and now, she has no leg to stand on, as they say."

"You definitely put her on her ass today," Makerson commented and grabbed his iPad from a nearby chair. "I was originally going to ask viewer questions to spice up the interview but I guess that wasn't necessary."

Paige laughed.

"I am enough spice on my own," Jorge replied and winked at his wife.

"I know you aren't interested in social media," Makerson replied while sitting on the edge of his desk. "But you're on fire. People are ranting about Big Pharma and how she's using the blame game for her son and not accepting that he had a problem."

"It is true," Jorge replied and moved closer to Makerson, glancing at the screen. "I am sure there are bad comments too."

"There are but you definitely got a discussion going," Makerson replied. "Elizabeth Alan met her match."

"Oh, *amigo,* I am more than her match," Jorge replied with a grin. "I'm her worst fucking nightmare."

CHAPTER 20

"The others, they will be here later," Jorge commented as Jesús joined him in the conference room of Hernandez-Silva Inc. Each with a coffee in hand, the two men sat across from one another at the table. "There are things that I do not wish for the others to hear about, as you know."

"I know, sir, I do understand," Jesús nodded as he pulled his chair closer to the table and reached into his shirt pocket for a piece of paper and placed it on the table. It consisted of a scattered bunch of names and poorly constructed drawings. "I jotted down where everyone was standing the night Paige was shot and I cannot figure where the bullet came from."

Jorge ignored the tension in his shoulders when he leaned in to look at the sketch. It was a bittersweet victory on the night they bombarded a group of white supremacists in cottage country. Their battle plan had been simple. First, they set a fire around the cabin to lure them out, then they shot at the group as they ran from the flames. However, when he glanced at the diagram Jesús jotted down, he felt the need to push aside his own emotions from the night. Despite their massive victory, the sight of Paige bleeding with fear in her eyes was humbling. Few things had frightened him as much as that moment.

"Sir, I do not know unless I am mistaken," Jesús confessed. "It happened so fast. At the time, I assumed the bullet came from the cabin where we found the men but maybe I was wrong."

"That's what I thought too," Jorge admitted as he stared at the piece of paper. Something seemed off about it but he couldn't figure out what. "Most of us were on the other side of Paige. I don't know if it would've been the right angle for someone to shoot from the cabin."

"But sir, do you really believe it was one of us that shot her?" Jesús wondered out loud and folded the piece of paper, glancing toward the door. "I think the only people on her other side was Chase and Diego. Chase, he will not touch a gun and Diego would do anything to protect Paige."

"Unless Chase shot her by accident and doesn't want to say?" Jorge asked but knew he was grasping at straws. That didn't make sense. At the time, Chase had watched everything closely to make sure they got away from the fire before it picked up. "But I do not think."

"Would someone be behind her?" Jesús wondered as he slid the paper back in his pocket. "Someone we didn't know about?"

Jorge thought for a moment. "I must talk to Chase in private and discuss this matter with him. The rest of us were busy focusing on the cabin, perhaps he noticed something we did not?"

"It is possible, sir," Jesús agreed as voices could be heard from the main entrance. "We will continue this discussion."

Glancing toward the door, Jorge saw Paige and Diego appear, each with a tray of coffee. Jesús jumped up to open the door for them. Diego glanced at the two cups already on the table as he sat his tray down and Paige did the same.

"What? We bring coffee and you already got some," Diego commented abruptly. "What the hell?"

"Miscommunication, Diego," Jorge replied and grinned at his wife. "I am sure we can drink two."

"I saw Jolene and Chase downstairs," Paige jumped in. "Michael's at work, didn't you say Diego?"

"Yes," He nodded. "He's always working."

"Ah, the good police, keeping our streets safe," Jorge quipped as he took a drink of his coffee and glanced at his phone. "Makerson is on the way and Athas is downstairs. We can start soon."

"We're talking about Paige's meditation CD," Diego said with a grin and Paige rolled her eyes, leaving Jorge confused. "Did you tell him?"

"No, he was gone when I saw the message," Paige replied and turned her attention toward Jorge. "A well-known spiritual book company wants me to record a meditation CD for them. I guess they have the music and the dialogue but the person they originally hired didn't quite work out."

"They think her voice is soothing and she's a natural," Diego spoke excitedly, his eyes expanding in size. "Ironic that one of the world's best assassins also has the voice of an angel."

They shared a laugh while Jorge gave Jesús a look, something that went unnoticed by Paige.

"*Mi amor,* of course," Jorge quickly jumped in. "To me, you have always had the voice of an angel. So this offer, it does not surprise me."

Loud, clicking heels could be heard in the hallway as Jolene walked in the door, followed by Chase. Had they arrived together? Jorge was curious but instead made eye contact with Alec Athas, who trailed behind.

"We are here," Jolene announced the obvious as they all took their usual seats. "Are we missing someone?"

"Makerson is on the way," Jorge offered as everyone grabbed their coffee. "I asked Marco too but he is tied up."

"But sir, how much should he know?" Jesús asked showing no judgment. "There are already too many of us who know so much."

"We are a family," Diego answer for him. "That's how it is."

"This family, it keeps expanding," Jesús replied. "Shouldn't everyone be in a need to know basis?"

"I don't want to know a lot," Alec spoke up. "I don't want any more blood on my hands."

"We all got blood on our hands," Jorge reminded him and Alec looked away. "That's how this game works. You're a politician. Show me a politician with clean hands and I show you a politician who won't be around for long."

The buzzer rang and Diego jumped up.

"That must be Makerson," He commented on his way out the door.

"Me, I want to do more," Jolene jumped in as if the meeting had already started. "You, you have this all boys club where the guys, they take care of problems but what about me? I can do too, you know."

"I know, Jolene," Jorge replied tactfully. "However, I don't see you taking care of what Jesús just did in Mexico."

"Ok, this falls under the category of things I don't want to know about," Alec interrupted just as Diego returned with Makerson while Jorge grinned. "I don't want to know what happened in Mexico."

"Sorry I'm late," Makerson muttered as he awkwardly walked in and sat down.

Jorge shrugged with disinterest.

"Speaking of Mexico, sir," Jesús cut in. "I heard this is the reason Elizabeth Alan supposedly hesitated on the debate with you. She soon has a vacation scheduled in Mexico."

"Really?" Jorge said with a grin. "A lady against drugs yet she chooses to vacation at one of the drug capitals of the world. What a coincidence."

"I thought it was the murder capital," Makerson commented as he reached for a coffee. "I just ran a story about a Canadian tourist that went to Mexico on a holiday and was killed at her resort."

"Us Mexicans," Jorge said with a sanctimonious grin. "We are pretty good at that too."

"You are changing subjects," Jolene abruptly cut in with her eyes on Jorge. "I tell you that I want to do more and you talk about other things. I want to do more."

"I will have something for you soon," Jorge replied and turned his attention toward the others. "Ok, we must get this meeting on track again. I want to talk about the Elizabeth Alan interview."

"Actually, if I may cut in here," Makerson spoke softly but with some assertion in his voice. "This just came across my desk."

Turning his iPad, he showed a poorly shot video of Jorge's interview with Meghan Willa, moving it forward to the end.

"Mr Hernandez, you're clearly not aware how interviews work but you do not ask me questions, it's the other way around," The reporter snapped as she jumped off her chair while across from her, Jorge gingerly rose from his seat with a sanctimonious smile on his face.

"Well, Ms. Willa," Jorge countered as he removed his microphone. "I do believe, it is the reporter's job to keep the interview in line, am I not correct? Perhaps, you would be better suited for a different career and asking people questions merely be, how do you say, a hobby?"

Everyone around the table began to laugh, including Jorge.

"Ah, see, too bad that wasn't on air too" Jorge commented as he winked at his wife. "Perhaps people would enjoy seeing this here argument."

"They are seeing this argument," Makerson calmly replied. "Someone at the studio that day recorded it and it's all over social media this morning."

"See, if you were on social media, you would've known this," Alec piped up. "You need accounts."

"I need for nothing," Jorge shook his head. "You people fall in line with this social media nonsense but me, I do not wish to join. People can do or say whatever they wish, I will not be sitting like a mindless moron staring at my phone all day, worried about how many likes a picture of my fucking dinner got or who is doing what. I do not care."

"Too bad more people didn't think that way," Chase offered as he shook his head. "It's too much. If it wasn't for my kids, I wouldn't be on at all."

"The point is that a lot of people are calling you a masochist because of how you spoke to Meghan Willa," Makerson continued to speak evenly. "That you were condescending and rude to her on and off camera and that this off-camera shot shows that you were also disrespectful."

"Of course!" Jorge countered. "I do not respect her. She walked in there with her short skirt, stripper heels and an inch of makeup. Is she a reporter because she look more like a *puta* to me."

"See that there," Diego spoke up. "Talking like that can get you in a lot of trouble."

"I say this to you, I don't have it blaring all over *social media*," Jorge replied. "So what? Is no one else thinking the same thing? That woman, she is a terrible reporter but the network she is on does not care because she is, how you say, eye candy?"

Glancing at his wife, she nodded with a grin on her face.

"You are sexist!" Jolene cut in and pointed toward her cleavage. "This is what I was saying earlier. You think I'm a *puta* too because I am dress sexy, no?"

"Jolene, you actually do real work," Jorge replied and shook his head. "You do not prance around in stripper heels and short skirts. You have had management positions in this company, you have been one of the people I have counted on to get things done. This woman, here, on the screen,"

Jorge glanced toward Makerson's iPad. "She does nothing but lay in a tanning booth and ask stupid questions that show her ignorance."

Jolene deflated slightly and nodded.

"I think what he means," Paige jumped in. "Is you're capable of more than Meghan Willa. You take pride in your appearance and look professional but you have more to offer and you've proven it."

"Yes, exactly what Paige said," Jorge nodded. "This is true."

"So, back to the story," Makerson interrupted. "I would like to have a quote from you."

"Are you sure that's a good idea?" Diego asked with bulging eyes. "You just heard him talking, didn't you?"

Chase snickered and others soon joined.

Makerson thought for a moment. "Hernandez maintains that he has great respect for women and his comment reflects the specific person, not her gender."

"*Perfecto!*" Jorge replied with a shrug. "You took the words right out of my mouth, Makerson."

"Politically," Alec jumped in. "I'm a little concerned with that comment as well as your interview with Elizabeth Alan because you were a bit abrupt with her too."

"Nonsense," Jorge insisted. "You people here in Canada, you are much too sensitive about everything and not offending someone and you know what? People, they are tired of tiptoeing around and worrying about saying something wrong. Me? I don't play that way. I say it how it is."

Makerson grinned as he tapped on his iPad. "He believes integrity is more important than political correctness and will continue to reflect this in his comments."

"That sounds just like me," Jorge replied as Diego rolled his eyes. "I am all about integrity. Even if sometimes, it has a bite."

CHAPTER 21

"Paige, we must talk about something," Jorge said as they sat in traffic on their way home from the meeting. He glanced toward the passenger side of the SUV, where his wife was checking her phone. "This is perhaps not the ideal place or time but sometimes at home, it is hard to talk, you know?"

"With the baby and Maria…" Paige replied and her words drifted off as she nodded in understanding.

"*Si, mi amor,* this is what I mean," Jorge replied and glanced at the traffic then back at his wife. "I have not said anything in the past because of the pregnancy, so much going on with taking over the pot industry and I did not want to worry you but.."

"What's wrong?" Paige immediately cut him off and sat her phone aside. "Are you having health issues again? I told you that you have to stop eating so much.."

"No no," Jorge laughed in spite of himself and reached over to touch her arm. "No, *mi amor,* it is not that. I am worried about you. I worry about the night you were shot."

"I'm fine," Paige insisted. "It was just a graze. That's nothing, all things considered."

"I know, Paige, but I wonder how it happened that night," Jorge replied as traffic slowly moved ahead. "I think about it a lot. Who shot you?"

"I assumed it was someone in the cottage," Paige spoke softly and the two shared a look.

"Are you sure of this?" Jorge countered. "it would not be someone else?"

"You think it's someone else?"

He didn't respond at first but looked at the traffic ahead.

"But who would it be?" Paige asked. "Do you think one of our own shot me? Could there have been someone else in the woods that night?"

"Me, I do not know," Jorge confessed and heard vulnerability in his own voice. "This is my worry."

Both fell silent as traffic started to move more quickly, as they edged closer to home.

"I…I have thought about it," Paige seemed reluctant to share. "But I didn't want to over think it. I didn't want you to worry."

"This here," Jorge swung his hand around as he replied. "You know, I will always worry, Paige. If anyone ever even *thought* of hurting you, I do not care who, you know what will happen to them."

Paige didn't reply. Both knew that the last time a man threatened her life that his own ended in a brutal and barbaric way.

"Do you think it was Jolene?" Jorge wondered out loud. "Because at that time, you two.."

"No," Paige cut him off as she shook her head. "Jolene was on the other side of me and we were working together that night."

Jorge nodded.

"Most people were on the other side of me unless they slipped away for a minute," Paige reminded him.

"This is true, my love, I have thought about this and so has Jesús," Jorge replied as they turned on their street. "Diego and Chase were on that side but, we know they would not do such things."

"Definitely not," Paige spoke with certainty. "Jorge, I don't think it was one of ours. There were shots coming from the cottage that night."

"Perhaps," He replied with a shrug. "Paige, I do not like to ask about your past, I know we don't talk about it much but would you say…have some enemies from that time?"

She didn't reply.

"Paige, if there is something," Jorge insisted as they turned into their driveway, opening the garage door. "You must tell me."

"It would be impossible to trace me to any of my work," Paige was insistent. "I was very careful."

"Then who?" Jorge asked as he turned off the SUV and the garage door closed. "Is there someone else?"

Paige didn't reply but shrugged.

"*Mi amor*," Jorge turned toward her. "You must tell me if there is something I should know. I am serious right now. Is there someone who wishes you dead? Someone you think might be a threat?"

"I don't think so," Paige quietly replied.

"Unless they are out to hurt me," Jorge quietly asked. "Is that what you think?"

"I don't know," Paige replied and shook her head. "We can't assume anything."

"If there is..."

"I know," Paige leaned in and gave him a kiss. "I know."

They slowly got out of the SUV, both lost in their own thoughts. Jorge feared she was holding back from him. There was something that felt unanswered but what was the right question to ask. Could it be someone out to hurt her to get to him? Did Paige know or suspect something and wasn't saying? Was there something in her past that was now resurfacing?

"Paige, you know," Jorge began as they reached the door. "Maybe just to be safe, I should..."

As soon as he opened the door, his conversation was quickly halted when met by a furious daughter.

"You tell me to not speak of her death," Maria ranted as she pointed toward her iPad with fire in her eyes. "Then you go in this interview and talk about my mother's overdose? *Papa!* How could you?"

Stunned for a moment, Jorge didn't know what to say but fortunately, Paige quickly took over.

"Maria, we were concerned if you talked about it in school that it would bring you negative attention," Paige calmly replied as she stepped through the doorway and Maria backed off, while Jorge continued to stand in stunned disbelief. "In this case, he brought it up because he wanted to point out how addiction affects us all. I thought it was brave of him to talk about such a difficult part of his life."

Jorge shot Paige an appreciative look before walking through the doorway.

"Yes, Maria, she is right," Jorge spoke gently. "I did not intend to talk about your mother's death but this woman, she felt that marijuana was the path to dangerous drugs and blames it for her son's eventual death. I was simply pointing out that this was just her belief that addiction comes along differently for everyone."

"But you had to use *her* as an example?" Maria fumed as Jorge closed the door.

"Yes, Maria, I had to show that I also knew what addiction can do to a family," Jorge spoke honestly. "Do you think it was easy to explain this to you when it happened? It was one of the more difficult conversations we have had, Maria. You know this. You were not close but she was still your mother."

The last words seemed to lower Maria's defenses and she nodded before looking at the floor. When she looked up with tears streaming down her face, Jorge felt his heart drop.

"*Papa,* but the journalist said that it was your fault," Maria sniffed and Jorge and Paige exchanged looks. "That you.."

"Maria, what are you talking about?" Jorge immediately cut her off. "Makerson did not say it was my fault and the other interview.."

"No, *Papa,* the journalist that called me tonight," Maria spoke with such innocent eyes that Jorge felt fury shoot through his veins. "She called and asked about my mother's death and she said it was because of you that she died."

"Maria, who are you talking about?" Paige jumped in. "A journalist called *you* and spoke to you about this? What did you say?"

"I said nothing!" Maria put both hands in the air. "I know that famous people always say 'no comment' and so, this is what I did."

"You didn't say anything else?" Jorge confirmed as he fought the rage that was taking over his body, Paige looked worried. "Maria, this here is important, please tell me if you said anything."

"No, I swear, *Papa,*" Maria spoke dramatically. "She asked how my mother died and I said 'no comment!' Then she asked how I felt about the fact that my father had something to do with her death and I told her 'no comment again' and ended the call."

"How did she get your number?" Paige asked in a calm tone.

"I think on social media," Maria spoke honestly. "I have it there for when a director wants to contact me."

"Maria!" Jorge screamed, unable to hold his fury back any longer. "You remove that immediately! You must never put personal information on the internet. No phone number, address, nothing!"

"I'm sorry, *Papa,*" Maria began to cry again. "I just…"

"Now, Maria!" Jorge cut her off. "And Paige, will you call the phone company. Have her number changed immediately. Maria, what was the woman's name that calls you?"

"Papa, it was that lady you did an interview with," Maria said as she wiped a tear from her face. "Meghan something…..she had a weird last name."

"Willa?" Paige asked and shot a look at Jorge.

"Yes!" Maria was wide-eyed. "That was her! She called back and left a message on my phone."

"Get it!" Jorge instructed. "I want to hear."

Maria didn't reply but ran upstairs.

"Don't yell at her," Paige spoke quietly as she approached him, touching his arm. "She didn't mean to do anything wrong. You have to relax with her or she'll never tell us anything."

Jorge considered her words as his daughter ran downstairs.

"Meanwhile, let *me* take care of this," Paige insisted. "I know what you want to do with Willa but let me."

"Paige, I…"

"Me and Jolene," Paige squeezed his arm. "Ok."

He reluctantly agreed.

"Meanwhile, you're going to call Makerson to tell him about this and he can act accordingly."

"*Papa,*" Maria was hitting buttons on her phone. "Here it is."

HI Maria! This is Meghan Willa phoning back. I think we got cut off. Could you please return my call so we can discuss my questions. I know you are nervous but this will just be between us, sweetheart.

Jorge wanted to kill that reporter. He wanted to wrap his hands around her scrawny neck and choke the life out of the fucking *puta* cunt! How dare she call his daughter and make such accusations.

Taking a deep breath, he looked into Maria's innocent eyes and his heart broke. She was frightened of him. He bit back his anger.

"Maria, I am sorry," Jorge spoke quietly as he reached out and touched her shoulder. "I did not mean to get angry with you but once again, I am concerned for your safety. You cannot have your private information out there. It is a dangerous world. A *very* dangerous world. This bitch..."

"Jorge," Paige cut in.

"No, Paige, I will say it how it is," Jorge looked into his daughter's eyes. "This bitch, Meghan Willa, she was wrong to call you. I am *very* angry with her. *Not* you. You handled yourself perfectly and I am *very* proud."

Maria smiled nervously through her tears. "I'm sorry, *Papa,* I just had my number online for acting stuff."

"Maria," Paige cut in. "Actors don't have their own private information online, they have agents who take care of these things."

"*Papa!* Can I have an agent?" Maria looked hopefully between the two of them.

"We will consider it," Jorge spoke reluctantly. "But first, I must take care of this situation. This woman was wrong to call you and I plan to make sure she knows it."

Maria nodded and folded her hands in front of her.

Leaning down, Jorge kissed his daughter on the top of her head and pulled her into a strong hug. Her tiny body was so fragile and that mere thought only insured that Meghan Willa would not see her next birthday.

CHAPTER 22

It was those eyes. In them, you could see a darkness that most wish for no one to know about. It is like they held you captive, defenseless, powerless and unable to escape. Perhaps that is why everyone either feared or loved Paige Noël-Hernandez. She could cast a spell with a single look with those crazy eyes.

Jolene had known better than to challenge her. It was a mistake that she had made in the past, to find herself locked in the fury of a woman who killed without a second thought. In fact, she was the ideal match for Jorge, a man who had either personally murdered or organize the death of anyone who got in his way. He wasn't a man who believed in second chances but through the grace of God, Jolene had been given one and it was something she was thankful for every day.

Of course, much had changed in the past year. She had worked hard to prove her loyalty to Jorge and Paige but had she not, even her brother would've turned his back on her. This she knew. Diego had a strong bond with Jorge Hernandez as he did with Paige. They were two powerful people and yet, they played the role of everyday citizens without a path of death and destruction behind them.

Since his move to Toronto, no one had connected the number of suspicious and unsolved murders to Jorge Hernandez. Police feared for their lives and the people above them wouldn't want to lose power and for that reason, the former cartel boss would always be safe. He owned everyone.

It was hard to believe that these two dangerous people could parent an angel like Miguel. The first day Jolene saw him, his big, brown eyes looked into hers and she broke down in tears. They all watched - Paige, Jorge, Diego, Chase, and Jesús - as she sobbed uncontrollably when reminded of the child she had lost a year earlier. Diego had quickly removed the baby from her arms while Chase ushered her into the hallway. Perhaps it was necessary to be ripped wide open in order to heal.

It was a private conversation with Paige a week later that changed their relationship. Once strained, a bond formed between the two women. While the men in the room thought she was losing her mind the first time she held Miguel, Paige understood in a way that only another woman could. It was then she asked Jolene to be the godmother; it was a beautiful gesture that had been like a lifeline to a sinking ship.

Since that day, Jolene would've done anything for Paige and Jorge. Her loyalty was more powerful than her fear. Her need for acceptance and family stronger than the voice that warned she could be stepping into a landmine and not the Garden of Eden. And Paige Noël-Hernandez could be as much *el diablo* - the devil - as her husband.

"So, the plan, what is it?" Jolene asked as she and Paige drove through downtown Toronto.

"You know, I'm not completely certain yet," Paige admitted as they headed toward the building where Meghan Willa lived. "I do know, it won't be pleasant."

Jolene shifted uncomfortably in her seat, purposely pushing away the memory of Jorge and Paige ambushing her the previous year. She had never been as frightened in her life. Yet, they had allowed her to live. Meghan Willa wouldn't have that luxury.

"I say, we just shoot and go," Jolene suggested as she glanced out the window. "Be done with it."

"We could," Paige calmly agreed, her voice consistently even. "But we also could give her the false sense of safety…then put her on the chopping block."

The statement sent a chill through Jolene's body.

"I think we should play it by ear," Paige replied. "I have a few thoughts."

Arriving at a newer building in the downtown area, the two women walked in behind another guest as if security didn't exist. The young, Chinese woman ahead of them was staring at her phone, oblivious to their presence. Neither said a thing but followed her into the elevator and pressed the button to Meghan's floor.

It was after the other woman got out and they were alone that Jolene spoke.

"The camera for this elevator, is there one?"

"Yes, deactivated."

Jolene nodded. Marco, the company's IT expert could hack into anything and often did as part of his job. This meant that security cameras in the building would be turned off.

They arrived at her condo and Paige stood aside while Jolene gently tapped on the door. It slowly opened and the white lady from Jorge's controversial interview answered. She wore a robe and slippers, with no makeup and her hair up in a bun. It was interesting how many women appeared so beautiful on camera and yet in real life, it became clear that this was an illusion at best.

"I live next door and my power, it is not working," Jolene spoke in a friendly tone. "I see you have no problems?"

"Ah…no," Meghan appeared confused as her eyes scanned the hallway. "I-

"Well," Paige was suddenly beside Jolene. "You're about to."

Meghan attempted to close the door but Jolene shoved her and the two women went inside. Locking the door behind them, she turned to see the frightened reporter regain her balance and rush toward her phone across the room but Paige was already there.

"No no no!" Paige spoke in her even tone as she grabbed a nearby Kleenex from the box and picked up the pink smartphone. "See, it's rude to check your phone in front of company."

"We do not like rude," Jolene confirmed and reached in her purse for a gun. "And screaming, it is also very rude."

"She's right," Paige confirmed and pointed toward the couch in the next room. "Shall we go have a seat? I think it's time we have a little girl talk."

Jolene grinned and followed the two women into the living room. It was posh with the same kind of expensive furniture that Diego had in his condo; but the gays, they always liked nice things. Jolene did too but was more frugal, more practical however, women like Meghan Willa wanted to impress others. It was obvious.

"I know who you are," Meghan spoke with fear in her voice, something that caused Paige to stand a little taller. "You're married to Jorge Hernandez. He sent you here to threaten me."

"My husband doesn't send me *anywhere* to do *anything*," Paige was quick to correct her with an even tone as Meghan sat on the couch. "I'm here of my own free will and for that, you should be grateful because what my husband wanted to do to you was pretty barbaric."

"He is Mexican," Jolene spoke loudly as she continued to point the gun at Meghan who started to shake. "You do not fuck around with Mexicans."

"She's right," Paige agreed as she sat down in a chair across from Meghan while Jolene continued to point her gun at the reporter. "I've spent a great deal of time in Latin American countries and they can be quite… brutal in their approach."

"They will cut you into pieces," Jolene offered.

"After they torture you," Paige reminded her and the two women nodded as if they were chatting about an everyday event.

"This is true, they do like torture."

"And my husband," Paige continued. "He was very angry when you called his daughter."

"You do not mess with a man's family," Jolene commented. "They do not like."

"Jorge felt that since you had such a big mouth," Paige continued to speak with a calm voice. "That he would start by cutting out your tongue…but he also played around with the idea of choking you. Neither are pleasant ways to die."

Meghan Willa appeared frozen, as if too frightened to cry or even speak. Her eyes begged for pity but she was too stupid to understand that Paige was a woman who had little compassion outside of her family.

"But that is messy…..and, I don't know," Paige said as she waved a hand in the air. "Maybe I'm getting old but I like to keep things clean now. I like simple."

"We can do simple," Jolene insisted and then made a face. "Or we could do fast, get it done with. I can shoot."

Seeing the fear in Meghan Willa's eyes, Jolene continued to speak to Paige "Her brain, it will be all over that wall behind her."

"Red would be lovely with this expensive decor," Paige nodded with arrogance in her voice. "I wouldn't want to be the person cleaning it up though."

"Please," Meghan barely whispered. "I promise, I will do whatever….." Her voice was shaking, causing her teeth to click together.

"You look cold," Paige observed.

"We did interrupt," Jolene replied. "Maybe, she was going to take a bath or shower?"

"How rude of us," Paige replied in her soft, soothing voice and turned her attention to Jolene. "You know, I once took care of a lady by throwing her smartphone in her bath water."

"You can do?" Jolene asked with surprise in her voice.

"Well, you make sure to have it hooked to an extension cord and frayed wires always help but…" Paige paused and checked Meghan's reaction. "Yes, it can be done."

"Oh, she does not know."

"Of course she doesn't," Paige nodded and looked into Meghan's eyes. "I'm one of the best assassins in the world. I can kill you and make it look like a suicide, an accident, however, I wish. I'm very skilled."

Meghan suddenly jumped up and reached for a nearby lamp but not before Jolene lurched forward and ripped it out of her hand, shoving the gun directly into the reporters face as she sobbed hysterically.

"Not smart," Paige spoke calmly as she rose from the chair. "See, Jolene, she is also a very dangerous woman. Contrary to what you might think, women are some of the most dangerous people in the world. We just hide it better than men."

Jolene smiled and nodded.

"I'm getting tired of this," Paige commented and approached Meghan. "Let's get this over with"

"What you think?" Jolene asked as Paige glanced around.

"I think that Meghan here was quite depressed," Paige replied as she glanced around. "Her career wasn't going so well. She felt she couldn't compete. Her beauty was fading. You know, her life... was worthless."

"But...I...I said I'd do anything," Meghan spoke in a child-like voice. "I will work for you. I know Makerson from *Toronto Am* does, I can too..."

"We don't need your help," Paige replied.

"But no one will believe that I....people who know me.."

"That's the thing about suicide," Paige spoke softly. "We are often surprised by the people who do it. And when the police go into your drafted email, they may find a letter you were planning to send to your mother telling her how empty and meaningless your life is....how fame never brought you the happiness you thought it would."

"What? I.."

"See, we take care of everything," Paige replied. "I have a wonderful hacker who has this email in your Gmail account. So it looks like you wrote it."

"You think the police will find?" Jolene asked.

"Well, they are pretty useless and lazy," Paige insisted with a girly laugh. "But this will be a high-profile death so they will have to actually do a little work this time."

"Ah, yes," Jolene nodded. "This is true."

"Please..." Meghan continued to beg, something that both women ignored.

"I enjoyed this girl talk," Paige continued as she glanced at Jolene. "We really must do it more often."

"Yes, it is nice," Jolene agreed as she glanced at the floor to see that the young woman had urinated down her leg. "Maybe next time, we do without this one."

"That won't be an issue," Paige grinned and thought for a moment. "I think she's a jumper."

"I still think electrocute in the tub," Jolene offered ignoring the reporter's pleas.

"Ah, but the chance to fly," Paige spoke dreamily as she reached forward to touch Meghan's hair as she sobbed hysterically, begging for her life. "Like an angel in heaven."

"You really believe in such?" Jolene asked.

"What I believe," Paige spoke with confidence. "Is that us women, we bring life into this world and sometimes, it's necessary that we also take it out too."

CHAPTER 23

….Meghan Willa left a note telling of her struggles with depression. Her family asks for privacy during this difficult time.

Jorge glanced across the table at Paige, who appeared unfazed by the news report as she leaned forward and kissed Miguel. The baby stared back at her while Maria swung around abruptly to glance at the television in the next room.

"*Papa!* Isn't that the lady who called me?" Maria asked as she turned back to face them both, her brown eyes widened in surprise. "The woman asking me about you?"

"Yes, Maria, unfortunately, we now see she was a very troubled woman," Jorge commented while Paige nodded sympathetically. "This is perhaps why she made up such terrible stories."

"People in pain often want to hurt others," Paige spoke softly while looking at her baby.

"*Si,* this is true," Jorge replied and quickly changed the subject. "Maria, you are now finished school, why are you up so early this morning."

"I'm working on my audition and Paige and me are going to look into ACTRA and agents today," Maria said as she danced in her seat. "I'm so excited."

"Well, take your time," Jorge reminded her. "You want to make sure to learn about this industry."

"Of course, *Papa!*" Maria said as she jumped up from her seat, reaching for her bowl and glass. "I can't wait."

Paige glanced at Jorge as Maria danced her way to the dishwasher before rushing upstairs.

"*Mi amor,* it will be a long summer if I must hear about acting every day," Jorge muttered and glanced at his phone. "Why can't my daughter be fascinated with science or math….history…anything but acting."

"I hate to say it but after going on a few auditions, it mightn't be what she thinks," Paige reminded him. "There's more competition than auditioning for a school play. It's a different world."

"I do not want my daughter heartbroken and disappointed but at the same time," Jorge said as he glanced at Miguel, who was watching him with interest. "I want more for my children. Much more."

"It will be fine," Paige assured him. "Don't worry."

"And my love, suicide?" Jorge asked as he rose from the chair, giving her a kiss on the top of the head. "Clever, very clever."

"There's more than one way to skin a cat," Paige reminded him, causing Jorge to laugh as he reached for his phone. Glancing at his messages again, he slid it into his pocket.

"Well that cat, it has been skinned," He spoke in a low voice. "I thank you, *mi amor,* you and Jolene did well."

"Who knew we would make a good team?" Paige replied as Jorge leaned down to kiss Miguel. "But as it turns out, she's stronger, much stronger than before."

"This is good because we need that strength," Jorge said as he started toward the door. "I will text you later."

Jumping in his SUV, he headed to the *Princesa Maria*, where he had scheduled a meeting with both Makerson and Athas. The first one to arrive, he entered the empty club to find Chase making coffee behind the bar. He turned around to reveal a black eye.

"Oh, *amigo!*" Jorge commented as he sat on a stool. "She is being a little too rough now. Black eyes are abuse, you know?"

"Oh no, this," Chase laughed. "This is from the gym."

"I did not know you were participating in fights now?" Jorge commented as he leaned forward to inspect the bruise more closely. "Is this something new?"

"I'm always training, you know," Chase replied with a shrug. "I saw they started a fight club and I thought, you know, why not?"

"Does this black eye," Jorge said as he pointed at Chase. "Does this mean you lost?"

"Nah, I won alright," Chase said with a grin. "But the other guy, he got a few good punches in."

Jorge nodded, his thoughts spinning with possibilities.

"But it was a rush, you know," Chase continued. "That feeling of being powerful, in control, even for a minute."

"*Amigo,* you do not have to tell me of such things," Jorge replied with laughter in his voice. "That is my life. Love, power, and loyalty. Do we need more?"

"I…I guess I never saw how addictive that rush is," Chase replied as he leaned on the bar. "You know, it's like you're nervous but once you do it, you want to do it again. Seeing that guy on the ground. Man, that was fucking powerful."

"Proving, my friend, we're all animals," Jorge commented as Chase nodded while turning toward the coffee pot. "We pretend to be civilized because it looks good, you know? But underneath it all, we are led by the need for power. This is something I learned about myself a long time ago and it seems, Chase, you are now seeing the same for yourself."

"I didn't think that was me," He admitted. "I thought it wasn't my nature. It was the rest of you but not me."

"Never think you are different from us," Jorge replied as Chase passed him a cup of coffee than starting to pour one for himself. "Every step, it has led to this moment. That much I know."

"Things, they will now change for you," Jorge continued. "You will see, *amigo,* you have opened your eyes to a whole new world."

The door suddenly opened, interrupting their conversation. Unsure of who was on the other side, Jorge reached for his gun but stopped when he saw Diego and Jesús walk in, followed by Makerson and Athas.

"What? Did you have a meeting outside I do not know about?" Jorge asked sternly but with humor in his voice, his eyes tilting up while his head leaned toward his chest. "You know me, I do not believe in coincidences."

"Yeah, well this time, you gotta," Diego informed him as he rushed toward the coffee pot. "Me and Jesús were coming here to talk to Chase. We're starting a singles night here."

"What?" Jorge shook his head as the other men exchanged looks. "We have pot stores across the country. Why do you worry about a singles night at the bar?"

"This guy, he started a dating app and he wants to hold events here," Diego replied as he poured coffee. "I figure, if we can do it here and it's a success, why not do the same at the pot shops? Having singles nights?"

"Sir," Jesús jumped in and Makerson nodded behind him, while Athas checked his phone. "They do this sometimes at grocery stores. It increases the number of people who visit."

"It's ideal," Diego insisted. "Think about it! They come out, meet someone, buy some weed, go home, smoke it, have great sex and we are forever their favorite company."

"We sell weed," Jorge reminded him as he glanced at both Makerson and Alec, who appeared humored. "We're *already* everyone's favorite company."

"We gotta lighten up our image," Diego insisted. "Because of these conservative assholes in the media, we're starting to seem too serious. And you," He pointed at Jorge. "Mr. Suit and Tie serious, you aren't helping."

"Diego, I am not going to look like some bum in an interview," Jorge complained and pointed toward the office. "Now can we have a meeting about the real issues."

"You're the real issue," Diego continued to dramatically insist. "We gotta get you out of the news, you're a buzz kill."

"Diego, let it go," Jorge insisted as he started toward the office and the others followed.

"Sir," Jesús spoke up. "I do think Diego has a good idea about singles nights but I also think that you must continue to be professional. It is important for the company. Your strength creates more confidence in our business."

Jorge didn't reply but waited for everyone to take their seats. Chase sat behind the desk and that's when Diego noticed the black eye.

"Hey, what's with…"

"Fight at the gym," Jorge jumped in with a reply. "Can we please not get so far off topic that we never return again? We have work to do here today. You guys can chit-chat about this after our meeting."

"Now," He turned his attention to Makerson. "You got something for me?"

"I got a few things today," He replied eagerly and pulled out his phone. "First of all, Meghan Willa's suicide?"

Everyone looked at Jorge.

"It was very... sad." He replied with no emotion in his voice. "What else?"

"Well, I see here that since the debate between you and Elizabeth Alan," Makerson slid his finger over the smartphone screen. "She's released a statement that 'We all share the pain of addiction and after my conversation with Mr. Hernandez, I feel I have better insight into this topic. My own personal circumstances involving my son's death made me closed to other opinions and although I still don't condone the use of pot or it's legalization, I also see no reason to fight it.'"

"*Perfecto!*" Jorge replied. "This here, it means that we have resolved this issue."

"Well, yes and no," Makerson made a face. "Elizabeth Alan has dropped her defenses on the topic, but there is still a push to make it illegal again and a lot of online propaganda suggesting the increase in violence is due to the legalized weed."

"Like the violence, it did not exist before?" Jorge asked with amusement.

"Ok, so I have to jump in here," Alec Athas suddenly spoke up. "Big Pharma wants you out. They're losing too much money so they're going to work any angle they can find. They want to take the government down."

"How?" Jorge immediately asked. "You got something?"

"Sexual harassment with one of his top staffers," Alec answered honestly. "It hasn't got out yet and it can't," He glanced at Makerson who nodded. "The prime minister knew and covered it up."

"This does not seem like a big deal," Jesús said with a shrug. "So what?"

"The problem is that now," Alec answered. "There's instability in the government and opposition is trying to find a crack so they can split it wide open."

"So what can be done?" Jesús leaned in. "Can we fix this controversy?"

"Unfortunately, no," Alec said as he ran a hand through his short hair. "The opposition is chipping away and once this story breaks, we're fucked because Big Pharma is pushing hard to get weed out but first, they got to push the government out."

"Fuck," Diego said. "Those fuckers."

"Oh Diego," Jorge said with a shrug. "We can take them on and we will."

"What we really need," Alec continued. "Is someone strong that can take the prime minister's place if he has to step down. Someone who can give people confidence in the party again and take on the opposition head-on."

A silence filled the room and everyone shifted their attention toward Jorge.

"Him? Are you kidding?" Diego jumped in. "A Mexican immigrant with a questionable past and the owner of the largest pot franchise in the country? Like the little old ladies and stuffy white women are gonna vote for him."

"Hey now," Jorge teased. "I happen to know white women, they like me, I even married one if you have forgotten."

"This is true, sir," Jesús offered as the others laughed. "Also, you must remember, there are many immigrants in this country."

"There are many immigrants that no one listens to," Alec told Jorge. "They're ignored. Politics, it's directed at middle-class white people. There is underlining unrest and it won't take much to shake things up. Normally, a controversy like this one wouldn't be a big deal but the climate is just too risky now and the opposition knows it."

"This, it does not make sense," Jesús appeared skeptical.

"That's what I'm saying," Alec spoke passionately toward Jesús. "We need a leader who speaks for the people who sacrificed to get to this country. They want to see someone who represents them."

Everyone looked at Jorge again. This wasn't the first time Alec had brought up this topic. It was, however, the first time he brought it up to the group.

"Of course, I'm flattered but this is of no interest to me," Jorge replied. "But if I ever ran, you know I would win."

"Oh my God," Diego dramatically rolled his eyes, causing Jorge to laugh.

"But, me, I do not think this is a good idea," Jorge admitted to a crestfallen Alec. "I understand what you say but still, even this recent attention on me through the media, it has been silly. I do not wish to part in such a ridiculous world."

"You know, everyone makes some interesting points," Makerson cut in. "But one of the issues here in Canada is lack of interest in politics. Most politicians are bland, saying what people want to hear and that turns people off. It's insincere. We need someone who will stand out in the crowd."

"Look, I'm not an expert in any of this shit," Chase spoke up. "But the way I see it, if they're going to attack your business then you got to take them head on. If you're in politics, it would give you the option to not only protect your business but to fuck with Big Pharma. I would think that would at least appeal to you."

Jorge raised an eyebrow but remained silent.

CHAPTER 24

"I'm not saying I will do it," Jorge reminded his wife as they sat together on the couch, each with a glass of wine in hand. Paige studied his face with uncertainty before she quickly looked away. "*Mi amor*, it is merely a possibility."

"They're trying to make it sound like you're the only option," Paige quietly replied while shaking her head. "I'm not saying you couldn't do it but I don't think you see the full picture. If you get involved in politics, our whole life will be under a microscope. We can't kill every journalist that ask too many questions."

"Of course not, Paige, I do see what you mean," Jorge replied and thought for a moment. "But, perhaps we can instead find someone who would be more ideal and help them get elected. Perhaps there is someone out there who can fill these shoes."

"Let's not get ahead of ourselves," Paige reminded him. "So far, it's speculation and who knows if the story will even break. Is there a way we can keep this out of the media?"

"It does not look good," Jorge admitted and shook his head. "These things, they get out."

"But still, that doesn't mean the opposition will get in and even if they do," Paige reminded him. "Pot is here to stay. It would be like trying to contain a forest fire with a bucket of water. Plus, public support is high."

Jorge considered her words and nodded.

"Look at your sales," Paige reminded him. "The company is growing. Look at the huge response to the pot festival. This isn't the kind of monster you can shove back into the closet."

Although Jorge wanted to believe what Paige was saying, he had an unsettling feeling. There was a lot of talk about the recent rise in murders in Canada's largest city and some suggestions that pot was the reason behind it. Although the idea seemed ludicrous to him, he also knew that when people wanted to justify anything, they found a way. He also knew that Big Pharma was losing money and they weren't about to go down without a fight.

There were few people who Jorge Hernandez looked to when seeking advice but there was one whose role was prominent in his life. The man he called his 'boss' with the cartel, carefully hidden away as if he were merely retired after many years of much success in the legitimate world. He hadn't been traced to the billions in drug money nor would he be. Even if the truth came out, no one would believe it because this man worked carefully to keep up his profile. He was untouchable and for that reason, so was Jorge.

Their phone call was brief. Jorge quickly explained his situation in the privacy of his office as he stared at a framed photo of his family. Paige had been right to insist that he think about everything involved because the media would attempt to devour him if he got involved in politics. He would be watched carefully and for that reason, Jorge was skeptical. The only positive side was the power and influence he would carry.

"I would suggest that instead, you find someone who can represent your interests," He told Jorge. "However, that person must be as strong as you. They must take on the dogs that nip at your heels. You've shaken up the pharmaceutical industry and they simply are not going away."

"I wonder who that could be," Jorge considered but came up with nothing.

"Can you not influence the politician you backed in the last election?"

"Too soft," Jorge immediately insisted.

"Well liked, is he not?"

"He is but this is not enough."

"I recommend you find someone who *is* enough."

Their call ended shortly after and Jorge sat alone in his office, deep in thought. He finally decided that perhaps Paige was correct. Nothing was threatening his business yet so it was better to not jump the gun.

He found Maria dancing around excitedly when he left the office while Paige turned and gave him a look; their eyes met briefly and he forced a smile on his face.

"*Bonita,* what is with all his excitement?" Jorge asked with some hesitation. "Did you win the lottery or something?"

"No, *Papa!*" Maria giggled with delight. "I'm going for my first audition next week!"

"Oh Maria," Jorge forced a smile on his face as his daughter rushed forward to hug him. "That is wonderful! I am so proud of you."

"It's a small role," Paige commented quietly as Maria reached for her father's hand and led him to the couch. "A commercial that wants kids from different cultural backgrounds."

"Wow! That is very exciting," Jorge continued to fake his enthusiasm. "So, what do you have to do?"

"I'm not sure yet," Maria replied.

"What is it for?" Jorge searched his brain for questions.

"A store," Maria replied and reached in her pocket for her phone and showed him the company's website.

"Very nice!"

"Chase is going to be so excited when he hears this," Maria said as she danced in her seat. "Maybe he can take me to the audition."

"No, Maria, it will be me or Paige that will take you," Jorge immediately insisted. "Chase, he is busy and it is better a parent accompanies you."

"I actually think a parent is required," Paige started as Maria rose from the couch, as if she hadn't heard anything and giggling, ran upstairs. Jorge turned and shook his head.

"I do not like this acting thing," He reminded Paige who shrugged in response. "Look at how ridiculous it is making her."

"She's excited," Paige replied.

"She's already acting like one of those self-obsessed actresses," Jorge complained as he leaned back on the couch and closed his eyes. "I do not like this."

Paige didn't reply but simply leaned over and gave him a kiss on the cheek before sitting beside him.

"I also got news today about the meditation CD," She added and Jorge's eyes popped open. "I'm recording it next month."

"Two celebrities in one house?" He teased.

"My role is more of a background thing," Paige insisted and raised her eyebrows. "Which is exactly what I want."

"And this commercial for Maria?" Jorge raised his eyebrows, turning toward his wife. "What do you think?"

"I think it will be a good experience for her but there will be a lot of other kids auditioning too," Paige spoke honestly. "I want her to be hopeful but I'm trying to get her to be realistic too. I explained that actors often go on many auditions before they actually get a role but she seems overly confident. I wonder where she gets that from?"

Jorge laughed. "Oh, *mi amor*, you must be overly confident in this world or it will eat you alive."

"Fair enough," Paige replied. "Speaking of which, did you talk to…"

"Yes, I did," Jorge grew serious. "It is a difficult decision and I see your point. He also feels that at this time, it would be better to have someone else groomed for the position but that is the problem, who? Who is strong enough to take on Big Pharma and win?"

"I don't think that's an issue," Paige spoke skeptically. "I know they'll have a hand in this battle but I don't think they can win the war. If anything, they'll try to push their synthetic pot pills."

"This makes sense," Jorge agreed and took a deep breath and turned toward his wife, his eyes fixating on her neck. "I must not allow this to dominate my thoughts anymore. I have too many things in my life that are much more relevant. Too many…more pressing issues."

Jorge leaned in and gave her a kiss. Moving closer, his hand slid around her waist, his fingers under the waistband of her pants. Very quickly, his breath grew labored, causing the kiss to grow in intensity as Paige reached for the back of his neck, encouraging his lust.

Finally tearing himself away, his eyes glanced toward his office. Maria was upstairs with her music playing while the baby was napping. Juliana was out for the afternoon. Everything was perfect.

At least, for now.

CHAPTER 25

The room was spinning. A heat started in his chest and slowly spread throughout his body, like a spark of energy that was attempting to light him on fire. A fear quickly replaced it as a chill overwhelmed him, his stomach turned, immediately causing him to sit up. He felt weak, vulnerable, as if suddenly alone in the world.

Glancing toward his wife, Jorge considered waking her but decided against it, instead he rose from their bed. His legs were wobbly as his feet touched the floor, his arms heavy as if attached to sandbags. Jorge attempted to not panic as his body betrayed him. He was powerless. Fear enclosed his heart as he slowly made his way across the room.

In the bathroom, he saw an eerie transformation take place in the mirror. As he stood in disbelief, it was as if Jorge were getting younger with each second that passed. The small lines on his face disappearing, while his hair grew darker and his eyes warmed in a beautiful light. The dark collection of experiences that ranged from lust and power to murder and destruction were falling from his consciousness, his soul growing light. It could've been an amazing experience except Jorge felt like he was slipping away, as if a huge vacuum was pulling him into another dimension and he couldn't stop it.

The transformation continued until he was a child again. The 12-year-old version of Jorge Hernandez stared back at him, with vulnerability in his eyes. This was him before his brother died, back when life looked much different; a time when he never would've believed the man he would become. It was humbling and it was painful.

Paige walked in the room with a confused expression on her face. She looked tired, older as if life had drained the passion and love from her eyes. There was a coldness that immediately filled the room. Expressionless, she shook her head and sighed.

"Miguel, I told you to use your own bathroom," Her voice was unrecognizable. No longer soft and beautiful, she sounded bitter. "Get out!"

"Paige, it's…"

"Do not call me by my first name!" She snapped back, lurching toward him, she suddenly slapped Jorge in the face.

Stunned, he was unable to speak. Wanting to point out that it was him, a glance at the mirror proved otherwise. Jorge could see his younger brother staring back, dressed in the same clothes he wore the day of his accident.

He had forgotten the blue t-shirt and grey pants.

How could he have forgotten?

Feeling Paige pushing against his arm, Jorge shook his head and attempted to speak until he suddenly was wide awake, a small light glowing from the nightstand. Leaning over him was Paige, her eyes full of concern.

"Jorge, are you ok?" She quietly asked. "I was feeding Miguel and when I came back, you were talking in your sleep, you seemed….disturbed or upset?"

"Oh, Paige, you will not believe what I dream," Jorge slowly sat up and looked around, his hand reaching out to touch the nightstand. His arms no longer felt heavy. "I was sick, something was wrong with me and when I went to the bathroom, I started to get younger while you, you were older."

"How come I'm the one that gets to be older?" Paige teased as she lay back down and pulled the covers up. "Although, that's probably how it would happen."

"No, you do not understand," Jorge insisted. "I was a child again. I was 12. You were older and then I was Miguel. It was strange."

"Miguel your brother or Miguel your son?" Paige asked, suddenly intrigued.

"Miguel...*mi hombre,*" He quietly replied and they exchanged looks. She reached out and touched his arm. "It was strange Paige. I do not know if this dream has meaning but it was very nervous for me."

"You mean you were nervous," Paige corrected him and ran a hand up his arm as he slowly lowered back down into the bed.

"Yes, sorry, my English..." Jorge drifted off.

"When you get upset, your English comes out wrong," Paige reminded him. "That's why I know this dream really scared you."

"*Mi amor,* it was creepy," Jorge insisted as he turned toward her. "Maybe I will die. I hope that is not what it mean."

"No," Paige quietly replied. "Death in a dream usually doesn't mean death."

"But I did not die," Jorge said. "It was as if everything in my life flashed before my eyes and I felt as if it were going away, into another place, you know?"

She didn't reply.

"I guess that does not make sense," Jorge continued. "Maybe it is my conscience?"

"Maybe," Paige considered. "Maybe you are wondering how your life would be different had your brother lived?"

"That is definitely true," Jorge replied. "Me, I think that every day. Especially since our son was born. I look in his eyes and wonder, how my life would be if my brother had lived."

"Would you want it different?" Paige asked.

"I would like this place I am now," Jorge reflected. "I would take a different path to get here. But to think about such things, it is too late now. We cannot change the past. I am where I am. It was not easy but would I be the same person had I taken a different route?"

Paige didn't reply as the question floated around the room.

The couple fell silent and eventually went back to sleep.

The dream haunted him the next morning as he got up and got ready for his day. Although Paige didn't bring it up, her eyes were full of concern when they shared looks across the breakfast table, as Maria chatted on about her upcoming audition. Had his wife recognized a dark omen and not told him?

His fears continued to grow as the morning moved along, even as he sat through a business meeting with Diego and Jesús. It was as it ended that Jorge made the rare admission of fear over his nighttime illusion. He expected both men to laugh, perhaps make a joke or two and lighten his mood but instead, their reaction was one of disturbance.

"That's fucking scary," Diego made the abrupt comment as his eyes bulged out. "That would scare the hell out of me. I think you should go to your doctor."

"I'm fine, Diego," Jorge said. "I do not need you causing me worry."

"I'm just saying," Diego continued. "You had that heart attack a couple of years ago…"

"It was a mini heart attack," Jorge reminded him. "I have since seen my doctor many times and he is happy with my current state. I'm a man of 18 again."

"Perhaps, sir, that is what your dream meant," Jesús suggested. "Maybe you are not getting older like the rest of us, but younger at heart and maybe your past, that you say fell away, is your conscience."

"He don't got a conscience," Diego argued. "We're not talking no made for tv movie here, we're talking Jorge Hernandez."

Jesús started to laugh.

"All I can think of," Jorge said and momentarily paused. "You know, when we are young, we do not care. We live like there is no tomorrow and with what I did, that was a very strong possibility but you know, I have lived many lives and here I am. And now, with my daughter and son and of course Paige, I must be here for them. I fear what would happen if I were to die."

"Paige is a very attractive woman," Diego teased. "She would have you replaced in a second."

"No one, Diego, would replace me," Jorge boasted. "This here is impossible."

"Sir, you know, this comes from all your worry about the potential election," Jesús suggested. "Alec and Makerson are both pushing you to run if the current prime minister were to step down but sir, is this a good idea for you? Maybe not."

"They only want you in because it suits them," Diego reminded him. "Makerson would get great stories for his paper and Alec….I don't know, what the hell he gets out of this?"

"He will learn what a real man does in these here situations," Jorge commented. "He is not powerful enough to run himself and obviously, most politicians are too weak to make an impact. I am powerful and fearless. I will fight for this country and not just say the words people want to hear. Where else will they find this combination?"

"Sir, there must be someone else," Jesús insisted. "And really, it would not be a simple time. I was reading about this and you would be first required to win a leadership competition."

"You do remember how Alec Athas won over other candidates in his district, right?" Diego reminded him. "They all dropped out when they heard Jorge was backing him."

"Officially," Jorge jumped in. "I was advising him. We are not allowed to spend much money on our politicians here."

"Officially," Diego reminded him.

"Yes, of course," Jorge grinned. "But he is right, it may not be that easy. Even if I ran and won for the party leader, that does not mean Canadians will vote for me. There are many racists in this country that would not wish to have a Mexican run their country and to be honest, I am not as familiar with Canadian politics."

"Still, sir," Jesús jumped in again. "Do remember that these men that want you to run, they have their own reasons. You must be careful. You've already brought attention to yourself. Have you ever considered, perhaps it is Makerson and Athas that are helping create these problems in order to serve their own purpose?"

Jorge glanced at each man and considered these words.

"You would make a great prime minister sir," Jesús continued. "But is this something you wish to do?"

"And is it *necessary*?" Diego added. "They tried to say that this conservative group wanted to criminalize weed again but pot ain't going nowhere. Not goddamn likely. They got their own agenda."

Jorge didn't reply. Instead he glanced at his beeping phone and raised an eyebrow at the words on his screen.

CHAPTER 26

Little did they know that everything would change that summer. It happened quickly, leaving many people disturbed as if their feet were no longer on stable ground. And it started with the weather.

"It is as if Mother Nature," Jorge pointed at the television as he carried Miguel into the living room early one morning. "She's gone *loco.*"

Toronto was hit by an intense rainstorm that included high winds and even some hail. The news was full of stories about residents barely escaping the large chunks of ice that fell from the sky, causing damage to vehicles, homes, and businesses. One shop was in the process of renovations when the wind tore through destroying the building, leaving a construction worker trapped.

The media, however, barely made mention of the homeless people caught in the furious storm. Fortunately, many were given a helping hand by quick thinking Toronto residents who cared enough to usher them into a business or help find them shelter until the intense weather passed. The whole incident left many in shock.

This weather hadn't been forecast. In fact, even meteorologists were having problems explaining the impromptu storm.

Hot and dry conditions followed resulting in many forest fires throughout the country. In fact, it was such a concern that the government encouraged people to create a plan of action in case they were suddenly forced to evacuate. The forest fire report became a regular lead in the news and for many Canadians, was as frightening as recent acts of violence in Toronto. One media outlet had been heavily criticized for calling it 'Mother Nature's version of a mass shooting'. To the less sensitive people, it was a fair comparison. People were dying because unlike those of the past, many fires were fast-moving, barely allowing residents time to escape before the flames charged through with ferocity. Many lost their homes while others, their lives. Canadians watched the news in fear, realizing that no one was immune to disaster.

The most devastating of these events took place in early August when the vicious flames took a sudden shift narrowing in on a remote indigenous community. Many of the residents were asleep in their beds when the fires blazed through, killing everyone in its path. The prime minister addressed the public in an emotional speech, pausing several times while delivering the horrendous news while media representatives struggled to report the tragedy. Many would later say it was one of the most difficult stories they had ever reported since a number of the dead were children. One famed reporter broke down, live on the air, later shamed by the network but respected by a public that said it showed humanity in a time when people needed it the most.

Paige stopped watching the news. Whenever it was on, she quickly escaped to the baby's room. There, she would hold Miguel and stare out the window, as if waiting for fires to terrorize their neighborhood. Even Maria grew subdued, her disappointment over unsuccessful auditions became a secondary concern. And Jorge watched with both anger and sadness but it was after one particular phone call from Makerson, that he grew furious.

"The government knew," Makerson broke the news to Jorge before it hit the media. His voice was lifeless, defeated, the summer taking a toll on him. "About the fire heading toward the first nation community. They had a choice. They had the resources available to help the people but instead, sent them to the white, suburban neighborhood. All hell is about to break loose."

That's when the protests started. At first, it was a few indigenous people outside the parliament building but after an emotionless statement from the government that demonstrated limited explanation and avoidance, the protests quickly grew to across the country. Indigenous leaders spoke openly about how they were often neglected by the government but this time, it caused the death of an entire community. One speech by a western Canadian chief would go viral across the country and eventually, the world.

"They forget us when our women and children go missing. They forget us when our water is toxic. They forget us when our people are living in poverty. But this time, we will not let them forget!"

The power behind the cheering crowd was undeniable. The audience was full of people from many demographics, all frustrated with the government's lack of sincere commitment to Canada's first people. Many enraged that the government was warned about the fire headed toward the small, indigenous community and did nothing to help. They instead focused on a middle-class neighborhood, primarily consisting of white people.

Protests grew through the summer months while government scrambled to get the country out of its hostile mode but it was too late. People of all ethnicities and backgrounds joined the indigenous people, expressing how they too felt ignored by the government. Many shared their frustration that leaders seemed more concerned with giving tax cuts to big business and wasting money when many Canadians were barely able to survive on low wages especially with the rising cost of food and shelter. They referred to themselves as the forgotten Canadians and related to the indigenous leaders who complained of being disregarded by their own government.

"We watched the tragedy of an indigenous community burning to the ground and thought 'those poor people, what a terrible tragedy,'" An emotional woman cried one night on the news. "And then we realized, that could be all of us. We're *all* Canada's poor. The government didn't care about the people on that reserve and they don't care about us either. They don't care about poor people. They don't care about our quality of life. We are nothing to them."

The protests that started over a small indigenous reservation quickly grew to an overall outrage from people living in poverty in a first world country. The fury grew stronger, louder and impromptu. It was not unusual for a popular street of a major Canadian city be overtaken by protesters, mostly young people, insisting on more fairness in the government.

Eventually, corporations and businesses added their voice, recognizing that it would be a public image nightmare if perceived as part of the problem, many encouraging employees to step forward and say they were part of a 'winning team' which became a phrase associated with a company that cared, rather than another soulless corporation.

Jorge Hernandez watched with interest. It didn't alarm him because he had happy employees who quickly jumped on social media, stating that his wages and treatment was fair. They talked about his immigration program that gave new Canadian residents and refugees fair employment opportunities, jobs that paid a reasonable wage to people who sometimes couldn't speak English and were still trying to adapt to their new country. His HR team also helped new residents with this transformation, something highlighted in a special edition of *Toronto Am* that focused on the companies that 'make Canada the best country in the world'.

Canada's cries of protest continued to grow stronger as the summer came to an end. By September, it was clear that something had to be done. The official opposition party took no responsibility in their former contribution to the problem but instead insisted it was the current government's fault and an early election had to be called.

"Clearly," The opposition leader said in a sit-down interview with Canada's largest news corporation. "The people of this country aren't happy. We've had nationwide protests all summer long. It's time to call an election and get this country back on track. This unsettled climate is affecting all aspects of government and business. We simply have to put the brakes on before we crash and burn."

It was dramatic and caused Jorge to merely roll his eyes as he watched but at the same time, the entire situation gave him an odd feeling of satisfaction. There was something about the general conscientious of the country that sent a fire through his soul, he loved how passionate the people were, the insistence that they had enough. He had greatly underestimated Canadians. No longer quiet and polite, the pussycat had turned into a roaring lion.

And now they needed someone with as much passion to lead their country. Someone who could tap into the current energy and it wouldn't be another docile white man who gave the same speeches over and over again. So many empty words. People no longer believed. They felt cheated and enraged. It was as if the tragic death of the first nations community was an attack on anyone who was ever at a disadvantage and yet, the politicians appeared blind to the facts. They hid in a secret room and talked to public relations experts who advised them on what to say next. They were robots. They were all fucking robots.

"It's like they don't understand," Jorge commented to Paige one evening as they watched the news. "They do not see that their little speeches are no longer working. Canadians, they want action not words but this government, it is too late. They, themselves, are surrounded by fire and there is no way out."

"I never thought I would see this happen in my country," Paige shook her head. "I can't believe that they allowed that community to burn down. At first, I thought, the fire happened fast and maybe they weren't able to do anything..."

"But the truth, it has come out," Jorge quietly reminded her as he leaned in and gave her a kiss. "They can deny it but that one man, he gave a confession that he was instructed to 'forget the fucking Indians'"

"Then he commits suicide..." Paige gently replied and the couple shared a look. "So they try to say he was mentally unstable. I can't even believe that our government is trying to convince us of that. It's completely unreal."

"That man, he was not lying in the interview."

"He was crying," Paige commented and swallowed back her own tears. "He was clearly devastated by what happened. All those people, children, died. It's horrific."

"Paige, government, they do not care," Jorge spoke gently. "I know, it is hard to believe for Canadians because you were brought up to feel that this is the best country in the world. And yes, in many ways, it is but Paige, never believe that it is perfect. This here, it is something you expect to hear in another country, maybe a third-world country, but not Canada."

"I think you're right," Paige sniffed and wiped her eyes. "I think we're all in shock. We always felt that things were more stable, that the terrible things in the world, would never happen to us. That we were better."

Jorge didn't respond. His wife's naivety was surprising and yet, he saw the same in the eyes of many Canadians. The words 'but this just doesn't happen here' were said again and again, on the news and in public. What started off as sadness and mourning of a nation had quickly turned to bitterness. However, not everyone's target of this bitterness was the same.

Counter groups that believed that immigrants were the problem and that indigenous groups were unfairly attacking the government began to gain a voice. Some suggested that the first nations people were always taking from the government and had special benefits that other Canadians didn't enjoy. It was only a matter of time before white supremacists started to gather steam. This disturbing reality came to light when an image of a group of teenaged boys giving the Nazi salute hit social media, causing one small Prairie town to hang its head in shame, insisting that this was not representative of the community.

Jorge had many meetings with Alec Athas around this time and eventually, some of the top ranking people in government, right to the prime minister. Paige said nothing. Although her original protest that he not get involved was still there, it grew weaker as the state of the country became frail until finally, after much pressure from Canadian people in the form of protests, petitions and constant outrage on the news, the government finally had no choice but call an election. The prime minister would step down.

"Rumor has it that the opposition is connected with the white nationalists," Alec muttered to Jorge one morning over breakfast, even though the restaurant was empty. He opened his mouth as if to say more but stopped, his eyes pleaded in silence.

"This here, it is not news," Jorge spoke with frustration in his voice. "They creep in everywhere and the government is no exception."

"We can't let them win," Alec spoke with defeat in his eyes. Regardless of his party loyalty, he had been horrified by the events that summer, disgusted with his own party but what could he do? They were pressured to stand together but the toll was clearly marked on Alec's face.

"I know, *amigo*, I know," Jorge replied as he glanced out of the window. "You know, Paige, she doesn't like me getting involved."

"I know," Alec slowly began. "But I originally thought the prime minister was going to get pushed out because he allowed one of his key members to get away with sexual harassment. But this….this is a whole other thing."

Jorge didn't reply but merely nodded.

"We need someone to take the reins here, someone who can get this country back in order before it gets worse," Alec spoke with pleading in his voice. "This isn't just an election. This will be the most important election we ever have in this country. It could change our entire nation for the worse if we're not careful."

Jorge continued to sit in silence, his stomach in knots.

"We need to find a new leader and we need to do it fast. The election date can't be announced until we find a new party leader."

"So first you must have the leadership convention…" Jorge spoke clumsily, unsure of what was involved.

"It will happen but let's face it, it's only a formality," Alec insisted and shook his head. "We can't fuck around. We have to make this happen fast."

Jorge didn't reply.

"We need someone who can do this," Alec spoke in a low voice as he leaned forward on the table. "*You* can do this. Let's not pretend that I don't know who you are, who you *were* in Mexico. Plus you took over the entire pot industry and changed the rules in half the time it took the government to even sort it out in the first place. You have a vision, instincts, wisdom, common sense…..this is what we *need* now. You're one of the most powerful men in this country. You speak for minorities. Think about it. No one else can do what you can do."

Jorge didn't reply but an electric current flowed through his body.

This would be the biggest decision of his life.

CHAPTER 27

"Everything said here today, it does not leave this room," Jorge spoke with an assertion in his voice while he observed his tribe around the boardroom table. Michael and Diego appeared defeated, while Jolene nervous, Chase angry, Jesús concerned as was Paige, who sat beside him. It was necessary to get everyone back on track. "Clara, has she been in to *clean*?"

"Yes," Diego answered from the end of the table. He lacked the usual vigor in his voice and this concerned Jorge. It was important to leap right in and get to the heart of the matter.

"I recognize that this summer, it has been difficult," Jorge said, pausing for a moment to take a deep breath before launching into his speech. "Despite the success of the pot festival, our country has been in misery and it has affected us all."

"The most tragic was at the indigenous community," Jorge paused for a moment. "The prime minister, we know now, was not told all the correct facts at the time and he made a terrible decision. For this reason, he has decided to step down, allowing others to try to rebuild the party again. This leaves Canada in a vulnerable position and we may have an even bigger problem if some of our enemies decide that it is time to take advantage of any weakness."

"As you know," Jorge continued. "I have been approached to run for leadership. Although the invitation, it was tempting, I do not want to be in politics."

Glancing at Paige, he saw the relief in her eyes. It had been the subject of many conversations and although she supported whatever Jorge wished to do, he understood the reasons why she discouraged it.

"However, having said that," Jorge said with some hesitation. "I also do not wish to see this country appear weak so tomorrow it will be announced that I am running for the party's leadership."

"But you say…." Jolene shook her head.

"I said I don't wish to get involved in politics and I don't," Jorge reaffirmed his position. "However, it is important for Canadians to not lose faith in this here party, so they need to…*believe* that we are coming back stronger than ever. They need someone who is not afraid to speak on behalf of them, who is powerful and can regain people's faith. My role is to get in the media and fight back until they find the person who *will* run the party."

"So, you're fucking with them to gain confidence in the party again?" Michael spoke up with skepticism in his voice. "Is that what you mean?"

"Fucking with them?" Jorge asked with a raised eyebrow.

"What he means," Paige took over, directing her comment to Jorge. "Is you're trying to mislead people and yes," She turned toward Michael. "That's exactly what he is doing. He's the…"

"Distraction," Diego cut in. "That's what you mean, Paige. He's got a mouth and they know he will make people forget the shitty stuff that happened this summer."

"More or less," Paige replied.

"I don't think I'm going to forget," Chase spoke bluntly and shook his head. "Half my family lives in a native community. That could've been them. The government turned its back on them because they think we are trash. I don't care if the prime minister made the final decision or not."

Michael nodded and Jorge wasn't sure what to say. He knew the officer had traveled to many of the areas affected by the fires, including the indigenous community. He saw some terrible things.

"It was very tragic," Paige said with sympathy in her eyes as she shared a look with Chase. "And it was wrong."

"So, sir," Jesús cut in. "Am I understanding you correctly? You are going to *pretend* to run for the party leader, which means if you won, you could also run for our prime minister? Is this correct?"

"Yes," Jorge was quick to reply. "I am, as you say, buying them time until they find a suitable candidate, however, it is my job to draw as much attention on myself and make the party strong again before they fall more in the polls."

"Is it just me who thinks this is ridiculous?" Diego suddenly spoke up with his usual vigor; his eyes large, animated like a cartoon character, he shrugged in an exaggerated fashion. "I mean, come *on*! Former *Mexican narco* and current owner of a *marijuana* chain is running for a party leader with hopes of becoming the next prime minister. Are they out of their fucking mind?"

"Diego, it is not exactly public knowledge that I was a narco for years," Jorge corrected him. "In their eyes, I'm a Mexican who worked hard with my father to build a coffee company that was successful and I'm now CEO of one of the largest retail chains here in Canada. I'm an immigrant who moved here for love and for my daughter to learn at one of your highly respected schools. I am relatable and yet, powerful and that, my friend, is what politics needs. The politicians here, they play a role and the people, they see through it."

"Oh my fucking God, he really believes this," Diego said to Chase, who merely shrugged.

"He *does* have a point," Chase replied. "People aren't interested in politics because it seems like a bunch of actors playing a role. Jorge is different. He's very direct and people respect that and yeah, he's an immigrant. He grew up poor. That's relatable to a lot of people."

"Oh come on!" Diego started to laugh. "Jorge Hernandez? King of the cartel? Prince of death? Are you fucking kidding me?"

"You don't think that some of these other politicians don't have a few skeletons in their closet?" Michael spoke smoothly with a humored expression on his face.

"Not *literal* skeletons," Diego replied and pointed toward Jorge. "Unlike this guy."

"Glass houses, Diego," Jorge said causing laughter to flow through the room. "Do not throw rocks, as they say."

"Yeah, but I'm not running for prime minister!"

"And neither am I," Jorge insisted. "It is, as they say, an illusion."

"I gotta say," Michael spoke up. "That's a good plan. It takes some heat off the party and helps to build them up until they find another guy to do it."

"Or girl!" Jolene spoke abruptly. "Why not a girl? A woman, she could do better."

Paige nodded.

"Paige," Diego suddenly widened his eyes and leaned forward on the table. "Maybe you should…"

"Not on your life, sweetheart," She calmly replied, causing everyone to laugh again.

"It was a thought," Diego said. "People actually like you."

"It is not about being liked," Jorge jumped in. "It is about being respected. It's about being seen as powerful. And tomorrow morning, *Toronto Am* will announce that I throw my hat in the race."

"Wow!" Diego shook his head. "I cannot wait to see what people think of that."

"So sir," Jesús jumped in. "Does this mean that once they find the person who will run…"

"I will drop out," Jorge replied. "Saying my business needs my full attention."

"It will be nasty," Jolene predicted. "This election, it will be bad."

"Who better to take on the vultures?" Diego commented.

No one could disagree with that point.

It was on the way home that Paige expressed her concerns.

"I'm scared that you're going to get hooked on that feeling, that power and you'll decide to go all the way with this," She spoke softly, almost in a seductive tone. "I know you. I know how you think."

"Paige, I do not want this," Jorge insisted. "Sure, I will enjoy the next few weeks because the attention, it will be fun. I will enjoy pointing out everything that is wrong in the government and my vision, of course, but that is all. You see, I will walk away from this and if anything, I will be more powerful especially when representing my company. It will allow me to bring more attention to Our House of Pot while the party, they find the right man….ah, person for the job."

"Let us hope so," Paige commented. "I'm worried they can't. And that your profile will be too strong because I know how you are....you're charismatic. People like that. I just....I don't know."

"Paige, you do not have to worry," Jorge insisted as he reached out to touch her arm as they stopped at a light. "After all this, I will be happy to step back. I feel that my life, it is about my family. I worked too hard for too long and now, I want to enjoy my wife, teach my daughter, make my son a real man."

Paige rolled her eyes and laughed.

"I do not know, I guess maybe I am mellowing out," He said with a shrug as traffic began to move again. "I had the adventure and now I want something else."

"You should spend time with Maria this week," Paige suggested. "She's heartbroken about not getting any roles this summer."

"Ah yes!" Jorge agreed. "It was difficult for her, the realities of show business. But it was important that she understand."

"She actually had a casting director tell her she didn't look Mexican enough," Paige replied and shook her head. "She was crying about that last night. I tried to tell her that the white lady doing the casting perhaps didn't have many Mexicans in her social circles."

"Ah, those white ladies," Jorge teased and winked at his wife. "What do they know about Mexicans?"

"What indeed," Paige grinned.

"Ah, *mi amor,* it was a tough summer for her," Jorge replied and shook his head. "I hope this new school is better than the last."

"I still wonder if public school might be the best option," Paige asked. "I mean, it would give her the chance to be around kids that aren't rich."

Jorge was skeptical. He did agree with Paige but at the same time, feared greatly for his daughter's security.

"We will see," He finally answered. "We will see."

"I think things will be better this fall," Paige predicted. "Maria will be settled into a new school and move on from everything that happened this summer. Miguel is getting a little older, I'm getting less scared of being a mom."

"Ah and your meditation CD, it will soon be released," Jorge reminded her.

"It's not my CD, just my voice," Paige reminded him.

"You will help many, *mi amor,* with the voice of an angel."

She rolled her eyes in response.

"But you know what they say," Jorge reminded her. "The devil is never far behind."

CHAPTER 28

"And *Papa*," Maria spoke enthusiastically as the two of them walked through the mall heading toward a coffee kiosk. People were occasionally giving them a sideways glance and pointing in their direction but for the most part, keeping their distance. He had, however, noticed one person taking his picture and that irritated him. "The school has a *way* better drama program. When I told some of the other girls about my former school, they said it was mediocre at best."

"Well, Maria, how would they know?" Jorge attempted to be diplomatic as he approached the stand and ordered his coffee. After finishing, he turned to his daughter. "*Bonita,* would you like something as well?"

Glancing at the nearby treats, she turned up her nose. "Just water."

"I guess the lady wants water," Jorge grinned at the barista and returned his attention to Maria who shrugged bashfully. Reaching out, he patted her shoulder, relishing her rare moment of shyness as they moved away to wait for his order. "So Maria, as I said, these people, they do not know. It is what you make of it that matters."

"But *Papa,*" She quickly jumped in, her brown eyes widening. "A better school may prepare me for a life on stage."

"I thought you wanted to be in front of the camera," Jorge reminded her as the young man at the kiosk called his name and they headed over to pick up their drinks. After thanking him, Jorge passed Maria her bottle of water and took a drink of his coffee. "This here, it has changed."

"*Papa,*" She continued with a dramatic sigh. "I see how they talk about you in the media and now I don't know."

This surprised and intrigued him. Was it possible that through his own experience with the press, he'd been able to remedy his daughter of her dreams of fame? Then again, Maria's summer had been full of rejection and discouragement as well, so perhaps it made her see the darker side of an absurd industry.

"Maria, in fairness, they are especially critical of me because it is politics," Jorge reminded her. "But I do think that you have made the right decision. Being famous is not what you think. Many get involved in the industry because they want to feel special. You, Maria, you are already special."

Glancing at his daughter, he noticed her attention was averted to one of the national newspapers sitting on a nearby table. Of course, Jorge had already seen the front page. His announcement had caused a bit of a scandal in the media. It was getting a tad ridiculous even though it was only a few days since he threw his hat in the race. Although Jorge had expected attention, even he had no idea what he was in for when he agreed to this scheme.

"*Papa,*" Maria said as she moved closer to the table, running her fingers over the picture of her father in the newspaper. "Why do they say you've brought division in this country? What does that mean? I don't understand."

"Maria," Jorge attempted to gather his thoughts but felt like a lion in a cage as people watched all around them. "I think maybe it would be a good time for us to leave."

"But I haven't bought anything yet," Maria complained.

"But Maria, you have said," Jorge continued to feel the weight of their eyes on them both. "You have even said you are not in the shopping mood. Perhaps we leave and try again another day."

When she didn't appear convinced, he continued. "I must stop by the bar to see Chase before it opens. If we arrive before that time, you can come in."

Seeing her disposition change, Maria quickly nodded with enthusiasm. Chase was the one carrot Jorge knew he could successfully dangle in front of his daughter when attempting to persuade her.

He felt relief once they reached the SUV and his daughter was safely behind closed doors.

"*Papa*," She continued. "You never answered my question about dividing the country, what does that mean?"

"Maria," Jorge thought for a moment as he pulled out of his parking space. "It means that because I am an immigrant, some, they do not believe I should be running to be party leader while others think that this is ok."

"But you live here now," Maria argued. "Why does it matter if you do a good job?"

Jorge shrugged. "Some, perhaps, think I cannot."

"*Papa*, many don't understand," Maria continued as she tapped on her phone. "Like that guy yesterday, who said that if you won, you would have everyone in Canada speaking *Mexican?*"

Jorge laughed when recalling the man featured in a parody show, displaying his ignorance.

"Does he not realize," Maria continued dramatically. "That we speak *Spanish*."

"I think that was why that program, Maria, wanted others to see his comment," Jorge said with warmth in his voice. "To show his ignorance. They were ridiculousing him."

"*Ridiculing, Papa,*" Maria corrected and with a serious tone continued. "And if you want to become prime minister one day, you must improve your English."

Jorge continued to grin and merely nodded his head. As if! The last thing he wanted or needed was to become prime minister however, it humored him to play the game. Many had already attacked his qualifications, pointing out that he couldn't speak English well enough, let alone French, Canada's two official languages. However, this same argument brought out many immigrants and sympathizers to his defense, stating that Jorge Hernandez understood how it felt to be new in the country and struggle to fit in. It was interesting how each side was attacking the another, while he merely stepped back. That, perhaps, was the division mentioned in the morning paper.

"Thank you, Maria, this here, it is a good point," Jorge replied as they headed toward the bar. "I will keep that in mind."

Of course, in the beginning, many ridiculed him. The CEO of Our House of Pot wanted to run in the leadership race with his sights set on becoming the next prime minister of Canada? Newspaper cartoon sections went on fire across the country, as everyone treated his announcement more as a joke. It wasn't long until many political observers pointed out that it wouldn't be the first time that someone rose on a celebrity status to take on a powerful position.

And that's when the racists came out.

"We can't have this man, a *Mexican,* running our country," A far-right reporter spoke out on social media a week after the official announcement. Pushing his glasses back, he proceeded to stroke his beard as he continued to speak with a rigidness in his voice. "This is obviously something we can't allow to happen. This man knows nothing about our country, our history, our laws…. he can't even speak proper English. He's the man you go to if you want to score weed, he's not the man you vote for to represent our country around the world."

It humored Jorge.

"What? I cannot do both?" He laughed to Alec after hearing these remarks as the two men sat in his office. Since he refused to deal with anyone else in the party, Alec had been given the duty of harnessing Jorge's campaign. "Would that not make me the best leader?"

"The best way to deal with this is to do an interview with a national news channel," Alec was quick to address the situation. "Talk about how you see yourself as a businessman, not a drug dealer and that the fact that your company essentially took over the Canadian pot industry is a clear sign that you are more than able to take on a challenge and win."

"Maybe, Alec, it should be you running for this leadership, not me," Jorge pointed out as he leaned back in his chair. "Have you not considered that? The people, they love you."

"In Toronto," Alec corrected him as he pointed at his iPad. "You, your face, it's known nationally."

"I got a handsome face," Jorge said with a shrug and laughed. "What can I tell you my friend, people like handsome."

"People like stable," Alec replied and glanced at his iPad again. "You're a family man with strong roots in the community."

"But it is like you say, immigrants, they love me, I am them," Jorge reminded him. "I am new to this country, my English not always so good, would that not be relatable."

"When you're talking to them," Alec reminded him. "Of course, if you're speaking to a group of white people who look like their ancestors came here over 100 years ago, then you use the best English you got."

"Ah, yes!" Jorge nodded. "It does depend on your audience."

"Women aren't sure about you," Alec continued. "They aren't sure if you're trustworthy."

"I get that a lot from women."

"You must convince them," Alec said and placed his iPad down on a nearby chair. "Seeing you with your daughter at the mall helped."

Jorge nodded. He was uneasy about using his daughter to gain attention. On that particular day, it was merely to cheer up a glum Maria but in retrospect, it shone a different light on him. People saw him as a caring father who wasn't out for a photo opportunity but a man who wanted to spend time with his child.

"I think you need to bring Paige with you more," Alec suggested with skepticism in her voice. "Do you think she'll do it?"

"She isn't crazy about this, you know?"

"I know," Alec glanced down and scratched his head. "But this is what we gotta do."

"The meditation CD, this helped."

"That's a helluva a lot of women," Alec nodded and looked back up. "What else do they know about Paige? She's a well-known life coach, she met and married you in record speed."

"I'm fucking lovable," Jorge said and laughed. All of this continued to humor him. "She couldn't help herself."

"You mightn't want to mention that in any interviews," Alec replied with a grin. "Tell me something, are you still speaking to that feminist group tomorrow afternoon?"

"Yes, *amigo,* I think so," Jorge said and glanced down at his phone.

"Do you still have that shirt with spit up on it?" Alec asked and the men exchanged smiles.

"Indeed I do, *amigo,* indeed I do."

CHAPTER 29

"We might have someone," Alec muttered as the two stood together, waiting for Jorge's opportunity to speak to an audience filled with mostly women. The group consisted of various ethnicities, gathered together to listen to speakers, visit retail booths and some non-profits interested in connecting with the community.

Jorge was one of five political contenders invited but the only one to show up. Then again, he suspected the others were playing the same game as him; it looked good for a party to appear strong to regain voter's confidence, even if contenders had no plans to follow through to the end. It also enhanced their own profiles by throwing a hat in the race. Everyone won; except for those who believed that his party was in good standing.

"*Perfecto!*" Jorge quietly replied and glanced around the room. "Because this here, it is not so fun as the days go by, *mi amigo.*"

"It wasn't meant to be," Alec reminded him with a smooth grin. "Is Paige…"

"She will be in the front row with Miguel," Jorge replied and glanced toward the stage. "I tell her to put on a fake smile."

"Unfortunately, politics isn't as glamorous as people think," Alec quietly reminded him. "It's a lot of events like this one, any opportunity to speak, really."

Out of the corner of his eye, Jorge saw a woman with bushy blonde hair approaching them, a skeptical smile on her face.

"Mr. Hernandez?" She reached out to shake his hand while her eyes glanced at the stain on his shirt. "I'm Suzanne Torode, we spoke on the phone earlier this week."

"Ah, *Señora* Torode, lovely to meet you," Jorge replied, throwing on a charming smile as he shook her hand. "Thank you for the invitation."

"I do appreciate you agreeing to speak to us," Suzanne replied and appeared to relax. "We asked some others too but I guess there were scheduling conflicts."

"It does happen," Jorge agreed with a nod. "It is a busy time."

"We are anxious to hear what you have to say," She replied and ushered him toward the stage. "Just allow me to give you a quick introduction."

Her 'quick' introduction ran on longer than necessary, speaking of his contributions in business, his immigration program at Our House of Pot, how Jorge was a new resident of the country, had married a Canadian woman and how they shared two children. After the awkward biography, he was finally able to walk on stage in front of a group of about 300+ women. Many looked tired, while others simply skeptical but most appeared engaged. A few were staring at his shirt.

"Good morning," Jorge addressed the crowd, an infectious smile crossed his lips, his fingers automatically touching the spit-up stain on his shirt. The spot was still wet from the water doused on it in the SUV, making it seem as though it was fresh. Glancing at the spot, he continued. "You must excuse me, my son, he is 4 months old and still does not understand when is a bad time to spit on his father."

Laughter filled the room as his gaze automatically landed on Paige. She was wearing a dress that was pretty, although conservative compared to her usual style. Alec had her choose an outfit like that of another politician's wife. Miguel slept in his seat on the floor. Jorge knew how much she hated dragging that awkward plastic contraption around so he'd make it up to her later.

"I am here to speak to you today but," Jorge paused for a moment. "I feel as though this here, it is backward. Maybe it would be better if *you* speak to *me*. After all, it is the normal thing for politicians to stand in front of a crowd such as this one and *tell* you what he or she plans to do. It is normal, to make promises, is it not?"

He noted that the audience appeared surprised by his comment and felt his confidence rise. Alec appeared pleased from the sidelines.

"And I believe this, it is the problem," Jorge continued. "Too many politicians, they stand in front of an audience, such as yourselves and tell *you* what *they* think you need. Me? I do not know what you need. All of you, you come from different backgrounds and lifestyles. It is not fair for me, as a man, to try to tell you anything. I need you to tell me what you need and me, I must listen."

He saw some looks of appreciation but was surprised when one woman's eyes watered as she looked down. That's when he knew he was on the right track.

"The problems with government in this country, in most countries," Jorge continued. "Is they say what surveys and market research tell them to say. They say what others tell them to say. They say what they *think* people need to hear. But I am a man who prefers to be direct. People, they want the truth. So I, I will give you the truth."

"This country," Jorge relaxed. "It is in some trouble now. We cannot pretend that it is not."

From the sideline, he saw Alec cringe.

"I can lie and tell you everything is fine but it is not fine," Jorge said as he touched his tie and glanced at his wife. "This summer, it was not our downfall so much as it was proof that we were already in trouble. This is not to say, we won't be ok but we need to…acknowledge this before we can repair it. And we have a lot of work to do."

"The fires that our country experienced were tragic," Jorge continued, his voice gathering more vigor as he sensed something changed in the audience. "The deaths….*unacceptable.* And yes, I do understand, some are unavoidable in these tragedies but when an entire community of our indigenous people die because the government does not send help, this here, it is a problem. A *big* problem. And I do…recognize that I am here as a member of the same party but I will not stand here and try to make excuses for those decisions. I will not lie to you."

"My wife," Jorge pointed toward Paige in the audience. "My daughter, they cried when they watched the news on that terrible day this summer, as many of you did. But not me and you know why? Because I was furious. Most of the people who were left to die, they were women and children. Many of the men were in other parts of the country for work, some were helping neighboring communities with fires, not aware it was also coming for their own. The women, the children, they were stranded in the middle of the night.."

He saw more tears in the audience. *Perfecto.*

"But this country, it will heal," Jorge spoke with enthusiasm. "It will not happen overnight but we can learn from this terrible tragedy. These communities, these families, they represent all of us. The protests that followed this summer, it was because people are tired. *Exhausted. Frustrated.* The government, for many years, they do not listen to the people who need them the most. They listen to corporations. They listen to rich voters, middle-class voters but what about those in our communities that struggle? What about the single mothers, the working poor, the homeless?"

"I want to hear these stories," Jorge spoke emotionally and could see he was connecting with the audience. "I recently started a website. It is for everyone to go on and share with me their stories and what they need from their government. As I said earlier, I do not know. I am not you."

He pointed toward several women in the audience.

"I do understand struggle," Jorge continued. "I am wealthy, yes, but I grew up in a small town in Mexico and my family, we were quite poor. My father, he decided to get into the coffee business because he read somewhere that Americans, Canadians, they loved their coffee!"

People laughed and Jorge paused and smiled again.

"He say, you know what Jorge? These people in first world countries, they pay a *lot* for a cup of coffee. We must get into this here business," Jorge lied and continued to grin. He never had this conversation with his father. In fact, they barely spoke. "And our business, it grew and grew..... but it was a lot of work getting there. I started from the bottom and I worked my way up."

This part was true. Except, of course, it was with the cartel. The ways he proved himself in this business were vastly different from that of a coffee company.

"Since those days, the company, it has been sold," Jorge continued. "My father, he has passed. My family, it is now in Canada. I feel privileged to live here, to be a part of your community. I am honored to have my daughter go to a wonderful school with children from all ethnicities. I have a beautiful newborn son. I am married to an amazing woman. I am privileged and I wish for everyone to have the chance to also feel this privilege. Everyone should have the chance to have their dreams come true. This is, after all, a rich country…so why, I must ask, are so many people living in poverty?"

"It is time to make this country stronger," Jorge continued and took a deep breath. "It is time to send a message around the world that Canada is not just known for kindness but for being powerful and *proud*. It is my belief that we have a lot of work to do but we *can* do it together."

He ended his speech on a high note and walked off stage to join his wife but before he was able to reach her, many women approached him with questions, concerns and some to simply have a selfie taken with the charismatic Latino. Paige stood back, a smile on her face as she talked to Alec, who appeared impressed.

Back in the SUV, no one spoke until they were out of the parking lot.

"Holy shit," Alec said with a nervous laugh. "I didn't know where you were going with that speech."

"Neither did I," Jorge confessed as they joined traffic on the main road, heading toward Alec's office, where they would drop him off. "It was….impulsive."

"Oh, you should practice ahead of time," Alec insisted. "It's very important."

"It comes across as fake and people, they do not like that," Jorge insisted as the baby woke and made a gurgling noise in the backseat. "They want real."

"You were definitely real today," Paige added before Alec could speak. "That's what they liked about you."

"That and admitting you aren't sure of what they need," Alec jumped in. "That was a terrific point."

"It is what it is," Jorge said with a shrug, he acted casual even though the speech had left him feeling an unexpected high. "People, they want to be heard and acknowledged. They are angry."

"And rightfully so," Paige added as she glanced back at the baby, while Alec stared at his phone. "I think I saw Makerson in the back of the room."

"Probably, there were other reporters," Alec said with a shrug. "So far, some live tweets were made, quotes from Jorge, it looks good."

"So, any luck finding a candidate yet," Paige abruptly changed the subject.

"We have someone in mind," Alec spoke mysteriously. "His family has been in and out of politics for years, so he would be a good possibility. We have a meeting tonight, so hopefully, there's some news. You can come if you want, Jorge."

"Nope," Jorge shook his head. "I don't got time for that. Just let me know when to step down, in the meantime, the Hernandez campaign rolls on."

Exchanging looks with his wife, Jorge noted the skepticism in her eyes. He winked at her and returned his attention to the road ahead.

CHAPTER 30

"*Furious Jorge!*" Diego sang out gleefully as he burst into laughter. The group around the boardroom table quickly followed his lead after glancing at the illustrated image of a monkey with Jorge's face jumping on the current prime minister. In his usual seat, Jorge merely shrugged and glanced toward the window at the dark skies outside before returning his gaze to the image on Alec's iPad. The comic was in a national newspaper.

"Sir, it does seem appropriate," Jesús commented as he glanced at Paige, who attempted to hide her smile behind a cup of coffee.

"I do not understand," Jorge replied with a self-conscious grin. "What is this about?"

"It's referring to a popular children's book called *Curious George*," Paige began to explain the joke to her husband. "They probably got the 'furious' part from your speech."

"When you said you were furious about the indigenous community," Alec confirmed as he glanced at the iPad while the others around the table continued to show amusement, including Jolene who laughed hysterically at the illustrated image of an angry Jorge Hernandez shaking his fist in the air, his face scrunched up in fury.

"So this, this is what they took away from that speech?" Jorge asked and shook his head. "Of all I say, *that* is what stood out to this paper?"

"What stood out was a catchy comment," Alec corrected him with a somber expression while the others around the table started to grow serious again. "That's what grabs readers and sells papers. That's all they care about."

"Obviously," Jorge replied as he watched Alec open another link on his iPad. This one was more serious featuring the overhead image of the burnt reservation. The headline said *Hernandez takes responsibility for government's lack of action.* "So, this one, it is better?"

"Not really," Alec insisted with a shrug as the others watched. "This one suggests you are saying that the government fucked up. It's like you're going against your own party."

"So, what?" Jorge said with a shrug. "We pretend that we didn't fuck up? Is that right?"

"I mean, I agree with what you've done," Alec spoke honestly. "But others in the party don't."

"Yeah, well, fuck them," Jorge said as Alec taped on his iPad. "Someone has to take responsibility."

"They're scared it will cost them."

"Are you fucking kidding me right now?" Jorge countered. "If you ask me to run for a party, this is what you get."

"I think they're seeing that now," Alec said with a shrug.

"Anything else, Athas, I don't got all day," Jorge bluntly replied.

"The rest is a rundown of what you said and some audience reaction," Alec quickly shuffled through different headlines. "Most were primarily positive including the one Makerson did but the point is that you *are* getting media attention. The other candidates aren't getting more than an occasional mention."

"So I'm the most popular candidate?" Jorge asked and lit up while Diego rolled his eyes and Paige laughed. "This is what you are saying, right?"

"Yes, I mean, you're resonating with the people much more," Alec said as he relaxed in his chair. "Didn't you say there's a lot of hits on the site from people with stories and concerns."

"Some are spam," Jorge replied and glanced at Jolene, who seemed to finally compose herself. "But yes, for the most part, people have written in with their thoughts, concerns and so on. Paige and Chase have been reviewing these comments and let me know the important ones, the general feeling…"

"This is research," Alec replied as his eyes widened. "Its the best way to see what people are looking for."

"So, Jorge is pretending to run for a party to manipulate people by telling them what they actually want in a prime minister?" Michael asked with skepticism in his eyes. "Why don't you guys just give them what they want and not bait them. Like a sincere government."

"It's complicated," Alec admitted as he turned toward Michael. "I'm not going to lie, I once had an idealistic attitude about government but then you get in and it's not what you think. There are conditions, situations and a lot of negotiating and compromising, unfortunately, it's never as easy as we want to believe from the outside looking in."

"This is some fucked up shit," Michael shook his head and looked at Diego, who gave him a warning glance. "It shouldn't be so complex."

"Life, Michael, is complex," Jorge replied and leaned back in his chair and glanced at everyone sitting around the table. "Everything always seems much different from the outside looking in. Running a company, joining the police, having a baby, joining politics, so many things seem easy until you are doing them. We all know these things."

No one could disagree with his assessment.

"The good news, sir," Jesús jumped in. "The company is getting more attention in the media, our sales and shares are growing, this is good."

"And now we are back to the beginning and the reason I am doing this," Jorge jumped back in with his usual zest. "To make my company stronger, better, a leader in this country."

"Enhancing your profile," Alec continued. "People like that you are direct and it remind Canadians that this is also how you run your company."

"But the pot festival this summer," Diego jumped in, his eyes widened as he leaned forward on the table. "*That* gave our company worldwide attention. We could expand anywhere now once it becomes legal everywhere."

"And Diego, that is my dream," Jorge insisted. "You must remember the world, is watching Canada now to see how legalized pot works out for us. They will see our challenges and the economic outcome, of course."

There was a brief pause as a few people nodded in silence.

"So, Alec, have you had any success finding someone to take over the party?" Paige spoke up with some tension in her voice. "You mentioned a meeting the other day…"

"It didn't go well," Alec answered with some hesitation. "Look, I know you want Jorge out but it's been a challenge to find someone who's willing to take on this mess and who has the credentials to do so. Don't worry though, we're still looking."

Paige didn't appear convinced.

"Ah, my wife, she wants to have my full attention," Jorge teased and winked at Paige. "And can you blame her?"

Alec didn't reply while Diego groaned and rolled his eyes.

"But sir, what if they are not able to find someone," Jesús spoke with some hesitation. "This is not a good idea for you."

"Relax," Jorge spoke casually. "Once I have the party built up, someone is going to jump on board because that's the toughest job. People won't buy a house that's falling apart but you throw on some paint, fix the walkway and plant some flowers and suddenly people are interested."

"I think you're gonna need more than a few flowers to pretty up this fucking mess," Michael commented and Diego quickly nodded.

"We're getting there," Jorge spoke confidently. "One speech at a time."

"You've got a few more this week and an interview," Alec reminded him. "And some people still think you're a misogynist even though you've been pretty clear that this isn't the case."

"How've you been clear?" Diego asked with a shit eating grin on his face. "When you were telling off that reporter…you know, the *dead* one."

"She had mental health issues," Jorge spoke defensively and glanced at Jolene who nodded. "I released a statement saying that I loved strong women and I surround myself with them. This is true. Paige, Jolene, my daughter, these are strong women that I respect. How can an argument with one woman suddenly make me hate all women?"

"Because they need to find something wrong with you," Alec calmly suggested. "It's their way of ripping you apart although, it doesn't stand a chance considering you just spoke to a room full of women who hung on your every word."

"Problem solved, no?" Jorge shook his head. Although he loved the power of standing on stage speaking, the rest of this political life was tedious and boring. Going over numbers, social media likes, this was ridiculous to him. "I keep playing the game, my shares keep rising and then someone else comes along and *terminado*."

"True," Alec agreed with some hesitation. "But you have to continue playing the game. Show up places, talk to people who approach you…"

"You, my friend, are very cynical in what?" Jorge glanced at Paige. "Less than a year in politics"

"Considering a narco is running for the party and people trust him more than the prime minister," Michael threw in before Alec could answer. "Shouldn't that tell you something?"

Diego shot his boyfriend a dirty look.

"Are we finished here," Jorge ignored Michael and started to move his chair out and turned his attention to Alec. "I got it. I keep playing your fucking game for now. That it?"

He had barely stood up when his phone beeped. It was Chase at the bar.

"What the fuck?" Jorge made a face as he read the message and shook his head. "There's someone at the bar, demanding to talk to me."

"The bar's not even open yet," Diego commented as he glanced at his phone.

"Chase couldn't make the meeting. Maybe something is wrong," Jorge commented as the others started to rise from their chairs. "Diego, can you take Paige home?"

"I'm coming with you," She replied as she started to stand.

"Paige, please," Jorge insisted in a softer voice. "This here, it's probably something to do with the club anyway, do not worry about it."

"Sir, I will come with you," Jesús insisted.

Jorge gave a lazy shrug while Paige seemed to relent, glancing at Diego, who nodded.

"If I need the rest of you," Jorge commented. "I'll let you know."

CHAPTER 31

"I'm here," Jorge announced as soon as he entered the club while behind him, Jesús locked the door. He glanced around noting the shades were still drawn, the lights dim and no one was in the room. Without skipping a beat, he continued, "So what's fucking going on?"

"Me, that's what's going on," A tall, bald, white man wearing jeans and a leather jacket came out of the office and Chase followed, his eyes meeting with Jorge's briefly as the four men kept their distance from one another in an empty area where chairs and tables had been pushed aside. "You and me have to talk, Hernandez."

"Is that so?" Jorge replied with a flippant tone, shoving a hand in his pocket, his fingers caressing a gun. "You tell me what the fuck we got to talk about. I don't know you."

"It doesn't matter who I am," The man was quick to reply as his eyes narrowed in on Jorge. "I know *who* you are and since you're in politics now, I could make sure that everyone else does too."

"Really?" Jorge appeared humored and glanced at Jesús who was glaring at the strange man. "You know *who* I am and yet, you stand here, threatening me? Tell me, does this seem like a good idea?"

"I know you were head of one of the largest cartels in Mexico," The man continued in a low voice as his eyes studied Jorge. "I know why you're here in Canada and why you're in politics."

"Is this so?" Jorge asked in a mocking tone. "If I were as powerful as you say in Mexico, why would I be here? This here, it does not make sense."

"Because you fucking immigrants think you can take over," The man continued and Jorge quickly realized that he was dealing with something different from what he originally thought. This man wasn't out to extort money from him, threatening to expose who Jorge was but instead, a racist. "You think you're going to come here, find an easy way to bring in your drugs and the next thing, Canada will be overrun by Mexican criminals just like down in the states."

A chill ran through the room while Jorge continued to stare in silence. Chase stood back with his arms crossed in an angry pose.

"We're not having it," he continued. "I'm a member of a group that monitors these situations to protect Canadians, *real* Canadians and it's time you drop out of the race."

"So, let me get this straight," Jorge replied with a smooth grin on his face. "You think you are going to come in here, *demand* to see me and then insist I drop out of the race and it is just going to happen."

"It's going to happen," The man's cold eyes continued to stare at Jorge who showed no fear. "I've dealt with your kind before. You're not in Mexico anymore, *amigo,* you don't have any power here. If you want to go back to your own country and do whatever, we don't care but you're not doing it here."

"You seem to have missed something," Jorge grew aggravated by this conversation. "I *am* a Canadian citizen and for that matter, I'm a successful, legal businessman but most of all, I do not need your permission to do whatever I wish. Perhaps, I will run for the leader of the party and win. And then, maybe I will run for Canadian prime minister and win that too. This here, it is not up to you. Now, leave my fucking club."

"Your club," The man laughed and looked around before suddenly unzipped his pants and proceeded to piss on the floor. "This is what I think of you and your club."

Jorge didn't react but could see Jesús reach for his gun while Chase appeared completely horrified. The man had barely zipped his pants up again, a sanctimonious grin on his face when he suddenly lost his balance. It took a second for Jorge to realize that Chase had punched him in the side causing him to hunch over, displaying the gun he tucked into his jeans. Chase quickly grabbed the weapon and placed it out of the man's sight.

"You know, maybe we should start this here conversation over again," Jorge quickly picked up where they left off, walking toward the large man who was now attempting to regain his composure. Reaching for his gun, he must've realized it was gone as he continued to try to stand up. "Let me introduce myself. I'm Jorge Hernandez and where I come from, you mind your own fucking business"

The man opened his mouth to talk but before he could, Chase lurched forward, punching him in the throat. Jorge grinned as he watched the man struggle to speak, to breathe, either way, he didn't care. If anything, he felt enormous pride for the group's most timid member's actions. It wasn't often Chase showed his fury but when he did, it was worth the wait.

"So, as I was saying," Jorge calmly continued as the man's face turned red. "This here is not acceptable. You, coming on my territory with the belief that you can threaten me and I will listen. If you feel that I am powerful in Mexico, would you not also realize that here, I am too?"

"You would think that would be obvious, sir," Jesús finally spoke up in his usual, diplomatic way as he continued to point a gun at the stranger. "After all, in Mexico, we do not play by the same rules."

"We know about boundaries," Jorge replied as the man started to stand upright again. "We also know about respect."

The man glanced at the gun in Jesús' hand as his eyes filled with desperation. Jorge calmly watched him while his heart pounded in fury but it was important that this man wasn't able to see his anger. It was important that he didn't know that he had any effect on him. In fact, Jorge showed no expression when Chase suddenly grabbed a bar stool and lifted it in the air before powerfully bringing it down against the man's back, knocking him face down on the floor and ironically, into his own piss.

"*Incredible!*" Jorge spoke triumphantly as he rose his hands in the air as he walked towards the man collapsed on the ground. "Chase, you should be one of those men, you know in action movies."

His face red, his expression still one of fury, Chase managed to muster a smile and shake his head as Jorge approached the degraded man on the floor as he struggled to get up.

"Except in movies, sir, they make it look real," Jesús reminded him. "It is not real."

"That's because those pussy actors couldn't lift a chair let alone break one," Jorge reminded him as he stopped inches away from the man's head. "And speaking of pussies, this one right here, he seems to think he can come in and piss on my floors, threaten me and then go home. But me, I do not see it that way. In fact, I find it very distasteful to do such things."

"And speaking of distasteful," Jorge continued as he placed one foot on top of the man's head and held it firmly against the floor. "You, sir, are going to lick up every last bit of piss on my floor and if you don't, I am going to snap your neck. And then, I will remove your head and send it to whoever you love the most. Do you have a grandmother? Mother? Wife? Women, they have strong emotions when receiving a severed head."

"Well, sir, it is not exactly like roses," Jesús laughed at his own joke.

"This here, it is true," Jorge calmly agreed, removing his foot from the man's head. "I would suggest, white boy, that you start licking my floors clean unless you want grandma to get a surprise delivery and it ain't gonna be no fucking Publisher Clearing House prize either."

Chase and Jesús flinched when the man followed instructions, his tongue reaching out to lick up the puddle of urine that surrounded his face. Jorge simply laughed and turned to walk away.

"You know what," Jorge stalled in the middle of the floor. "Chase, you might want to put on the club's Facebook page that there will be a delayed opening today due to…plumbing issues. Piss on the floor, I would say, is plumbing related, is it not?"

"Kinda falls in that category," Chase replied. "It's hardly sanitary."

"No, see this is true," Jorge started to walk back toward the man and hesitated for a moment before he added. "And it's about to be even less sanitary."

With one quick movement, he stomped down on the man's head causing him to let out a primal scream that filled the room. Fortunately, the building was soundproof so no one could hear outside the four walls.

Turning toward Jesús, he started to walk away.

"Make sure he is dead and I don't care what you do with the fucking body."

"I will call in some of the boys to help out," Jesús reached for his phone while Chase showed no expression, staring at the man on the floor.

"How did he even get in here?" Jorge directed his question at Chase. "Bar is closed."

"He came to the back door and I thought it was another truck," Chase admitted. "He pushed his way in. I should've checked more carefully, I'm sorry."

"This is perhaps a lesson for the next time," Jorge pointed out. "There are some crazy fuckers out there. We must be careful."

Jesús was already on the phone. To someone who didn't know better, the irrelevant conversation was about the weather and family events but those inside the room knew differently. It was over as quickly as it started.

"Our own delivery truck will come around the back," Jorge predicted as he pointed toward the doors close to the bar. "I want him out of this fucking place. Then we got to clean up. A delayed opening sign on the door. You think you can handle that or should I stay?"

"We got it, sir," Jesús answered as he slid his phone in his pocket. "If you need to leave…"

"Find out who he is and who he's connected to," Jorge muttered as he walked toward the door.

"I will drop by your house after," Jesús replied and Jorge nodded.

It wasn't until his drive home that Jorge's anxiety took over. Was this man connected to a group that wanted to attack him? Hurt his family? The funny thing was Jorge had already grown bored of the political circus but could he back down now? Would that send the wrong message? First, he had to learn this man's identity before making any decisions. Paige would not be happy.

He arrived home to Maria's loud pop music. It echoed through the house while his wife met him almost immediately.

"Paige, I will tell her to turn it down," Jorge insisted and started toward the stairway but felt a hand on his arm, causing him to turn back around. Their eyes met and he immediately knew the music wasn't her concern.

"The music is fine," Paige insisted.

"Did you hear what happened at the bar?" Jorge asked, slightly confused.

"What?" Paige hesitated. "What happened at the bar?"

"I will tell you later," Jorge shook his head as fear filled his chest. "What is wrong, Paige?"

"I think..." She suddenly hesitated. "Jorge, I had Marco hack some personal emails from top government officials."

"Can this be traced?" Jorge seemed hesitant. "I don't want..."

"No," Paige assured him. "I was trying to find out if they had anyone in mind to take over this campaign so you could get out. I found out...I mean, it kind of looks like..."

"Like?" Jorge asked.

"Judging from an email I was reading," Paige hesitated for a moment. "Jorge, I think some people in the prime minister's own party wanted him out. The fire? They let it happen on purpose because they knew he would take the fall."

CHAPTER 32

"His name is….ah, was, Claude Rexdale, sir," Jesús said shortly after his arrival when he, Jorge and Paige gathered around the desk. The mood was somber as they shared expressions of concern. "Marco is looking into it but so far, it would seem that he is with a racist group based in the US who believes in something called a *white genocide*? Sir, what is such things?"

"It's a white supremacist group that feels that the Caucasian population is disappearing," Paige answered the question, while Jorge watched her with interest, raising his eyebrows. "For example, Miguel is a mixed race baby. To them, I should only be having children with a white man."

"But genocide?" Jorge said with laughter in his voice while everyone around him appeared quite serious. "My English, it is not so good but is that not an exaggeration?"

"It's fear-mongering," Paige gently replied. "Create the threat and then convince others that it's a cause for concern. That's how these people work."

"They perhaps believe this to be true?" Jesús inquired with some hesitation. "But does it really matter?"

"It does when you think your race is superior to others," Paige reminded him and Jesús nodded. "These people are convinced that white people are superior intellectually and otherwise so they see this is a real threat."

"Superior and yet, they believe this nonsense?" Jorge commented with laughter in his voice. "Do they not see the irony? Perhaps they are not so superior after all."

"In Mexico, we do not worry of such things," Jesús added with a shrug.

"In Mexico, we got bigger things to worry about," Jorge said and hunched in his chair. "It is these kind of people that makes me hire a *niñera* that also carries a gun. I want my children protected from these racist pricks."

Paige didn't reply but appeared concerned. He knew she wanted him out of the limelight and although Jorge understood why he also felt that it was necessary to not back down.

"So, it would seem," Jorge continued as he glanced at his phone. "That these people may be involved in the current downfall of the government, no?"

"It kind of seems that way," Paige quietly replied. "They usually work behind the scenes…"

Her voice drifted off and Jorge could see the fear in her eyes. His own experience since moving to Canada had taught him that some people didn't appreciate an immigrant with a great deal of power or money, often questioning their trustworthiness. It had happened to him many times but he mainly saw it as a nuisance and not a real problem.

"We need to make sure that this does not happen," Jorge insisted and watched Jesús give a quick nod in agreement. "It is important that the people recognize the dangers of voting for parties that share these values."

"But sir, if they think the same way," Jesús reminded him. "They will vote for them because they share the values. This could be a problem."

"I'm worried, Jorge," Paige spoke quietly and touched his arm. "These people are dangerous."

"And me, I am not, *mi amor?*" Jorge replied with a seductive grin. "This here is not for you to worry about. I can take them on."

"I am worried they'll expose you," Paige reminded him. "What if they reveal your connections to the cartel? I'm scared of what they know and what they can prove."

"I understand, Paige but we cannot back down," Jorge reminded her. "We must take on these people."

"Like you did today with Claude Rexdale?" Paige gently asked.

"We must do what we must do," Jorge insisted. "That body, it will not be found. I've made sure of it. If these people start disappearing, then the message will get back to the top. Once that is accomplished, the party will have found another successful candidate to take over and we will be finished here."

Paige didn't appear convinced.

"It will be fine," Jorge insisted and looked toward Jesús for reassurance. "Things, they always work out."

A message appeared on his phone indicating that Diego was outside. Paige volunteered to let him in. As soon as she opened the office door, Maria's music could be heard as she continued to sing upstairs. Relieved that her passion hadn't dispersed even though the entertainment industry had temporarily broken her heart, Jorge considered that the only thing that mattered was his family. Their safety was his priority.

Diego could be heard talking to Paige long before they arrived in the office. As soon as they walked in the room, he jumped into an explanation.

"Jolene is tied up at the bar….helping Chase before he opens tonight," He said while heading to his usual seat while Paige closed the door, muffling the music. "Everything else is taken care of."

"No evidence that Claude Rexdale was ever in the club?" Jorge asked for reassurance. "Cameras? Nothing?"

"Just ours and they were erased," Diego insisted. "He came in the back so not like if he walked in the front door. It wasn't smart for him to show up alone."

"*Did* he show up alone?" Paige asked with some hesitation as she sat down.

"Yes, believe me, I have checked," Diego insisted. "We got it covered."

"It is interesting," Jorge said as he leaned back in his chair. "In Mexico, my biggest concern was other cartels and in Canada, my biggest enemy is racists. It is, what you say, a disturbing surprise?"

"That's one way to put it," Diego replied as he nervously fixed his tie. "I don't like it. We got to get you out of this political shit. These guys are poking around way too much."

"And they are poking at a bear," Jorge replied sternly. "We cannot back down from our enemies because it does send a message, wouldn't you say?"

"What we must do, sir," Jesús commented. "Is quickly find another candidate so you can move out of the public eye. That may relieve some of these issues."

"But what if I does not?" Jorge contemplated the possibilities. "What if I took it more seriously? What if I pushed harder? What if I called out these racists for who they are and air this information publicly?"

"You would need proof," Diego abruptly commented as his eyes bugged out in alarm. "We got none."

"I must start talking in interviews about the racism I have dealt with since moving to Toronto," Jorge suggested. "In general terms. I will make it sound like passing comments from business associates, that kind of thing."

No one replied so he continued.

"What if, I say, talk about the racism I see every day," Jorge continued. "And tell people the truth, that it is a problem. That we need more education. Those laws must be stronger against hate groups."

"If we shine the light on them," Paige spoke with hope in her voice. "This might force them to back down especially if they're exposed and it affects their employment, their future and maybe even cause legal issues but it could also shake things up a little too much."

"It is the only way," Jorge assured her. "We must take them on."

"Sir, in fairness, we've already taken them on in our own way," Jesús spoke with humor in his voice. "There are definitely less white supremacists here in Canada since you arrived."

Jorge gave a hearty laugh when he considered those whose lives had already come to a bitter end. Their deaths were often brutal and torturous, for which he had no regrets.

"As Paige said," Jorge spoke slowly. "We must shine a light to something that they do not wish exposed. This government, it is working against their own prime minister so we must find out who is the enemy in their party and make it public."

"Maybe they all are," Diego suggested as he reached for his phone while Jorge nodded.

"This is true," He said as he shuffled in his chair. "We already know the prime minister was misinformed on the night of the fire. It does not matter that this was exposed because there is already a dark cloud over him. People, they only listen to half the story."

"Suppose we find out who is behind all this?" Diego asked. "They may not be so forthcoming to admit the truth."

"They will confess their sins," Jorge insisted. "Believe me, the other options are not so pleasant."

No one replied.

"Unfortunately," Jorge commented. "This may not be so easy. My suspicions are that there are many. My fear is that this is a problem that will take a long time to resolve."

CHAPTER 33

"Sir, I have a theory," Jesús muttered as the two men walked to the door. He stopped and glanced at Diego and Paige as they headed upstairs to see Miguel. "Regarding, what you had me look into a couple of months ago?"

Jorge didn't reply but pointed toward his office. The two men made their way back and once they closed the door, Jorge wasted no time diving into the topic.

"Is this about Paige?" Jorge asked and his heart started to race in anxiety. "What you got?"

"It's not that I got anything," Jesús quickly clarified, creating some ease in the situation and pointed toward the desk. "Perhaps we should sit down."

Jorge nodded and they returned to their original seats.

"I have given this much thought," Jesús spoke slowly, his forehead wrinkled as he spoke. "I say this bullet, it hit Paige in an awkward position. It barely grazed her arm so it was either an inexperienced shooter or it was a mistake. It is unlikely anyone else was in the woods that night, we monitored the area too closely. I do not see it shot from the cabin because the men we targeted were rushing to get away from the fire plus the angle would've been unusual. Paige and Jolene were more to their right. If they were to shoot, it would have been directly ahead, so closer to you."

Jorge listened, his mind weighing the information.

"Boss, I do not see that bullet being meant for Paige," Jesús continued but briefly paused. "I believe it was meant for Jolene and Paige, she just happened to move in the way. With the smoke, it would be hard to see."

Jorge didn't reply. He felt a sense of relief, followed by anger. Jesús was suggesting one of his foot soldiers had been disloyal. Nothing angered him more than having his trust broken. Anger crept up Jorge's body, grasping him tightly as he continued to listen.

"Sir," Jesús continued with apprehension. "It almost certainly had to be one of our own. I have given this much thought and I cannot see another option that makes sense."

Jorge didn't reply as his mind went over everyone who was there: him, Jesús, Chase, Paige, Diego, Jolene....Michael.

"It would not be Diego plus he was too far away," Jesús continued with some hesitation. "I know it wasn't me, I know it wasn't you....Chase, the man will barely touch a gun.."

Jorge waited.

"Sir, I do not know," Jesús continued after some hesitation. "But Michael, since that day has been around less and his attitude is unusual. Do you think we can trust him? I know he helped with Paige after she was shot but sir, did you ever consider that perhaps that was out of guilt?"

Jorge felt a spark run through his body and his eyes widened.

"I originally thought he was farther away," Jesús continued and took out a roughly drawn sketches to illustrate his point. "But then I remember seeing him move around. At the time, I thought it was for a better angle because it was closer to the cabin but when I think, he would've had a good shot at Jolene. Paige was quite close so if she moved, it may be enough to graze her arm. Plus, sir, there was so much smoke and difficult to see."

"But why?" Jorge felt anger grip at his soul. "Why Jolene? Are you sure it was not for Paige?"

"As I said, how he react to Paige being shot. It was not for her," Jesús shook his head. "But why Jolene? I do not know but sir, this is the only thing I can think of..."

"And he wouldn't have tried again because it was too risky," Jorge continued to let his mind travel down that path. "But he was much closer to the cabin so he could've blamed it on the men who we were targeting."

"Sir, I have gone through it again and again, all summer..."

"I will talk to Jolene and if we suspect he is…."

"Sir, we must watch him carefully," Jesús replied. "I tell him as little as possible but what if he is undercover?"

"I don't think that's the case," Jorge considered. "But just because he is not helping the cops does not mean he's not helping someone."

"This is a good point, sir," Jesús nodded.

"Let's keep this from Diego," Jorge insisted.

Jorge sent Jolene a quick message before showing Jesús to the door and thanking him again. Returning to his office, he sat behind his desk and thought about everything he had just learned. Reaching into the mini fridge beside his desk, he took out a Corona and opened it up. What he wanted was a cigarette but he had done so well since quitting, reminding himself that it was during times of stress that the temptation returned.

Eventually, he heard footsteps coming downstairs and voices in the hallways, leading toward the door, indicating that Diego was most likely leaving. After a few minutes, a gentle tap on his door caused him to jump as Paige stuck her head inside.

"Is it ok to come in?" She asked with some hesitation. "We thought you had gone somewhere?"

"No, *mi amor,* please come in and shut the door," Jorge said in a low voice, noting Maria's music had stopped. She glanced at the beer as she entered the room and closed the door. "I had a conversation with Jesús after you went upstairs."

"About?" She asked while heading toward the desk.

"Remember I had concerns about the night you were shot?" Jorge asked as she sat down. "Jesús, he made a good point today. What if that bullet was meant for Jolene? You were beside her, there was a lot of smoke that night, perhaps you moved and got hit by accident."

Paige thought for a moment but didn't reply.

"Can you remember being shot?"

"It happened so fast and I think I was in shock," Paige admitted. "At first, I didn't realize I had been shot. There was so much noise and smoke and confusion. I remember putting my head down and turning slightly but I was a bit disoriented so I probably turned…I'm not sure."

"We have another theory," Jorge continued with reluctance. "It was one of our own."

Paige raised her eyebrows.

"We are thinking Michael based on his positioning and how he seems to be moving away from us lately."

"But he helped...." Paige immediately stopped and began to nod. "I see where you're going with this."

"Maybe not," Jorge shrugged. "But Jolene, she is on the way over. I wish to ask her if she had any issues with Michael. Perhaps, there were problems?"

Paige thought for a moment.

"I remember when they first got together," She started. "I think there was something about Jolene not trusting Michael."

The couple made eye contact and Jorge nodded.

"At the time, I thought it was normal that she would be concerned where he was a cop," She continued. "But I knew you had him thoroughly checked out."

Jorge showed no emotion.

"Paige, if I learn he is working against us..."

They shared a look. No words were necessary.

"*Mi amor*, I am glad that this bullet, it was maybe not meant for you," Jorge spoke honestly. "But I am not pleased by this turn of events either."

"Let's see what Jolene has to say first," Paige spoke evenly. "This theory might be wrong."

"The more I think about it, the more it fits," Jorge commented just as he got a message on his phone and leaned forward. "Jolene, she is here."

"I will let her in," Paige rose from her seat. "Maybe you should talk to her alone. I think I should swing by and see Alec. I'm curious what he thinks of this deception within his party. Maybe he knows something."

Jorge didn't reply but nodded as she walked away. He had mixed feelings on the subject.

As soon as the front door opened, he could hear Jolene's loud voice.

"The baby? Can I see?" She was saying while walking loudly toward the office.

"Jolene, I'm in here," Jorge called out as heels could be heard approaching the door.

"I see you first," Jolene said as she entered the office and hesitated before closing the door. She appeared nervous as she approached the desk.

"What is wrong?" Jolene asked as she lowered herself into a chair. "Your eyes, they are beady and funny looking like when you are mad. What did I do?"

"Nothing, Jolene," Jorge said with laughter in his voice, recalling some of the confrontations he had with the Colombian in the past. "This time, it is not you."

"Ok..."

"Jolene, I must ask, have you ever had any issues with Michael?"

His question seemed to throw her off guard. At first, she shook her head but something caused her to hesitate.

"No, not recently."

"Not recently?"

"Well, you know, in the beginning, I was suspicious," Jolene admitted. "I did not like Diego being with a cop. I thought it was uncomfortable. What if he lie? What if he is trying to hurt us? I try to respect your decision but I do not know, I was suspicious."

"Did you say anything to him about this?"

"I question him, yes," Jolene answered and appeared to relax. "I thought everything, it happened way too fast. And Diego, he is not easy, you know?"

Jorge grinned.

"So it seemed unusual that he want to be so serious so fast," Jolene continued as she relaxed. "It did not fit together for me."

In truth, Jorge had been so preoccupied at the time that he had merely accepted the research done on Michael and hadn't thought beyond it. Maybe Jolene had been right to be suspicious.

"I confront him and he get mad."

"Diego?"

"No no, I mean, I confront Michael and he got mad," Jolene corrected him. "It was me, I guess being an overprotective sister. Diego, he pretend to be tough but he's not so tough, you know? He pretend nothing hurt him but he is very...what is the word? You know, hurt easily?"

"Vulnerable?" Jorge asked.

"Yes! That is it," Jolene nodded. "But both got mad at me so I walk away. Figure it was not my business."

"Jolene," Jorge suddenly wasn't so sure about the theory. "Jesús thinks that when Paige was shot, it was actually meant for you and she moved in the way at the last second."

Jolene widened her eyes but didn't reply.

"And he thinks it was Michael who did it."

"What? Me?" Jolene appeared shocked. "But I say I had resolutions about him but to shoot me?"

"Reservations," Jorge corrected her. "But Jolene, what if you were getting close to something?"

She paused for a moment, her eyes widened as she stared at the desk.

"I did see something," Jolene confided. "I see him talking to a strange man. I thought, this is another man he has relations with so I confront…. oh! What if that was…"

"Something else?" Jorge finished her sentence. "What if you saw something you shouldn't have?"

"But what?"

"Have you seen anything since?" Jorge asked, ignoring her question.

"No," She shook her head. "But Diego, he complains that Michael, he is not around much anymore."

Jorge picked up his phone and hesitated before making his next move.

CHAPTER 34

"This time, I'm going to ask tougher questions," Makerson informed Jorge as the two men sat down in front of the computer while a young intern helped to angle the computer before sitting on the other side of the desk, tapping on another laptop. "These are questions from the public from some of your peers…"

"My peers?" Jorge asked with amusement in his voice as he straightened his tie, a smooth grin crossed his lips as he tilted his head. "You don't say."

"Your *political* peers," Makerson muttered with an awkward smile and glanced toward his assistant but she appeared busy with her work. "People questioning your abilities, your motives, why the sudden interest in politics…."

"Do not worry," Jorge was quick to reply. "I assure you, I have an answer for all your questions."

"I'm sure you do," Makerson replied just as his assistant commented that everything was ready to go.

Makerson started off with the usual song and dance; he introduced himself, then Jorge, using his uplifting, for the public voice. On the other side of the desk, the assistant was watching her screen closely while Makerson held an iPad in his hands to check live reaction as the event took place.

"Thank you for dropping in today," Makerson finally addressed Jorge who threw on his own fake smile and nodded.

"I am most gracious for this opportunity," Jorge replied. "I enjoy addressing any question, comments, concerns you might have for me."

"I see that you're getting a lot of response to the website," Makerson said and Jorge nodded. "Canadians are reaching out and letting you know how they feel and what the current government is lacking?"

"*Gracias,* and yes, the public has been very forthcoming with me," Jorge hesitated for a moment. "I set this up because, in truth, I really did not know what people wished from their government. I could guess and do lots of expensive research but to me, that was ridiculous. Just ask, make it simple and they will tell you."

"And the website is getting an outstanding amount of hits from people from all over the country?"

"Yes, this is true," Jorge replied and turned more toward Makerson to show his openness. "We have had an incredible interest from throughout Canada, from people of all ages, expressing their concerns. What I have learned is that people, they want jobs, they want stability, they want affordable housing they want to feel secure and not worry about how they will pay for their children's braces or look after their ailing parents. The people, they do not ask for anything unreasonable. This is something we share, regardless of our ethnicity, age, whether we live in rural or urban areas, we all want to feel safe. We want to feel that the government is there for us when we need it the most."

"Do you feel that the current government, your *own* party is providing that?"

"I believe they are doing some but not enough," Jorge spoke honestly, knowing that he was breaking a rule by speaking up against his own party but he wasn't playing their game.

"Housing prices, renting prices in this country, they are gouging people," Jorge continued. "So, even if they do have a wonderful job that pays well, it is difficult to get ahead financially when the wolf is always at your door. We are having a brain drain in larger cities because people simply cannot or will not pay these ridiculous prices to have the luxury of living in a major city. We are losing great people in cities like Toronto for this reason and can you blame them? You are a young person, leaving university with a large debt, do you want to add to that debt by moving to a large city, paying big rent, probably making less than they are worth and trying to keep food on the table? This here is too much."

"What would you suggest is a solution?"

"I believe," Jorge thought for a moment. "I believe there is no easy solution. The government, they often throw a band-aid on a problem but me, I think there are better ways. More regulations so that rent prices aren't inflating, perhaps the government can help first time home buyers, people with limited income, these are things I am looking at but in honesty, I do not have all the answers here and now. I simply feel that renting should be more competitive."

"If I walk out of this office today and go to buy, say, a new car," Jorge pointed toward the window. "Everyone out there has a sale, a deal to lure me in. Why not landlords? When did it become a situation where they do us, the consumer a favor and not the other way around. We, the public, are the customer. Why is there no competition for anyone but the rich?"

"But if you were to push that ideology, wouldn't that maybe discourage companies from developing? If they feel that the government is against them?"

"I'm not going up against them," Jorge insisted. "But I can work with them too. They must let me know what is their concern. Is it taxes? Do they need something from me? See, this here, is how the government has to work. They must listen to everybody and try to find solutions."

"Let's move on," Makerson said as he glanced at his iPad. "Now, earlier, you mentioned that you are getting a lot of feedback on your site. Has there been much talk about refugees and immigration? Recent polls have suggested that many Canadians are hesitant about allowing refugees into this country. What are your thoughts?"

"Well, personally, I like immigration," Jorge said as he threw on his charming smile. "It has worked well for me, you know? I think it has also worked well for Canadians because I have created many jobs since moving here, since creating my company."

Makerson laughed his fake laugh.

"This is true, Mr. Hernandez, you certainly have helped our economy grow but there are many people who suggest the pot industry was fine before you stepped in. Why did you feel a need to take over nationwide?"

"The problem was that things were not consistent throughout the country," Jorge reminded him. "Different rules in different provinces, private versus government operated, supply issues, all of this was not consistent throughout the country. Our House of Pot stepped in and made this our priority. Small town and large cities, it does not matter, the product, the price, everything is the same. That is what people want."

Makerson nodded. "And the pot festival this summer?"

"We brought in many tourists," Jorge jumped in with enthusiasm. "Large numbers, it was more than we originally expected. This here is terrific for Canada. This is what we want. We want that tourism dollar. We are as entitled as some of the more popular destinations. We have a lot to offer."

"Some people have suggested," Makerson started and hesitated as if to find the right words. "That you are the exception and not the rule. That many immigrants come here and are draining our resources rather than adding to them. Have you heard this much since joining the leadership race?"

"No," Jorge lied. "Actually, it is funny we hear this so often in the media because it does not seem to come up often when I am out speaking with people."

"Really?" Makerson did his fake surprise. "That's interesting. So you don't feel this is an issue?"

"I believe that some parties want you to believe it is an issue," Jorge said and glanced up at the ceiling as if looking for the answer.

"You have to remember, Mr. Makerson, that many politicians, they want you to feel that there is an 'enemy' that we must fight against. This, of course, is a distraction. So, for example, it is the immigrant's fault that your taxes are too high, that you cannot find affordable housing, that you didn't get that job….this, it is the blame game. Very popular in politics. It takes your eye off the real issue, which is often greedy corporations, the government not doing their job, this kind of thing. Immigrants are a vulnerable group of people and unfortunately, they are often used as a scapegoat. It is like if you set a fire and then rob a bank. Everyone is looking at the fire and are afraid it will spread, fearful that people will die, wondering how it got started, who is to blame? Meanwhile, their money is long gone."

Makerson made eye contact with Jorge and nodded.

"So, you feel that it's to the government's advantage that there is prejudice against immigrants?"

"I think it's to the government's advantage that they look the other way," Jorge replied. "Right now, immigration is a hot topic and this is what they see, so they stir that pot."

"Are you suggesting there's no racism in this country?" Makerson read from his iPad. "This is from Carol in Toronto."

"Not at all. Racism," Jorge calmly replied. "I experience it every day but I see that more as ignorance. I do not think that it means people want to stop immigration to this country but that they heard many negative messages about various cultures, mostly through the media. For example, I am Mexican, so people have said that I must be involved with the drug cartel."

Jorge laughed. Makerson joined him.

"This here, this is what I mean," Jorge spoke smoothly. "If I was with the cartel, why would I be here? In Canada? With a business? It does not make sense. Come to my home. It is quite modest for a man in the cartel, I will tell you that."

Makerson laughed.

"But you see, that is what media tells us," Jorge continued. "Turn on the television, most shows about Mexicans, about South American people, are they not about men and women in the cartel? So of course, that is what people think they know but there is so much more and my wish is that we learn about one another, to end these prejudices."

"There was a comment recently made by one of your peers for the party leadership, that I would like to read and get your thoughts."

Makerson glanced down at his iPad.

"'Just to let you know, Jorge Hernandez was born in Mexico and became a Canadian citizen within a year of being in Canada. Which is pretty fast if you're familiar with the Canadian immigration process. Why was he able to establish citizenship so quickly and what can he possibly know about Canadian values, Canadian laws, Canadian politics? Why is he even being considered?'" Makerson returned his attention to Jorge.

This was the question they agreed to end on and that was for a reason.

"You see, my friend," Jorge replied with a mixture of strength and calamity that would be noted for weeks to come. "This here is exactly why I am running. It is unfortunate that these *old* and *limited* ways of thinking still exist in Canada and they certainly have no place in politics."

"This country is beautiful because it is made up of people from every background," Jorge gained more strength in his voice, more fire in his eyes as he dramatically swung his hand around. "Ask *anyone, anywhere,* they will tell you that Canada is the greatest country in the world because it represents peace, inclusion and freedom. It represents a place where anyone, from any walk of life can go to prosper. It represents people who are striving to be better. It represents a government who cares for its people. This is why I am in this race. This is why I have immigrated here, why I raise my children in Canada. I will not apologize for moving here, for starting my business here, for raising my family here. I value, I appreciate being a Canadian citizen everyday."

"Just as I have learned English," Jorge dramatically continued. "I strive to learn everything about this country, about its government but I do so through a different set of eyes because it carries value. It is because I am *not* from here, because I have seen extreme poverty growing up in a third world country, that I look at this country with adoring eyes. This here, it is the ideal. If you must learn, you learn from the best."

CHAPTER 35

In truth, Jorge had no idea what he was doing. The concerns brought up by other politicians were right; he wasn't very familiar with the Canadian political system and spent a great deal of time researching information, asking Paige, Makerson, and Athas many questions. They held him up on his two feet for these interviews but it was starting to wear thin. His enthusiasm for this game was running out. Unfortunately, the public's interest in him wasn't.

"Now there are buttons with his picture on them," Paige told the group the following afternoon, when they met in the boardroom. "Maria brought one home from school yesterday. We didn't even know they existed."

"Buttons?" Jolene automatically spoke up, glancing down at the buttons on her blouse. "How do you fit picture of Jorge on there? I do not understand."

"As if his big head would fit on that little button," Diego chimed in from the end of the table. "She's talking about like pins, you know...." He stopped to point at his chest. "Remember back when we were kids, you had a pin with Madonna on it..."

"Oh!" Jolene's face lit up "Yes, oh, I see.."

"The problem is," Paige continued. "Where did they come from? Not from us."

Everyone's eyes switched to Alec.

"It wasn't my idea," He quickly replied. "And I didn't do it."

"But someone in the party did?" Jorge finally spoke up. "Is that what you are saying?"

"It would seem that way," Alec replied. "Honestly, I kind of heard a third-party made them."

"As in?" Chase asked as he shrugged, a look of cynicism on his face.

"I'm guessing someone who wants Jorge in as much as the party," Alec replied. "Someone who has something to gain. It's hard to say."

"I will not lie," Jorge hesitated for a moment. "I enjoy the power that has come with this political bullshit but at the same time, it is getting out of hand. This was never meant to go this far."

"And sir," Jesús quickly jumped in. "I see you in Mexican news. I go online and last night, they talk about you running for Canadian politics. People in our home country, they are very excited and wish you were running there."

"That's the other thing," Alec said with some hesitation. "You're hitting a lot of international news since this last interview."

"But I did not say anything too exciting," Jorge commented as he thought back to his last interview. "Just the usual political talk."

"But people think you're inspiring and authentic," Alec attempted to explain. "They're tired of the same political bullshit and you represent a more direct, honest approach. You're going up against your own party and saying that although you're running for them, you want to swoop in and… well, change politics. That's unusual."

Jorge didn't reply.

"Sir, I am looking here," Jesús spoke up again. "I see you being featured in other news in both Europe and Latin America. The fact you are running as a new Canadian is very exciting to the people."

"I believe the words I saw yesterday," Alec jumped in casually. "Is that you're the rock star of Canadian politics."

Jorge knew this comment was purposely catering to his ego but unfortunately, it worked. There was something exciting about getting international attention for his role in Canadian politics however, he also could see from the look on Paige's face that she wasn't happy.

"Still, this here, it is too much," Jorge spoke with a calm voice. "It was never meant to go this far. We talked about it in the beginning. You wanted someone to divert attention and bring us back in the polls. I have done this so I would recommend you find someone fast."

"The problem is," Alec jumped back in. "If you suddenly leave now, people might realize that this is a gimmick and you never meant to stay or even worse, that you only did this to get more attention for your own brand."

"This is exactly why I did do it," Jorge said with laughter in his voice. "But yes, I see what you mean and I guess, the best solution to have someone who outshines me."

"Sir, I'm not sure this is possible," Jesús continued to look at his screen. "You are quite popular. I do not know who would be able to stand up to you."

Jorge sat up a little taller but noted that Diego was rolling his eyes.

"We've created a monster," Diego quipped from the end of the table.

"In fairness," Jorge said with a smooth grin. "I was already a monster, long before politics came along."

Everyone laughed and Jorge felt the mood lighten.

"When I step down, I will say that I want to spend more time with my family," Jorge glanced at his wife who appeared skeptical. "As for the person to replace me, that is not my problem, is it?"

His eyes gazed at Athas who looked away.

"It is up to the party to figure it out," Jorge continued. "I am holding them above water so you do not drown in your own fucking stupidity. What better way to show that your party isn't racist than having a Mexican run? You can't expect me to solve all your problems. This was only supposed to be temporary."

Everyone's eyes were on Athas.

"They want to meet with you again," He quickly directed his comment at Jorge. "The prime minister and his top people want to speak with you. They don't want to go through me anymore."

"I do not wish to meet with them," Jorge reminded him. "I have in the past. What do they want?"

"I think you know."

Jorge didn't reply. He could see the concerned look on his wife's face and this time, he felt the same but for different reasons. He had no fear that his past would get dug up however, the political game reminded him of wading through mud while trying to keep clean.

"I want out," Jorge spoke abruptly. "By the end of this week. *Terminado.*"

Alec didn't reply but simply nodded.

"If that is all," Jorge pushed his chair out. "I got things to do today."

"Sir, we do need to talk…" Jesús started and they made eye contact but he quickly shifted gears. "To Marco, before we leave."

"Yes, of course, you go and I will meet you shortly," Jorge nodded and switched his attention to Diego. "And you, we must talk as well before I go."

Everyone else rose from their seat but Paige and Diego stayed behind with Jorge. Jesús gave a knowing look before heading for the door behind Jolene, Chase, and Alec.

"Diego, I must ask," Jorge started after everyone else left. "I have not seen Michael much lately and when I do, his attitude, it is funny. You know?"

Diego shook his head with despair in his eyes. "Things haven't been good with us."

"You did not think this was a reason for concern?" Jorge countered. "That maybe we have something to worry about?"

Diego looked away.

"I do not like to pry," Jorge spoke bluntly. "But he knows a lot so we must be careful. Your relationship is it…"

"It's…complicated," Diego confessed.

"What does this mean?"

"Our relationship," Diego slowly continued. "It's open. It's not just him and me anymore and now it's falling apart."

"So, this means, what?"

"It means," Diego said with some hesitation, "It means, he'll probably leave. It means that I'm old and alone. It means that I had my chance and I fucked it up."

"Diego, that's not true," Paige immediately jumped up and rushed over to give him an awkward hug before sitting beside him.

"Diego, you're mi *hermano,* why did you not tell me these things?" Jorge asked as he shook his head. "Why did you not come to me?"

"I wanted to handle it myself," Diego admitted. "Plus, once you say it out loud, it's real, you know. You can't deny it anymore."

Paige reached out and touched his arm and the two shared a look, Diego's eyes full of desperation.

"This here, it is running from the truth," Jorge quietly added. "I have some concerns of my own about Michael. I would rather wait until I know more to say anything because for now, it is just a theory."

"Tell me," Diego jumped in with concern in his eyes. "I need to know."

"Diego," Paige was quick to jump in. "Honey, we don't know anything for sure so let's not go there yet."

"Paige," Diego turned toward her. "I feel like a fool for bringing this man into our world. I was desperate to make it work that I jumped in with both feet. If there's something I should know, please tell me."

"Diego," Jorge said and saw the vulnerability in his friend's eyes and had to look away for a moment but quickly looked back. "This here, it is not your fault. He was in our world before you and he got close. Sometimes, we get caught up in the moment and do not see clearly."

"But look at you and Paige," Diego gestured toward Jorge. "How happy you are and how fast it happened."

"Oh, *amigo,* that is not every day," Jorge reminded him. "You cannot compare us with you. It is never a good idea to compare to anyone. We are all different."

"Everything is going to be ok," Paige quickly added.

"Please tell me," he looked at Paige than back at Jorge. "What do you think he did?"

Jorge exchanged looks with his wife who nodded. Things were about to get very messy.

CHAPTER 36

Loneliness runs deep. It's not something you can understand unless you've truly experienced it in the depths of your soul. Diego believed it was a pain like no other. There wasn't anyone who could tell him otherwise. It was a reality that he experienced since his teenage years and no matter where he was in life, or who he was with, there was always an isolated part of him that few saw.

The problem was that being around people who didn't share these despairing feelings sometimes made the pain stronger. However, being around other broken people made him feel whole but it was only temporary; the moment they left the room, he was back to his empty self, struggling to keep his head above water. It was that sink or swim feeling that caused many to desperately grab on the person closest in order to survive. It was sad and pathetic but was there any other way?

As a young man, Diego arrived in California from Colombia as a lonely, poor immigrant with little English and big dreams. However, the feeling of isolation hit him immediately upon arrival and fear filled his heart. What was he doing? What was he thinking? There was a sense of dread along with the realization that he couldn't go back home either. It put him in a vulnerable position and regardless of his status in life, in many ways, Diego Silva remained that frightened, immigrant kid grabbing a life raft. Back then, it was a rich sugar daddy named Ralph Borowiak who saved him but who would save him now?

Michael Perkins had originally seemed like the perfect match. After all, as a dirty cop, he was essentially one of them. He knew what Diego was really about and accepted him. There were no secrets. At least, not many. The two had formed a quick bond that was exciting in the beginning but grew tired until Michael suggested they see other people while maintaining their own relationship. Diego reluctantly agreed, suddenly faced with that ironic karma resurfacing from his youth, when he was the one suggesting the same arrangement to Ralph so he could have his cake and eat it too. It was that selfishness that slapped Diego in the face and suddenly everything came back full circle.

The other men were never to be brought home. That was the agreement. Diego didn't abide by this rule. It didn't seem to matter since Michael was never around. Essentially, it was over but neither was ready to say the words.

The news that Jorge and Paige told him changed everything. Although all the facts weren't in yet, it was clear that Jolene also shared their fear and at the end of the day, these people were his family. They were looking out for him.

After their meeting, Diego returned home and sat in silence. He thought about everything; the day Paige was shot, the events since then including Michael's many mysterious disappearances and he silently blamed himself for not seeing it sooner. Had he been so desperate for this relationship to work that he was blind to what was really going on?

That afternoon, he ripped his condo apart, looking for anything that revealed some clues but he found nothing. It never occurred to him before that it was strange Michael had so few possessions in their shared home. Like Diego, he was a man in his 40s so wouldn't he have books, movies, photos, anything? This was when he began to wonder if he had a second home. He messaged his theory to Paige, who said she would look into it.

Grabbing Michael's computer, he checked the history and emails. Nothing. Like his home with Diego, it was a shell of his life. His email account was mostly newsletters he had signed up for but nothing of substance. He claimed to have no social media due to his line of work but was that true? His history was empty. Either he wasn't using this computer or he was cleaning it out as fast as he did.

Sitting in silence, Diego's mind went over everything. He thought about conversations and moments he thought mattered. A million ideas floated through his head while a sense of doom filled his soul.

The doorbell rang, tearing Diego from his trance. He glanced at the clock. Hours had passed. Checking his phone, he saw it was Jolene waiting outside. He buzzed her in and slowly made his way to the door.

"Oh Diego," She met him with sadness in her eyes. "We must talk. Are you alone?"

With a lump in his throat, he nodded and moved aside as she entered the room. Closing the door behind them, he followed her to the couch where they both sat.

"Diego, I talk to Jorge," She said and took a deep breath as she turned toward him. "He and Paige, they were helping Marco look into Michael, to see...."

Neither said a word for a moment but shared a look.

"Diego, a long time ago, I see Michael," Jolene started and hesitated. "He was talking to another man and I confront him. I was scared he was doing something behind your back. I did not trust but I didn't want to hurt you so I say nothing. Now, I regret this."

"Jorge, he tell you his theory?" She continued to speak slowly with pain in her eyes.

"Yes," Diego finally found his voice. "He thinks that Michael shot Paige, meaning to shoot you instead."

"It was because I see him with this other man," Jolene continued to speak as she slid closer to him. "He tell me, at the time, that it was no one. That you were the only man he was with and I believe him because I thought, I should not get involved. I was being paranoid. I left alone."

Diego didn't take his eyes off his sister as she spoke. He could tell she was uncomfortable.

"I was asked to return to the office today," She continued and looked down at her hands then back up. "They looked to see about your idea that maybe Michael has a second home."

"He does, doesn't he?" Diego asked with no emotion in his voice.

Jolene nodded with tears in her eyes which she quickly blinked away.

"Diego, he is married to a woman," She quietly said as she reached for his hand. "He has been married for many years. When he go away, that is where he is going. And when he come here, he is obviously telling her the same reason as he tell you."

Stunned by the news, Diego couldn't speak.

"This is why he isn't on social media," She continued. "He tell you that it was because of his work, did you not say?"

"But I'm…"

"I know, Diego, you are not on too and that is why you weren't suspicious," Jolene squeezed his hand. "That is why, he has so little. You even say how he travel light when he move in, this is why. He has two homes."

Diego felt his mouth go dry as he looked away. A chill ran through his body. It made sense but it was still a shock that reached into that dark, lonely place that he detested so much, the place that made him fall victim to situations like this one. The pathetic, sad person that gave him great shame. He felt like an idiot.

"Diego, I am so so sorry," Jolene said and sniffed. "I wanted to tell you myself, away from the others. Jorge ask me. He wants to see what you want to do."

"He might've shot Paige," Diego finally found his voice; it was weak, hoarse, almost as if someone had kicked him in the stomach and he was attempting to recover. "He might've tried to shoot you. He lied. He so fucking lied about everything. How could I be so blind?"

"Diego, we do not know everything yet," Jolene said and leaned in to hug him, her perfume filled his lungs. "He fool us all, Diego. Not just you."

"I have to take care of this," Diego said in a small voice as Jolene let go of him and moved away. "I brought him into our world, it's up to me to take care of him."

"You did not bring," Jolene insisted as she sniffed and took a deep breath. "Jorge, he brought him to us and now, he blame himself. I know, he say that when I was at the office. He feels terrible, Diego. He is furious but not at you. He is upset with himself but mostly, he is angry at Michael."

Jolene's phone beeped. She reached in her purse and glanced at it.

"It is Jorge," She commented. "He ask if we can have him meet us tonight? Do you think?"

"I...I guess...."

"Diego, it is up to you," Jolene said as she tapped on her phone and looked back into his eyes. "This is for you to decide. If you wish, you can talk to him alone but....but Diego, we are your family. We want to do this with you. But if it is too personal..."

"No, I want to...." Diego said as he ran a hand over his face. "I don't know what to say or what to do. I...I don't know..."

"Diego, this, it will be ok," Jolene said and leaned in to hug him again. "We are your family. We will be there and ask the questions and it is up to you.....how you want to do this, you know?"

He knew.

"Ok," Diego finally replied and reached for his phone. "He began to tap a message. "At the club?"

"VIP room, yes," Jolene replied. "Tell him, we are having a private celebration for something."

"For what?" Diego was suddenly blank as he closed his eyes to fight the wave of emotion that was rising inside of him.

"We are celebrating..." Jolene thought for a moment. "We are celebrating Jorge's political success. Maybe he decided to take this more seriously?"

Diego nodded and stared at the phone for a minute before tapping a message. His fingers felt like rubber. It was as if his whole body was shutting down.

"Here, let me do," Jolene said as she ripped the phone from his hands. Her fingers moved quickly as her face tightened. She showed him the phone before hitting send. "Does this sound right?"

Reading the message, Diego simply nodded.

She hit send and placed his phone on the nearby table.

Neither said a word. A 'ting' sound alerted them both. She grabbed the phone and read the message.

"He say, he will come," She announced and placed the phone back on the table. Her eyes searched his face. "Diego, are you going to be ok?"

He nodded slowly.

"Can I do anything for you?" She asked in a soft voice.

He shook his head.

"Maybe, a nap? A shower?" She glanced around the room. "A drink? Would this help?"

"No," Diego answered honestly. "I don't know what I want right about now."

"I do not want to leave you alone."

"I'll be fine, Jolene," Diego spoke much more hastily than he intended. "Thanks, I will be ok."

"Ok," She spoke in a gentle voice before reaching over to give him another hug and then, she was gone.

Diego sat and he thought. He glanced at his phone to see a message of compassion from Paige. Did he need her to go to see him?

Did he?

I'm fine, Paige. I just got to work some things out. I'm sorry for everything.
I'm coming over.

Sitting the phone aside, Diego felt his pain subside as anger moved in. Michael had deceived him. All these months, it was a lie. He had tried to kill Diego's sister and in the process, could've killed his closest friend. And yet, he looked into his eyes with love and Diego was left the fool. The Joker. As if his life wasn't even real. As if his feelings were nothing. And what else was he hiding? Why was he trying to kill Jolene? What was she getting close to?

Who was the man Jolene saw Michael with? Do we know?

He sent the message to Jorge knowing that he wouldn't say much in a text.

Paige, she is going to see you. She will tell you. The party is on for tonight. VIP room is booked.

Diego suddenly felt his pain turn to fury. Pure, black fury. No one fucked with his family. No one.

CHAPTER 37

"People are getting high on Hernandez," Jesús read the headline out loud to the others who gathered with him in the VIP room of *Princesa Maria.* His comment was quickly followed by laughter as the group looked at Jorge, who was giving a sideward glance to Diego. He was keeping his shit together so far.

So far.

"Well, you know, I like to think that I bring a certain something to this whole political debate," Jorge commented as he grinned and winked at his wife. "You know, the people, they like my honesty and directness. No one ever told them that this here could be a part of politics."

"We certainly don't see it much," Michael spoke up, completely unsuspecting of the underlying theme in the room. He would find out.

"The people," Jesús continued as he powered off his phone and set it down before reaching for a drink. "They are sheep who need a leader. This is you."

"This is me," Jorge held his glass of wine up in the air and everyone did the same. He noted that the only person who looked tense was Chase. It was only a matter of time before he crossed the line to become like the rest of them.

Diego continued to show a fake smile but was much quieter than usual which made Jorge fear that Michael would suspect something. However, if he did, it was not obvious. He seemed joyful, completely unaware that he was one of those sheep that was about to be slaughtered.

"Well, sir," Jesús spoke up. "They could not find a better leader."

"So, you're doing this for real?" Chase asked. His innocent-like expression made the entire 'celebration' seem even more authentic. "Both feet in?"

"Both feet in," Jorge replied as he sat his drink down. "I always say, if you are going to do something, make it all or nothing."

There was silent communication between him and Chase.

"So the private party out there," Jorge pointed toward the door. "When does it start?"

"Not for a while yet," Chase glanced at his watch. "There's some award thing, then they're moving the party here."

There was no party. They closed the bar for a reason.

"I was wondering why no one was here tonight." Diego finally spoke up. "Thought you might still have those plumbing problems from the other day."

The two men shared a grin. Michael had no idea about Claude Rexdale although it had been in the news that he was missing.

"You know me," Jorge commented airily. "I take care of problems quickly and efficiently."

"Yes, this is true," Jolene said and cleared her throat. She had barely looked up from her phone since arriving.

"What the hell is so interesting on that phone," Jorge asked with a shrug. "You cannot enjoy our company, Jolene?"

"Baby pictures," Paige quickly spoke up. "I sent her some pictures of Miguel."

"He is so beautiful," Jolene gushed as she swiped quickly and turned the phone around to show them a picture of the baby. "I miss! I have not had the proper time to spend with my godson lately."

"I know, he keeps complaining about that," Jorge teased her and everyone laughed as he watched Jolene turn her phone off. He had to lighten the mood so Michael wouldn't be suspicious. He wanted to catch him completely off guard. However, the clock was ticking and Jorge wasn't sure how much longer Diego was going to keep his cool.

"Speaking of not being around much lately," Jorge turned his attention toward Michael. "Where have you been? The police, they have you on one of their wild goose chases? Every time I turn on the news, there is a story of something being 'under investigation' and yet, no crimes seem to ever be solved."

"Many aren't," Michael confirmed. "They just go in limbo. If you don't find something right away, the chances of ever finding the truth decrease with each day."

"Interesting," Jorge said while nodding his head and reaching for his wine. "Well me, I cannot complain about that."

There were a few snickers around the table. He noted that Michael hadn't answered his original question.

"It's the nature of the beast," Michael continued. "Too many crimes, not enough resources and we fell behind this summer when some of us went to places hit by fires."

"What did you do, exactly?" Paige quietly asked, her eyes fixated on Michael.

"For me, I mainly went afterwards," He replied and tilted his head to the side. "To help families in distress, look for bodies, evaluate everything and report back."

Paige nodded. "That must've been so sad. I still can't believe the devastation that took place this summer."

"There's something about seeing people in that situation," Michael continued. "Vulnerable. It makes you believe in humans again."

"Ah yes!" Jorge said as he finished his glass of wine. "Terrible situations bring emotions to the surface. This is what I find. It also brings the truth. And the truth, it is so rare."

An awkward silence fell over the group.

"Tell me, Michael," Jorge spoke abruptly, turning in his direction. "How do you feel about the truth?"

With all eyes on Michael, he appeared stunned.

"Let us hear some truth," Jorge continued as Diego turned to give Michael a dark glare. "You know me, my campaign, I like speaking honest and I appreciate the same in others. So, tell us about your wife. I suspect this one, Diego would like to hear. Also, tell us about shooting *my* wife or did you mean to shoot Jolene? What was she getting close to? We want to hear your secrets. Please share them with us."

Michael sat upright and looked around the table and began to shuffle uncomfortably in his seat. Jolene was the first person to pull out a gun and point it at him but Jesús and Paige were quick to follow. Chase glared at him and Diego finally turned and looked into Michael's eyes in silence.

"I..I don't understand," His reaction was one of panic as he pushed his chair back, causing everyone but Diego to jump up including Chase, who rushed for the door and stood in front of it, arms crossed over his chest. There was no way Michael was getting out and Diego had already made sure he didn't have a gun on him and his phone was turned off.

"Look, I can…" Michael started and turned Diego. "It's not what you think."

"Ah! But it is!" Jorge replied as he walked toward Michael with his phone pointed in his direction, swiping through various images. "You are married to a woman. I have your address. A few pictures. Looks like you're a very happy couple. I guess not that happy since you had Diego on the side. This is confusing to me. So you are not gay… but bi? And you're not honest… but a liar?"

"See to me, this here is personal between the two of you," Jorge gestured toward both Michael and Diego as he powered off his phone. "But when you shoot my *wife,* it becomes very fucking personal. And I do not care that you helped us that night. And I do not care that the wound was superficial. And I do not care that the bullet maybe wasn't even meant for her. The fact that you wanted to shoot someone else in this here family, now that is a problem. *Un gran problema.*"

"You want to shoot me?" Jolene loudly exclaimed as she continued to point her gun at Michael, her face full of fury, causing her resemblance to Diego to shine through. "I want to shoot you."

"See, this here is the problem," Jorge cut her off. "We *all* take everything that happened quite personally but not as personally as Diego. He is the one of us that was truly misled. It is much more to him."

"Why?" Diego asked in a hoarse voice as he shook his head. "Why, any of this, why?"

"Can I explain?" Michael appeared to panic with fear in his eyes. "Please!"

"Ah *Lucy,* you got some 'splainin to do," Jorge grinned as he reached for his own gun. "And you got a lot of people right here that can shoot you and not miss, so you better make sure to tell the truth."

"Things...I..." Michael attempted to speak but began to stutter. "I... didn't tell you about my wife, Diego because our marriage it was...it was coming to an end and I..and then things happened and I...things got so complicated so quickly..."

Diego didn't respond. He just stared with sadness in his eyes.

"You could not *try*?" Jolene loudly complain.

"I thought I could resolve it myself and...." Michael drifted off and attempted to control his breathing. "I..."

"Let's move on from this here soap opera," Jorge spoke abruptly as he quickly got hold of the situation. "Now, let's talk about *my* wife and why you shot her? Were you trying to shoot Jolene? We need some clarity in this here situation."

"What was I getting close to?" Jolene asked as her eyes narrowed on him. "What did I see when you were talking to that guy. That day I confront you?"

"He... was an informant and it was crucial that you keep quiet or he and I would both be dead," Michael insisted. "It had to do with work."

"Then why shoot me?" Jolene yelled and the tension in the room grew. "You tell me now!"

"I wasn't trying to shoot you or Paige," Michael started to hyperventilate, now with tears in his eyes. He turned his attention toward Jorge. "I was trying to shoot you."

Before Jorge could respond, before he even had time to comprehend what he just learned, an emotional Diego jumped up, pulled out a gun and shot Michael in the head, causing Jolene to gasp in shock while the rest of the room fell silent.

CHAPTER 38

"I was bamboozled!" Diego commented sharply as he knocked back another drink later that night as he, Jesús and Jorge sat at the bar and Chase stood on the other side with a sullen expression on his face. This was after the body was removed and the men returned to the *Princessa Maria* to make sure everything was back in order. Paige left after the shooting and Jolene after they got rid of the body.

"You were, what?" Jorge asked after taking a moment to process the comment. Finishing his beer, he slid the bottle aside and turned toward Diego. "Is this here, a real word? It sounds like something out of Disney. You know, for the kids?"

"Nah, it means duped," Diego insisted with sad eyes that stared off into space. "He tricked me. He used me and thought I would never find out. I can't believe I trusted him."

"In fairness, Diego," Jesús began before knocking back another shot of tequila. "We do not know everything. All we know is he was married and clearly not happy if he was also with you. We do not know why he wanted to shoot Jorge."

"Yeah, about that, Diego," Jorge jumped in. "You couldn't have waited a minute or two to find out *why* he wanted to kill me before you shot him? Would that have been too much?"

"I know, I know," Diego spoke quietly as he looked down at his hands. "But as soon as he said it, as soon as I heard the words from his mouth, my first reaction was to shoot him. I couldn't think beyond that. I had to do it right then. I couldn't second guess myself."

"Hey and I am not saying it was wrong," Jorge quickly clarified with a hand in the air. "I would love to know *why* he would want to shoot me. I mean, it does not make sense."

"Sure it does," Chase finally spoke up. "There was probably someone else wanting it done and he was just the errand boy. He was able to get close to you, gain your trust and someone found out."

"I'm not sure," Jorge replied and shook his head. "Around that time, I was having a lot of issues but mostly with white supremacists. I somehow doubt he was working for them."

"Who fucking knows!" Diego spoke dramatically with his hands swinging in the air. "I didn't think he liked to fuck women too and here we are!"

Jorge couldn't help but grin at Diego and shrugged.

"You make an interesting point, Diego," Jorge replied. "But we cannot dwell on it."

"But what if there are others?" Chase appeared concerned.

"This here, it happened months ago," Jorge reminded him. "If there are others, they have not done well."

"Paige, she's going to worry," Diego reminded him. "Maybe she can find out."

"Maybe there is nothing to find out," Jorge suggested. "We can never know. The man to me, he was a lone wolf."

"He did seem...you know, like he thought you had too much influence on me," Diego suddenly commented with a strange look on his face. "I had forgotten. He said this a long time ago. He thought you would eventually let me take the fall for you. I remember because we argued about it and he actually seemed jealous that you were like a brother to me. I don't know why."

No one responded.

"It's buckets of sunshine and piss," Diego finally continued and shook his head. "Just when you think you got the sunshine, you got the piss instead."

"Diego, it's not always that way," Jorge reassured him and touched his arm. "You know this."

"I don't know it though," Diego turned to him with vulnerability in his eyes. "There aren't many people you can confess your heart to and be accepted. Most people don't even bother to listen… or care if they do. I thought he did. Less lately but in the beginning, I thought he did."

"I think things just got too complicated for him," Chase gently offered. "He was married and thought he could manage everything but maybe getting away from his wife wasn't so easy. I've been married. Trust me. There are so many complications to consider. It's never cut and dry."

"He is right," Jorge agreed. "This here, it is not you. You did nothing wrong and *amigo,* you sacrificed a lot tonight. I will never forget what you did. This is why you are my *hermano* and I want you to know that I would do the same for you."

"I know," Diego said and managed a small smile. "That's why I did it."

"And everyone else here," Jorge continued, gesturing toward Jesús and Chase. "We would all do the same. That is what we have here. It's not just that we work together, we are *familia.* No one and nothing will take that away."

With his arms crossed over his chest, Chase nodded as Jesús stared solemnly into his glass.

"We are here for you, *mi hermano* and we always will be," Jorge spoke with strength in his voice.

"I know," Diego spoke emotionally. "I know."

"This is something you don't get out there," Chase spoke calmly as his rigid demeanor grew more relaxed and he pointed toward the door. "Out there, loyalty, it means nothing. Family, it means nothing. They're just words that are convenient from time to time but that's all they are…words."

"This is true," Jorge agreed. "But really, do any words mean anything to some people?"

"They mean something here," Chase insisted and glanced briefly at Diego before returning his attention to Jorge. "With us. We look out for one another. We're here for each other. Family? My family back home? Forget it."

"You mean that hick town?" Jorge teased and watched as Chase laughed.

"Yes, that *hick town.*"

"But small towns," Jesús spoke up. "I thought they, you know, look out for one another. Support one another? No?"

Chase shook his head.

"That is why he's here, Jesús," Jorge reminded his friend and watched him nod in reply. "We are all here because we are, to a degree, without family. We make our family. This is it here."

"It's not just family though," Chase insisted and crossed his arms again. "It's the loyalty factor. I mean, I've worked places, got laid off, got used and for what? You get paid nothing and when they're done of you, they toss you aside. They don't care. Your loyalty, your work, it means nothing. You mean nothing. But here, this stuff counts."

"It goes both ways," Jorge reminded him. "Loyalty does not always mean much to employees. They work somewhere then on to the next thing. They do not care. Loyalty, it is rare in our world today. I have loyalty and in return, I am there for whatever is needed."

No one commented. That evening had been proof of his words.

Jorge felt his phone buzzing and pulled it out of his pocket.

"Paige, she is wondering where I am," Jorge said and stood up from the stool. "And she said to make sure you are all ok to drive home."

"I can drive anyone home," Chase insisted. "I didn't drink."

"Diego?" Jorge asked.

"I'm fine."

"Drive him home," Jorge said to Chase. "He says he's fine. He's not fine."

Diego didn't agree but slowly stood up as did Jesús.

"Sir, may I get a drive, if that is ok?"

"Of course," Jorge agreed. "I hadn't realized you drank too much."

"I didn't sir," Jesús said. "But me, I walked here."

"Why?" Jorge asked.

"Exercise sir," Jesús replied as he moved closer. "I must lose some weight."

Jorge grinned as he glanced at his friend's protruding stomach.

"Ok, let's roll," Jorge pointed toward the door. "I gotta get home. Paige is awake, maybe she wants to seduce her husband."

"It is quite late, sir," Jesús reminded him as he turned on his phone and waited for Chase to set the alarm.

"Yes, but I am irresistible," Jorge joked as they opened the door. They walked into the chilly October night.

Diego grunted and rolled his eyes while Chase merely grinned.

"We will talk tomorrow," Jorge commented as he headed for his SUV. "*Si?*"

Tired, everyone agreed. Diego followed Chase and Jesús jumped in the passenger side of Jorge's vehicle.

"Sir, I do not like that we didn't have a chance to learn why Michael shot at you," Jesús immediately started once they were inside. "This does not make sense plus he was way off....."

"I know."

"Do you think.....you don't think Diego knows more and will not say?"

"No," Jorge answers automatically and then rethought his answer as they pulled out on the street. "Do you?"

"I do not think so," Jesús replied after hesitating. "It does not make sense, you know?"

"A lot of things don't make sense," Jorge replied as they headed toward Jesús' building. "It's late. Too late to have this conversation here."

"Paige, she will find out," Jesús suggested.

"I think you might be right," Jorge spoke with hesitation. "But there was a lot of smoke and hard to see. Also if I was dead perhaps it would mean that Diego would take over and in turn, that would give Michael more power."

"Perhaps sir."

"Power, it is an aphrodisiac," Jorge insisted. "Trust me, I know."

Both were silent for the rest of the drive. After dropping off Jesús, Jorge was relieved to arrive home. After putting the alarm back on, going upstairs to look in on Miguel, he finally made his way to his bedroom. Paige was sitting up in bed, reading.

"Mi *amor,* you are still awake," Jorge commented as she put the book aside and he began to remove his clothes. "You should be sleeping."

"I was worried," She quietly replied.

"Diego, he is fine," Jorge insisted as he tossed his clothes on the chair. "It is me who needs your attention tonight."

Down to his underwear, he walked across the room and wasted no time crawling into bed beside Paige and leaning over to kiss her. His hand automatically slid under the covers and down her body.

"I'm worried about you," She whispered.

"Do not worry about me," Jorge commented, his breath laboured. "Just for tonight, do not worry about me. I am fine and I'm exactly where I want to be."

Their lips met and the world fell silent.

CHAPTER 39

"It is, how you say, one of the beautiful moments of life," Jorge commented as he tickled Miguel, once again causing the baby to laugh. On the other side of the table, Maria was giggling as she watched while Paige dug into her breakfast. "It used to be every time I pick him up, he either cried or fell to sleep but now, he actually seems to like me."

"For a while, I wasn't sure if he liked any of us," Paige muttered while chewing on her eggs.

"He loves me the best," Maria said as she leaned in and made eye contact with her brother and he smiled. "He's always loved me the best."

"Well, that is good Maria," Jorge replied as he reached for a cup of coffee while juggling the baby in his other arm. "Miguel will always need his sister. Family, it is the most important thing."

"*Papa*, did I laugh a lot when I was a baby?"

"Maria, you were the most serious baby I had ever seen," Jorge answered as he sat the coffee cup down and Miguel stared at his face. "At one time thought your mother had sedated you because you were so quiet."

"Not really, right?" Maria said with apprehension in her voice.

"No, of course not!" Jorge said and began to laugh. "You have just proven my point that nothing has changed."

"*Papa,* I am an artist, we can't help but be serious," Maria insisted. "The counselor at school said that I'm very disciplined with my art and that I need to not be such a perfectionist."

Jorge considered these words. "Maria, perhaps you should listen. You need to be a kid. This here, the acting thing, it does not happen overnight and once it does, most, they wish they had time to do normal things. Take advantage of this time. You won't be 12-years-old ever again. Remember that."

Maria seemed humbled by his words. He noticed she had been unusually quiet in recent weeks and it concerned him. Her summer of audition rejections hadn't helped her confidence level but it was good that she was able to experience this reality. Many people brought up their kids to feel like they were the center of the universe which made them unprepared for the real world.

"I have to go finish getting ready for school," Maria said as she stood up and took her dishes to the dishwasher. Jorge noted that she had barely touched her breakfast but didn't comment until she was upstairs.

"Did she eat at all?" He whispered as Miguel stared at him, his little finger touching Jorge's tie.

"A little," Paige said with a sigh. "I'm worried. She picks."

"We must watch this closely."

"But really," Paige said as she pushed her plate aside. "That's always been the case. I don't remember her ever eating a lot."

Jorge made a face and looked down at his baby.

"This is what I was saying the other day," Paige reminded him. "This political thing, it's taking so much of your time and...I feel like your family needs you now. The kids are young. It's like you said to Maria. She's only going to be 12 once. Miguel is only going to be a baby once. You've often said you regret the time you were away from Maria when she was this young. I...I don't want you to have the same regret with Miguel."

"I know, *mi amor,* you are right," Jorge replied as his wife stood up and took her plate and fork to the dishwasher, leaving her untouched coffee behind. "When Alec gets here today, I must insist he find someone else immediately."

"But the problem is," Paige reminded him as she opened the dishwasher. "You're outshining everyone. You're getting the most donations and if you're bringing in the most money, they're not going to let you go easily."

Jorge didn't reply but looked back down at his son. He gurgled and drool fell on Jorge's tie.

By the time Alec arrived, Jorge had an idea.

"I have some thoughts," He began before reaching his chair behind the desk. "About who could maybe run in this leadership race."

"I gotta talk to you about something first," Alec cut him off as he sat in his usual chair, a pensive expression on his face. "Unfortunately, you're not going to like what I have to say."

"And this is something new?" Jorge asked as he sat down. "What you got?"

"It's kind of a good news, bad news thing," Alec continued as he ran a hand over his lower face. "The good news is that you're miles ahead of everyone else in the race for leadership but the bad news is…"

"Is that not the bad news you just tell me?" Jorge didn't bother to hide his irritation. "How many times do I have to tell you that I'm not doing this for real?"

"I know but….Jorge, if you run, you could win," Alec insisted. "Like, not just for leadership but in the election, for prime minister. People find you intriguing."

"Do not cater to my ego," Jorge said and shook his head. "This here, it is not going to work for me. My life, it is not going to be a political game. As you recall, I only did this to help out and rise your party out of the shithole that you got yourselves into. Now, this, it is your problem, not mine."

"I….I don't know if I've ever seen anyone that connected with people like you do," Alec said while he shook his head. "I know-

"Look, I am done," Jorge insisted. "I have enough work with Our House of Pot, I do not have time for this too. My family, they need me here. I cannot be traveling all the time. I cannot be in this insane political world. This here, it would be better suited for someone like you."

"Me? No, I-

"What?" Jorge cut him off. "You're what? People like you. People *know* you. Look how you did in our last election. This is not impossible. You do what I'm doing."

"I'm not you," Alec said and shook his head. "I don't have your charisma. I don't have your power. That's what people are drawn to."

"Then get it!" Jorge insisted and leaned forward. "Figure it out."

"There's something else," Alec continued. "This, you really won't like."

"This, of course, is no surprise," Jorge said and leaned back in his chair.

"Remember how the campaign buttons came out of nowhere?" Alec began to speak slowly and waited until Jorge gave a vague nod before continuing. "I heard Big Pharma had something to do with it. They want you in so they can try to take over your company while you're busy with politics."

"Like fuck, they will!" Jorge spoke with fury in his voice and hit his fist against the desk. "Over my dead fucking body, they'll take over my company. Fuck you, fuck your party, fuck all of you because my company, it is more important than this fucking election. Figure it out!"

"But, hear me out," Alec said defensively with a hand in the air. "Don't you think it's kind of convenient that it was leaked? Don't you think that they wanted it to get back to you for a reason?"

"All I know is that I will always fight Big Pharma until I'm dead in my grave and then, I'll return from my place in hell to fight them some more," Jorge spoke with a steady voice even though he felt his face burning up. "Those fuckers, they will never win."

"See that's the point," Alec calmly replied as he leaned forward. "They wanted to make sure you knew this information because they knew how you would react. As much as they are trying to build you up, don't think they aren't working on the other side too. They know that the minute you hear this, you'll drop out and that we have lost our key player. It makes it easier when the election rolls around."

Jorge didn't respond and shook his head.

"The problem is we need to find someone as strong as you and fast," Alec spoke with some reluctance. "The alternative is…"

"There is no alternative," Jorge snapped. "This here, it has to end."

"But if Big Pharma gets their way and gets their party in," Alec gently reminded him. "That could affect you too. They want to criminalize pot again. They want you out so they'll find a way."

"Once again, the solution is clear," Jorge reminded him. "Find someone else, someone strong who can do this. There are how many people living in this country? There has to be at least one that fits."

"It's not that easy," Alec insisted. "If you'll meet with.."

"No!" Jorge sternly replied. "I've met with these people before and yet, this temporary situation wasn't so temporary, was it?"

Alec shook his head.

"Look, I know you don't care what I think," Alec said with some apprehension. "But you would be the best person to run this country. You know all sides of things. You know what it's like to be rich and poor, to be an immigrant, how to deal with business, there are so many advantages."

"Look, I do understand," Jorge found himself relaxing slightly because he could sense Alec's sincerity. "But I do not want this and really, neither should this party. The people who say I do not know much about Canadian politics, they are right. I do not."

"That's why you hire a good staff. That's what they're for," Alec spoke slowly. "We're here to give our advice and tell you what you need to know. You're the CEO in this case, you're the face of the country. You don't have to know everything about the history of Canada or politics, you just have to listen to your advisers. That's how this really works."

"To me, that shouldn't be," Jorge replied. "That seems like a deception."

"Maybe," Alec agreed and seemed to relax. "But isn't it all to a degree?"

"Alec, do you know what I want?" Jorge spoke thoughtfully. "Right now, my life? Do you know what I want?"

Alec shook his head.

"I want a peaceful life," Jorge replied. "I want to control my company and take care of problems, then go home at night, see my family, have dinner, have sex and go to sleep. That's all I want. I don't want to be traveling all over the world and pretending to like people who I do not like. I don't want to be making speeches and kissing asses. I don't want to be dealing with asshole leaders from other countries and some, they are genuine assholes, I've met a few in my day. I don't want any of that. To me, that's politics."

"I understand," Alec replied uncomfortably. "I really do."

"I know you do," Jorge considered his words for a moment. "Because at the end of the day, you are a simple man. You appreciate the simple things."

Alec nodded.

"Look, find a great candidate," Jorge insisted. "Maybe a woman, that would be more ideal. I am finished."

"You've already helped a lot," Alec replied and gave a stiff nod. "I will bring this back to them."

Jorge nodded and watched the man across from him. He knew Alec meant well but he also knew he was a puppet on a political string.

CHAPTER 40

"I will take them out before they take me over," Jorge commented as the group shared a drink following their 'family meal' at the Hernandez residence. After an evening of listening to Maria talk about her disappointing summer auditions and a few minutes of the group gushing over the baby, the children were now upstairs allowing the *familia* to discuss business.

"Big Pharma, they will never take you over," Diego immediately jumped in with his usual vigor even though his eyes told another story. "If they think they can win, they're sadly mistaken."

"Well, they won't win this round just as they haven't won any round before," Jorge reminded the group. "This here, it is a game. But me, I don't play by their rules. I will do whatever it takes to send a message to these fuckers."

"But sir," Jesús spoke up as he gently placed his utensils on the plate. "These people, they do not scare easily. Even if we were to take out a CEO, you know they'd have someone replace that person. It will look quite suspicious if all these people….you know.."

"Make it look like an accident," Paige threw in with ease. "Or suicides. After a while, people get the message."

"Regardless," Jorge decided to switch gears. "I must get out of politics and they have to find someone else. I am no longer interested in playing this ridiculous game. My focus must be the company."

"But who?" Jolene was quick to throw in. "It does not sound like they find someone."

"That's because they aren't trying hard enough," Chase reminded them. "Jorge, they want you so they're not gonna look."

"If they think it's that easy to manipulate me," Jorge said and took a deep breath. "They got another thing coming to them."

"Maybe *we* have to find another candidate and build them up," Paige considered and Jorge leaned in and touched her arm as the two shared a look. "Someone relatable...."

"Chase?" Jorge turned his attention to the youngest member of the group. "He is half indigenous, nice looking, young, down to earth, all these things."

"I don't know politics," Chase said and began to laugh. "As if this country would vote for someone who's young *and* indigenous. Not likely."

"Well, they were ready to vote me in," Jorge commented with laughter in his voice. "At least you were born here. Fuck, I haven't even been here that long, you know?"

"When you have to find an immigrant to do the work Canadians don't wanna do," Diego mocked. "Clean your house, do your pedicures, run your country....you know.."

Everyone laughed and Jorge quickly joined in.

"That will be my campaign slogan," Jorge joked. "Immigrants, we do all the things you don't like to do...and more!"

Everyone laughed again.

"Hey, how about you, Diego," Jorge continued to joke. "First gay prime minister."

"That we know of!" Diego laughed and clapped his hands together.

"Hey now, do not start rumors," Jorge teased.

"I say, Jolene," Diego replied. "A woman, an immigrant..."

"Yes, in the House of Commons arguing with people," Paige joked and shared a look with Jolene who widened her eyes and began to laugh hysterically.

"And sir, if she didn't get along with the other members," Jesús jumped in. "She would take out a gun and threaten them."

Jolene's laughter grew louder.

"Calm down," Diego instructed her while shaking his head. "This is what I always tell you, Jolene, you're embarrassing when you laugh like a crazy person. You're gonna wake up the baby."

"Oh Diego, you are joyless," Jolene immediately defended herself. "You do not know how to laugh at yourself and enjoy life. This is why you're so stressed and cranky."

"Ok, let's not argue," Jorge quickly cut in before the two got off track. "Listen to this. When I talked to Alec the other day, you know, telling him to find someone else. He was so nervous when he left that he turns to me and said, 'I'm not going to be the next person who goes missing, am I'?"

Everyone laughed again.

"I say, not if you find another candidate," Jorge continued to grin as he reached for his wine and the others continued to laugh. "I told him to do it himself. People, they like him."

"But not as much as you," Paige reminded him.

"Then find someone they do like," Jorge insisted. "This here is getting out of control. I told him he has a few more days and that's it, I will be dropping out, one way or another."

"I feel like they're using you for your charisma," Paige said as she pushed her plate aside. "All they want is someone to build up their party and to get the most funding. You've done that and if you decide to drop out for family reasons, people would understand. The party only gains from this deception."

"This is true" Jorge agreed.

"We must solve this problem," Jesús insisted. "It is taking too much time."

"I agree," Jorge nodded and turned toward Paige. "I haven't the time or interest for politics. I have worked hard for many years and now I wish to enjoy my life."

Something caught the corner of his eye. He turned to see Maria sneaking downstairs with a strange look on her face. Immediately locked in fear, he could barely find his voice.

"Maria! What is wrong?"

Everyone turned toward the child as she hesitantly walked down the stairs and entered the dining room. Her eyes full of fear, causing Paige to jump up from her chair.

"Is it Miguel?"

"No," Maria quickly answered. "He is fine. Juliana is with him."

"Then what is the matter?" Jorge asked as she made her way to the table and Paige hesitantly returned to her chair. "Maria, you are scaring me."

At first, she didn't speak, her eyes scanning the faces around the table before landing on Diego then Jorge.

"Papa, I have something to tell you."

He felt his heart race and feared the worst even though, logically, Jorge knew that his daughter was often overly dramatic. She had been fine over dinner.

"What is it Maria," Jorge reached out and touched her arm, coaxing her to move closer. "Are you sick?"

She shook her head.

"Maria, you are worrying me, please tell me what is wrong."

"Why isn't Michael here tonight?" She directed her question at Diego. "Did you two break up?"

His eyes widened, as if unsure of how to answer her question.

"Did he do something?" Maria continued and everyone around the table grew serious. "Something bad?"

"I...we...it wasn't working out," Diego finally said. "I haven't seen him in days."

"Did he do something to you?" Maria continued to pry and Jorge wondered where this was coming from since she hadn't been close to Diego's former boyfriend.

"Well," Diego began to answer and glanced at Jorge before doing so. "He....he was actually married, Maria. He was married to a woman and I had no idea."

"He lied?" Maria quietly asked.

"Yes," Diego calmly replied with sadness in his eyes. "It was complicated but...you know, things weren't good."

"Maria, why do you ask these things?" Jorge asked suspiciously. "Did something happen that made you wonder."

"I just saw online that he was missing," Maria started and everyone exchanged looks, Jesús and Jolene were the first to pull out their phones. "It's on the news."

"Oh, well, Maria," Jorge quickly took over. "He is a police officer, so you know, his job, it is dangerous."

"Don't worry," Diego quickly jumped in. "I'm sure they will find him."

Maria studied his face for a moment before she replied, "I hope not."

Stunned, Jorge looked between his daughter and an equally shocked Diego.

"Maria!" He quickly jumped in and squeezed her shoulder. "This here, it is rude not to mention…cruel."

"*Papa,* they broke up and he did something mean to Diego," Maria reminded him. "He deserves what happens to him."

Jorge was genuinely stunned by her comment and didn't know what to say. Fortunately, Paige jumped in.

"Maria, where is this coming from?" She spoke gently. "This isn't like you. I thought you liked Michael."

Jorge watched his daughter shrug then finally shake her head as her nose curled up.

"He was not a nice man, Diego," She quickly informed him with a serious expression. "He was a very bad man."

Diego appeared stunned and shared a look with Jorge.

"Maria," Jorge spoke calmly even though his heart raced. "Did Michael, did he do something to you?"

He noted Chase's face harden while Jolene leaned forward.

"He threatened me," Maria admitted and made eye contact with her father. Jorge immediately knew she was telling the truth. "I saw him. He was looking in your office one day and I asked him why. He said if I told you that he was in there, he would arrest you and Paige….everyone….and me and Miguel would be in foster homes."

Jorge was too stunned to reply.

"I was so scared he was going to take you all away," Maria's voice caught and huge tears formed in her eyes. Jorge promptly pulled her into his arms while everyone at the table fell silent and exchanged looks. Feeling his body grow weak, Jorge couldn't even speak.

CHAPTER 41

"You were very brave tonight," Jorge spoke gently to his daughter after walking Maria to her room and giving her another hug. The anger he felt seething through his veins was carefully hidden in case she mistook it as being directed at her. Above all else, he would always protect his daughter. "I am sorry you had to experience this terrible situation."

"It's not your fault, *Papa,*" Maria slowly let him go and stood back. She had grown so tall over the summer but her eyes were full of innocence. "I was very scared. I don't know what I would ever do if you all went to jail."

"Maria, that is simply not going to happen," Jorge insisted even though in reality, it was a possibility. "He was trying to frighten you because he knew he was in the wrong. Was it only that one time?"

Maria nodded. "I think you had forgotten to lock it."

"And this was?"

"In the summer," Maria answered. "Everyone was in the kitchen. Maybe he went to the bathroom or something?"

Jorge nodded.

"*Papa,* maybe I shouldn't have said anything in front of everyone," Maria said as she began to fidget. "It's just that I saw that story on the news.."

"This is good, Maria," Jorge replied. "I thank you for being honest with us and I promise, he will never bother you again."

Maria nodded and didn't reply.

When Jorge returned to the dining room, he could see that everyone was already discussing the topic and looking at their phones.

"Is she ok?" Diego immediately asked as he rose from his chair, his eyes full of worry. "Was there anything else?"

"She is fine," Jorge replied as he returned to his seat and Diego hesitantly did the same. "This was very unexpected."

"I'm sorry," Diego said and started to shake his head. "I had…"

"Diego, this is fine," Jorge replied and put up his hand to indicate that he stop speaking. "No one here blames you. It is in the past but now, we must focus on finding who he worked for, if anyone."

"What if he was working for himself?" Jesús asked as he looked up from his phone. "Or for the police?"

"Nah, he hated his work," Diego insisted. "He was crooked."

"Maybe he had no choice?" Jesús asked with a shrug.

"It is a possibility," Jorge considered. "But he was a dirty cop. He could've been taking money from anyone."

"But when he tried to shoot you," Jolene said in a quiet voice and glanced toward the stairs. "Do you think he was hired? Would he not try again?"

Jorge thought about everything for a moment and finally shook his head.

"I do not know," He admitted. "In truth, we are only guessing. He is no longer a threat but it is important we learn if there are others to worry about."

"But why break loyalty to us?" Chase asked as he sat his phone down.

"He never had it to begin with," Jorge said with a shrug. "He led us to believe the opposite but as time went on, we saw him less."

"But if he was trying to kill you," Jolene spoke slowly. "Should we not be seeing him more?"

"Not if he thought we were on to him," Paige immediately picked up the conversation. "That's probably why he was looking around the office. He probably got paranoid over time and wanted to see if we suspected anything. Maria caught him and he threatened her so she wouldn't tell us."

"But what?" Jorge asked. "What would make him think this?"

"Let's start back at the beginning," Paige gently replied. "At first, he wanted to be part of everything."

"He was very anxious to get the white supremacists, remember?" Diego piped up.

"That was an excuse," Jesús replied. "He knew in the confusion, he could shoot Jorge and no one would probably ever suspect him."

"Except he got Paige instead and he knew if I ever found out," Jorge glanced at his wife. "It would be the end of him."

"He was doing it for someone," Chase added and shrugged. "What other reason would he have?"

"None that I know of," Jorge replied. "And let's face it, there is probably someone who would pay the price."

"He was part of two households," Paige gently replied. "It could've been about money."

"Maybe he was pressured by someone to do it," Jolene suggested with a knowing look in her eye. "They find out he's with Diego and has a wife… blackmail? Is that the word? Blackmail?"

"That would make sense," Diego said, ignoring her question and turned toward Jorge. "What do you think?"

"I think we are only guessing again," Jorge suggested. "We must find out who he is connected with. That might be our answer."

"He wanted to make it look like an accident and then when it didn't work," Paige thought for a moment. "He avoided us."

"Guilt," Chase commented. "He shot a pregnant lady."

"We are going in circles here," Jorge reminded them. "We must look at the next step. Marco has already been checking his computer. I will talk to him tomorrow and explain why it is important that we find any connections. I think we may never know the truth."

Everyone fell silent.

The thought plagued him well into the night. While Paige slept beside him, Jorge went over everything again and again. He wasn't getting further ahead but instead, only growing more confused. He eventually drifted off.

The next morning, Maria seemed more chipper than she had been in weeks. It made Jorge see how much the entire secret had weighed on her heart. She even ate a reasonable breakfast for a change. If nothing else, there was that.

Diego had promised to speak with Marco and work with him to find something on Michael's computer but it seemed unlikely. He was a cop so chances were good, he knew how to cover his tracks.

After Paige returned from dropping Maria off at school, she found Jorge on the couch with a drink in hand.

"It's a little early for that, isn't it?" She gently chided him as she sat beside him. "We'll figure this out."

"Paige, I don't like this," Jorge admitted. "Not just what Maria told us last night but the political thing, everything. It is like, I want to have a peaceful life and yet, no one will let me. There is always something else around the corner."

"There always will be," Paige said as she moved closer to him, her hand reaching for his as she smiled. "That's life but maybe you're making this too complex. You can drop out of politics today. This minute actually, you don't owe anyone anything. As for the Michael situation, remember when you guys went to see Dolores Stumples? You told me that you were going to shoot her but he did instead."

"Yes, he went crazy," Jorge said, remembering the lady from Big Pharma that had a hit out on Makerson months earlier. "I mean, he shot her with every bullet in his gun."

"Exactly, that's unusual," Paige reminded him as she curled her legs up on the couch. "Then remember, Diego said he had PTSD?"

"Yeah," Jorge rolled his eyes. "If you ask me, that was just to get the attention of Diego."

"Perhaps but it does suggest a pattern," Paige gently pointed out and Jorge turned his attention toward her. "He overreacts and then repents or grows anxious. He wanted to shoot you for whatever reason. He got me instead. His conscience built up over the months and he started to panic, searched your office, was caught and threatened Maria so she wouldn't talk."

"This does make sense," Jorge said as his phone began to ring. It was Alec. "I wish I knew for sure."

"It's a possibility," Paige suggested as Jorge reached for his phone.

"Yeah, what you got Alec?"

"One last event and you're done," Alec confirmed. "After that, you'll be in the race but keep a low profile while we move the other person in."

"Excellent!" Jorge replied and felt relief in his heart. "And who's the guy?"

"You're not going to believe it."

CHAPTER 42

"You've got to be fucking kidding me, right?" Jorge said as soon as he sat across from Alec in the quiet coffee shop. They had purposely chosen somewhere away from the downtown area, a place where little attention would be given them. "This here, it is not real? I gotta tell you, today, I am not in the mood for these kinds of jokes."

"It's not a joke," Alec quickly reassured him with a straight face as he reached for his coffee. "I promise."

Jorge didn't reply at first, instead, he looked out a nearby window and shook his head.

"If you fucking pissed in your coffee and drank it, I wouldn't be more surprised," His comment was abrupt as he let out a loud sigh. "This is fucking unbelievable."

"Ok, at least hear me out," Alec insisted as he leaned forward on the table. "There's a little more to the story."

Jorge simply shrugged and rolled his eyes.

"She met with the prime minister and some of the key members of the party and managed to convince them," Alec continued and lowered his voice. "She's serious about this."

Jorge didn't speak.

"I know what you're thinking…"

"No, Athas, I assure you, you do *not* know what I'm thinking."

"But Elizabeth Alan *is* well-known for the work she did with Canadians for Conservative Values. People like and trust her. People listen to her."

"Have you lost your fucking minds," Jorge jumped in angrily. "She's for *conservative* values. Us here, that is not what our party is about and if you have forgotten, she wanted to criminalize pot again. So what? Now the party wants to take it away? I don't fucking think so."

"No no!" Alec's eyes grew in size. "No, she doesn't want that now. She doesn't believe that anymore. She went through this whole transformation."

"I bet."

"She did, she really did," Alec insisted. "I was skeptical too but she managed to convince all the people who matter. Look, this is good for the party because she can use that narrative, that story to show why we need the pot shops to continue. She'll be on your side."

"The white lady who was against me not long ago?" Jorge asked as he reached for his coffee and took a drink; it was bitter. "You expect that her and I, now we become best friends and she wants to help me out? You do not think people will see through this? That you want to whore out the recognizable faces in Canada? That is what this is about, right? Why you want me? Why you want her? People know us."

"That's not true," Alec insisted and shook his head. "She's changed her mind and if the people see that *she's* changed her mind, they might too. She gives a powerful case for increasing marijuana consumption."

Jorge raised an eyebrow.

"Apparently," Alec looked away and back at Jorge. "Her sister, she has some serious health problems. She stumbled on a documentary talking about the healing effects of cannabis and out of desperation, started to use it and it helped. It helped a lot. She felt better than she had in years. Apparently, she told this story to Elizabeth Alan, who in turn started to do her own research, talk to different people and now, she sees the other side of the coin."

Jorge felt his ears perk up but he was still somewhat skeptical.

"Ok, so maybe, she does believe all of this here," Jorge said and paused. "Even if she does, will that be enough? What else does she got?"

"She has a huge following, that's what she's got," Alec took out his iPad and showed Jorge a Twitter account and pointed at her followers. To this, Jorge showed no interest.

"I know, you don't care about social media," Alec continued. "Look, she's speaking openly about her change of heart and people are responding. Some are going to jump ship but others, they'll listen. It's not just the pot angle, it's the honesty factor. People trust her like they trust you. They believe you because of your...extreme honesty and that's why they like her too."

"I do not think she's strong enough," Jorge shook his head.

"Have you seen her lately?" Alec challenged. "Because she sings your praises."

"Me?" Jorge asked and began to laugh.

"Yes, you," Alec insisted as he searched his iPad. "She recently recorded a video talking about how she had misjudged you. How she held you in great esteem for being brave enough to push against strong opinions and even your own party. She's been very vocal on the subject."

Turning the iPad around, Jorge watched as Elizabeth Alan's face appeared on the screen.

....he has forced us, as Canadians to take a hard look at ourselves. We want to believe that Canada is a nation that is built on multiculturalism and acceptance but Jorge Hernandez has been very vocal on the fact that he experiences racism every day. His campaign has demonstrated the division in Canadians because on one side, you have people walking around Toronto wearing his buttons, speaking of how refreshing his campaign is and on the other, you have people who started to feel it was acceptable to spew hatred. It's very sad, especially considering the terrible tragedy that took place this summer.....

Alec turned the iPad around and hit a button causing the screen to go black.

"I'll send it to you later," He commented as he shoved the device back in his bag. "I know it's hard to believe but she talks about you all the time. She admires you."

"I am shocked."

Leaning forward on the table, Alec briefly studied his face.

"If she gets in...and you *know* how to get her in," Alec spoke in a hushed tone. "This is someone you can control. You can make her exactly what you want."

"Are we sure about this?" Jorge asked with some hesitation. "This is not a thing where she tricks us, gets in and changes her entire point of view."

"She can't," Alec insisted. "She's locked into the party's ideology. Trust me, you got to almost sign it in blood it's so sacred. To go against it, would be like going against you."

Jorge grinned and raised his eyebrows.

"So this here," Jorge pointed toward the bag Alec had put his iPad in. "Before I believe anything, I must meet with her. I need to know if I trust her and if I do, then we can figure out how to have my grand finale."

"We still need you to do that one last speech later this week," Alec insisted. "We're at an all-time high now. Our polls are even higher than we ever anticipated when this started. It's important that you give them one, last strong speech before you gracefully bow out."

"I can do that."

"But Jorge, for what it's worth," Alec said as he looked into his eyes. "You could win this thing. The leadership, prime minister, all of it. If you wanted to, you could have power over the country."

"You know that power," Jorge laughed self-consciously. "You know that this is what I strive for and as you say, my weak point. I believe that few things are as important as power. Love, it is the only thing and unfortunately, *mi amor*, she does not want me involved in politics and yes, I do understand why. If I were a single man, I would throw it all at the wind but as a man with a family, I must be more cautious. I must try to keep my dirty laundry out of sight, you know."

"It makes sense," Alec replied and nodded. "But you have managed this long."

"Alec, I will tell you a story," Jorge said with some hesitation. "It was brought to my attention that Diego's former boyfriend, he threatened my Maria. When she found him snooping through my office months ago, he said if she were to tell me he would make sure me and my entire family was arrested."

Alec's eyes grew in size.

"Of course, Michael and Diego, they broke up and the man, he is missing," Jorge continued and ignored the skeptical look in Alec's eyes. "But that does not matter. What does matter is the look in my daughter's eyes when she tell me this here story. She was frightened. I knew something was wrong for weeks but I thought, it was because of the fires, because of the disappointment with auditions this summer. You know, a new school this fall. She's a teenager now, who knows, right?"

Alec nodded and his expression softened.

"Instead, it was because this man threatened her," Jorge paused and saw Alec nod in understanding. "It is better to keep a low profile sometimes and not tempt fate. I see that more than ever. I am usually the ultimate fate tempter but in this case, I have to think of my daughter when she tell me the story about Michael's threats. I cannot ever let this happen. Her mother, she is dead. Her grandparents, they are all dead. If we go to jail, my children have no one. Paige is right. We must keep a low profile."

Alec's face filled with sadness.

"And you, you know what I mean," Jorge reminded him. "You have lost family, your sister. And you also have…..well, you know what you have done."

Neither spoke for a moment. Of course, it had been many years since Alec had sought out retaliation toward the man he held responsible for his sister's death but it was his one, dark card that played against the ones full of light. It was leverage and in Jorge's experience, it was always good to have leverage.

"You know, Jorge, that I'm on your side," Alec finally replied. "Whatever you need."

"Right now, I need to meet this lady in private," Jorge replied. "Unless you would like to join us, that would be fine. I'm quite curious what she has to say."

"I will make it happen," Alec replied. "You can count on it."

CHAPTER 43

"You will excuse me if I find it hard to believe that you had such a change of heart in a few short months," Jorge bluntly commented as he walked into his office followed by both Alec Athas and Elizabeth Alan. Ignoring the look of disbelief on the middle-aged woman's face and the warning glance from Alec, Jorge gestured for both of them to sit down as he walked behind his desk. "I take it, you are no longer the moral police, Ms. Alan?"

"Well, I…" She stuttered and glanced at Alec as they sat across the desk from Jorge. "I will admit, it must seem a little hard to believe."

"A little?" Jorge gave an impish grin as he plunked down in his chair. "I would say so. You were my biggest opponent at one time and now, you want to work together?"

"Her situation changed," Alec reminded him. "A series of events have changed her views."

"So now, you what?" Jorge asked, purposely taunting her. "Smoke one when you got PMS or you want to get in the mood for your husband? Do tell me, Ms. Alan, what caused this sudden change of heart."

"It's not like that," Elizabeth put her hand up as if to insist on peace. "Please let me explain."

Jorge gestured for her to continue and listened with interest.

"When we had our debate a few months ago," She began with some hesitation, her eyes briefly looking toward the ground with the same shame as a teenager who was just caught fucking her boyfriend in the back of her parent's car. She finally looked up again with genuine sadness in her hazel eyes.

"What?" Jorge coaxed her.

"I was forced to face some harsh truths. The most important of which was that I had to stop trying to find someone or *something* to blame for my son's death. The truth is you *were* right. I couldn't blame pot for being a gateway drug. He was going to do what he was going to do regardless. I didn't want to admit that I saw it coming. I didn't want to admit that my son always had a very...erratic side to his personality. I was left facing a lot of things that I didn't want to deal with."

"I am sorry for that," Jorge spoke sincerely. "I do, also, have children and I can understand these feelings."

"Thank you," She replied and Jorge felt his original reluctance soften. "Then you can understand that burying my son was....." She stopped speaking and cleared her throat.

"Ms. Alan, we do not have to go through this," Jorge said as he sat forward in his seat. "I do, I understand. We often want to see the world as if it were black and white and often, there is a lot of grey, no?"

"Yes," She spoke softly and nodded. "It has been a very difficult journey and this summer, it was as if after our debate, all my theories, all my blame, everything, it fell apart. Piece by piece until there was nothing left."

Jorge noted that Alec put his head down and was quiet.

"So, I had to rebuild," She admitted and sat up a little straighter. "Part of that was discovering pot wasn't the root of all evil. This happened when someone close to me began to experiment with THC oil to deal with a debilitating illness. It completely changed her life. That's when I started to research it and discovered that maybe I had a lot to learn."

"This is fair," Jorge replied and nodded. "Once again, I am sorry for your loss and of course, all you recently dealt with. It does not sound like an easy journey."

"Thank you," She nodded with a small smile. "As much as I hated you the day of the debate, you forced me to do the work that I didn't want to do but it was necessary."

"This is good," Jorge said with a smile. "Everything, it does happen for a reason, no?"

"Absolutely," She softly replied.

"There's more too," Alec gently cut in. "Remember the group Canadians for Conservative Values? Wait till you hear this."

Jorge noted that Elizabeth was nodding, her original smile stiffened and her eyes turned cold.

"They used me," She spoke up bitterly. "They saw me doing these little videos talking about grief and losing my son and they swooped in and took advantage. They realized that I had a lot of anger and sadness, that I was vulnerable and needed a cause so they pretended to care only to get me as a sympathetic spokesperson for their group."

"She had thousands of hits on social media," Alec added. "That was the draw."

"Yes and to be honest," Elizabeth continued. "I didn't care about that. I didn't look at the Facebook likes or shares or whatever and think 'Wow, look how popular I am!'. I did it because I needed to do something or I was going to lose my mind. I did it because I thought maybe I would connect with another parent who needed to know they weren't alone. I never did it to manipulate anyone and I certainly didn't do it to be manipulated."

"Yes, they showed her a lot of....*facts*," Alec said with some hesitation. "Facts that helped her form an opinion on marijuana."

"Yes because as I said," Elizabeth jumped in. "I was vulnerable. I wanted someone to blame so when they come along with this so-called *research* that said that pot was a gateway drugs then asked if my son ever smoked it....they made it too easy. They made it too *fucking* easy."

"Woo!" Jorge said as he widened his eyes and began to laugh. "I did not expect this language from you."

"It infuriates me," Elizabeth seemed to ignore the two men who were grinning from ear to ear and exchanging looks. "You don't understand. I'm so angry about how they weaseled their way into my life. It actually makes me sick."

"That's how cults work," Alec gently offered. "They find people in vulnerable situations and take advantage."

"They showed me research and information that suggested that our family values in Canada were shattered, that media, pop culture is to blame," Elizabeth added. "I can't believe I fell for it. My friends, my family were so worried about me but were willing to put up with my craziness because I sounded a bit like myself again."

"This here, it does not surprise me," Jorge spoke with compassion in his voice. "There is a time after someone we love dies where….our world can be reshaped. Sometimes, it is for the good and sometimes, it is not. But Ms. Alan, I do not wish to focus too much on the past and I believe, neither should you. You must move on and the best revenge, I believe, is success."

A smile lit up her face and she nodded.

"I'm not sure how much Alec has told you about me," Jorge continued as he glanced at Athas briefly who gave a skeptical look. "But I'm no longer interested in running for the leader of this party. I am….preoccupied with both my business and my family. I have young children that need my attention. This is time I can never get back so I am sure you can appreciate why I must bow out gracefully."

"I do understand," Elizabeth nodded and moved forward in her chair. "Mr. Hernandez, if I were me in your shoes, I would do the same thing. Believe me, I would." There was something in her eyes that made him trust her. A depth, a warmth, filled with many regrets and sadness. He had to look away. Taking a deep breath, he began to nod.

"I am ready to drop out very soon," Jorge continued, his voice softer than it had been earlier in their conversation. "I am prepared to endorse you, of course. Provided that you have a reasonable platform."

"We're working on that," Alec commented. "Her beliefs are similar to yours; immigration, health care, reasonable rent rates, better paying jobs…."

Jorge nodded but didn't reply.

"She has experience in politics and working with campaigns," Alec added. "Has served on various boards, volunteered, owned her own business…"

"What kind of business?" Jorge asked with interest.

"Nothing too fancy," She laughed. "Just a bakery."

"Ah! Do you know of this French bakery downtown?" Jorge said. "With the amazing pastries…the little one, it is near our offices?"

"Yes!" Elizabeth spoke enthusiastically. "Isn't it amazing?"

"My wife, she will not allow me near it anymore," Jorge joined her in laughter. "Too many pastries."

"The only concern we're having is that people may feel she's not qualified enough," Alec continued, getting back to business. "She has been involved in politics but never ran. She's well known in Toronto but not the rest of the country."

"I've volunteered during many elections since finishing university," She shrugged. "I even worked for an MLA but never took the plunge even though people said I should."

"But I must ask," Jorge said as he leaned on his desk. "Why this? Why politics? Why not the city council? Why not, you know, something smaller? Why the leader of this party and potential prime minister?"

"Because I'm tired of sitting on the couch yelling at the tv," She replied. "I'm tired of seeing so many people struggling. I'm tired of the rich getting richer. I'm tired of people falling in the same situation as my son."

"Do you know," She glanced between the two men. "After my son died, I found something he wrote to a friend on his computer. It was an email where he talked about how hopeless he felt about the world. He talked about unemployment rates, how a couple of his friends had gone to college or university and now flipped burgers for a living. He talked about how expensive it was to live and how he wasn't sure he would ever be able to afford an apartment, a car.....anything. He talked about how hopeless it seemed because he didn't have talents, or gifts, how he had nothing to give the world."

Jorge listened with interest.

"And it occurred to me," Elizabeth slowly continued. "There's lots of young people who feel the same. That's not because we, as people or parents fail. It's because of our country, our economy has failed us. The jobs aren't there. The expenses keep growing. Someone has to get this under control and I'm tired of sitting back and watching."

"Ah! Yes," Jorge nodded in agreement. "What you say, it is true. That is what people need and what you have to do is to share this story but you must also be ready to fight. There will be people who try to tear you down."

"I'm a mother who lost my son," She spoke with fire in her eyes. "Nothing and no one can ever rip me down after that."

Jorge saw the sadness in her eyes and merely nodded.

CHAPTER 44

"You don't really believe this, do you?" Paige asked with some hesitation as she placed Miguel in his crib. "That she has a chance in hell of winning? Nothing you said convinces me."

"Paige, she just...she had a compelling way of expressing this, you know?" Jorge searched for the words but found he was falling flat.

Avoiding her gaze, he walked over to the crib and looked down at his son. Miguel had grown so much since the day of his birth. Had Maria at this age? He shamefully couldn't remember. Jorge had been away so much and missed more milestones in her development than he cared to admit. Miguel briefly opened his eyes, looked directly at Jorge then closed them again.

Turning away, he took a deep breath. Scratching his head, he looked at Paige who had watched him carefully with interest. Her face was expressionless.

"To tell you the truth," Jorge finally admitted as he moved away from the crib and Paige followed as they headed toward the door. "I do not know. This here, it has spun out of control."

Paige didn't reply but took his hand and led him out of the room. Standing in the hallway, she looked into his eyes and finally spoke.

"Let's make a pot of coffee," Paige calmly suggested. "And talk about this once and for all. The house is quiet. Maria is at school. Juliana is out. Let's avoid our phones and really talk."

Jorge nodded and followed her downstairs. Paige went to work making the coffee while he glanced at his phone quickly then set it aside. He briefly considered turning it off however if there were an emergency, especially with Maria, it was imperative that it be nearby.

"Paige, have you ever considered having a phone," He pointed toward the wall and searched for the word in English. *"De linea fija?"*

"A landline?" Paige asked as she turned on the coffee maker. "Really?"

"I was thinking, maybe for times we do not want to deal with our phones," Jorge considered. "For emergencies. Only the school, Diego, the others have it."

"But aren't they the same people who have our cell numbers?" Paige asked evenly.

"Yes, but you know, our phones are more distracting," Jorge commented and took a deep breath. "And do you really want to be attached to it every second of the day? This here, it gets tired. Why not have a house phone for emergencies. We are too dependent on technology, no?"

Paige considered the idea and nodded.

"I…I do not always want to carry my phone everywhere," Jorge pointed toward the door. "Out there, yes but in my house? Sometimes, I would like to turn it off completely."

"I will look into it tomorrow."

"Sometimes Paige," Jorge continued. "I think the old ways, they are coming back. Books and not e-readers. Phones attached to the wall and not in our pocket. Maybe the world isn't making us insane maybe *we* are making ourselves insane."

"I think you're probably right," Paige nodded in agreement. "Maybe it's time to slow down a bit."

The coffee finished brewing and Paige quickly fixed them each a cup. She knew exactly how Jorge liked his while ironically, he never seemed to get it right. He smiled as she passed him his cup and they made their way into the living room.

"Let's start with Elizabeth Alan," Paige spoke thoughtfully as they sat on the couch. "Do you really think she can win?"

"No," He answered automatically before taking a drink of his coffee. "This here, is really good, Paige."

"Don't change the subject," She teased. "So you don't think she can win?"

"Not even for a second."

"But you'll endorse her?"

"Sure."

Paige paused for a moment.

"So are you encouraging her because you want your way out," Paige ran her finger over the rim of the mug. "Or are you encouraging her because you plan to continue to run and know you can squash her?"

Jorge laughed and looked away.

"I'm just...curious," She appeared to choose her words carefully. "Ever since this began I haven't been able to shake the feeling that you actually want to do this. That you love the power, the idea of running this country. I know you keep saying you don't but..."

Jorge stared into her eyes for a moment and thought about what to say.

"I will not lie, it has crossed my mind many times," He replied and moved closer to her. "When I am up there, giving a speech or during an interview. I feel powerful. I feel like I'm stronger than I ever have been before but yet, I do not like the everyday nonsense. I do not like every word I say being analyzed or having to apologize because I have offended someone. That is not me."

Paige nodded and showed no judgment.

"But do I want to take the good with the bad?" Jorge asked and glanced across the room, his eyes drifting toward the stairs. "Do I want to be separated from my family all the time? Do I want to put my company on the back burner while I focus on an entire country? Do I want to learn all the details behind Canadian politics and history? Do I want to learn French and be criticized always for my broken English? Do I want my past dug up?"

"You know," Paige started and tilted her head. "Some of the most powerful people in the world are involved in politics but only from behind the scenes. Aren't politicians merely the puppets on the string and not the ideas people? Aren't they there as the spokesperson more than they are the visionary?"

Jorge raised his eyebrow and nodded.

"Remember when you first met Alec?" Paige reminded him. "You said you were just getting started with him. That you wanted to take him all the way to the top. What changed that? Why can't we do that? You know he will do whatever you say. You know he believes in you and your ideas. That's why you're in *this* situation in the first place. I think it should be him that takes over. Make him see that he *can* do this."

"Yes, I agree," Jorge considered. "I must convince him to join the race then make him into me. He will be the lion that devours them all to make it to the top."

"Exactly," Paige said as her hand gently touched his thigh. "As I said, the most powerful people in the world aren't the leaders. They're the people in the background, the ones no one knows about or suspects has any influence. Trust me, this is the best idea for everyone."

Her hand slid further up his thigh and his original stress quickly disappeared, replaced instead with sensations that flowed through his body. Suddenly, everything looked much different from only moments before and a sense of relief filled him as his passions grew.

Noting his wife was putting her coffee cup down, he quickly did the same before reaching forward to gently touch her face. Their lips met with an unexpected gentleness that quickly turned passionate. Leaning in closer, he felt his pants being unzipped, her fingers quickly moving inside to focus on the one spot that sent him over the edge.

"The door, it is locked?" He spoke breathlessly. "No one is coming home?"

"No time soon," She replied. "Juliana is gone all day. Maria's in school."

Hearing these words, Jorge ripped off his pants while she removed her shirt and pants, revealing only a bra and thong. He started to unbutton his shirt as he leaned forward to kiss her while she attempted to remove his tie, finally giving up instead using it to pull him even closer. He quickly moved on top of her as his breath increased, his heart pounded ferociously like an animal about to attack its prey. Previous thoughts of power disappeared as he fell into a world of pleasure, as his hands roamed over her body. Jorge's lips moved to her earlobe and she gasped as his fingers and tongue worked simultaneously, hitting her two weakest points at once, causing her to moan loudly, her body arched in response.

Pulling down his underwear, he slowly moved inside her causing Paige to let out a loud, animal-like sound that only caused him to want her more as he drove deeper and deeper inside of her. She wrapped her arms and legs around him as he thrust deep inside of her, disappearing into a world of pleasure as his face slowly moved against hers while unfamiliar sounds came from the back of his throat. He pushed a little harder and she let out a loud moan and as her body grew weak beneath him.

For a few moments, they laid in silence.

"This here," He finally began to speak in a hoarse voice. "This here has been a very compelling argument to spend more time at home, *mi amor.*"

She giggled and ran her hand through his hair.

"I was merely pointing out the possibilities," She whispered. "It's better to put everything on the table."

"This is true," He spoke lazily, not feeling compelled to move. "Do you think it will work? Can we convince Alec?"

"I'm positive," Paige replied.

"So I throw Elizabeth Alan to the wolves?"

"You mean, you weren't going to anyway?" Paige quietly asked.

"Possibly, yes," Jorge agreed. "But I wonder, where that leaves her?"

Paige looked up with a coldness in her eyes. "I really don't care. Do you?"

CHAPTER 45

"This is what I've been saying all along, *amigo*," Jorge spoke sternly from behind his desk while on the other side, Paige enthusiastically nodded as she turned toward Alec. "You, *you* should be the one. Not me. Not Elizabeth Alan or any of these other clowns. It should be you."

"I...I don't think," Alec shook his head. "I don't think I'm ready for this and people don't know me..."

"But they know Elizabeth Alan?" Paige cut in and laughed. Jorge quickly followed her lead. "If anything, her entering the race is proof that you don't exactly have to be a household name to enter."

"Exactly!" Jorge spoke with abruptness in his voice and raised his hands in the air. "Who the fuck is Elizabeth Alan? I don't care if she has a following online or whatever she says. We need strength. She, she doesn't have it."

"But you said you'd endorse her," Alec reminded him as he exchanged looks with both Paige and Jorge. "You can't turn your back on her now."

"Really? And why the fuck not?" Jorge quickly replied. "I do not think I owe her for anything. I can change my mind."

"I was behind her too," Alec replied nervously. "Suddenly, we both turn our backs on her."

"*Amigo*, let us be honest here," Jorge lowered his voice and leaned forward on his desk. "Do you really think she can win? She's lukewarm, at best. That is why she needed my endorsement. She knew she did not have a leg to stand on without me behind her, but me, I am a man who changes his mind. I go behind the powerful one and it is not her."

"You seemed convinced it was her the other day," Alec tested him skeptically. "I was there, remember?"

"Look, Paige had a discussion with me earlier today," Jorge commented with a shrug. "I was so anxious to step down that I saw what I wanted to see. Now, as I reflect, it is clear that I made a huge error. However, as Paige pointed out, this error has opened my eyes to how much stronger you would be in the leadership race."

"Look, with exception to Jorge," Paige quickly picked up the conversation. "The race is pretty soft. Most of the people who put their name in only did so to make the party seem solid, just as Jorge only got involved because you needed the boost after the disastrous summer. Your job was to find someone who would regain their trust and to prove that the party wasn't as neglectful."

"And that man, it is you," Jorge insisted enthusiastically. "You are trustworthy, people like you and you won your district by a landslide the last election."

"I think I had a little help from my friends," Alec reminded him as darkness covered his eyes.

"And my friend," Jorge leaned forward and stared into his eyes. "You will again."

Alec considered the idea for a moment and Jorge saw this is a good sign.

"Alec, you know I do not lie to you," Jorge commented as he leaned back in his chair and briefly glanced at his wife. "This here, it is your time. You must grab this opportunity."

"But I don't have the following you have," Alec returned to his original train of thought. "They want Jorge Hernandez. You're powerful and you give them a sense of hope."

"And you cannot?" Jorge spoke gently with a shrug. "You have heard my speeches, my interviews, you know what I tell people. All you have to do is to do the same. It is not difficult. You must talk about jobs, immigration, reasonable rent and give them a sense of hope, of comfort.

Elections are about promises. They want the boy next door as much as they want the powerful man and you're it."

"If Jorge endorses you and says he plans to advise you through the campaign and beyond," Paige jumped in. "That might give you the push you need. You will get his followers plus pick up some of your own, especially here in Toronto."

"Exactly," Jorge agreed. "My wife, she is always right."

Winking at Paige, Jorge noticed that Alec was leaning against his hand, deep in thought.

"*Amigo,*" Jorge jumped in. "Of course, you must go and think about this but do not look for reasons why it will not work. Instead, find ways it will and why you should do this. I assure you, I am right. You can win the leadership race and then we will make sure you win the election."

"I will…..I'll talk to the people at the top," Alec spoke with some hesitation. "And see what they say."

"They will, of course, say yes," Jorge said with enthusiasm. "When you explain everything we just discussed. Clearly, Elizabeth Alan, she will not be the one."

"My fear is that she is riding the party with no intentions of going with their beliefs," Paige suggested. "You know, she could say she's all for pot until she gets in and then starts making restrictions, going against the party on issues like abortion, immigration…"

"This is true, *mi amor,*" Jorge nodded enthusiastically. "She may have had a change of heart but perhaps, the change of heart, it is not that strong."

"You seemed convinced when we spoke to her," Alec reminded him again.

"I am convinced that at this moment, the lady thinks she has changed," Jorge commented and took a deep breath. "But when push comes to shove, perhaps not. She might crumble."

"We don't need to talk about her anymore," Paige shook her head. "This is about you, Alec. You need to put your hat in the race. You can win."

Alec's face softened when he looked at Paige.

"You do remember," Jorge abruptly added. "It was Paige that you wanted advisement from when you first decided to get into politics. You respected her opinions at that time. If you will not listen to me maybe you should consider listening to her. You know that she would not suggest something unless it was in your best interest."

"He's right," Paige quietly replied. "I've honestly thought it all along but could tell you were reluctant. However, since there's no promising candidates...."

Her voice trailed off and she looked away.

"Other than me, right?" Jorge teased. "*Mi amor,* my love, come on!"

She laughed and rolled her eyes.

Alec appeared lost in thought.

"So, what you think?" Jorge gently coaxed him and glanced briefly at Paige. "Do we make a good argument?"

"You do," Alec confirmed and glanced at both of them before standing up. "I..I'm going to have to think about this though."

"Don't think too long," Jorge insisted as he rose from his chair and Paige did the same. "This here has a short shelf life. I give a speech tomorrow and it is at that time I plan to step down and make my recommendations for who I feel would be a better candidate. My friend, I hope that this is you."

"Alec," Paige gently added. "Talk to whoever you need to but in the end, do what you feel is right. You'll have much more power to do what you've always talked about if you're prime minister. Right now, you're limited to your riding. This will give you the ability to do more."

"And of course," Jorge quickly jumped in. "You always have me and Paige as advisors. If you're ever not sure how to handle a situation, just think about what I would do."

Alec's eyes widened slightly and a humored grin crossed his lips.

"Within reason, of course," Paige said and began to laugh. "Maybe with a little more restraint than my husband."

"Restraint, *mi amor,* it is not my style," Jorge teased and winked at Paige. Alec seemed to relax as Jorge walked around the desk and offered his hand to shake. "We are here for you Alec, for whatever you need. *Anything.*"

Alec looked into his eyes and nodding, reached for Jorge's hand. The two men shook in silence.

It was after Paige showed Alec out and returned to the office that the couple shared a silent look. Paige with a grin on her face and Jorge with a pensive expression.

"It will be a whole new world, my love," Jorge finally spoke. "And we will run it."

"And the beauty," Paige replied as she sat down and crossed her legs. "Is that it'll be from behind the scenes. You don't have to have your face out there, you won't be under a microscope..."

"I don't have to learn all these details that I do not care about," Jorge added with a nod. "It will be easier. This is how we should've done it from the beginning."

"No, I don't know about that," Paige said and shook her head. "After everything that went down this summer, the country needed a distraction and for that, you were perfect. You're very charismatic, charming and you captivated them simply by being bold, blunt, that's what people liked about you. It rebuilt the party. I don't think Alec could've done that but now that the tedious work is required, he can step in with ease and with your guidance, we can make this happen."

"My love, we've got this," Jorge spoke with a smooth grin on his face as he leaned back in his chair. "We always win."

CHAPTER 46

As much as Jorge wanted to believe that he would have control over his last speech, he was wrong. Since he represented the party and they were already on shaky ground, Jorge was forced to meet with various people including the current prime minister and a PR specialist to discuss his strategy. By the time the early morning meetings were over, he was growing frustrated and exhausted by the ordeal.

"*Mi amor,*" Jorge turned to his wife shortly before they joined the *familia* for a quiet lunch at the *Princesa Maria*. Chase ordered in food before the press conference. "I am happy this is the last day. I will never be as relieved as when this is over and I can finally step away from the insanity."

"Need I remind you that this is why I suggested you get out of it," Paige muttered as Chase started to put the food on the table. The aroma from the Mexican cuisine filled his lungs and gave him comfort. "This isn't for you, Jorge. This isn't what you want at this point in your life."

"Oh, Paige, you do not have to convince me of anything," Jorge replied and looked up as Jolene, Diego, and Jesús entered the room. "After the insane meetings this morning, I am *done*. They picked apart my speech, criticized my English and suggested that I 'also' recommend Elizabeth Alan because she is a woman. Not because she is qualified. Not because they think she can win. Not because she has a unique platform but because she is a woman. They said 'we need to show we are supporting the female demographic'. Can you fucking believe this?"

"Can you *not* fucking believe this?" Diego was quick to jump in as he sat down. "It's politics. That's how these fuckers work."

"But sir, were you ever serious about this?" Jesús spoke in his usual slow tone as he sat down. "Did you really hope to be prime minister."

Jorge didn't reply but merely shrugged as he glanced over the food.

"So, you couldn't make the announcement here like you wanted?" Chase asked as he continued to open bags and place the styrofoam containers on the table. "It would've been nice."

"No, they insist that I need a larger venue or something like this," Jorge said and shook his head feeling slightly distracted. "There will be press from all over as well as those involved in politics and the party itself, supporters, that kind of thing. I guess this here is a big deal."

"Are you nervous speaking in front of all those people?" Chase asked with interest.

"Tell you the truth," Jorge said with a shrug. "I never really thought about it...you know until *now*."

"Sorry," Chase said with regret on his face as he found his own seat and sat down.

"This here, it is ok," Jorge said and laughed. "It will be good. You will see. You all must come."

It was later that afternoon before Jorge considered the crowd again. Glancing at the audience, it was bigger than he anticipated and he began to understand why the party picked such a large venue.

"Chase is getting Maria from school so she will be here any minute," Paige quietly commented as she gently touched his arm and looked into his eyes. "Are you ready?"

"*Mi amor,* I'm always ready for anything," Jorge whispered and pulled her close, kissing her on the forehead.

What Jorge hadn't anticipated was the audience reaction when he walked out. Along with the many reporters, there were also people who supported him, including a group of people wearing t-shirts that said 'Latinos for Hernandez'. A spark ran through his body when he looked into their faces. They showed the same excitement for him as they would a rock

star or a celebrity. It was invigorating and at that moment, he understood
Maria's quest for fame.

"Good afternoon," Jorge spoke into the mic. He was immediately
welcomed with cheers. He smiled and stepped back as he looked around
the room, trying to take it all in. Stepping forward again, he began to
speak.

"My wife, she always says to live in the moment, to be present," Jorge
said and paused for a moment when he heard more applause from the
audience. Glancing to his right, he saw Paige with Maria now standing
with her, wearing her school uniform. "This here is what she means because
this is a moment I will admit, I feel very flattered."

There was appreciation in some faces while the media continued to
hover like vultures. From the front row, he could see Alec Athas nervously
watching and the two men briefly made eye contact. Elizabeth Alan was
nearby with a fake smile on her face.

"But I do not say this because of my ego but because this here, it
demonstrates to me that there is a renewed hope for a party that deeply
disappointed you this summer," Jorge continued and the room grew quiet.
"And for me, it was deeply disappointing too. We must never forget the
grave error that was made. It has since been revealed that the prime
minister had been misinformed about that horrific fire that took one of
our indigenous communities but this does not make it less of a tragedy. It
broke this country but we have since proven that Canada, Canadians, we
are stronger than any tragedy that can happen to us. Together, we can get
through anything."

Jorge paused for more applause. Glancing at his speech, he pushed it
aside and looked up to notice Jolene, Diego, and Jesús standing together
in the audience, watching with anticipation. He felt his heart begin to race
but he took a deep breath and continued.

"Today, I am here to make a couple of announcements," Jorge clarified
and noted reporters watching him with interest. "But first, I want to speak
to you about a few things that I believe are very important and what needs
to be our focus in this country."

"As you know, I am a new Canadian and although many of my critics
have used this against me," Jorge said as he glanced toward a specific media
personality who was known for his right-winged views. "I feel that this

actually gives me a huge advantage. It allows me something to compare to and in many ways, this country is superior. Canada has many social programs that ensure that its people have access to free health care, that you are supported if you lose your job or if you have a new baby. There are so many things that you have that other countries, do not have. This here, to me, is beautiful."

"But as an immigrant, I see things that maybe need some improvement," Jorge spoke honestly. "I have spoken to many immigrants who feel that they are not necessarily represented. Many of you have sent me emails that tell about how you've been a target of violence or racism. For some, it is because of their religion and others, it is because of the color of their skin. So what can we do?"

He glanced around the room and paused for a moment.

"We can educate children, starting at a young age," Jorge answered and spoke slowly. "We can educate adults too. We can have zero tolerance for this behavior. We can strengthen laws for hate crimes. There are many things that we can do and we must. We cannot allow this situation to grow worse. History has taught us that terrible things happen when people are racist. We do not have to look further than what happened this summer."

There was dead silence in the audience. Alec continued to look nervous.

"Through this campaign," He slowly edged toward his original speech but pushed it aside again. "I have learned more about this country than I ever could from books. I learned it through all of you. Your stories, your comments, who you *are* tells me a story. Your words, they matter to me. You have allowed me a look into each of your lives, into your world and that is very significant. This is what we need. Not market research. Not surveys or polls. We need to know the people of this country. We need to listen more…this is something I have said from day one. It is true that politicians like to talk a lot but not all of them listen."

There was some laughter from the audience. That's when he noticed Makerson mixed in the media crowd.

"When I first threw my hat in this race," Jorge said with a grin on his face. "I did not know how people would react. I am new here, to this country. My English, it is broken. I do not speak French, one of your official languages. People accused me of terrible things. It was almost as if the media wished to find ways of insulting me."

"But then, I see something very different," Jorge continued and put his hands together before pulling his arms apart as if to gesture toward the crowd. "I began to see buttons with 'Latinos for Hernandez' which I did not make. I had people approach me on the street with their stories, their hopes, their dreams and suddenly, politics, it had a face. It was not a cold, structured part of our lives but it had a heart and that heart, it was you."

He specifically pointed toward the group of Latinos with a sign. An older woman was wiping a tear from her eye and he had to look away.

"Politics, it is not numbers or ratings," Jorge continued and took a deep breath. "It is not who is winning and losing. It is not arguing with the opposition like children in a playground. It is to represent the people of this country. It is your voice. It does not matter what your color is, how long you live here, how much money you make, who you love, where you worship or if you worship at all. Politics is supposed to be about you and you must always be represented by someone who cares about people but isn't afraid to be strong. Someone who isn't afraid to stand up to bullies whether they be in our own country or another. It is the person who brings us together and doesn't pull us apart. It is the person who will continue to prove that we live in the greatest country in the world."

He heard cheers sweep through the room and fill him up. For a moment, for a split second, he reconsidered his original announcement but then he looked toward Paige, who was standing on the sideline. Beside her was Maria watching with excitement and pride on her face.

"Unfortunately," Jorge continued to speak. "I regret that this person, it will not be me."

A stunned silence followed.

"I have given this a great deal of thought," Jorge continued and felt a weight fall from his heart and his body felt light. "I have decided to step down from this race because, at this time, I have a young family that needs me."

On impulse, he turned and gestured for Maria to come to him. Hesitant at first, she shyly walked on the stage and appeared stunned when met with applause.

Enthusiastically pulling his daughter close, he gave her a kiss on the top of the head and watched a gleeful smile appear on her face.

"This is my daughter Maria," Jorge announced as he continued to hold her close and he felt her arm around his waist. "And my son, Miguel, he is home today. He is not one for crowds, you know?"

There was laughter in the audience.

"I do thank you for the support, this here, it was not an easy decision," Jorge spoke honestly as he continued to hold his daughter close. "But I do have one last thing to announce. Since I will no longer be running to lead this party, I would like to make my endorsement and to officially announce a new contender for this party leadership."

Glancing down at the audience, he saw Elizabeth Alan move closer to the stage. It was in that moment that he sent her a burning look before moving his gaze behind her.

"When I just described the person who should be running this party and eventually this country," Jorge continued. "Someone who cares about the people, not the numbers. Someone who isn't in this to win an argument but to work for you. It is my great pleasure to endorse my friend, Alec Athas."

CHAPTER 47

Pictures of Jorge Hernandez embracing his daughter and kissing her on the top of her head became the most tweeted picture from the announcement. Even before news outlets were able to write a story about the events, many were using this picture as an explanation for why the popular candidate dropped out of the race. Although there were speculations and rumors on social media, many people appeared disappointed to see this turn of events.

Of course, the surprise announcement of his endorsement of Alec Athas created a wave of excitement. The second most popular image from that press conference was Jorge Hernandez shaking the hand of Alec Athas with his usual, charming smile while Maria stood poised beside her father.

However, not everyone was happy with his announcement. Only moments after Jorge took his daughter's hand and the two left the stage so Alec could speak, Elizabeth Alan appeared in his path. He didn't even blink as she stared him down with fury in her eyes.

"What the fuck was that?" She snapped, alarming some of the onlookers. "Was this your plan all along?"

Maria appeared stunned by how this woman spoke to her father and quickly stood a little taller.

"Papa, la mujer es loco."

Jorge couldn't help but laugh as he let go of his daughter's hand and pulled her close to kiss the top of her head.

266

"Maria, this is fine," Jorge insisted in a gentle voice. "You go over there with Paige. I will only be a minute."

Although she appeared skeptical, Maria shot Elizabeth Alan a nasty look before heading toward her step-mother, who was also watching with interest.

"You stabbed me in the back," She immediately accused in a hushed tone. "We had a deal. You promised that you would endorse me."

"I had, what you call, a change of heart," Jorge spoke solemnly as he touched his chest. "Is it not my right to change my mind?"

"And you couldn't have told me about this change of heart?" Elizabeth retorted with some pain in her face. "Was it better to humiliate me?"

"And how could I humiliate you?" Jorge countered with a shrug. "Your name, it was not even mentioned. These reporters, they had no idea of any of this."

"Some of them were here by my request," Elizabeth argued. "Now it looks as if I wanted them here to see you endorse Alec Athas!"

"And Ms. Alan, I am sure he appreciates that," Jorge spoke with sincerity and then leaned in. "And really, did you not realize that this here is a dirty game. Welcome to politics, baby, where there's a smile on your face and a knife in your back."

With that, he walked away as if they had finished a civil and warm conversation.

It was on the way home that Jorge admitted to Paige and Maria that he felt relief that it was over.

"I feel so light, you know?" Jorge commented as they sat in traffic. "It is like I have my life back. I can focus on my company and my family. I will work from home as much as possible, it will be beautiful."

"*Papa,* you said that before," Maria quickly reminded him from the back seat as she continued to stare at her phone. "But it never happens."

"This time, it will happen," Jorge reassured her but suspected his daughter was probably right. Things never slowed down but merely shifted. "I want to be there for all of you and to see Miguel grow up. I regret I missed so much with you, Maria."

"*Papa,* there are people saying mean things about us on Twitter," Maria said as she looked up from her phone with a dismal expression on her face. "They say…."

"Maria!" Jorge immediately cut her off. "What do I tell you about social media?"

"That you hate it."

"What else?"

"To ignore it," Maria replied and sat her phone aside.

"Exactly," Jorge replied. "This here, it means nothing."

"But they said I was ugly."

Jorge felt anger burning through him and he took a deep breath.

"Maria, you're not ugly," Paige immediately insisted. "Sweetie, people say mean things just to be hurtful."

"You're going to say that because you're my mother," Maria said in a faint voice.

Jorge glanced in the rearview mirror again and the sight of his daughter's sad eyes broke his heart.

"Maria, this here, you cannot listen to," Jorge immediately began to lecture, cautious to not sound harsh. "These people, they are no one to you. Just strangers. You are a beautiful young woman and do not allow strangers to make you feel differently. This is why I tell you that I do not like you getting into television. This is what these celebrities deal with every day."

"He's right," Paige gently commented. "It's not all glamorous when you're in the limelight. You can't base how you feel about yourself on what others say especially on social media. Your father, he dealt with the same thing throughout this campaign."

"Why are people so mean?" Maria asked as she smoothed out her skirt. "What did I ever do to them?"

"You are famous this afternoon," Jorge attempted to explain. "You're on social media and you will be on the news tonight. People, they get jealous, Maria. Weak people, they only want to hurt or insult others because they are miserable fucks."

"Jorge," Paige muttered and gave him a warning glance.

"But Paige, it is true," Jorge said and glanced toward his daughter and noted she was laughing. "This here, she should know. These people, they are nothing. They should mean nothing. Maria, this is an important lesson for you. You cannot take this to heart. You must always be stronger than your enemies. This is important."

"You mean like that crazy lady after your speech," Maria said as she continued to laugh. "*Ella es loco!*"

"*Si,*" Jorge agreed. "Maria, that woman, she was mad because I promised to endorse her today, not Alec. That is why she acted that way."

"So you did the wrong thing?" Maria asked and forced Jorge to consider the truth.

"Yes, Maria, you are right," Jorge agreed. "I did not keep my word however, I do not trust this lady and I do trust Alec. He will go far."

"His speech was quite good," Paige commented. "Not as good as yours but it was good."

"Well, you know, he had a tough act to follow," Jorge muttered and winked at his wife who grinned in response.

"Is anything going on tonight?" Paige asked as she yawned.

"No, my love, tonight is for my family and tomorrow," Jorge said as they stopped at another light. "We will meet with Alec in the conference room."

"I thought you had that interview with Makerson?" Paige asked as she looked out the window.

"Ah! Yes, this is true," Jorge replied. "I will call him after I arrive home to discuss today. He would like to do a story for tomorrow morning's paper and to put on social media this evening. It will be my first official interview after dropping out. I purposely did not give the reporters a chance to ask anything after announcing Alec entering the leadership race. The last thing I wished to deal with at that time was their ridiculous questions."

"*Papa,* were you nervous when you spoke today?" Maria asked with interest. "I was nervous and I was just standing there."

"Oh, *bonita,* I would not say nervous but anxious," Jorge replied with a smooth grin on his face as he glanced in the rearview mirror. "It is, as they say, a weight off my shoulders to have this finished."

"But, *Papa* did you not see why I love being on the stage so much?"

"Maria, I will admit, there was a moment," Jorge replied but halted. "It was brief, but there was a moment where I saw why you loved being on stage with applause. It is very powerful and it is that power that you enjoy. It's not the applause or the audience excitement, Maria, it is the power you feel when you have all that attention on you. And for that, you are very much like your *papa* because I, too, I also enjoy power."

"Is that why you own a company?"

"Yes, Maria, that is why I enjoy running a company," Jorge said with a nod. "But Maria, you must be careful because power, it can sometimes take over your life. For example, I did not wish to lead this party or become prime minister. It was the idea. When you find power exciting, you sometimes can find yourself doing things that you do not enjoy simply to feel this way, do you know what I mean?"

"I think so," Maria replied but didn't look convinced.

"What I mean, Maria is that for me to continue in politics," Jorge said and glanced at his wife. "It was not something I wanted to do every day. It was the idea of power that excited me, not the actual work."

"I think I understand," Maria replied and began to dance in her seat. "It would be like if I were to do something like a play I hated because I wanted the attention."

"Yes, that is what I mean," Jorge said with a nod. "You must always follow your heart."

"Maria," Paige jumped in. "And when you want to do something like, say, a play you don't actually like, you have to ask yourself why? Maybe it's good to do the play because it gives you more experience or maybe you don't like it because it poses a challenge and you're scared. With your father and politics, he knew that it would take him away from his family and that the day to day work would be tedious and not necessarily interesting to him. So if he were to continue, it would be for the wrong reasons."

"Power," Maria replied.

"Exactly," Paige answered and turned in her seat. "He would've had power but would he be happy?"

Jorge could feel the strength of these words and he hoped that his daughter did too.

CHAPTER 48

"Oh, *mi amor,* what a beautiful day this is," Jorge said as he stretched and slowly sat up in bed. Across the room, Paige was reaching for her robe underneath a pile of clothes, her hair up in a messy ponytail and her short nightgown rising to expose her thighs. His mind returned to the night before and the intimate moments that they shared after he removed it. "What is your rush away? Marla and Miguel, they are both sleeping."

"It's just a matter of time before Miguel cries," Paige reminded him. "Juliana has today off, remember?"

"Ah yes, this is true," Jorge slowly rose from the bed and pulled on his boxers before walking across the room. "I will look in on Miguel."

Paige stopped in the middle of the room with a shocked expression on her face.

"What is it?"

"You didn't check your phone," Paige said as her blue eyes grew in size and she glanced toward the nightstand. "Or did I miss it?"

"Oh Paige, today, I do not care," Jorge said before leaning in to kiss her. "It can wait. My son, he is more important."

Jorge found Miguel sleeping soundly, his tiny chest rising and falling with each breath. He was absolute perfection. Jorge could've stared at his son all day but eventually returned to the bedroom, just in time to hear the shower stop.

Sitting on the bed, he reached for his phone and glanced over the messages. Most were from the others, confirming the time of their meeting while Makerson informed him of rumors that Elizabeth Alan had met with the leader of the opposition about representing one of their districts looking for new candidates. To that, Jorge laughed out loud and shook his head.

Paige walked out of the bathroom in her red robe, brushing her wet hair. Glancing in Jorge's direction, she noticed the phone in his hand.

"I guess it was just a matter of time," She teased as she sat beside him on the bed.

"Look at this here," Jorge said as he showed her the message from Makerson. "The lady, she does not know what she want. You were right, Paige. She is weak."

"I was concerned that you were rushing to get away from politics and it was clouding your judgment," Paige spoke gently and continued to brush her hair. "The beauty of it is she can't complain publicly about what you did to her because it makes her look unreliable if she flips from one party to another so quickly."

"Ah, yes, this is true," Jorge agreed and sat his phone back on the table. "But I am happy to not have to deal with this anymore. Me, I slept like a baby last night and I feel like a million dollars this morning. Maybe even more than a million, maybe ten million."

"Now you can just focus on the business," Paige said and made a slight pause. "You can slow down and enjoy everything you have otherwise, what's the point?"

"Speaking of enjoying what I have," He leaned in and kissed her. "Next weekend, we should go away to our hotel suite. What do you say?"

"Sounds good to me," Paige said and looked into his eyes. "I'm sure we can arrange it."

It was later that morning when Jorge stopped by the office and met with Diego, Alec, Makerson and Jesús in the boardroom office. The four men were staring at an iPod when he arrived.

"Clara? She has already been in?" Jorge asked as he closed the door and headed for his chair. "Everything is good?"

"She was in," Diego replied and jumped up from his seat. "Coffee?"

"No," Jorge shook his head as he sat down. "This here meeting, it will be fast."

"We're looking at some of the online comments," Makerson remarked as he pushed his iPad aside. "For the most part, people are looking at you favorably for your decision."

"But they aren't sure about Athas," Diego jumped in excitedly and pointed toward Alec. "They think he don't got enough experience."

"And me, I did?" Jorge responded with laughter. "So what?"

"There's some speculation that Alec was thrown into the race at the last minute because you were leaving and the party didn't have anyone else that stood out," Makerson attempted to explain. "And this theory comes from our friend Elizabeth Alan."

"She's pissed because you fucked her over," Diego bluntly reminded him. "Now she's digging her nails in."

"I'm hardly worried about that lady or her nails," Jorge said with a shrug. "But they always have a spin on things, this is not surprising."

"The problem is that I have to prove her wrong and fast," Alec commented. "My speech went well yesterday but people aren't as sure about me as you."

"Again, I got no political experience," Jorge said as he leaned back in his chair. "Give them time."

"But, you're the CEO of a large company," Makerson reminded him. "That suggests that you can take on something of this…magnitude. We have to find a way to show people who Alec is too."

"Boss, he says what you did," Jesús spoke slowly while tilting his head to the right. "But for him, this is not enough."

"What we got to do," Jorge said after a moment's thought. "Is show the people you are listening to them and are serious about making changes. That is what they want. They do not care about this other stuff. They want someone who is going to make their lives easier."

"I'm thinking maybe you should have a live chat with people," Makerson jumped in. "Say you have reviewed a lot of comments and you feel that it's important that you have an open discussion in various formats including online."

"You get the trolls online," Alec complained. "Maybe in person is better."

"Maybe both?" Diego jumped in. "Not everyone is going to make the effort to go to a meeting but they might turn on a computer."

"Why not both at the *same time*," Jorge suggested. "Have someone monitor the questions, only give you the serious ones to answer."

"I can do that," Alec nodded.

"In the meanwhile, model your campaign off of mine, add a few things and wait for the leadership debate," Jorge suggested with a shrug. "And that, you must win. You must rip apart the other candidates like an animal that hasn't eaten in weeks. When people see that, you will be this here party's leader."

"You don't have much competition," Makerson reminded him. "It shouldn't be too difficult. Jorge is right, tear them apart and show you're the most powerful. That's what people remember.."

"People, they love a good fight," Jorge reminded him. "Be passionate, be abrupt, be crazy…"

"Nah avoid the crazy," Makerson corrected him. "There's enough crazy in the world of politicians, let's keep it to a minimum here."

Jorge laughed and glanced at the clock. He was bored.

"So if that is all…."

"And Elizabeth Alan, she won't be a problem?" Alec directed his question at Makerson.

"Not unless she has insider info," Makerson commented and thought for a moment. "She doesn't know that Jorge was planning to pull out all along, does she?"

"No, she knows that he was going to drop out this week," Alec insisted. "She wasn't aware of anything else."

"Even if she knows anything," Jorge said with a shrug. "She got no proof and you know me, I will shoot her down if she tries to attack me in the media."

"Interesting choice of words," Makerson muttered with a grin on his face.

"Not literally," Diego quickly jumped in and then turned to Jorge. "Right?"

Jorge laughed and pushed his chair away from the table.

"That lady does not need my help to destroy her," He said as he stood up. "My guess, she will do it herself."

In the upcoming days, Jorge's words were proven true when Elizabeth Alan started off strong, running for a seat with the official opposition party and by the end of that week, was starting to unravel. She acted erratically when confronted by a group of women questioning her opinions on abortion while recording the conversation for social media. Saying that it was 'God's will' for every child to be born and that she didn't believe abortion was a logical choice for any woman proved her downfall. Despite the party's conservative views on such matters, they felt she took the issue too far, therefore causing unwanted negative attention. She was forced to step down.

Meanwhile, Jorge was enjoying the quiet. He started to look for property to build their dream home but later decided instead to shop around for a house, since it required less planning and headaches. As Paige constantly reminded him, it wasn't always necessary for each goal to be monstrous. Simply finding a new home was enough. They didn't need to build a castle.

The days rolled by and Athas continued to gain support. His original fears were for nothing as he grew in popularity simply by being himself and perhaps a bit of Jorge Hernandez. It was a beautiful thing to watch from a distance. Life, looked different when it was observed and not controlled. All was quiet and peaceful. Then again, perhaps it was the quiet before the storm. The real question was, how big was the storm.

CHAPTER 49

"You're not fucking with me, are you?" Diego bluntly asked, causing Jorge to laugh and Paige to quickly join in as the three sat at their favorite restaurant. "Because you know, we've been down this road before."

"Diego, I promise," Jorge insisted as he leaned closer to his wide-eyed friend. "When Paige and me find a new home, it will be quite big and it is our wish at that time, to finally have a wedding. If you want to plan it, you may do so."

"We'd be honored," Paige added as she leaned closer. "It never was the right time before."

"But you're sure," Diego asked with some hesitation. "Because you've said this before and got all wishy-washy on me."

"Wishy-washy?" Jorge asked, confused. "What does this mean?"

"It means we keep changing our mind," Paige explained and directed her attention back at Diego. "In the past, there was too much going on but now that things will slow down…" She glanced at Jorge who leaned in and gave her a kiss. "We might actually have time to celebrate our marriage."

"Two years after eloping," Diego reminded them. "And you know, of course, I will say yes to helping you out. This is exactly what I need now."

"You know if you want to move things along quicker," Jorge added as he turned his attention back to Diego. "You can help us find a house. We wish to have something bigger."

276

"No, *you* wish to have something bigger," Paige corrected him. "I think our house is plenty big."

"Compared to what, my love, a shack?" Jorge teased. "No, we must have a larger home. Also, too many negative things have occurred in this house. It is time to start fresh somewhere new. Let us forget about everything in the past. The good and bad. Let's move on from here."

"I like the sounds of that," Diego said with some hesitation. "Maybe I will do the same. I have to get out of that condo. Maybe I will buy a house too."

"You must dream big," Jorge reminded him. "This life, we only live once."

The waitress stopped by the table to drop off the bill and Jorge quickly paid for everyone. The three of them headed outside into the cool night air and Jorge stopped to look around. Glancing up at the sky, he took a breath and put his arm around Paige.

"You know, winter, it is coming soon," Jorge commented as he looked from Paige to Diego. "You can feel it, you know? It is as if something suddenly changed and the dark clouds, they are looming overhead. There is a heaviness that I feel that was not here a week ago."

No one replied but the three of them exchanged looks. Diego said good night before heading toward his Lexus while Jorge and Paige found the SUV and climbed inside.

"I worry about him," Paige said almost as soon as they closed the door. "He's alone."

"He will be fine," Jorge insisted. "I do not think Diego needs a babysitter."

"I don't mean that," Paige warmly insisted. "I...I wondering if when we move if we can..."

"What? Have him move in with us?" Jorge asked with laughter in his voice.

"Maybe not *with us* but close," Paige said with a shrug. "I think it would be nice for him to live in a different atmosphere. His condo is so dreary."

"You know, in Mexico, my family lived close when I was a child," Jorge commented as they turned down the Toronto street. "My mother's sister, she was down the road. My cousins were all around. We were close as if we were brothers, you know? It was so different back then and in a way, I miss that."

"Do you talk to your cousins anymore?"

"We lost touch," Jorge replied. "After Miguel died, I don't know. It was as if they did not want their children near me. I became the 'wild child' and well, you know how this turned out. I am the black sheep to them. But sometimes, you know, I do wonder. I think of them. I wonder also if they think of me."

"Have you considered reaching out?" Paige asked and watched him with interest.

"No," Jorge shook his head. "Their lives are so different from mine. I do not think they would want to connect."

"It doesn't hurt to try."

Jorge merely shrugged.

"I know you miss Mexico," Paige continued. "You've given up so much for me."

"What?" Jorge said with laughter in his voice. "Paige? Are you serious right now? I gave up nothing."

"Well yes, you gave up your home, your home country," Paige reminded him. "You started a new life to be here with me."

"It was not such a change," Jorge reminded her. "I was already in Canada a great deal. Maria wanted to go to school here too. It worked out. There was never any sacrifice to be here with you."

"But you must miss it."

"Sometimes," Jorge replied. "But even when I go back now, it feels strange. I think perhaps I have changed too much to belong there now. It is like I cannot believe how I once lived. It is better for me, for Maria, to be here in Canada. And our lives, my life, it would not matter without my family. You know this."

They drove the rest of the way home in silence. Paige yawned a few times and Jorge turned on the radio. It was peaceful. It was perfect.

Back at home, they slowly got out of the SUV and went into the house. Juliana met them at the door and said Miguel was upstairs sleeping and Maria was in the living room. She said good night and slipped downstairs to her apartment.

Jorge opened a bottle of wine and sat in the living room with Maria. She rattled on about school and he felt distracted. His thoughts couldn't settle even though he had every reason to feel relaxed. Perhaps, Jorge considered, it was merely out of habit that his monkey mind never stopped. He was relieved when Paige joined them and started talking to Maria.

Excusing himself, he went upstairs to look in on the baby. Miguel was sleeping like an angel and then, he suddenly opened his eyes and looked up at Jorge with a smile.

"Oh, baby!" Jorge reached into the crib and picked up Miguel. Crossing the floor, he sat down in a chair next to the window. Pulling him close, he made faces to make Miguel laugh, something he did often and with almost no effort. He was a happy baby.

"Oh Miguel," Jorge said as he caressed his son's cheek as he looked up at him with his big, brown eyes. "I wish I had spent more time with your sister at this age. You know, you look like her. You're a Hernandez but you're also very much like your mother. This is why you are the perfect child."

The baby appeared to be listening as he stared at Jorge in a trance-like state.

"You will be the strongest Hernandez yet," Jorge continued as he ran his fingers over the baby's fine, soft hair. "You will do so much better than me. You will rule the world. You are not just my son but my legacy."

Kissing Miguel on the top of his head, Jorge returned the baby to his crib and watched him drift back to sleep.

Feeling at peace, he turned to leave the room when shots suddenly rang out from downstairs, sending waves of panic through Jorge's heart.

Flying across the hallway into the bedroom, he grabbed his gun and rushed toward the stairs. Fear gripped him as he grabbed the banister and hurried down to find Paige standing in the living room, holding a gun, while Maria ran toward him crying. It took him a minute to realize that a man was on the floor, bleeding. At that very moment, Juliana tore into the room with a gun in her hand. Quickly taking in the scene, she gasped.

"*Papa!* He said he was going to get all of us," Maria cried hysterically. "He said that he already got one of us and he was going to get the rest. What does that mean?"

"Sweetheart," Jorge took a deep breath. "You must go upstairs and check on your brother. Juliana, go with her!"

Without replying, she rushed toward Maria and both bolted upstairs while Paige hurried to the bleeding man on the floor. He was still alive.

Jorge felt fear turn to rage as he approached. Seeing a gun lying nearby, he gestured for Paige to pick it up before he pointed his own gun toward the man's head.

"You better start talking motherfucker or your family, they will not even recognize you when I am finished," Jorge spoke curtly with fury in his eyes. "Who the fuck sent you?"

"And what did you mean, you got one of us?" Paige asked with a calm voice even though Jorge could see the panic in her eyes.

"If you want to live, you will answer these questions," Jorge said. "Tell me now."

"My brother," The man's voice was weak as his eyes watered. "Claude Rexdale, You killed...I kill your family."

"Who is here with you?" Jorge demanded as he processed the information.

"No one," The man replied as a tear fell from his eye and slid down toward his ear. "Other family. You...next."

Jorge felt his heart race but hid his emotions.

"What do you mean, my other family? This here is my family."

"Thugs," The man fought for his breath. "I was.. you next."

Jorge thought of his last moments with Diego. Had this man been watching them at the restaurant? Had he killed his *hermano?* He heard a whimper come from Paige as she moved away.

"Text them!" Jorge instructed his wife before turning his attention back to the dying man on the floor. "What did you do?"

But the man was slipping away and not even coherent.

"I texted them all." Paige sobbed.

"And?"

"Only Chase has replied so far," Paige cried. "I will send another message and tell them it is urgent."

Jorge felt his fury replaced by sorrow. This couldn't be happening.

"Call them," Jorge instructed as he felt his arm shake and he lowered the gun. The man was dying.

He heard Paige crying and couldn't look in her eyes as she tapped on her phone.

Jorge shot the man one last time before he sat the gun on the nearby table. Paige cried as the phone shook in her hand. Feeling his legs grow weak, he sat down on the couch.

"Hello?" Paige was saying in a weak voice as she sobbed.

Jorge couldn't move.

CHAPTER 50

Power. It makes the world go round. The romantics will say it is love and the stoic will insist it is money but our world thrives on power. All the money and all the love can never fill an empty heart the same way power does and yet, when is it too much? When do we cross the line? Who wins when there is nothing left to take?

Jorge Hernandez had been a man obsessed with power. At one time, he would've taken down anyone who stood in his way without a second thought. It was a way to prove that those who tried to kill his spirit were unsuccessful. His father hadn't beat it out of him. His mother hadn't shamed it out of him. His brother's death hadn't killed Jorge's spirit but forced it to grow stronger. He had spent many days trying to regain the power life had ripped away. But it was never enough.

Paige made him see that it no longer mattered. He could've run for the party and become their leader. He could've become prime minister. He could've taken over the world, but for what? What more did he want? How much power did he need? Why did it matter? What would he lose to inflate his ego?

Death reminds us how little time we have on earth. It was God's way of letting us know that the clock was always ticking and one day, it would stop forever. We just never knew when that time would be.

Jesús Garcia López was *familia* and his murder tore out a piece of Jorge's heart. Life's fragility was suddenly much more prevalent to him. A stranger wanted to kill his *entire* family and what if he had been successful? What if Jorge had walked downstairs that night to find his wife and daughter dead on the floor? What if the man also killed Chase, Diego, and Jolene too?

Jorge continued to expect to see Jesús walk through the door but it never happened. It would never happen again.

The death sent a wave of shock through their tribe. Each took turns falling apart, sharing many tequila shots and memories over the next couple of days. Jesús had always been an important part of Jorge's life. The loyal foot soldier had proven his value when they were young men in Mexico and had always been there for him; but the one time he needed Jorge, he failed him.

"You have to forgive yourself," Paige insisted the day of the memorial service as they sat on the bed, she reached for his hand. "You had no way of knowing this was going to happen. If you thought for a second he was in danger, you would've been there with no hesitation."

"I should've been there," Jorge spoke in a hoarse voice. "I should've been there."

"He wouldn't want you to feel this way," Paige insisted and gripped his hand. "You *know* that."

Jorge merely nodded and took a deep breath. Looking into his wife's eyes, he quickly looked away.

"That man, he could've killed you, Maria…"

"He didn't," Paige reminded him. "Please, you have to let this go. We will get a new house, we'll have as much security as you want….but for now, we just have to get through today."

A small cry from the next room immediately alerted Jorge. It was Miguel waking up.

"Go to him," Paige glanced toward the door. "You'll feel better if you spend some time with the baby."

"I cannot believe he slept through the shooting the other night," Jorge managed to find his voice as he slowly stood up and Paige did the same. "We were all screaming, crying, shooting….and yet, there is my son, sleeping as if nothing was happening."

"He's a Hernandez," Paige teased. "This is normal to him."

Jorge laughed, welcoming a break from the sorrow. He leaned ahead and kissed his wife before heading out the door.

Miguel's watched when his father entered his room. Reaching into the crib, Jorge picked up the little boy and silently held him in his arms. Taking a deep breath, he briefly wondered how he would get through the memorial service but instead decided to focus on his son. If even for a moment, it would help him escape the bitter reality of the day.

"Miguel," Jorge whispered as he walked toward the chair and sat down. Holding his son carefully, as if he would break, Jorge looked into his eyes and cleared his throat. "I must tell you the story about the devil and the squirrel."

Settling in, he sat back and paused briefly before continuing.

"See there was this little boy who liked to feed the squirrels," Jorge slowly began. "He would put food out and watch the squirrel from his window. But also, he had a cat who would watch the squirrel with him. His eyes, they would get very wide. His tail, it would puff out and he would run from window to window, to get a better view of the squirrel."

"And in the forest nearby, was a wolf," Jorge continued as his son watched him with interest. "And that wolf, he also watched the squirrel. One day, the devil, he came along and asked the squirrel why he was so nervous? 'Why you always looking into the woods? What do you see?'"

"The squirrel said, 'There is a wolf watching me. I think he wants to eat me.' And the devil, he said, 'If he wanted to kill you, do you not think he would've already?'"

"Time went by. Then one day, the little boy accidentally left the door opened and the cat got out," Jorge continued. "And the cat, he was so excited, he headed right for the squirrel but before he could, the wolf attacked and killed him."

"And the squirrel, he was frantic because you see," Jorge continued and looked up to see Maria standing in the doorway. "He now realized that the wolf used him to lure out the cat."

"And the devil, he comes back," Jorge spoke with a grin on his face. "And the squirrel said, 'you told me that I was safe but now that the wolf killed the cat, now he has no reason to not kill me too.'"

"But he said," Maria interrupted and walked into the room. "'I'm the devil and the devil may lie.' I remember you telling me that story too."

"Yes, Maria, I did," Jorge said with a slight pause. "I know it is no Disney fairytale but what kind of father would I be if I only told you stories of princesses and unicorns? Too many parents, they shelter their kids and then they get into the real world and are not ready. You, Maria and Miguel, you will be prepared for anything. Both the best and the worst that this world has to offer. That is my job and I take it seriously."

"Like what happened here the other night?" Maria asked as she moved closer and sat on the arm of the chair, leaning in and Jorge put his other arm around her. Realizing he was embracing both his children at once, a soft light caught his eye and he thought it was Paige entering the room but when he looked up, no one was there. A powerful presence filled him and for a moment, he felt a warmth flow through him. Taking a deep breath, he nodded.

"I'm sorry I opened the door," Maria spoke with tears in her eyes. "It's my fault."

"Maria, he pushed his way in," Jorge reminded her and quickly continued. "In the future, you will be more careful but he would've found a way even if you hadn't opened the door. He was out for revenge because of an…unfortunate transaction I had with his brother. I am relieved no one else was hurt or killed."

Maria nodded and a tear escaped her eye.

"It will be ok, Maria," Jorge insisted feeling his strength surge. "We will be ok. We must get through this service today and everything will be fine."

The doorbell rang and Maria jumped up.

"That must be the others," She said and reached out for Miguel. "Here, *Papa*, I will change him for the service. You go see them."

Rising from the chair, he gave his daughter a quick kiss on the top of the head before passing Miguel to her.

"Maria, the maturity you have shown the last few days, it warms my heart," He said and kissed her again. Her reply was a sad smile.

Walking downstairs, Jorge noted that Paige was already with Diego, Chase, and Jolene. He discovered a somber room that was almost too much but he managed to push through and give each of them a warm hug. Diego looked the most emotional while Jolene simply appeared in disbelief as she had since Jesús died. Chase had pity in his eyes. Jorge looked away.

"As I just told Maria," Jorge began. "We just need to get through the service this afternoon. I do not know what is next but no one takes one of ours. No one."

Paige lowered her head and didn't reply but Diego quickly shook his head.

"You're goddam right," Diego insisted. "This isn't over."

"Please," Paige raised her hand. "We got two of their men and they got one of ours. This is where it has to end."

Diego slumped over and tears formed in Jolene's eyes.

"This isn't going to bring him back," Paige gently reminded them. "If we go after someone else, then they'll come back at us. We can't do this anymore. Please, haven't we lost enough this year?"

Her eyes met with Diego's and he slowly nodded as she swooped in and pulled him into a hug. Jorge had to look away as his closest friend began to sob uncontrollably, which in turn caused them all to break down, one by one. It was only Paige who remained strong.

Finally, they all collected themselves just as Juliana walked upstairs wearing a black dress, a tissue in her hand.

"Maria, are you ready?" Paige called out and they began to shuffle toward the door.

"I'm coming," She sang out, walking downstairs holding the baby. "Miguel peed *all over* his outfit and *me*, so I had to wash him up and change *both* our goddamn clothes."

Jolene was the first person to laugh. It was her strong, hearty laughter that was contagious and soon, they were all laughing at Maria's dramatic comment as she approached them.

"It feels good to laugh," Jorge remarked as he reached for his son. "This is what Jesús would want, you know? He would want us to be happy. He would want us to laugh. We will always mourn him in our hearts but we must also remember the good times. Life, it isn't just about our deaths but our lives."

"But it was him this time," Diego spoke dramatically. "And who next? We're all going to die....and..."

"Diego, please," Jorge put his hand in the air. "This is not something we must talk about," He paused for a moment and slowly continued. "Today, we must focus on the legacy of Jesús Garcia López and tomorrow, we all must think about our own."

No one replied but they shared a quiet moment before heading to the door.

Want to learn more about Jorge Hernandez and his gang? Go to <u>www. mimaonfire.com</u> to check out the rest of the series.

Printed in the United States
By Bookmasters